the

MERCY
TREE

A NOVEL BY SHARLENE
MACLAREN

WHITAKER
HOUSE

Unless otherwise indicated, all Scripture quotations are taken from the *Holy Bible, Darby's Translation.* Maintained by the British and Foreign Bible Society. Scripture quotations marked (KJV) are taken from the King James Version of the Holy Bible.

THE MERCY TREE
A Novel

www.sharlenemaclaren.com
sharlenemaclaren@yahoo.com

ISBN: 978-1-64123-956-1
eBook ISBN: 978-1-64123-957-8
Printed in Colombia
© 2023 by Sharlene MacLaren

Whitaker House
1030 Hunt Valley Circle
New Kensington, PA 15068
www.whitakerhouse.com

Library of Congress Cataloging-in-Publication Data
Names: MacLaren, Sharlene, 1948- author. | Whitaker House (New Kensington, Pennsylvania), other.
Title: The mercy tree : a novel / Sharlene MacLaren.
Description: New Kensington, PA : Whitaker House, [2023] | Summary: "A romance novel set in 1955 in Michigan featuring a respected pastor who receives an unsettling letter from a missionary in Japan that forces him, his family, and his congregation to tackle tough questions about faith and redemption"-- Provided by publisher.
Identifiers: LCCN 2022042482 (print) | LCCN 2022042483 (ebook) | ISBN 9781641239561 (trade paperback) | ISBN 9781641239578 (ebook)
Subjects: BISAC: FICTION / Christian / Romance / Historical | FICTION / Romance / Historical / American | LCGFT: Novels.
Classification: LCC PS3613.A27356 M47 2023 (print) | LCC PS3613.A27356 (ebook) | DDC 813/.6--dc23/eng/20220909
LC record available at https://lccn.loc.gov/2022042482
LC ebook record available at https://lccn.loc.gov/2022042483

1 2 3 4 5 6 7 8 9 10 11 ⊔⊔ 30 29 28 27 26 25 24 23

To Bethany "Betsy," my lifelong friend with whom I've shared a lifetime of experiences, a year-long singing tour around the country (40+ states), trips to Florida to bask in the sun, lunches, shopping trips, and times spent at each other's homes catching up on everything. You make me laugh so easily. I always smile at your sign-offs after we finish talking on the phone.

You say it as one word: "Loveyoubye."

I love you too.

TRUST

Sharlene MacLaren

Whatever you are going through, God knows.
Lay down your heavy load, your cares, your woes.
He knows that you are tired, can hardly face the day.
Take heart; the Lord, your God, will make a way.

To you, the road ahead is insecure,
But to our God, the path ahead is sure.
He hears your pleading cries; He sees each fallen tear.
Be brave; do not be overcome by fear.

When burdens are much more than you can bear,
Don't worry, weary one; your God's aware.
He knows your troubled heart; His love is deep and wide.
Look up! The Lord, your God, is on your side!

PROLOGUE

There is not a creature unapparent before him; but all things are naked and laid bare to his eyes, with whom we have to do.
—Hebrews 4:13

July 1946 · Tokyo, Japan

The smells of fish, nicotine, and sweat lay heavy in the hot, sticky air. Shipping docks littered with cigarette butts, animal waste, food scraps, and whatnot bustled with activity as soldiers carrying haversacks hurried past, and gulls swooped down to peck at the muddy earth. Hot bodies pressed together in a none-too-straight line, all vying for a spot on the monstrous steamer, a converted battleship, that would take them back to their beloved homeland, America. Ever since the United States had started occupying Japan, American troops had come and gone, serving months-long stints to help keep the peace among military and civilians as well as rebuild the war-torn country.

Private First Class Henry Griffin held his place in line among hundreds of other soldiers and their wives, awaiting his turn to board. He adjusted the thick leather strap of his overlarge backpack across his shoulder. It was heavy with souvenirs and a myriad of belongings he'd collected over the past year. Babies wailed, dogs barked, seagulls squawked, and men laughed and talked loudly over the din. Some smoked while they stood in line, others read American newspapers or magazines, and still others simply waited impatiently on the dock, shifting their weight as a grueling sun beat down on them.

Orders from one of the commanders rang out from a crackling loudspeaker, but the words were lost to Henry's ears due to the cries of a discontented baby squirming in his mother's arms just ten or so feet in front of him. The mother reached for a bottle under the flap of a bag she carried, her soldier husband trying to lend assistance. She shoved the nipple end into the infant's mouth, and sweet silence followed. The line moved forward a few steps.

For the hundredth time that day, Henry thought about his wife Nora. How would it be when they first locked eyes? A twinge of excitement mixed with guilt stirred inside him. They had talked about whether she should join him in Japan, but with a new baby, they'd decided it best she move in with her parents until his return. He wished now he'd insisted she come. No doubt it would've been better in the long run. He tried to push aside his tangled emotions by withdrawing his wallet from his back pocket and taking out the wrinkled photograph he kept stored between a few dollar bills. Nora had sent him the photo of his daughter Paige just after her first birthday. Now she was a full sixteen months old. How much had she grown? How many teeth did she have? How long was her wispy blond hair? Was it long enough for a barrette? Babies grew so fast. He tucked the photo carefully away and stuffed his wallet back in his pocket. He'd wanted a leave of absence more than anything before carrying out his overseas orders, but the Army rarely granted soldiers wartime leave, not unless you were sick, wounded, or going home in a body bag. He'd have to ease his way into his child's heart and hope that Nora had showed her his picture every day so that when they finally did meet, he wouldn't be a stranger to her.

Up ahead a ruckus erupted, two privates fighting about one thing or another, probably something as simple as their place in line. He'd grown accustomed to hotheads. Tensions were always high, even in a place where peace rather than war had become the order of the day. The pushing and shoving persisted along with the exchange of a few loud curse words until an officer intervened and another soldier stepped up to help separate the two. In time, the fellows calmed down, one of them sauntering off to light up a cigarette.

"You goin' home to family, soldier?" someone asked from behind. He turned at her voice. She was a small woman, probably in her sixties by the look of her wrinkled skin and graying hair pulled tight into a severe bun. She gave him a kindly smile.

"Yes, yes, I am. And you? Are you preparing to hitch a ride on this ageless warrior with all these bumbleheaded men? I hope you're not expecting a peaceful journey."

Her smile remained. "It won't bother me. I'm just glad to have received permission to board. My sister who lives outside of Chicago is quite ill, and I haven't seen her in three years. I'm worried if I don't get this chance to visit her, I may not have another one."

"I see. Well then, I'm glad it worked out for you. You must have a special connection to have gained permission to board."

"Oh, I do." She winked at him. "My son is an army captain so he pulled a few strings."

"How did you find yourself in Japan—in such uncertain times?"

"Oh, goodness, this is more my home than America. My husband and I both came here as mere youngsters, newlyweds we were, and, in fact, raised four sturdy boys here, two of whom are married. The oldest is living here in Tokyo with his wife, and the second oldest is serving in the Army. He too is married. The younger two went back to the United States and are attending Moody Bible Institute in downtown Chicago.

I'll have a chance to visit them when I go see my sister, so my trip has a twofold purpose. We're a missionary family in case you were wondering."

"Ah! Missionaries." Henry had been raised in a Christian home himself; in fact, his father was a preacher. He'd even married a fine Christian woman. Too bad he'd wandered off the straight and narrow over the past several months. He'd never let on to Nora though. As far as she knew, he'd been living a saintly life, ministering to his fellow soldiers and spreading the good news. And to quell any doubts she might have about his testimony, he always ended his letters with a passage of Scripture and a brief prayer.

It hadn't taken him long to learn the Army was no place to live a holy life, especially not in wartime when the government itself encouraged smoking breaks and the occasional drinking challenge if you happened to have a night off. Even the officers were known to partake—in different, more sophisticated circles. A man had to do something to drown out the sordid images of death and demise that haunted everyone's heads. If a few beers didn't do the trick, might be a pretty Japanese lady could help. He cringed at that reality, but the woman engaging him in conversation brought his mind back into focus.

She leaned in. "Oh, it's not the sort of news we publish, that we're missionaries, that is." She cleared her throat and lowered her voice. "We could well be sent back to America if the government should get wind of our work. Instead, we carry out our church work under the guise of operating a laundry service. It's pretty successful too. In the evenings, we hold Bible studies in a small room at the back of our house. We have been spreading God's Word for years—with the Lord's protective guidance, of course."

"That's amazing. Don't know as I've ever met a mission—er, an American laundress—before." He gave her a little grin, quite pleased, if not surprised, to have been made privy to such secretive information.

"Oh, goodness." She placed a hand on his arm and cast him a worried glance. "You aren't going to report me to the authorities, are you?"

"What? Good grief, no. I'm heading back to America. The last thing I want to do is speak with the Japanese authorities. They might come up with some reason to detain me."

"Oh, my, we wouldn't want that."

There came a brief pause in their exchange. Another announcement crackled on the loudspeaker, an officer announcing the boarding of another cavalry unit, although not Henry's. *Just get me on that boat so I can start preparing myself for going home. Home. Where Nora and Paige patiently waited.*

"What of your family? Do you and your wife have any children?"

Her question took him quite by surprise. She gave a low chuckle. "I noticed you're wearing a wedding ring. Women always notice such things."

He glanced down at his left hand where his gold wedding band glistened in the sunlight. "Oh! Ha! That's quite comical. Yes, I'm married, and I have a daughter I haven't even met yet. She's almost a year and a half now."

"Oh, my! You must be so excited to reunite with them!"

"I sure am! I married my wife fresh out of high school when I was a sophomore at Michigan State. The government caught up with me, though, and drafted me in late forty-four. After that, it was off to training camp for me and then once the United States bombed Tokyo in Operation Meetinghouse, I received my overseas orders to report to Japan. Been working with the Allied Forces throughout the occupation. When I came here, the city was in quite a mess."

"Oh, don't I know it. Beginning with the Doolittle Raid in forty-two, we sat on pins and needles wondering when the next bombs would drop. Miraculously, throughout all the bombings, our laundry service went untouched. Of course, the last raid was the one that prompted Emperor Hirohito to begin the peace talks. We were never so thankful as when Japan surrendered. So many innocent lives lost in that tragedy. I know that General MacArthur saw the mission as necessary, and I don't doubt it was, but to see so many innocent citizens perish was heart-wrenching."

"That's always the case in times of war. Innocent bloodshed is often a result."

"Yes." There was a bit of a pause in conversation. "So, you did not bring your wife with you. I have noticed many American soldiers having family here."

"We decided it best she stay back, being that she was with child. She moved in with her parents back in our hometown, Muskegon, Michigan."

"That makes a world of sense." She smiled, bit down on her lip, and pondered something before speaking again. "You and your wife are churchgoers?"

"We sure are!" This he said without hesitation. "I was raised in the church. My father is a Wesleyan pastor, and my grandfather, rest his soul, pastored in the Pilgrim Holiness denomination." Why were his nerves starting to get the better of him?

"That's lovely. And your wife? Was she too raised in a Christian home?"

"Yes, my wife is a fine Christian woman. There was a time I—" As soon as he spoke the words, he wished he could take them back. She lifted graying eyebrows in a silent question—as if to encourage him. He weighed his thoughts with care. "Well, there was a time I considered going into the ministry."

Her hazel eyes brightened. "And what should keep you from fulfilling that passion now?"

He thought a minute, tilted his head upward to gaze at a single cloud amid a sea of blue, and then gazed back at the woman missionary. "I suppose my faith has waned a bit since I joined the Army."

Her mouth turned up into what appeared to be an understanding smile. "It happens, young man. Seek the Lord, and you will find Him. He hasn't moved, not even a particle, so you needn't look far for Him. But you must do it with a true sense of longing in your heart."

He gave a slow nod. "I thank you for that."

They seemed to have run out of things to say, at least for the moment, so he turned himself around and faced forward again, eagerly awaiting the next boarding announcement.

"Henry," came a soft voice. He felt a light touch on the arm and quickly turned. His stomach dropped to the ground at the sight of her. "I see you one more time," she said in her broken English.

"R-Rina." His voice cracked. "What are you—why are you here?"

"I come—say goodbye." She sounded desperate. He dared not look at the missionary, even though he heard her tiny gasp. He coughed and then jumped out of line, taking the Japanese girl by the arm and leading her away, out of everyone's earshot, knowing with certainty that the older woman had to be drilling fiery holes into his back. He should have known better than to divulge anything personal to her.

Once away from the bustling crowd of tired and impatient soldiers, he found a shady spot and halted the girl in front of him, looking down on her nearly flawless face. Yes, he'd been attracted to her; he'd admit that. She worked at the military commissary and a lot of fellows flirted with her, but he'd known from the start that she had eyes only for him. To be honest, the notion flattered him. She'd asked him more than once to take her out, but he'd laughingly turned her down, telling her he was married and even had a child.

"You bring me to States," she'd said imploringly. "I make you happy. I have lot of love in my heart."

At that, he'd laughed again. Silly girl, he'd thought. Days, then weeks, then months passed. He saw her nearly every day, not that he necessarily sought her out, but she was just there—in the dining commons feeding hungry soldiers, working in the commissary, selling cigarettes and rations, and flashing her warm smile at everyone she met. Soldiers admired her, but mostly from afar. It was no secret she had her sights set on Private First Class Henry Griffin, never mind that he was a married man with a young child. He could have, *should have*, nipped it in the bud, but he allowed her to play her little game. Maybe even encouraged it to boost his ego. He was no Cary Grant, after all.

Then came that fateful night when he and a number of his buddies decided to saunter down to the local drinking club. As soon as he entered the place, he'd seen her sitting at a table with some of her girlfriends. The local women always patronized the drinking establishments in hopes of hooking up with an American soldier who, with a little luck, might eventually whisk them off to America. Their glances immediately connected, and he'd foolishly encouraged her with a wave and a smile. Servers plunked drinks on their table, and like everyone else present, he started imbibing. Loud music, laughter, dancing, and raucous conversation filled the place.

Next thing he knew, Rina coaxed him onto the dance floor, where he got lost in the twangy tunes and their swaying bodies. By the wee hours of the morning, he'd totally lost all sense of reason and found himself outside with her, his head whirling with dizzying drunkenness, and his body staggering, as they made their way, arm in arm, up the littered, narrow street to her rundown, two-room flat. He had little memory of the night, only that he'd very quickly and shamefully used her for his own pleasure, and she'd encouraged it, afterward proclaiming her undying love for him and begging him to return the sentiment. He recalled too the relentless guilt that settled in on him in that fateful moment and his urgent need to escape. Once outside, he'd retched on the street, then like a pitiful drifter, made his way back to his barracks.

"I told you not to come today, Rina," he said, gripping her narrow shoulders. "We said our goodbyes at the commissary the other day."

Tears streaked down her bronze cheek. "I tell you one more time I have love for you." She placed her hands, one on top of the other, across her heart.

Guilt seared through his veins. "I'm sorry, Rina, truly I am, but I told you I'm married. I have a daughter at home. I—what happened between us was wrong."

"No, no, it very right." She shook her head. "I have great love for you."

"No, you don't. You love the idea of coming to America—like so many other women here."

She sobbed quietly but he dared not show her a bit of comfort lest she take it the wrong way. He dropped his hands to his sides. What a heartless, idiotic fool he'd been to have led her on! He seriously doubted the Lord would forgive him despite what the missionary had said. Henry had stepped out of God's grace. Was there *any* hope for him? Could he ever find his way back to God after all the wrong he'd done? Why, he'd even taken up a filthy smoking habit, one he'd have to drop before going home to Nora. He'd also learned a few choice curse words that would shock the shoes right off his wife's pretty little feet if his tongue should ever slip up.

Rina looked up at him with anxious longing as tears filled her deep brown eyes.

"I'm sorry, Rina. I'm sorry for all of it. None of it should have happened."

Rather than argue, she gave a quiet nod. "I want—I *need* to, to tell you something."

"No, don't say another word."

"It very important."

"Rina, I don't want to hear it. This is goodbye." He reached into his pocket, withdrew his wallet, and removed all of the Japanese currency he had. "Here, take this money. I was going to exchange it for American bills when I returned to the States, but you need it more than I do."

She slapped his hand away and gave her head several fast shakes. For the first time ever, he saw flashes of anger spark in her glittery dark eyes. "You take my body, and you offer money? I no play woman! You not buy me!"

Despite her strong accent and poor English, Rina's rage was loud and clear. Henry felt like cow dung.

"No, no, that wasn't my intention. I just thought—" Before he could finish, she spat at him, just missing his face and hitting his collar instead. He stepped back and took a deep breath, letting the spittle slide down his shirt front. He understood her anger. God forgive him, he truly had taken something sacred from her. As far as he could tell, she'd been a virgin. His heart filled with deep regret. There was nothing he could do. Nothing. The loudspeaker crackled, and this time, it was his regiment's turn to board. He hesitated before turning. "I—I have to go now. Listen, Rina, I know you copied down my father's address from one of my envelopes from home. Please, I beg you, don't try to contact me. It won't do you any good."

She swiped away at her remaining tears and held her head high. "Who want to contact *you?* Ha!" she scoffed, tossing her long, shimmering black hair.

But Henry knew it was all bravado—and all his fault. Her shoulders slumped as she turned and walked away from him.

So that was it then. With resolve, he swiveled on his heel and walked away, the sun scorching his shoulders as he came back into its punishing light. He took great care not to look back. And reminded himself he'd have to take every precaution not to cross paths with that missionary woman during the voyage back to the States.

He was turning a page in his life. Going home. And putting the past and this ugly war far, far behind him.

ONE

For there is nothing hid which shall not become manifest, nor secret which shall not be known and come to light.
—Luke 8:17

September 1955 · Muskegon, Michigan

Daddy, pass the bacon."

Henry Griffin lifted the platter from the center of the table, tilted his head at his feisty ten-year-old daughter Paige, and waited for the all-important word.

She tipped her pigtailed head right back at him and gaped—until it dawned on her. "Plee-ease," she sang out.

"That's better," he said, reaching for the plate of bacon and handing it to her. He winked at his wife Nora, who sat across the table from him. She smiled and gave a little shake of her pretty blond head.

Paul, their seven-year-old second-grader, took a bite of toast, set it down, and took up his glass of orange juice, gulping like he hadn't had a drop of fluid in days. In his haste to quench his thirst, some juice splattered on the front of his plaid, short-sleeved shirt.

"Oh, Paul, look what you just did to your shirt," Nora said with a slight grimace. "I just laundered and pressed that last night. Now we'll have to go look in your drawer for another one."

Paul looked down at his shirt and shrugged. "It don't look bad." He swiped at it with his palm, then wiped his palm on his pant leg. "Sorry, Mom. We're just going to Sunday school and church. Nobody's gonna care that I got a little spill. 'Sides, you can hardly see it."

"Yeah, you can hardly see it, Nora," Henry said with a smile while pushing his chair back and rising. "Sorry to run, but I have to spend a little time in the office to go over my sermon notes again."

"What ya' preaching about, Daddy?" Paige asked. "Is it going to be boring? Are you going to tell any funny stories about us? You can tell that story again about me when I fell off my bike then blamed you for not holding the seat."

He chuckled at his daughter. "I don't think I can fit that one in today. Besides, people don't necessarily want to hear stories repeated. Once is usually sufficient."

"Well, then tell a different one—about me."

Standing up, Henry pushed his chair back under the table, picked up his plate and utensils as Nora had taught the family to do, and carried them to the sink. Glancing down at his daughter, he said, "I don't think I have one about you this morning, but maybe I can talk about that little stain on Paul's shirt, how just rubbing at it won't remove it, but how surrendering it to Mommy's wringer washing machine will make it clean again."

Paige wrinkled her nose. "What does that have to do with your sermon?"

He cast a glance from her to Paul. "You just make sure you listen to my message, and then see if you can make sense of it."

"You should tell everyone that Paul is a fumble fingers," she said.

"Hey, no I'm not."

"Yes, you are."

"Ain't."

"Are."

"Then you're a—a booger nose."

"All right, that's enough," Nora said with just the right amount of sternness to get the kids' attention. "Finish your breakfast so I can wash up these dishes before we walk over to church."

"Can I go over with Daddy? I won't pester him," Paul asked.

"No, Daddy needs his private time."

Henry grinned at his wife, ever the one with the last word. He'd been about to tell Paul he could come along, but, as always, Nora knew best. He did need those extra few minutes to pray about his sermon and reflect on his notes.

"Do you and Herb have the songs worked out for the morning service?" he asked Nora. She was a highly accomplished pianist and played for Sunday services.

"'Holy, Holy, Holy' and 'Rejoice, the Lord Is King,'" Nora answered. "They should fit nicely with your sermon since you said you're speaking about the sovereignty of God."

"Those sound perfect."

Besides playing a fine piano, Nora also sang solos, and occasionally, she and two other ladies performed as a trio. There was also a men's quartet, the Shoreline Gospel Four, which provided special music at least once a month on Sunday mornings and sometimes Sunday nights. Church of the Open Door didn't lack for musicians. In fact, during the summer months, the church held biweekly Saturday evening concerts and advertised them as a means of outreach. Folks came from miles around to enjoy the church's musical talents, with many returning on Sunday mornings. People told Henry that it was his sound biblical preaching that kept them coming back, but he was sure it was the music. He didn't dare think it was his sermons lest he acquire a prideful spirit. Open Door's active Sunday school program was another draw for both children and adults.

Henry kissed his wife and children goodbye before scooting out the kitchen door, which opened to a small side yard with a walkway to his church and office next door. A single red leaf fell from the old maple that stood tall in the middle of the yard. It was nearing that time of year when the leaves would turn color and fall, but for now, the last of summer still hung deep in the air, today's sunshine indicating another scorcher. He paused and glanced up at the beautiful tree.

Years ago, long before he took over the pastorate, the church folks had dubbed it the Mercy Tree. Someone had started a tradition of carving his or her initials into the trunk after choosing to invite Christ into their lives. Some folks had added a date, while others just left their initials. Out of habit, he always gave the tree a glance when passing; it never failed to give him warm feelings. He knew of at least fifteen people in his congregation who had carved their initials into the smooth bark of that tree since he'd come to Church of the Open Door on Wood Street.

As was usually the case for the Sunday morning service, the church was packed wall to wall. The singing went well, and Edgar Warner gave a wonderful solo rendition of "Great Is Thy Faithfulness." Henry had delivered as fine a sermon as he could in hopes of reaching some lost soul who needed words of encouragement. It was always his hope and prayer that his sermons would make an eternal difference in someone's life. Tonight's message would be a continuation of this morning's, only more concise and hitting upon the main points.

After the closing hymn, Henry gave the benediction and then moved down the center aisle to the lobby area to greet parishioners, hear their thoughts about his message, and speak with anyone who might need a word of counsel. A pastor's job took many hours of dedication—everything from daily prayer and studying to visitation if someone took ill, marrying and burying parishioners, going to hospitals to pray with the sick, and calling on church members so that by year's end, everyone would have received at least one pastoral home visit.

His secretary, Marlene Baskin, kept a close eye on his schedule and saw to it he didn't miss any of his appointments. The mother of four had been with him for as long as he'd been at Open Door, almost five years now, and more than once, he wondered what he'd do without her. Most pastors didn't have it in their church budgets to afford a pastoral secretary, but his congregation was big enough and financially stable enough to afford him the luxury. He pondered whether the day would ever come that churches would be able to afford assistant pastors. More and more, churches in larger cities were hiring assistants other than secretaries who could help with visitation duties and occasional preaching, thereby allowing ministers to take off a rare Sunday, but he didn't see that happening at Church of the Open Door any time soon. For now, he was just grateful for Marlene's kind servant heart and organizational skills.

"That was one terrific sermon, Reverend," the elder Thomas Bunyan told him at the door, shaking his hand with a firmness that always made Henry wince a bit. Henry was no weakling, but old Tom, a former sawmill worker, lived up to his last name with his weight, muscle, and stature. Some folks teasingly referred to him as *Paul* Bunyan.

"Well, thank you, Brother Tom. I appreciate your kind remarks. How is Carla doing these days?"

"Oh, you know, good one day, not so great the next. Her back's been givin' her fits the past few weeks. She said to pass on her regards to you."

"Well, you tell her I'll keep praying for her and that I hope she feels better real soon."

"I'll do that."

Tom moved along, making way for Arletta Morehead, the church busybody. He sucked in a cavernous breath, forced a smile, and extended his hand.

"Your sermon was quite good for a change, Reverend," she offered, shaking his hand.

"Why, thank you, Sister." Arletta never failed to sneak in a subtle dig along with her haphazard compliments.

She shook her head and a few strands of wispy gray hair flew out of her bun. "I dare say your stories about your children are going to make their little heads puff right out. Nevertheless, the one you told this morning about the stain on your son's shirt was a good illustration."

"Thank you. I assume you meant that as a compliment."

She tilted her face up and her blue-green eyes narrowed as she peered at him. "Well, you take it any way you please, Reverend." She started to move forward, but abruptly stopped. "Oh! One thing I've noticed of late. That picture on the wall of Christ standing at the door and knocking is starting to slant to one side. Perhaps you can have the janitor fix it this week."

"It's slanting? I hadn't noticed. I'll be sure to tell Sam Cordelle to check that out. Thank you for mentioning it."

"Did I hear someone mention my name?" The rather short but wiry janitor emerged through the crowd. He wore a tidy suit and tie, a far cry from the khaki work attire he sported on Mondays, Wednesdays, and Fridays. He kept the church and office clean and the yard maintained. He also took care of any electrical or mechanical problems if the job was within his skill set.

"Ah, Mr. Cordell. Mrs. Morehead seems to think the picture at the front of the church is slanting to one side. Perhaps you can look at that tomorrow or Wednesday."

"I have a sharp eye about such things," Arletta said with a sniff. "Florence noticed it too after I pointed it out last Sunday. I meant to mention it then. I'm surprised no one else brought it to your attention."

"I am too," Henry said, knowing full well that any slant had to be so minute that the average person wouldn't notice it. He swore Arletta Morehead came to church every week for the sole purpose of finding something to complain about.

Sam pursed his lips. His pale blue eyes, set amid the wrinkles of his deeply tanned face, twinkled. He looked for all the world like he was trying not to laugh. "Mrs. Morehead, in the future, when you see a specific need, try not to bother Reverend Griffin with it. I'm the one you need to seek out."

"Well, I should think he'd want to also keep abreast."

"The reverend has more pressing issues, ma'am."

That seemed to shush her. "You have a wonderful afternoon now, Mrs. Morehead," Henry said.

She gave a little wave as she turned. "Oh, I'll try. I plan to pull a few weeds. Yes, I know it's the Sabbath, but I don't think the Lord will mind if I do some light work."

"Not at all."

"Well, you fix that picture then, Mr. Cordelle." With that, she turned and headed for the door.

Henry let out a heavy sigh. "Thank you, Sam."

"You're mighty welcome, Reverend. I've known that woman a long time, so I know she thrives on keeping everyone on their toes." Someone came up behind Sam and tapped him on the shoulder, drawing his attention elsewhere.

Henry extended well-wishes to a few more parishioners until at last, the crowd had thinned to only a few stragglers. He greeted each one by name, including several teens and the few children who hadn't scooted out the door ahead of their parents to play in the churchyard. Most Sundays, Nora stood at his side, but this morning, something had waylaid her. A quick glance across the lobby, and he spotted her speaking with her good friend Veronica Hardy. They looked deeply engaged, so he turned his attention to the last of the attendees, his parents being two of them. They were always among the last to leave, as both enjoyed talking. He smiled at his father when he approached.

Lester Griffin extended his hand and gave Henry's a hearty shake. "Great message as usual, Son. I like how you tied in that little story about Paul spilling on his shirt this morning, and how it had to be put through the wringer before the stain would wash away. Sometimes, that's how life goes. We can't always expect to be forgiven without paying some sort of consequence. Can be painful sometimes. You always manage to relay one story or another to make it come to life for folks."

"Well, thanks, Dad, and you're right. Sometimes sin requires more than mere forgiveness, especially when it affects others."

His mother, Lillian, gave him a quick kiss on the cheek. "Oh, Henry, sometimes I still marvel that we raised you to be such a fine man of God—and a preacher at that!"

He chuckled. "Your prayers made all the difference, I'm sure, but Mother, you do say that every Sunday. I think you may be a bit partial."

"Now, now, it's not just me. Other people tell me they enjoy your sermons. By the way, don't forget you're coming over for dinner today."

"Of course, Mother, Nora mentioned it a couple of days ago."

Lester winked and leaned forward. "She's got a roast in the oven along with carrots and potatoes."

"My favorite," said Henry, smiling at them both.

"Oh, and the Parkers are joining us," his father added. "We figured Paul and Paige would enjoy having some children to play with."

"That's going to be a houseful."

Lester gave Lillian a playful little jab in the side, and she giggled. "You know your mother. She's always up for entertaining." He started to turn then stopped. "Oh! I almost forgot." He reached into his suit jacket and pulled out an envelope. "This came for you Friday. It's addressed to you, but was sent to our address. It's an airmail letter."

Henry felt his brow furrow. He took the feather-light envelope and gave it a quick glance. He didn't recognize the extra small handwriting in the upper left corner or the sender's last name. The only thing he did recognize was the Japanese postage stamps. "Humph. No idea." He stuffed it in his own suitcoat pocket. "I'll open it later. Might be an old Army buddy. I have a couple of friends who married girls there and are still living in Tokyo."

"Huh. Interesting. Well, we'll see you in a bit," Lester said.

"Nora and I need to tidy things up a bit in preparation for tonight's service, but we'll be over as soon as we can."

"We'll take Paige and Paul with us now," his mother said.

"They'll love that."

His parents waved and walked out into the lovely September sunshine.

⌒

Conversation at his parents' house had freely flowed along with spurts of laughter. His mother's roast had been so tender that it fell apart with a fork. Of course, her apple pie, still warm when served, had drawn a lot of oohs and ahhs. Ken and Sandra Parker were close in age to Henry and Nora. They had four children ranging in ages from four to twelve—all boys, much to Paige's chagrin.

"All they wanna do is boy stuff," she complained in the car on the way home that afternoon.

"Well, they are boys, honey," Nora said with a half-turn of her head, giving a little chuckle.

"And they're fun!" said Paul, bouncing like a rubber ball on the back seat.

"Of course, you'd say that. I hope Grandma doesn't invite them again when we go there for Sunday dinner."

"Paige, that's not a nice thing to say," Nora said. "They are a very lovely family, and the boys are well-mannered."

"Well, Howie kept chasing me outside and trying to pull my braids. I don't call that well-mannered. That's why I came in the house."

"You're definitely pretty enough to chase," Henry told her. "He might have a crush on you."

"Ewww. Daddy, don't make me barf."

"Paige, that's not a lady-like word," Nora said. The girl quieted.

Through his rearview mirror, Henry watched his daughter sulk, her blond braids blowing away from her face due to her half-open window. As the day grew longer, it had also grown hotter. Tonight's service would be unseasonably warm, even with all the church windows open. Henry loosened his tie.

They rode along, the sun lower in the sky these days compared to midsummer. He gave a quick glance at Nora. The way the sun's rays caught her shoulder-length blond hair made it shimmer, and the wind from her window blew it like a wild kite. Gee-whiz, she was so beautiful. Henry smiled to himself, once again thinking how blessed he was to have her for a wife.

"Can we go to the lake today?" Paul asked. "It's hot."

"Sorry, buddy," Henry said. "It's too late, I'm afraid. Maybe next Sunday."

"Did you forget? Mother has invited us to her house next Sunday," Nora said. "She's out of town this weekend visiting Aunt Martha, but she's already counting on us for Sunday dinner next week. She's invited your parents as well."

"Oh, I did forget. Seems we're always going to someone's house. When can we stay home on a Sunday afternoon, just the four of us?"

"The Sunday after next," she said with a winning smile, reaching across the seat and putting her hand on his knee to give it a little squeeze.

"Good grief, do you have to be so fetching?" he whispered to her.

She tossed back her head and gave a tiny, almost bashful, snicker. "And do you have to be so hopeless?"

"It's your fault," he said, winking at her.

"What are you guys talkin' about?" Paige asked. "I can't hear with all these windows down."

"Oh, nothing much," Nora answered, swinging her head around again.

The children took to bickering about nothing important. At four-thirty, Henry steered his green 1952 Ford sedan into their driveway and cut the motor. Both kids beat them out of the car, slamming the doors behind them and racing to the red-brick, three-bedroom, ranch-style house with the detached one-stall garage, screaming about who would make it to the front door first. The wild pair clamored up the porch steps and reached for the doorknob, but as it turned out, Paige, the faster of the two, if not the more determined, opened it first and rushed inside. Paul shrugged his shoulders in defeat and followed on her heels, failing to close the door behind him.

"Oh yeah, they slam the car doors but leave the house door wide open to invite all the flies inside," Henry murmured.

"Of course."

They both sighed, almost simultaneously. Nora giggled. Just then, Paige came back to the front door, yelled something at her brother, and slammed it shut.

"They are quite something, aren't they?" Nora said. "Sometimes, I don't want them to grow up. Ever. And the next day, I want them fully grown and living one hundred miles away."

Henry nodded. "Not one thousand?"

"No, I want them at least close enough to visit. I need to find a way to keep my thumb on them."

At that, they both laughed. Henry sank down into his seat, rested his head on the back of it, and then lazily turned to gaze at her. "Maybe we should start loaning them to our parents every other weekend. Then I could have my way with you whenever I wanted."

"Reverend Griffin! You have your way with me enough as it is! The last thing we want is more children. Lucky for you, tonight is a safe time."

"No more children, eh?"

"Absolutely not. We agreed on that a few years ago, remember?"

"Hm. I guess we did." He reached up, took hold of the back of her neck, and dragged her close to steal a kiss and rub her left thigh. It lasted all of ten seconds before she sat up.

"Good gracious granny!" she exclaimed. "The neighbors might have seen that."

"So?"

"Well—" She pressed at the wrinkles in her skirt and gave a little cough. "We don't want to make them jealous."

A good chuckle rolled out of him. "Good point." He sat up, then turned to give her a good perusal. "I think I failed to tell you I love you today."

"No, you told me when we first got up this morning."

"Did I? Did you say it back?"

"Of course. You don't remember?"

"Oh, that's right, I was about to go down the hall to the bathroom when you pulled on my arm and dragged me back into the bedroom, kicked the door shut, and pulled me into a ravishing embrace, hoping to get me back into—"

She slapped his arm, "Oh, stop it. I did no such thing."

"But you were thinking about it."

She rolled her eyes. "I am getting out of the car now."

Just as she reached for the door handle, he snagged her arm and bent over the seat to steal one more kiss, this time, deeper and more intense.

When he pulled back, she took a big gulp of air. "My stars in glory!"

He lifted her chin with a curled index finger. "Just a little something for you to think about today."

She fumbled with her ruffled collar. "Well, thank you for the warning." She wrestled with the door latch and escaped before he could grab hold of her for one more smooch. Her giggle rang through the air as she skipped like a teenager up the walk.

TWO

Ye have sinned against the LORD: and be sure your sin will find you out.
—Numbers 32:23 (KJV)

Henry and Nora had been playing romantic games with each other for the rest of the day, until it came time to walk over to church. Of course, they'd been secretive about their actions, throwing playful glances at each other, sending wordy innuendos that neither child could possibly interpret as suggestive, but phrases both adults clearly read as they were intended.

Nora found herself blushing throughout the afternoon, not that her husband embarrassed her, but that she was afraid her children would somehow catch on. Occasionally, Henry would nudge against her and whisper a sweet nothing in her ear to which she'd give a nervous giggle then glance around to see if either Paul or Paige were paying attention. Thank goodness, they were either busy working the family's latest jigsaw puzzle or reading a book or playing a game of checkers. At one point, they went outside to play marbles, leaving Henry and Nora alone and allowing him to take full advantage of the situation by continuing his flirtatious play and kissing her silly. She had to admit his actions had certainly got her thinking about how things would go tonight once they put their children to bed, the very notion of which set her heart to wildly pumping.

The evening service was sparsely attended, probably because folks were anxious to fit in as much as they could of the last of summer. Sunday afternoons meant long car rides for some families, picnics at a park, a walk along the Lake Michigan shoreline, or visiting with friends and family. Those kinds of days were running short, as October would arrive before long—and with it would come cooler air, the turning of leaves, rain, and everything else that went along with fall weather. Both children were growing like little weeds and would soon need new clothes for the winter months, so Nora had been trying to pinch pennies so she could buy them a few things, shoes and boots high on the list. She considered herself a good seamstress and thus planned to make a few new dresses for Paige and some new shirts and pants for Paul. However, sewing took a large chunk of time, and it wasn't a task she entirely loved. She would check out the secondhand shops first before going to the downtown department stores like Hardy-Herpolsheimer's or Sears and Roebuck. Anything to cut corners.

Pastors didn't bring home much of an income, so Nora had been giving serious thought to finding a job. In fact, she'd spoken to Bill Wittmyer, the grocer, just last Sunday, and he mentioned that he needed a bookkeeper. He had said she'd be well-suited for the position, and she had to admit the very notion of making money to contribute to the household excited her. Of course, she would have to talk to Henry about it.

At eight o'clock, Nora told the children to start preparing for bed. "Go get your pajamas on and brush your teeth and then we'll come read the evening Scriptures to you and say our nighttime prayers."

"Can we read in bed for a while?" Paige asked.

"A little while," said Nora. "But you have to get up bright and early for school tomorrow."

They sauntered off, Paige carrying her book with her, and Paul expelling a yawn as he rose from the card table where he'd been working a puzzle. It was the end of another busy weekend.

Later that night, still awake after lovemaking, Henry and Nora lay tucked under a lightweight blanket facing each other, spent but wholly satisfied, his arm resting over her hip, hers positioned across his side, their faces just inches apart as they quietly stared into the other's eyes. His dark brown eyes looked like the sweetest chocolate.

"It was a nice day today," he whispered.

"The best kind. I love the Sabbath for its rest and slower pace. Today, I reflected on how blessed we are. Our children, while they aren't perfect, are truly little gems, and our marriage—well, it's about as good as any marital union could be."

He gave a lazy grin. "I must agree with you on all points."

"You gave two fine sermons today, Reverend."

"Why, thank you, Mrs. Reverend."

She chortled, even as her eyes grew heavy. "Hm. Morning comes quickly."

"Indeed, it does, and I have an eight o'clock appointment with Brother Samuel from Lake Drive Methodist Church. He wants to pick my brain about how to handle a problem that's arisen in his congregation. He says he needs my younger point of view even though I'm sure he's fully capable of handling the matter on his own."

"He puts a lot of stock in what you have to say, as do many of our parishioners. What sort of problem is he dealing with?"

"Apparently, the church Sunday school superintendent appears to be having an affair with one of the deacons. Of course, they're both married to other people, so it's a rather dire situation."

"Oh, I'm sorry to hear that. I hope Reverend Samuel can lead them to repentance and help them to reconcile with their spouses. I'll be praying about the matter in the morning while I get the children ready for school, and I'll ask the Lord to lead you in just what to say to dear Reverend Samuel."

"Hm. Thank you." They both gave tired nods, granted one another a quick goodnight kiss, and then turned over to go to sleep.

For a change, Nora drifted into a deep sleep before Henry. For some reason, bringing up the matter of his appointment with Brother Samuel tomorrow had him thinking about what he would do should that sort of situation pop up in his own congregation. For sure he would take the scriptural route, first confronting the persons and encouraging them to turn from their sin. If that didn't work, he would then call together the elders of the church, pray about the matter, and then as a concerned body of leaders, confront the guilty parties again. If they continued in sin, discounting the church leaders' every word and flaunting their immorality before the masses, they would be left with no choice but to ban the parishioners from reentering into worship until they showed true signs of repentance. He sighed at the thought. It was a tough tenet to contend with, but should he ever come upon it, he would have to follow through as the Lord led.

He turned over, now looking at Nora's slender back. He closed his eyes and tried to drift into sleep mode, but then his thoughts carried him back to the morning service. He pondered his message, going over every phrase he could recall speaking and then criticizing himself for not having included this point or that. It became a vicious battle in his mind, as he wrestled around, pulling the sheets one way and then another. For some reason, his mind took him to his parents and their kind, supportive ways—and that's when it hit him.

His eyes popped open. The letter! How could he have forgotten? His father had handed him a letter that morning, an airmail letter of all things, which he'd only pondered for a second or two before stuffing it into his suitcoat pocket. And he'd not given it a thought the rest of the day. He flipped over onto his back and stared upward where the reflection of a single street light glanced off the ceiling. Should he go fishing for the letter now or wait till morning? But he had that early appointment tomorrow. It would be a tough morning, showering, then grabbing a quick bite to eat, and leaving the house before his children thought up some reason to delay him. He sighed and glanced at his wife. Her steady breaths told him she slept soundly, so Henry quietly removed the covers. Sitting on the side of the bed, he gave a lazy stretch, then stood and walked to the closet they shared. He opened the door and flinched when the thing squeaked. He needed to oil that stupid hinge. He pushed through the garments hanging in the closet and with what dim light he had to work with, finally located his suitcoat and the pocket containing the letter. Once it was in his hand, he padded out of the bedroom and down the hall to the kitchen.

Henry flipped on the light switch, walked to the sink, and took a glass down from the cupboard above it. He turned on the faucet to fill it. Sitting at the kitchen table, he took a couple sips of water and then placed the envelope in front of him. The name neatly printed in the upper left-hand corner was "Helen Felton"—certainly nobody he knew. He carefully peeled back the sealed portion of the letter and opened it. That's when a small photo fell out, along with another piece of folded paper. He took up the picture first and studied it. His first thought was that someone was sending him a picture of himself, for it resembled him as a boy, but upon closer inspection, he saw a child of at least partial Asian descent. Mildly curious, he unfolded the paper and found a letter penned to him.

Dear Mr. Griffin,

I am quite certain you are wondering who I am and why I would be writing to you. First, let me refresh your memory about the day in Tokyo some nine years ago when you were preparing to board the ship that would take you back to America. Perhaps you won't recall it, but you and I had a brief conversation while standing on the docks. I told you that my husband and I were missionaries, and that we had four sons. Well, my husband died two years ago, and while I have enjoyed continuing the missionary work, I am getting up in age and it is time that I return to the States for my retirement years. Three out of four of my sons live in the States, which gives me more incentive to move back. My fourth son will remain in Tokyo so he and his Japanese wife and their five children can carry on the work that my husband and I began 52 years ago.

The reason I am posting this letter to you is because of a young Japanese girl named Rina Hamada who you met in Tokyo. She passed away from a very progressive form of cancer four months ago. She had located our family mission about six months after you and I met. I recall she wanted to say goodbye to you that day, so I, of course, remembered her when she came to our mission requesting assistance. She was pregnant, you see, and because she had no family, we invited her to live with us until after her baby was born.

At this revelation, Henry's body gave a terrible jolt. Why was this woman telling him all this? He raised his head and stared across the room, mouth agape. *Surely not. It couldn't be.* There'd only been that one time with Rina. One careless slipup—and he'd been drunk, so he wasn't even in his right mind. Before reading further, he picked up the picture of the boy and stared hard at it. The facial structure, the nose, the jaw line…the mouth. Even that faintly showing dimple in his left cheek, all features Henry himself had. The eyes were different, Asian—and the hair color was a deeper shade, almost black, compared to his dark brown. He did a quick mental calculation. *Eight.* If—*if*—it was possible that this boy was his—he would be about eight years old, two years younger than Paige, one year older than Paul.

It was then that he broke into a cold sweat and fought off a wave of sickening dizziness. His chest cinched as he tried to catch a breath, but that woozy wave of confusion made breathing hard. What would he do—if it were true? His stomach quivered with nausea while a knot started to form there. For a moment, he thought he might have to vomit. Several deep, slow breaths seemed to calm him to the point of being able to pick up the letter and finish reading. It was the least he could do—if for no other reason than to collect all the facts. Perhaps this was nothing but a big misunderstanding. He swallowed hard and continued.

Since getting to know Rina, we remained very close to her and once Emiko was born, we did all we could to help her raise him, providing her with all she'd need to get back out on her own. Now, if you haven't already figured it out, Emiko is your son. Rina told me she had never been with a man before you, and to tell you the truth, she became so busy helping at our mission and working in our laundry service to support her son, she never did date another man.

He paused again, his heart racing, his stomach clenched into a terrible, rock-like ball as a mixture of terror and shock overtook him. He forced himself to read on.

I am leaving Tokyo by jet with a crew of dignitaries and will be bringing Emiko with me. I have obtained legal custody of him, but also have permission and legal backing to turn him over to you, his legal father. (I do have the birth certificate in my possession.) I am in my 70s and not as healthy as I once was, so I am not the best choice for continuing to raise Emiko, although I deeply care for him. I would like you to meet him—since he is your son, and I would hope once you do, you will wish to keep him with you. He is a brilliant young man and quite handsome as you will see from the picture I am including. Rina told me he favors you, and from what I remember of you, I would have to agree. The child has learned to speak good English, all thanks to his mother who was quite insistent. If you cannot raise him, Mr. Griffin, I will find an American family affiliated with my mission that will gladly adopt him. To set you at ease, I have not told Emiko about you, so if he does not have the opportunity to meet you, he will not suffer any disappointment. Rina kept very mum about you as well, so the boy knows very little about his father, only that he is an American.

I know this must all come as a tremendous shock to you—that you have a son you didn't have an inkling about. Rina told me she sat down at least a hundred times to start a letter to you, but every time, she tossed it into the wastebasket, deciding it best not to burden you. She also told me you made it very clear she was not to contact you under any circumstances, and although I disagreed with her decision, I did not interfere. However, now that she has passed, I feel it only right that I inform you—on the chance you will choose to raise your own son.

I will be in contact with you when I arrive on American soil. From there, we will arrange to meet in person. Please be on the look-out for another letter from me soon.

Yours very truly,
Helen Felton

Feeling distraught from the top of his head down to the heels of his feet, Henry shakily folded the letter and quite mindlessly put it back in the envelope, but not before he gave the photograph of Emiko one final study. He had a third child. *Emiko.* He tested the name on his whispering lips.

Nora. What was he going to tell her? Shoot, *how* was he going to tell her? His stomach roiled with a new wave of nausea. A bitter taste pooled in his mouth, and he knew he had to make a dash for the bathroom. He threw the envelope down on the table, jumped up and ran down the hall. Once there, he lifted the toilet lid, bent over, and heaved. He stayed there till he was sure he'd finished, gasping for breath and mopping his forehead, which by now was dripping with perspiration.

"Henry!"

He jumped at Nora's voice. She hit the light switch. "Uhhh," he moaned, straightening while also splaying his hand over his gut. The sight of her standing in the doorway, deep concern etched in her brow, her blond hair disheveled from their earlier lovemaking, made him feel worse.

"Honey, what's wrong?" she exclaimed. "You were fine when we went to sleep. Here, sit down." She reached across him, flushed the toilet, and put the seat down. "Sit. I'll go get you a glass of water."

"No!" The letter! She might see the envelope lying there on the kitchen table. "No, I'm—fine. I don't need a drink."

"Of course, you do." She turned, but he stood and took her by the arm, stopping her mid-step. "I'm fine. Go—go back to bed. I'll join you soon."

She frowned. "What on earth? You're as pale as if you'd just seen a ghost."

"Well, I—Maybe I—I just ate something that didn't settle with me."

She stood there hesitating, worry in her eyes. She laid a palm against his forehead in the same way she did her children when checking for a fever. He covered her hand. "I'm fine. Really. Go back to bed."

She stood there a few seconds longer, studying his face, as if she didn't quite believe him. And for good reason, he thought to himself. "All right then. Are you coming back to bed then?"

"Yes, I'll be there soon. Just give me a minute to make sure my stomach has settled."

She scratched her temple and wrinkled her brow. "You're sure I can't go get you a glass of water?"

"I'm sure. If I want one, I'll get it myself. Go on now."

She didn't go readily, but she did finally amble back to their bedroom. And that's when he expelled a heavy breath of relief. He had to get that letter and burn it. No, he couldn't burn it. He'd need to reread it. Then he had to put it in a place where Nora wouldn't find it. But what of the boy, Emiko? What was he going to do about him? Mrs. Felton said something about finding someone in America who could adopt him. Yes, yes, that was it. He'd give her permission to do that. That way, he would never have to confess a word to Nora about anything. Ever. It had to be that way. There was no other option, not for him, a well-respected pastor of a thriving evangelical church.

THREE

I said unto the LORD, Thou art my God: hear the voice of my supplica-
tions, O LORD...Grant not, O LORD, the desires of the wicked: further
not his wicked device; lest they exalt themselves.
—Psalm 140:6, 8 (KJV)

N ora did not awaken again, and she had to assume that Henry
had slept well the remainder of the night for she'd never heard
any stirring. She'd had little chance to talk to him this morning though,
as he'd had to leave in quite a hurry. As a matter of fact, he had even
risen ahead of her. He'd given her a hasty kiss goodbye, told her everything was fine, and headed out the door even before the children made
it to the kitchen table for their breakfast. That was nothing unusual,
though, since he was a busy man and often liked to arise well before
dawn to pray, read his Bible, and then leave extra early for his office,
especially on Mondays. He spent all week researching and preparing for
the following Sunday's message. He was a fine speaker, even charismatic
in his delivery, which seemed to be drawing more and more people to
their congregation.

She had gotten the children off to school without incident for a
change. There'd been little fussing between them, which meant they'd
both gotten a good night's sleep. Once they departed with the other

neighborhood kids for their six-block walk to Moon Elementary School, she sat down in her living room to have her own quiet time with her Savior. She would admit she wasn't nearly the spiritual giant Henry was, but she aimed high and always prayed the Lord would make her worthy of her calling as a pastor's wife.

The telephone sounded two quick rings, indicating someone was trying to reach her. Any other ring code would have meant someone else on the party line had received a call. Having a telephone was a necessity for a minister, even though 40 percent of Americans still didn't have one. It hardly seemed possible, but she'd read the other day in the *Muskegon Chronicle* that sometime soon, every American, and perhaps citizen across the world, would own a telephone. She shook her head at the very idea and made her way to the ringing apparatus, picking it up on the caller's third attempt.

She recognized the woman's name right away. Shirley Roberts was one of their newer church attendees. She was married with four children and attended weekly, almost always sitting in the fourth row from the front on what Nora called the piano side. From her vantage point on the bench, she could easily make out who attended on any given Sunday morning and on what side of the church they preferred to sit.

"Well, good morning, Mrs. Roberts. It is so nice to hear from you. Were you hoping to speak to Reverend Griffin? If so, I'm afraid he..."

"No, no, I—I was actually hoping to speak to you, Mrs. Griffin. If it's no trouble."

"Oh, goodness, it's no trouble at all. What can I do for you?"

"I—it's difficult for me to say."

"Would you like to drive over for a visit? My children are in school just as I'm sure yours are. I happen to be free."

"That's very kind of you, but I'm afraid I can't get away just now."

"Alright, well then, please tell me how I can help you."

A click sounded, meaning someone on the party line had either picked up to eavesdrop or hung up after realizing the line was busy. More likely it was the former. For that reason, most folks knew better than to speak about private issues on the telephone—unless they didn't mind having their news spread around town.

Shirley Roberts sighed. "I would like to request that you pray for my husband. He has no use for church. He doesn't mind that I come and bring the kids, but he himself has no interest."

"I would be honored to pray for him." Nora thought a minute. "Are you sure you don't want to come over for tea or coffee? I made some fresh muffins just this morning. You could talk freely here."

"That's so very kind of you, but it would be hard for me to get away. We only have one car, and my husband is off playing golf right now. He likes to play while the weather's nice before starting his shift at the furniture factory."

"I see. Well, I would offer to visit you except that our spare car is currently not working. Henry has tried working on it, but I fear he's done more harm than good." She gave a little laugh. "He now needs to take it to the shop, so there it sits in the driveway being quite useless."

"Oh, good heavens, I certainly wouldn't ask you to come here. I think for now, prayer will suffice. It's the first time I've ever asked anyone to pray for my husband. He would probably be mortified—and perhaps even mad at me if he knew."

"Well, you don't need to worry that I'll tell him. Besides, Christians are meant to pray for one another. I've just been reading about the early church in the book of Acts and how they learned to lift one another up in prayer and care for one another's needs. In the future, don't be afraid to ask me to pray. Have you invited your husband to come to church with you?"

"Oh yes, but as I said, he has no use for it. He always says church is full of hypocrites. I think one day, he may come, just to see what all the commotion is about. I talk almost every day about how wonderful Church of the Open Door is—and the music—my, oh my, it's amazing. Everyone is so talented, you most of all."

"Thank you so much. I'm thrilled you're enjoying our church. The people are lovely too, and, yes, there is a good deal of talent. As far as your husband thinking the church is full of hypocrites, that does seem to be many folks' standard excuse for not attending. Everyone has his and her own reasons. Unfortunately, the world is full of imperfect people, perhaps not all hypocrites, but plenty of sinners for sure. That's why we need Christ and His church."

"That's what I tell Fred. He grew up attending regularly, but after we married, someone said something hurtful to him in church. I don't even recall what it was, but it damaged his ego. He can be a difficult man to live with, and truthfully, he doesn't have many friends because of it. Once he makes up his mind about something, it is very hard to get him to change it. Anyway, that's when he stopped attending—about ten years ago I'd say. I had been attending that same church ever since, but about a year ago, the Lord started nudging me to try Open Door. I got to thinking if I started going somewhere else, he might give church another try, but so far, he's shown no interest. Instead, he drops us all off, then drives straight to Ryke's Bakery for a doughnut and coffee—and sits there till he figures church is over. Oh dear, now I fear I've plain talked your ear right off. I'm sorry."

"No, no, I'm glad you're talking to me. It seems you need to get it off your chest. I'll start praying that your husband has a hunger for spiritual things, and that he'll agree to return to church."

"Thank you so much. I appreciate it."

Another click sounded on the line. It was clear they had eavesdroppers. "Listen, Mrs. Roberts, I'm sorry we only have one working car, and Henry is driving it. Let me just tell you I will be in prayer for you this week. I'll look for you in church next Sunday, and perhaps we can set aside a bit of time for talking then."

"That would be lovely, except I can't talk long. Fred is not the most patient man."

Nora chuckled. "What man is? I'll be praying for Fred—and you as well."

"Thank you for listening. People are supposed to keep things to themselves and work out their own family matters, but I just felt I could talk to you."

"Everyone needs a listening ear now and then."

"Thank you, Mrs. Griffin."

"Please, call me Nora."

"But you're the preacher's wife."

"That doesn't make me anyone out of the ordinary. May I call you Shirley?"

"Please do!" She could almost *hear* the woman's smile of relief.

"I'll look for you next Sunday."

They said their goodbyes, and with her hand still resting on the phone, Nora sat in the cushioned seat of the little telephone table, the hum of the refrigerator in the other room her only distraction. She bowed her head. "Lord, in times like these, You alone are our answer. Please intervene in this situation, and help Fred to realize church is not a place full of hypocrites, but rather a place of love where sinners can come together, imperfect as they are, and learn of Your amazing, forgiving love. Amen."

She opened her eyes, stood, and returned to the sofa to reengage in her study of Acts.

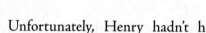

Unfortunately, Henry hadn't had much insight for Reverend Samuel's congregational matter that morning. His mind was too occupied with his own past sin to have the wherewithal to deal with someone else's indiscretion. The whole time he'd sat in the empty sanctuary on the front pew with the elder Reverend Samuel, guilt sizzled in his heart. He could barely even concentrate for all the shame, not to mention the confusion and disbelief that raced through his blood. A couple of times, Brother Samuel had asked if he was all right, mentioning that Henry seemed troubled by something. The elder preacher had insight for certain. Guiltily, Henry had said all was well and apologized for being distracted. He'd tried to listen with his whole heart to the pastor's troubling situation, and in the end, had even prayed aloud over it, asking God to lend direction and wisdom to the minister as he dealt with the guilty parties in his congregation. But the whole while he prayed, he realized he was the guilty one. Who did he think he was praying for someone else when he could barely see past his own major flaw? He'd left Reverend Samuel's church carrying a weight of defeat.

He supposed he needed to talk to someone about the letter from Mrs. Felton, but he knew exactly what they'd say: "You must tell Nora." And they'd be right. In fact, he should have told her about his infidelity upon his return from Tokyo, but no time had seemed right to him, and so weeks turned into months, and months into years. Besides, he'd gotten his spiritual life back in order, had sensed a call to the ministry, and prioritized his marriage and personal life. He couldn't imagine messing it up.

Now, however, the whole thing was a rotten, fumbled-up mess! He had a son he never knew existed. A very faint memory returned to him of that day at the docks when Rina had come to say goodbye. In a desperate tone, she'd said she had something to tell him, but he'd shut her down, saying he didn't want to hear it. He'd thought she simply wanted to proclaim her love one last time. Instead, had she wished to tell him she was pregnant? Had it been eating at her to let him know before he got on the ship? Had she thought telling him would make him change his mind about leaving? Whatever the case, she'd failed to tell him that day, and every day after that—until the years came and went. They were an ocean apart. Maybe she feared telling him would prompt him to come back to Japan and take his son with him, making it impossible for her to ever see him again. Oh, how the thoughts sped through his mind all that morning and all that day!

He'd barely had it in him to come up with a sermon topic for next Sunday, and when he did, he couldn't concentrate enough to make it come together. He needed to find someone else to preach for him. That's what he needed. And he needed to take Nora away for the weekend so he could spill the whole sordid mess to her. He'd had a sorry, one-night stand, he would tell her. But just admitting the words to himself was more than he could handle.

How in the world would Nora take such news? How would his parents, his brothers living in Pennsylvania and Wisconsin, his mother-in-law, who already viewed him as less than ideal? How would they all react when he announced, "Surprise! I have another son!"? And what of the church busybody, Arletta Morehead? Once she got the first word about his wretched sin, he could kiss his tenure at Church of the Open Door goodbye. As a matter of fact, his entire career as a minister could well be over, save for divine intervention. Would the board of elders tell him to pack up his office and leave immediately? His head spun with all the worst scenarios.

After leaving Reverend Samuel's church, he'd pulled over into a little city park and sat under the shade of a tree in the parking lot to look at Emiko's picture. He had traced his finger over the boy's face, memorized each feature, marveled at the similarities between the two of them, and shed a few tears at the notion of giving him to another family. Then he'd quickly swiped at his face, stuffed the picture back into his pocket, and driven away.

Now, he sat in his office, fumbling through paperwork, flipping through study books, opening and closing his Bible, and staring out the window at the Mercy Tree, its branches swaying in the wind. Through his open window, it felt as though a storm were brewing. Overhead, clouds moved, their shapes ever-changing, the sun peeking in and out.

He'd carved his initials in that tree when they'd first moved back to Muskegon after accepting the pastoral position at Church of the Open Door. For him, it had served as a symbol of new beginnings and heartfelt gratitude. He didn't know if Nora had ever carved her initials in the smooth bark. Truly, the Mercy Tree tradition was more for new believers. But he'd done it nonetheless and felt better for it. Now, here he was five years later, staring out the window of a late summer day and viewing himself as the most inept, sinful, deceitful human on earth. "Lord, what am I going to do?" He whispered the prayer, but no feelings of comfort or reassurance filled his heart. He wasn't worthy of God's listening ear. Far from it.

FOUR

Let us therefore use diligence to enter into that rest, that no one may fall after the same example of not hearkening to the word. For the word of God is living and operative, and sharper than any two-edged sword, and penetrating to the division of soul and spirit, both of joints and marrow, and a discerner of the thoughts and intents of the heart. And there is not a creature unapparent before him; but all things are naked and laid bare to his eyes, with whom we have to do.
—Hebrews 4:11–13

The children arrived home at precisely three-thirty with Paul instantly begging for permission to run next door to his friend's house. The neighbors had just gotten a new television set on Saturday, and Paul was eager to see one up close, since he'd only seen one while peering into a store window on Western Avenue.

Nora nodded her head. "All right, but don't stay long. I don't want you wearing out your welcome over there."

Paul gave a gleeful cheer and disappeared quick as a wink. Out the front window, she caught sight of him racing across the yard to the house next door.

Paige plopped her ten-year-old self on the overstuffed chair. "When are we going to get a television? All my friends have sets at home. They talk about watching the coolest shows, like *The Adventures of Ozzie and Harriet* and *Father Knows Best*." Dramatic by nature, she swept the back of her hand across her brow and released a loud sigh.

"I know, I know, Hollywood converted those wonderful radio shows into television shows. It's a shame. I so enjoyed listening to them."

"Well, if we had a television, you'd be able to watch them. It's not fair."

"It's plenty fair. First, I sincerely doubt all of your friends have television sets. They are very expensive. Goodness, we have a car sitting out in the driveway needing repairs. How could we possibly afford a silly box with moving pictures if we can't even scrape up the money to fix our spare car?"

"I don't know. Other people do."

"Do you have homework?" she asked, thinking a change of subject might help.

"I have a dumb state capitals test tomorrow. And Mrs. Johnson said we have to spell every single word correctly or it will be marked wrong even if we got the right city."

"Well, then I guess you do have homework."

Another long sigh spilled out of her. "Can we ever get a puppy?"

"What? Where did that come from?"

"My friend Lizzie got a puppy yesterday."

"That's nice."

"Well, why don't we have one?"

"I suppose because they're a lot of work."

"I'm old enough to take care of one. And Paul could help."

"Let's talk about this another time, shall we?"

"So, you're saying maybe?" The girl brightened.

"I said no such thing." She picked up the rug in the entryway, opened the screen door, and stepped outside to give it a good shake. Then, returning, she spread it back out on the floor, allowing the door to close with a little whack behind her. A quick glance over her shoulder revealed that Paige had not yet moved. "Do you want some help studying your states and capitals?"

"Maybe after supper. When are we gonna get a television?"

"Paige, you need to find something to do. How about you go outside and water the patio flowers for me?"

The girl dragged herself up out of the chair and sauntered into the kitchen. "Can I have a snack?"

"Just something light. I don't want you spoiling your supper."

"What are we having?"

"Meatballs."

"That's all?"

"No."

The refrigerator door squeaked open. "Where's the milk? Oh, never mind, I found it."

"You'll water the flowers for me?"

"Yes, Mother."

Mother? Good glory, sometimes it felt like her daughter was ten going on fifteen.

"Listen, I'm going to run over to the church to see Daddy for a minute."

"Okay," was all she got in return as she pushed through the screen door and headed across the lawn. She had been thinking about her husband a good share of the day, remembering last night and his strange bout with nausea, and then wondering too how his visit with Reverend Samuel had gone.

Had Henry's secretary Marlene Baskin been in, Nora would have asked her if Henry was busy, but she only worked Tuesdays and Thursdays, so she gave his office door a gentle knock on the chance he might be counseling an individual or even be on his knees praying. It wouldn't be the first time she'd caught him in the middle of a prayer session.

"Come in," Henry said.

She pushed open the door and peeked her head inside. "Hi, honey." The first thing she noted was how drained he looked. The color had gone out of his face so that it took on a pallid cast. Before entering, she'd caught him shoving something into his desk drawer, but she didn't give the matter a second thought. "How have you been feeling today?"

He sat up straighter. "Oh, you know, like the song goes, 'Fit as a fiddle and ready for love!'" He cut loose a little chuckle, but there wasn't much ring to it.

"You weren't feeling so chipper last night—after our lovemaking that is."

"Oh, that." He waved a hand. "It must have been something I ate."

"Oh, Henry. None of the rest of us got sick."

He shrugged. "I'm sorry, honey, I don't know what it was. I'm feeling better now though."

She walked around to his side of the desk, sat down on his lap, and looped her arms around his neck. Clasping her fingers, she pulled his head toward hers so that their foreheads touched. "Well, I'm glad you're feeling better." She planted a light kiss on his cheek. "How did your visit with Reverend Samuel go this morning? I prayed for you."

He cleared his throat. "Thank you, honey. It went fine. I think he will handle the matter in the right way." His answer felt rushed, as if he didn't wish to discuss it, so she didn't press it.

She unlooped her arms and straightened but did not remove herself from his lap. "I got a phone call from one of the ladies from church today."

"Oh? Who?"

"Do you remember Shirley Roberts?"

"The one with the four children who comes in every Sunday and sits close to the front?"

"Yes, that's the one. She asked me to pray for her husband."

"Why? Did she share any specifics with you?"

"She said Fred thinks the church is full of hypocrites."

"Our church in particular?"

"No, the church in general. I invited her to come over for a cup of tea today, but her husband had the car."

Henry wore a troubled frown. "It's too bad Fred views the church as full of hypocrites."

"I told her I'd pray for him. He probably needs a Christian friend."

"He probably does."

"Perhaps you can pay him a visit someday soon."

"I—yes, I'll try to do that." He frowned and looked out the window.

"Henry, what's wrong? You're usually so chipper when I come to your office. Something's bothering you, I can tell."

"Nothing's wrong. I'm just a little tired."

"Well, come home and lie down for a while then, take a little nap. Mondays are always your busy day, gathering notes, doing research, preparing for your next sermon."

He squared his eyes on her and wrapped her in his arms. "I love you, Nora. I just want you to know that."

"I love you too, honey," she returned, touched by the unexpected sentiment, yet somehow confused by it. Why did he sound so desperate?

"I'm going to find someone to preach for me this Sunday."

"Seriously? You're that tired?" She studied him closer, waiting for him to settle the sudden thumping in her heart.

His shoulders slumped a bit. "I've decided to take you away for the weekend."

"What?" She couldn't have been more surprised if he'd pulled the moon out of the sky and handed it to her. "How—?"

"I want to take you away—just you and me—and leave the kids with my parents—or your mother."

"Oh, Henry, just us?" He gave a slow nod and a tiny smile. "But—where would we go, and—and what in the world brought this on? You and I haven't gone anywhere together since—well, I can't even remember the last time."

"That's precisely why I want to drop everything and go somewhere. Imagine a cozy little cottage on a quiet lake, just you and me."

"It sounds lovely, but"—she sat back and tilted her head. "Henry Griffin, have you gone daffy? You know we don't have any extra money, and we have a broken car sitting in the driveway to prove it."

He traced her chin with his index finger and looked at her lips. "I'm aware, but what if I told you I've already made arrangements?"

"I'd be shocked."

"It's true. I put in a call to an old high school friend a half hour ago. He owns a cottage on Twin Lake, and back in July, I happened to run into him at Harvey's Hardware on Laketon Avenue, and we got to talking about the cottage he owns. He told me I could use it some weekend on the off-season. I decided to call him and ask him if he was serious. He said he was serious as a grave marker and, in fact, it's open this weekend if we want to use it. So I took him up on it."

She couldn't close her gaping mouth. It took a moment for the words to sink in. "Are you kidding me, Henry Griffin?"

"Nope. According to him, it's rustic, but it comes equipped with indoor toilet, cold running water, a compact kitchen with pots and pans and utensils, a tiny stove and icebox, and towels and bedding. Even has a rickety dock with a rowboat and some fishing poles."

A smile began to blossom. She set her hands on his shoulders and pushed herself back to see straight into his eyes. "Are you sure you're not toying with me?"

He kissed the end of her nose. "I'm not toying with you. All I need now is a stand-in preacher."

"Ask your father. He'd gladly fill in."

"I thought about him, but I don't want to impose on such short notice."

"But you'd impose on someone else? You know good and well he'll do it. He's a retired preacher. Who better to fill the pulpit on short notice? He's done it before, and folks love him."

He gazed off again, silent in his thoughts for a time. She held her breath. "All right then. I'll give him a call."

"Excellent." She started to jump up, but he stopped her with a hard kiss to the lips—an almost punishing one that rang of some kind of frantic emotion she couldn't quite pinpoint. A tiny shiver shimmied up her spine. "I—I'll call Mother to make sure she's fine with having the children spend the weekend with her. It's better to ask her to watch the kids than your parents because your father will be busy studying for Sunday's message."

"Good idea. Oh, and when you talk to her, tell her we'll pick the kids up late Sunday afternoon and not to expect us for dinner after all."

"I'll let her know." She slipped off his lap, and this time he didn't try to stop her. She walked to the door, and opening it, turned for one more glance at him. "We're having meatballs and mashed potatoes and gravy for supper tonight. Your favorite."

Rather than give his usual cheer, he issued her a tiny smile. "Sounds good."

Moments later, she made her way back to the house, excited about going away with her husband for a weekend…and yet strangely bothered at the same time. Something about Henry's demeanor wasn't right, but she couldn't put her finger on it.

Well, there'd be plenty of time for talking about it this weekend.

FIVE

The heart is deceitful above all things, and incurable; who can know it?
—Jeremiah 17:9

All week, Henry fidgeted, unable to focus on anything, even missing out on much of the family's dinner conversations due to his wandering thoughts. He knew Nora was concerned, but every time she asked him what was wrong, he came up with one excuse or another. Weekdays found him at his office even though he didn't have to prepare for Sunday's sermon. Instead, he tried to prepare for future sermons, but his mind kept telling him he might not even be there to preach if folks got wind of his past indiscretions.

Oh, sure, he'd told himself he wouldn't even meet the boy, that he would tell Mrs. Felton to go ahead and adopt the kid out, but even thinking such a thing made his stomach churn. Could he truly do that? Wouldn't it eat him alive knowing he'd rejected his own son? Is that what God would have him do? On the other hand, wouldn't telling Nora wreck his marriage and everything they'd built together? Moreover, what of Paige and Paul's feelings? He could hardly discount their reactions. They might very well hate learning they had another sibling. And how mortifying for him, their father, to have to try to explain how it could even be physically possible.

Lester Griffin was pleased as punch to accept his invitation to preach and had even told Henry it was about time that he took Nora away for a weekend. "Everything all right though?" his father had asked.

Henry had hemmed a bit, but in the end, told another fib. "Couldn't be better, Dad. Thanks for asking."

Even Marlene, his secretary, had noticed something amiss when he forgot to attend the Muskegon League of Evangelical Ministers Luncheon on Thursday. "How could you have forgotten that, Pastor Henry? You were supposed to deliver the invocation." She was probably fifteen years his senior, not quite old enough to be his mother, but that day, she'd treated him like one of her adult children. And with good reason.

That afternoon, he'd called the league president and apologized profusely, admitting he had no excuse other than his mind had been elsewhere. He couldn't even blame Marlene because she'd reminded him that morning. Of course, the reverend had accepted his apology and asked him to be on notice to deliver the invocation at an upcoming luncheon—to which he'd agreed, halfheartedly thinking he'd soon be forced out of the Muskegon League of Evangelical Ministers due to his hideous sin.

He kept wondering when the second letter from Mrs. Felton would arrive, praying he'd be alone when his father delivered it to him. A second letter from the same woman was sure to raise questions, but his father was never one to pry, so chances were, he wouldn't ask. Still, the notion of having to be secretive with his father pestered him.

Nora had been so busy preparing for their weekend getaway that she barely paid heed to his forgetfulness—never asking him if anything was wrong, or if he had any second thoughts about going to the lake cottage. In fact, she had started packing on Wednesday and was still putting items into her suitcase Friday morning.

"Honey, we're only going to be gone for two nights," he told her. "Why are you packing so much? Look." He pointed to the single overnight bag on their bed. "I'm only taking one change of clothes, a couple pairs of underwear and socks, and my shaving kit."

She gave him what he liked to call her high school grin, her blond ponytail bobbing from side to side as she flitted about their bedroom. "Well, good for you. I'm taking an outfit for every occasion."

"What is every occasion? We're going to a cottage on the lake."

"I know, but you might want to take me out for supper tonight."

"Oh, I might?" He smiled now, then advanced on her from behind, making her jump. "And what if I want to stay in?" he whispered in her ear. He took her by the shoulders and gently turned her, bending so that their noses touched. "I thought we could stop at the grocery store halfway there and find a couple of steaks to grill. Then we could build a fire tonight and sit by the lake to eat. It's a quiet night. We might even see some fish jumping. Then tomorrow, we can take the rowboat out, maybe fish a little. If we catch anything, we can fry it up for lunch or dinner. Who knows? It might even be warm enough to swim this afternoon and tomorrow. We've been having some great weather."

Her breath came out in short gasps because he kept drawing little circles on her back and planting kisses around her mouth while he talked. He couldn't imagine what would happen to the romance between them once he told her about his tryst with Rina some nine years ago. Would confessing everything shatter all they'd built together? Moreover, when should he tell her? How would he know when the time was right? How did one choose a right time to tell his wife he'd been unfaithful to her? Would it be tonight, before or after supper? Or perhaps tomorrow while in the boat in the middle of the lake, where she couldn't run away from him? While her heart thumped against his chest with passion, his thumped out of a basketful of nerves.

"You seem to have everything all planned," she answered, pushing back enough to fit both palms flat against his chest. She looked upward, her blue eyes shimmering with extra color this morning. "Don't I get any say?"

The Mercy Tree 53

He smiled down at her. She would never guess he had to force it. "I'll have to think about that one. Now, come on, let's finish up so we can be out of here."

Ten o'clock found them on the road with last-minute packing done, the breakfast dishes washed and put away, a light left on in the living room, and the house locked up tight. Nora talked almost non-stop on the half-hour drive, commenting on how some of the trees had started to take on a few fall colors, how the children were excited about spending the weekend at Grandma's house, and how relaxing it would be not to have a care in the world for one entire weekend.

Yes, not a care in the world, he thought. If only it were true.

They found the little cottage in Twin Lake, Michigan, without incident. It was situated on a narrow dirt road with a sparse number of cottages on the lake side and nothing but thick woods on the other. He pulled into the drive and cut the engine.

"Oh, my goodness, it's so peaceful here," Nora said. "Listen. Not a single sound but singing birds. Isn't it lovely?"

He gazed at her beautiful face. "Yes, indeed. Lovely."

Henry had hit the jackpot some seventeen years ago when he'd managed to catch her attention. Nora Harrison had been a popular, sophomore cheerleader, while he had been a senior and a quarterback on the Muskegon High School varsity football team. He hadn't been allowed to date her until her sixteenth birthday. Nora's mother hadn't approved of the courtship, even though he was a preacher's son. She'd thought he was too old, too forward, too playful, or too popular with the rest of the girls. Nora's father approved, however, taking Henry aside one day and telling him his wife would be fine in time as long as he took things slow and treated their only child with utmost respect. He'd promised he would, for he'd known since their very first date that he would someday marry her. And after a few months of dating, her parents started attending the church his father pastored. Nora said her parents were looking for a different church anyway, but Henry always figured they'd made the switch so that her mother could keep a close eye on him.

After high school graduation, Henry went to Michigan State on a full scholarship. Nora's mother had wanted them to break up, giving Nora time to date other boys, and so they were apart for a brief period, but they'd both been miserable. They corresponded via letters, and when the rare occasion occurred that he could hitch a car ride home for the weekend, he did, just to see her.

Everyone said they made the perfect couple, and by all accounts they had, but, looking back, they probably should've waited to get married till he finished college. Her mother had not approved, and truth was, their first couple years were tough with Nora working full-time to support them so he could attend classes, and he picking up a few hours of work to help carry the load. Yes, he'd earned a full scholarship, but they still had housing and living expenses as well as a car to maintain. They'd been madly in love but ill-prepared for the responsibility that came with marriage. Oh, they'd made it work, and God was on their side, but many times, they had argued over petty matters that often spiraled out of control, resulting sometimes in anger and hurt feelings that dragged on for days. They'd started attending a church in Lansing that helped them get back on track spiritually and relationally, but then his draft number came up, and the Army called him into active duty. They weren't entirely surprised when it happened because of all they'd read in the newspapers leading up to it, but the timing had been off. Nora was pregnant, although they had tried to avoid that, and he had not even been home for the baby's birth…

"Henry?"

Her voice called him out of his whirlwind of memories. "Yes?"

"Shall we go explore the inside of the cottage?"

Casting aside all thoughts of yesteryear, he smiled. "Let's do it."

The cottage was rustic all right, with a small kitchen holding the bare necessities, a tiny living room and bedroom, and a bathroom with sink, toilet, and a smaller than normal bathtub. It lacked insulation, meaning nobody inhabited it in the winter months—unless a few critters invited themselves in. Fine by Nora, for today, the sun shone bright, and it was as warm outside as a midsummer day. She suspected tonight would bring cooler air, and they would appreciate the big comforters piled on the double bed. She ran to the window overlooking the lake. The cottage stood on a sloped lot, with a well-trodden path leading down to the dock where a rowboat floated, secured to the dock by a rope. My, but it was a pretty sight. "Look, honey, there's an island on this lake."

He came up behind her and looked over her shoulder. "Indeed, there is. We should row over there and investigate. I wonder if there are any walking paths."

"Hm. I wonder the same." Since she felt his breath on her neck, she leaned back until she rested securely against his broad chest. He wrapped his arms around her and clasped his hands under her breasts. There they stood in serene moods. She nestled close, while he nuzzled the top of her head with his chin. Both gently swayed, as if some romantic tune played in the air, each caught up in their own thoughts and emotions. It was a lovely moment.

After a light lunch, the afternoon found them taking the rowboat to the island, where they walked its perimeter hand in hand, their bare feet sinking into the muddy shoreline. There were ducks and geese swimming among the lily pads, a couple of blue herons standing on the shoreline scouting for food, and a bald eagle circling overhead, swooping down in search of prey then soaring upward to gracefully land in the treetop of one of the many ancient oaks on the island.

"We should have brought our lunch over here and had ourselves a little picnic," she said.

"Yes, we should have. Maybe we can do that tomorrow."

After a time, they got back in the rowboat. She sat on the narrow seat in the front facing forward to get a better view, and Henry sat on the middle seat doing the rowing. They ventured out toward the middle of the lake on the other side of the island to admire the blue, sparkling waters. Nora spotted a few year-round homes, but from what she could gather, most were summer cottages, humble structures sitting on sloping land with narrow paths leading down to wooden docks. Most also looked empty and quiet. She could only assume the owners lived in southern places and drove up on summer weekends to escape the noise of the city.

"It was nice of your friend to loan his cottage out to us for the whole weekend."

"Yes, Harv Miller is very generous. Do you remember him?"

"Hm. I don't think so."

"We were good friends all through high school, although we ran in different circles. We were neighbors on Maplewood Street, so we enjoyed each other's company after school and in the summer months until we moved over to Lake Shore Drive. Occasionally, we run into each other at the hardware store or somewhere when we least expect it."

"It's funny how the people you think you'll always be friends with somehow drift away from you as your interests change—or you move away."

"Or you get married," Henry put in.

"True. Once we got married, most of our friends steered clear of us. Ha! It was like we had joined some sort of exclusive club and no one else wanted to join."

He gave a little laugh. "You're right."

"Getting married did change a lot of things for us. We had some growing up to do."

"Yes, we did. You grew up before I did," he said.

"Women usually do," she teased.

He allowed his oars to rest in their locks for a moment so they could let the breeze carry them. "Do you ever have regrets?"

She gave a slight turn of her head. "About getting married you mean?"

"We were awfully young. Do you wish we'd waited?"

"I was just barely eighteen and you were twenty. But do I have regrets? Not a one. Do you?"

"Me? No, of course not."

She breathed a little sigh. "I'm glad because I used to wonder if you felt robbed. I mean your college years were not spent in the traditional way, living in dorms, making close friends, joining campus clubs, that sort of thing. Ours was a very nontraditional start, wasn't it? You going to school full-time and me working forty hours a week so we could eat and pay what few bills we had."

"Yeah, those were some crazy years for sure," he murmured. "I'm glad you don't have to do that anymore. I appreciate so much that you sacrificed for us, but it's nice that you can stay home with the kids now." He picked up the oars and began rowing, the oars propelling them forward and making small waves that spread out into large, mesmerizing circles. Across the lake, a few fishermen had anchored their boats and were no doubt hoping to catch their supper. She picked up a little twig on the boat's floor and tossed it into the water.

"I was thinking the other day that it wouldn't hurt for me to get a job again. It might even be fun for me. And we could use the extra income."

He stopped rowing again. "What are you talking about?"

"I wouldn't mind it, Henry. We do have to pinch pennies, and the kids could use some new clothes."

"Well, your working outside of the home is completely unnecessary." His answer came so abruptly that it caught her off guard. "You have children to raise."

"Don't you mean *we* have children to raise?" A slight annoyance rose from deep down. She did not wish to get into a squabble on this lovely weekend getaway, but it was, after all, a good time for talking things out with no children to break into their conversation.

"Well, yes, of course. You know what I'm saying. If you took on a job, we'd have to make a lot of adjustments."

"Not really. Our children go to school every day. I'm sure we could work something out so that my hours would coincide with theirs."

"I can't believe you're even thinking about this."

"Why not? It makes perfect sense."

He didn't answer right away, and she kept mum for the next minute or so. Finally he spoke. "We really don't need the money, honey. We're doing fine."

"Oh? Then why has our second car been sitting in the driveway for the better share of two months?"

"I have the money put aside to fix it."

"You didn't tell me that."

"Well, I've been putting some extra money into our savings account."

"Why didn't you tell me?"

"I didn't think it was necessary."

"Well, if it involves finances, then I have a right to know."

"Are we arguing?" he asked, maneuvering the boat so that it pointed back toward their cottage.

"We might be. I'm not sure."

With their backs to each other, neither could read the expression in the other's face. "Can we talk about this notion of a job another time?"

"You know we can. I just wanted to throw the idea out there."

He kept up a steady rowing pattern, failing to respond further so that the only sounds they heard were the quacking ducks and the oars lifting and dipping in the water, lifting and dipping, lifting and dipping.

They made it to shore. Henry rowed the boat up beside the dock, then reached down and tossed a rope over a dock post. He finally spoke. "Look, honey, I'm sorry I snapped at you about the notion of your getting a job. We'll discuss it soon, okay? Just not this weekend."

"Fine, but just let me say this. Some days, I feel like I could help make life a little better for us if I brought in a little money. Maybe we actually could get a television set for the kids."

"You're not serious! Ever since they invented that contraption, you've said, 'I'll never have one of those hideous things in my house. Who wants to sit around and stare at a box all evening?'"

"I know, but…"

"Can we both turn around? Your back is plenty cute, but I'd rather look at your face."

She swiveled her body on the narrow seat, lifted her legs over and set them on the boat floor. He did likewise, so that their knees touched, she in her blue pedal pushers and floral short-sleeved shirt, he in his short-sleeved, button-down cotton shirt and casual shorts that fell just an inch or two above the kneecap. He took both her hands in his and dipped his head down so that their eyes met. He smiled first, and she followed suit. "We can talk about all this later, I promise. And I'll try to keep an open mind. We have the whole weekend, but for now, can we just enjoy each other's company without any tension?"

She freely agreed, then on a whim, stood up, albeit with a bit of wobbling, placed her hands on his firm shoulders, and then kissed him squarely on the mouth. After a few seconds, she withdrew and said, "I love you, Henry Griffin, and I wouldn't want to be the cause of a rift between us."

He looked like he had something further to say, but if he did, he held it in. They exited the boat and climbed the hill to the cottage.

SIX

Strive diligently to present thyself approved to God, a workman that has not to be ashamed, cutting in a straight line the word of truth.
—2 Timothy 2:15

The weekend went far quicker than either anticipated. What Henry had thought would be plenty of time for bringing up the topic of his affair with Rina and the son he just discovered shrunk into oblivion when up against Nora's adventurous spirit and constant need to chatter. If they weren't fishing, she was dipping a long-handled net into the water's depths to see what she could come up with. Most times, it was nothing but muck and seaweed, but occasionally, a poor turtle would get tangled in the netting, making her squeal with delight. Every time she caught something, she acted as if she'd just come upon a hundred-dollar bill. Then just as quickly, she would release it so she could try again. He laughed at her enthusiasm, but worried at how fleeting time had become.

Interspersed with their adventures were times of intimacy when ravishing each other's bodies became as much a necessity as eating and drinking. On Saturday afternoon, they headed to a town further north and found a nice little diner where they sat in a booth next to a window, ordered fish and fries, and talked about their children. He longed to tell her then about a third child, one that wasn't hers but could be if she'd welcome him into their home, but of course, he lost his courage. He just couldn't seem to find the right moment to broach the subject because he knew once he did, it would shatter their nearly flawless weekend. Lord have mercy, it could shatter their entire *future*.

Nora had not mentioned the idea of getting a job again. She probably didn't wish to throw a damper on their weekend either. He might not have been opposed to the idea of her finding work if it weren't for the fact that Emiko might be moving in with them. The boy would need a replacement mother, someone to ease him into his new environment, to introduce him to his new teacher, to help him get ready for school every morning, and to greet him when he came home, someone to—but what was he thinking? Just the term *replacement mother* was unrealistic. No one would replace Emiko's mother, and shame on him for thinking Nora should assume such a role. Equally unfair was the idea that the boy would even take to Nora—or *him* for that matter.

That night, he lay in bed staring at the ceiling and listening to a steady rain. Nora lay next to him, snuggled close. He loved her more than his own life, and he couldn't imagine inflicting pain on her. Yet telling her about his affair would cause her unimaginable anguish. He tried to envision her reaction. Of course, she would cry, but would they be tears of sorrow or deep-seated anger? Henry almost hoped for the latter. He felt like he could handle her anger better than her pain. He rolled over, and took a few of the covers with him. Nora stirred, but she didn't awaken, and he was glad. A part of him wanted to spill the whole thing, but a bigger part wanted to pretend none of it was real—that there'd never been a sordid affair, Emiko didn't exist, and there was no such person as Helen Felton.

His heart pounded with angst. Fear was something foreign to him. For one thing, he preached against it, always telling his parishioners it was sinful to allow fear to creep in, for it indicated a lack of faith in God. The Bible even warned against fear in Isaiah 41, verse 10: *"Fear not, for I am with thee; be not dismayed, for I am thy God. I will strengthen thee, yea, I will help thee, yea, I will uphold thee with the right hand of my righteousness."*

What would his parishioners say if they knew he was lying in a pool of sweat, his nerves so shattered he could barely think straight? What would they say when the story of his sinful act came to light? Was there any way to avoid telling the whole truth? He started imagining ways. They had adopted a child from Japan—an orphan? But that would be an outright lie. They were fostering a homeless child? Partially true, but not enough to appease a guilty conscience. They were looking after an orphan? A total lie. Yes, Emiko had lost his mother, but the boy had a father who was very much alive.

Of course, the easy way out would simply be to call Helen Felton and tell her he did not wish to meet Emiko, that meeting him would cause too much emotional upheaval, and that the boy would be better off getting a fresh start with some well-deserving Christian family—or even a young couple unable to conceive and longing for a child of their own.

Yes, that was what he continued telling himself to do. It would indeed be simple, and he could then wash his hands of the matter and never utter a single word of any of it to Nora—or anyone. But in good conscience, could he go through life knowing he had another son who he'd abandoned? And what of Paige and Paul? Didn't they deserve to know they had another sibling?

When sleep came at last, it was restless and filled with bad dreams. In one, he'd fallen out of a rocking boat and lost the ability to swim. The harder he tried, the more his legs became tangled in seaweed. Moreover, when he reached for the edge of the boat, it drifted away so that he was left flailing in the water while Nora reached for him and called his name. He gasped for air as the boat drifted even further, his head bobbing up and down in the murky water, making it hard to breathe, which ultimately woke him.

Somehow, all his tossing and turning had tangled the blankets around his ankles. Uncovered, chilled, and disoriented, he lay in a pool of sweat in only his boxer shorts. And still, Nora slept like a baby, completely unaware of his torment. The rain had stopped—at least for now—replaced by the steady chirps of tree frogs, crickets, and bullfrogs. There were other night sounds known only to the lake residents, sounds a city dweller like him wouldn't recognize. The sound he did recognize was that same old loud pounding of his pulse echoing in his head. He had to get this dreadful secret off his chest, but how—and when?

He said nothing to Nora about his nightmare and what had brought it on as they sat in the kitchen Sunday morning enjoying their bacon, eggs, and toast. Instead, they talked about their plans to leave mid-morning and drive out to Lake Michigan's beautiful Pere Marquette Park. The sun had peeked out amid a cloudy sky, so there was still hope for some nice weather to finish out their weekend. They would climb a sand dune or two, buy a hot dog at a local eatery by the beach, and take a couple of towels that they'd brought from home to lie on the sand, weather permitting. The beach would be sparse compared to the usual summer crowd, so finding a parking spot close to the water would be easy.

By eleven o'clock, they jumped in the car and headed toward Muskegon, a lovely weekend mostly behind them—and one giant secret still tucked away.

~

After her morning devotions, one of the first things Nora did on Monday morning after sending the children off to school was call Shirley Roberts to apologize for not being at church yesterday.

"I'm sorry I missed seeing you at church," Nora said. "As you probably know by now, my husband swept me away for the weekend."

Shirley chuckled. "Yes, I heard that. Your father-in-law delivered a very nice sermon yesterday. Of course, I missed hearing your husband."

"Both are good speakers. My father-in-law is a retired minister. His father, Henry's grandfather, was also a preacher."

"So, it runs in the family. Perhaps your own son will follow suit."

"I've wondered that myself."

"By the way, I must tell you I so enjoy your piano playing. I missed hearing you yesterday."

"Well, thank you very much. I'm sure Mrs. Hamstra was every bit as good though."

"She plays fine, but she doesn't hold a candle to you, Nora. You are one of the reasons I love attending Open Door. I could listen to you play all day. I also love the church's name: Church of the Open Door. It has a very welcoming ring to it."

"Doesn't it? It appealed to Henry and me as well when he got the invitation to come and serve as their new pastor. We do strive to open wide our doors to anyone seeking to know God better or are simply just curious about Christianity."

"You know, yesterday, Fred remarked about the church's name when he dropped the kids and me off. He said, 'Pfff. They say Open Door, but what does *that* mean? All hypocrites welcome?' I told him to stop being so judgmental and come and find out for himself. I was quite proud of myself for standing up to him for a change. I know wives are expected to be submissive, but sometimes I just have to speak my mind."

"Good for you. I probably would've done the same. What did he say when you told him he should come and see for himself?"

"He actually said he might attend next Sunday, just to prove his point."

"Really? Well, let us both agree to pray that he will. He'll see first-hand that we are a loving bunch of folks. We're not perfect, mind you, but we are learning how to love better I think."

They talked on a few minutes longer until there was a knock at Nora's door. "Oh, I'm afraid I have to go now. Someone's at the door."

"Thank you so much for calling," Shirley said. "I hope to see you next Sunday."

"I will be there."

After replacing the receiver on its cradle, she hurried to the door. When she opened it, she was delighted to see her father-in-law standing on the porch. "Dad, come in!" She looked beyond him to the car. "Where's Mom?"

Lester didn't come inside. "Oh, I'm not going to stay, Nora. I just wanted to drop off this letter that arrived on Saturday afternoon. It's addressed to Henry. It's the second letter that's come to my house with his name on it. He probably told you about the first one. Anyway, I'll just hand it over to you. I intended to deliver it to him at his office, but the church doors are still locked, and I don't think Marlene works today."

She took the letter and gave the return address a quick glance, not allowing her eyes to linger too long on it. More than likely it had to do with his pastoral duties. "Thank you, Dad. I'll see to it that he gets it. I just got off the phone with a lady who started attending Open Door a few months ago, Shirley Roberts. She told me she enjoyed your message yesterday. How did it feel to get behind the pulpit again?"

"Oh, you know. It sort of feels like going home—no matter whose pulpit I'm standing behind. I'm invited to speak at the Church of the Nazarene in a few weeks, and a couple of weeks after that, at Lakewood Baptist. Of course, I most enjoy standing in for Henry."

"He appreciates it, but he never wants to take you for granted either."

"Pfff, I don't feel put upon at all. You two kids needed to get away. Did you enjoy your weekend?"

"It was wonderful." In fact, the weekend was dreamy if she wanted to sum it up in one word. "We enjoyed every minute of it. I can only speak for myself though. I did notice Henry growing a bit quiet yesterday. I imagine he was thinking about all the work that awaited him in the week ahead. I don't know why he's not in his office right now. He may have had an early appointment."

"Probably so. Well, I'm off to meet some of my old cronies at the Doo Drop Inn for breakfast. I'll see you later, honey."

"Bye, Dad, and thanks again for preaching yesterday."

"It was my pleasure." He stepped off the porch and gave a little wave. She watched him until he climbed into his car, and then she closed the door and leaned against it, picking up the letter and giving it one more little gander.

Lester had said it was the second piece of mail he'd received for Henry at his address. He'd also said Henry had probably told her about the first one—which he had not. Some tiny bit of worry nagged her at the core, but she couldn't quite determine why. She had absolutely no grounds for worry. She did recall thinking something wasn't quite right with Henry's demeanor last week, but she hadn't dwelled on that either. He was by nature a very even-keeled sort of guy, so she had no reason to believe anything was wrong. Surely, there was some logical reason he hadn't mentioned the letter he'd received prior to this one.

Then like a streak of lightning, a memory flashed across her mind. Last week, when she'd stopped by his office, he had hurriedly stuffed something into his desk drawer, then quickly closed it. Maybe he thought she hadn't seen him do it, but she had. Still, she hadn't dwelt on the incident. Why would she?

She studied the return address again. Helen Felton from Naperville, Illinois. She knew no one by that name and couldn't think of a single individual they knew from there. She walked to the lamp on the coffee table next to the sofa and guiltily held the letter up to the lampshade to see if any words showed through, but it was indecipherable. Anyway, it was none of her business.

"Well, no point in thinking about it," she said aloud. "I'll just set it right here up against this lamp." And so, she did. And then she stepped away from it and walked to the kitchen, but not without one last glance back at the mysterious missive.

SEVEN

All have sinned, and come short of the glory of God.
—Romans 3:23

Henry had purposely driven to his parents' house first thing Monday morning to explain that a second letter would be arriving in the mail for him and that he'd like his father to deliver it directly to him and not to Nora. It was church business, he would explain, nothing Nora needed to bother herself with. Of course, that would've been a lie, but he was willing to tell it just to get his hands on the letter ahead of her. He was too late, though. His mother said that, yes, indeed a second letter had arrived on Saturday while they were at the cottage and his father had taken it already to drop off at Henry's house either before or after meeting some friends for breakfast.

Hoping to confiscate the letter before Lester gave it to Nora, he'd asked Lillian where he was having breakfast.

She clucked. "I don't even remember if he actually named the restaurant, honey. But don't worry. He'll give it to Nora, and she'll then pass it on to you."

"I know. I just wanted to get it first. I should have thought to talk to Dad about it before we left for the weekend, but I guess my mind went somewhere else."

"Humph." Lillian wrinkled her forehead and gave him a curious look. "So, Nora will just hand you the letter. I don't see what the problem is."

He shouldn't have voiced his concern to her, for now he'd puzzled her. "You're right, of course, there's no problem at all, Mom. I'll just be on my way."

"Don't you want to come in for some coffee and a cinnamon bun—made fresh this morning?"

"No, sorry I can't."

"Well, at least let me wrap one up for you."

He started to decline, but she hurried off to the kitchen before he had a chance. Impatient to leave, he stood there, shifting his weight until she returned with the delicacy. He took the sweet offering and bent to give her a light kiss on the cheek. "Thanks, Mom. I'll see you later."

He felt her eyes on him as he made his way back to his car.

"Please, Lord, may it be that Dad hasn't given the letter to Nora." But even as he muttered the words under his breath while starting the engine, he doubted God would grant such a request. He had gotten himself into this pickle, and until he dredged up the entire story to Nora, there'd be no answered prayers, no hearing God's still, small voice, and certainly no peace.

Rather than park at his house, he chose a spot on the other side of the church where his car would be out of sight. He had to see if by chance his father had slipped the letter under the locked church door. He climbed out of his car, and locating the key in his pocket, took it out and let himself into the church. No letter there. On he walked to every door leading to the outside, but there was nothing lying on the floor anywhere. His heart sank. Well, there was still a chance his father hadn't stopped by yet. Perhaps he could stand at this door overlooking his side yard and wait for his dad's '53 Plymouth to pull into the driveway—unless of course he'd already been here, in which case, Nora would've seen the letter and wondered who in the world Helen Felton was. What was he going to do?

He stood there pondering things for a bit, trying to pray, but not receiving any clear direction, not even knowing if God heard. "Oh, Lord, I've botched things up in a big way. Help me get through this."

Only then did he feel the slightest hint of something—it was a sort of sense of peace that came over him. Be honest, were the words. And that was it. *Be honest.*

He entered his house through the back door and stood for a moment on the landing. There were two ways to go, either down the stairs to the dark basement housing the furnace, water heater, and a wringer washing machine with wintertime clothesline, or up two steps into the kitchen. He stepped into the kitchen. It was a light and breezy room; cozy would probably be the word a woman would use. Nora kept it tidy as a new baby's wardrobe.

They didn't have the most modern house on the block, but neither was it old and run down. It had a relatively new roof, nice red brick siding with white trim around the blue front door and black shutters at the front and side windows. On the north side of the house were three bedrooms and a family-sized bathroom; on the south end was the living room with fireplace and coat closet, the kitchen, and the dining room. With their well-manicured yard, most would consider the preacher's home quite lovely. Henry dutifully mowed the lawn once a week, sometimes twice in the middle of summer, and often, folks would walk by and call out a compliment or two about the home's appearance. If he took pride in anything other than his family, it was in his neat little house with the trimmed shrubbery and healthy green grass.

Most churches of the day provided their pastors with parsonages, but Open Door chose instead to give their pastors a housing allowance with which they could buy their own home or rent. Five years ago, when they'd accepted the pastorate at the church, Nora and he had prayerfully decided buying made more financial sense. Only God could have orchestrated how it came to be that they bought the house next door to the church. An elderly couple had lived in it. Their health was declining, so their daughter encouraged them to move in with her. Soon after, the decision was made, the house went on the market, and it happened at almost the exact time Henry and Nora were about to move from Wilmore, Kentucky, to their hometown of Muskegon, Michigan. Many times over the past several years, Henry and Nora talked about God's perfect plans and how He always made things work out for their good when they placed their full trust in Him.

But what of this situation? Somehow, Henry had to bring himself to spill the secret he'd kept from Nora for nine years. Would all things still work out for their good, like it says in Romans 8:28, after she learned about his eight-year-old son? He quivered deep inside thinking what could easily happen after telling her. Either she would yell and scream and cry, but eventually find it in her heart to forgive him…or she would allow her anger to fester until she no longer had it in her to continue living with him. *Oh, Lord, those are both brutal scenarios. Please tell me how to handle this horrible situation. Please, Lord. If the letter is indeed here, do I confess the whole sordid story today—or do I just take the letter back to my office, open it there, and then wait on my instincts to tell me how to proceed?*

Once again, those two little words seemed to whisper in his ear. *Be honest.*

He found her in the living room playing her piano. Not for the first time did he feel appreciation for her special talent, the way her fingers flew up and down the keyboard with precision. The hymn was one of his favorites: "There's a New Name Written Down in Glory!" He had a vivid memory of the day he'd knelt at an altar as a young teen in the church his father pastored. Afterwards, his father had said, "A new name's been written in God's Book of Life tonight, Son, and no one can erase that name! Ever." It had given him a sense of peace then, and it gave him peace now. What didn't give him peace was the secret he held tightly to because of the *what-ifs* that lay on the horizon.

He folded his arms and leaned against the doorframe, legs crossed at the ankles, his presence yet unknown to her. When Nora played the piano, she lost herself in the craft. She could play classical, gospel, jazz— any style she had a mind to play. Just set her down in front of a set of black and white keys, and let her loose. It was wonderful being married to this talented, multi-faceted woman who was giddy one moment and serious the next, Godly, playful, dutiful, loving, and dedicated were just a few words that described her. When she finished the song, she very seamlessly moved right into the next, "Victory in Jesus," an equally rhythmic, spirited hymn, unaware that he watched on. He wondered if she was working on next Sunday's hymn selection already.

At the close of that second hymn, she paused, and so he took the opportunity to applaud her. She gave a little jolt, obviously surprised. "I didn't hear you come in!"

He moved away from the doorway and approached, putting his hands on her shoulders and giving her a light massage. "Hmm, that feels heavenly," she said, leaning into his touch.

"Are you choosing your songs for next Sunday already?"

"Not yet. I was just playing for my own pleasure."

"Well, it was lovely as usual."

"Thank you." She swiveled on the piano bench so she could face him. She wore a comely house dress with yellow flowers on a blue background. Her blond hair fell down her back, although it was pinned up on each side with silver barrettes. She had no bangs, like so many girls and women of the day did, thanks to the president's wife, Mamie Eisenhower. And Henry was glad because bangs would only serve to cover up her pretty forehead. Nora never had been one to follow popular trends. She was confident enough as to carve her own way, providing God Himself took the lead, and he admired her for it. She had a bit of stubbornness to her also, a streak of feisty independence that most men would resent. But he loved that about her, loved that she wanted to mingle with people and do her part to make an eternal difference in their lives. In fact, that's precisely why she wanted a job, he was certain of it. Oh, she said she wanted to contribute to the family's finances, but he knew there was more to it than that. She wanted to associate more with people outside of the church, folks who might not know Jesus, and an outside job would provide that opportunity. They would have to discuss it again, and soon, but not until they came to terms with this looming secret. Looking at her now, he found he loved her more than ever before, and he wished to the heavens he could keep things this way forever. *Help me, Lord.*

"What brings you home already?"

He bent and kissed the top of her head. "Oh, I don't know. I guess I just wanted to see you, that's all—and thank you for the weekend."

"It was grand, wasn't it? Are you feeling more rested now and ready to dive into next Sunday's sermon preparation?"

Next Sunday. Where would the two of them stand with each other in just one short week? An uncomfortable knot formed in his chest.

She tipped her head to the side. "Are you all right, Henry?"

"Yes, yes, of course. Did the kids get off to school on time?"

"Yes, but they missed seeing you. Oh! I almost forgot." She slid off the bench and walked to the end table next to the sofa to pick something up. When she turned, he saw it—the *letter.* Fear kept his feet nailed in place. She came close and held it out to him, but he didn't readily take it. He was too frozen. "It's a letter with your name on it, but it was sent to Mom and Dad's address. Dad said it is the second such letter that's come to their address with your name on it."

Henry's heart thrummed hard, stealing his very breath.

"He stopped by just after the kids left," she continued. "Anyway, take it." She held her arm straight out so that the letter dangled practically under his nose. "Henry, what is going on? You have the most worried look on your face." She withdrew the envelope and perused it carefully. "The return address has the name Helen Felton on it. Who is she?"

"Someone I met years ago."

"Okay. Now I know that much. Like Dad said, this is the second letter you received from this person. He said you probably told me about the first one. But you didn't, Henry. Why not? What is there to hide?"

He sucked in a breath that came from the deepest parts of his lungs, then slowly let it out. He took the offered letter.

"I'll explain everything." Sweat beads popped out on his forehead almost immediately, and it wasn't even a hot day. In fact, it had been raining off and on for the last thirty-six hours, bringing much cooler air. They hadn't yet turned on their furnace, but it certainly seemed hotter in the house than usual. "If you will excuse me, I just want to go someplace alone to read this, and then I'll be back."

"Henry, you're scaring me. Should I be worried?"

He hated like everything that it had come to this. If he could think of one good thing about spilling the whole truth today, it was that the children were in school.

He didn't answer her question—just shuffled down the hallway.

He closed the bedroom door behind him then walked to their neatly made bed that showed not a single wrinkle, the extra blanket at the foot of the bed perfectly folded. "I don't even know if I'll be sleeping in this bed tonight," he said in a whisper.

He opened the envelope, withdrew the letter, and began to read.

Dear Mr. Griffin,

As promised, I am sending you a second letter to let you know Emiko and I have arrived in the States. I am currently living with one of my sons in Chicago, but this coming Wednesday on September 21, I'm riding with him to Hope College in Holland. My grandson is a student there, and my son is taking him back to the campus. I plan to borrow my son's car and drive up to Muskegon so you can meet your son. The boy still does not know about you as I don't want to cause him any undeserved grief should you decide not to meet him. I realize you had no idea he existed and that it's taking you and your wife a good while to adjust to this new development. Emiko is the grandest little boy, a fine gentleman, so I am quite sure you will love him in an instant.

You can reach me at my son's house by telephone. Simply call the operator and provide the following information so that we can talk before Wednesday: Samuel Felton, 740 East Jordan Street,

Naperville, IL. I will bring Emiko to the address at which I mailed this letter and the prior one. I believe Rina told me that's your parents' address.

All of this said, I will see you <u>this</u> <u>coming</u> Wednesday—unless I hear otherwise from you. May God bless you.

Helen Felton

Henry refolded the letter and inserted it back in the envelope. He stood up, straightened his shoulders, and blew out a long sigh. The moment of truth was upon him.

EIGHT

The LORD is nigh unto them that are of a broken heart;
and saveth such as be of a contrite spirit.
—Psalm 34:18 (KJV)

Nora had never been a nail biter, but as she sat on the sofa in the living room awaiting Henry's return, she'd chewed off a hang nail, pulling too hard on it. Now the blamed thing hurt.

At long last, the bedroom door opened, and she heard Henry's footfall coming down the hall. He certainly wasn't in any big hurry. He rounded the corner and entered the living room, his face as solemn as a judge who'd just handed down a life sentence. She wanted to reassure him, but strangely, she was too busy reassuring herself, though she knew not why. She instinctively moved over and patted the place on the couch next to her. "Have a seat."

"I'll—just sit here." He lowered himself on the chair directly across from her, the marred pine coffee table between them. Her morning coffee, now cold, sat there in its saucer next to her open Bible.

Only seconds passed, but they felt like several minutes. She cleared her throat. "Henry, what's wrong? You've been carrying something around for a week or more now. You might as well get it out."

"Yes—I know."

"Well, what is it? It can't be so bad that you and I can't work it out together. Have the elders done something? Have you lost your pastorate? If that's it, we can deal with it. We'll look elsewhere. We'll—"

"No, no, nothing like that."

"Well then, has someone hurt you?"

"No—not exactly."

"What do you mean, not exactly?" Nora felt chills run down her spine. "Henry, you're scaring me."

"I know, and I'm sorry, Nora. You can't know how sorry I am."

Her heart had taken to pounding like a bass drum. It thumped in her head.

His head hung low, his shoulders drooping like a baseball player who'd just lost the game because he struck out.

She wanted to remove herself from the sofa and go kneel beside him, but he'd chosen to sit away from her for a reason. *Dear God—has he found another woman?* That was something that had never occurred to her, but now it struck her like a brick. Why hadn't she thought of it before? "Oh, Henry..." she mumbled just audibly enough for her own ears.

At last, he cleared his throat. "First, Nora, I love you. I love you very much."

"Yes?" She wasn't going to say it back because she didn't know what lay ahead.

"That's the easiest part of this whole thing. The rest is not so easy."

"Get on with it, Henry. If there is someone else, just tell me now and get it over with."

He jerked his head up as something like horror washed over his expression. "What? No! No, there isn't another woman in my life, Nora. Good grief. I just finished telling you I love you."

"So? It's possible for a man to love two women at the same time."

"It is? I wouldn't know."

Now, ire like she couldn't ever remember feeling toward her husband or anyone else rose in her, and a loud scolding shout rolled out of her. "Well, then, for crying out loud, Henry Griffin, tell me what's going on!"

"All right. All right." His voice came off surprisingly calm. "I will tell you—and straight out." He drew a deep, abysmal breath. "Last Sunday, after church, Dad handed me a letter. It was an airmail letter sent to his address with my name on it from someone named Helen Felton. It came from Japan."

"Japan? Why Japan? You served in Tokyo, but that was, what—nine or ten years ago?"

"I came home in 1946."

"All right, nine years ago then. What about it? Is Helen Felton someone significant to you?"

"She wasn't then, but she is now."

Her brow creased as confusion simmered. Was this the woman with whom he was having an affair? As much as it hurt, she had to know the truth. They had two children to think about in this hideous love triangle. "Go on."

"This is not easy, Nora."

"And you think it is for me? If you want a divorce, your life is over, you know that, right? No church will ever take you…"

"Nora." He scooted to the edge of his chair and tried to reach for her across the coffee table, but she slid as far away from his touch as possible. "I don't want a divorce," he said.

"Well, I'm sure this—this—Helen person certainly wants you to get one."

"No, no, she certainly does not want that. She's in her seventies, Nora. She's a retired missionary, moving back to the States to be near three of her four sons."

That bit of news gave Nora a good jolt. It took her a moment to let that bit of information digest. "Oh. Then—exactly why did she write a letter to you?"

"I'm getting to that."

She said not a word, just stared at him, awaiting his explanation, wanting it, yet dreading it at the same time.

"I found out that I—in that letter that Mrs. Felton sent, I found out that I—I have another son, Nora. His name is Emiko. His mother is Japanese. She—she died four months ago."

He stared at her, his eyes as soft and as penetrating as she'd ever seen them, but she held clasped hands in so tight a squeeze, it felt as though the blood flow had stopped, and perhaps it had. She sat, unmoving, unfeeling, her body frozen, her eyes gazing straight at him, and yet not seeing, her muscles paralyzed, her throat unable even to swallow. Somewhere in the recesses of her mind, she had heard words, and yet, they'd made no sense to her. They echoed now, but she dared not listen to them repeat themselves, so she simply sat there, still as an ancient boulder, feeling the beat of her heart, yet too numb to acknowledge it.

He got up from his chair now and came to sit beside her. He took up her hand between his two. "Would you say something, honey?"

Gradually, reality, ugly and hideous, began to creep inside. Nora withdrew her hand and jumped to her feet. She clutched her head with both hands and turned a full circle. "You—you what? Did I hear you correctly, Henry?"

"Yes, yes, I'm afraid you did."

"You have another son—besides Paul?"

"Yes, I do. He is eight, one year older than—P…"

"You don't have to do the math for me, Henry James Griffin. I'm not stupid. But, wait, apparently, I am." She glared down at him. "You have had a son for eight years that I knew nothing about because I've been married to a man for fifteen years that I don't even know. You have lied to me all these years, and…"

"No, I haven't lied to you. I didn't know about him."

"Well, you had an affair and kept that from me. That equates to lying, Henry. And all these years, you've been leading a congregation, preaching against sin, telling people to seek forgiveness, to repent of their sins, to live clean lives…"

"And I meant every word of it. The Lord did forgive me of my sin, Nora. I confessed it on the ship coming home from Tokyo."

Nora scoffed. "Oh, how convenient for you. You confessed your sin once you knew you weren't going to see her again. Or did you see her again? Did she come to the States to visit you?"

"What? No, no, I never saw her again after that last day."

"How do I know that?"

"Because I'm telling you."

He reached for her again, but she moved further away. She did not want him coming near her. She did not want him massaging her hand, nor even touching her for that matter. "How could you, Henry?" She walked to the opposite side of the coffee table, in front of the chair he'd occupied just moments ago. He sat on the couch looking up at her, his handsome face now long and pained.

"I could try to explain, but I'm afraid you wouldn't accept any explanation I'd give. It was wrong. That much I know, Nora. Very wrong."

"But—how could you? Paige and I—we faithfully waited for you."

"I know. I'm ashamed."

"I never suspected."

"I know. You had no reason to suspect. If I may, can I try to explain how things developed?"

"I'm not sure I want to know."

"I think it's best if you let me try."

She narrowed her eyes on him. "Don't think it's going to make me understand because even in a million years, I won't."

"I wouldn't expect you to, Nora. I just—I just ask that you hear me out."

She walked to the chair that was furthest from him, a tan wingback that showed lots of wear from grimy little hands. She lowered herself into it, but didn't lean back. Instead, she sat on the chair's edge, back pin straight, feet poised in case she needed to bolt. She glanced out of the picture window and then down at her hands, folded in her lap. "I'm listening."

He had to swing his body around to see her. He swallowed hard, his Adam's apple bobbing, and she imagined the pulse in his neck racing the way his breathing was so jagged. "I wasn't on the front lines, but I heard and saw plenty," he told her. "When the Army drafted me, I wasn't in the best place spiritually. You remember. You and I fought off and on about foolish stuff. I guess you could say I fell off the spiritual wagon. I was immature and ill-prepared for what lay ahead. When I arrived in Tokyo, it wasn't to a pretty sight. There was the smell of death everywhere I went. About a hundred thousand lives were lost in the final bombs dropped on Tokyo. Operation Meetinghouse is what the government termed it. When I arrived there, I had to help in the cleanup, which meant cleaning away debris from fallen buildings and helping to identify and dispose of dead bodies. It was horrible. After a time, a part of me grew hardened, and I'm ashamed to say my faith dwindled. I know I confessed to you when I got home how I'd taken up some pretty bad habits."

"Somehow you failed to confess breaking your wedding vows though!" she inserted, red-hot anger and anguish so intertwined she could hardly distinguish one from the other. She wanted to feel sorry for him and all he'd had to endure, but right now, it wasn't in her. It felt like a big excuse on his part, and she wasn't swallowing it.

"You and I—we felt worlds apart there for a while. I remember we had a big fight about something before I left."

"You wanted me to stay with your parents instead of mine after the baby came. Your parents had the parsonage and more people around to help take care of the baby. My parents had a smaller house, and Dad wasn't well. You thought it would be too much responsibility on my mom. I didn't want to stay with your parents because I didn't know them that well, and my mother wanted me to live with them. I honored her wishes above yours."

"Yes, I remember. Regardless, when I left, we weren't on the best terms. In retrospect, we should have waited to get married. We were both too young."

That much was true. They were both under a lot of stress. They had wanted to wait till he graduated from college before she got pregnant, but it didn't turn out that way. Then when the Army butted in, things got worse. Still, none of that gave him license for an affair. Her chest grew heavy, and a new thought emerged. "Did you have more than one affair?"

He gave a jerk of his head. "No! It wasn't even what you'd call an affair, Nora. I had no feelings for her. In fact, I was only with her—um—*intimately*—one time—and I was drunk at that. You must believe me."

"Oddly, believing you doesn't change a thing. It doesn't make me feel any better. You were married to *me*, Henry, and yet you took another woman to bed!"

"What I did was wrong. I know that."

"Pfff, that's an understatement."

"I'm so sorry, Nora. Please know I'd give anything to turn back time, but—I can't. It happened. And I have a son I never knew about."

She gave a little grunt of disgust and shook her head then lifted her gaze at him. "I can't forgive you, Henry. I don't know if or when I'll be able to."

"What do you want me to do?" He raised his voice to a desperate pitch.

Nora covered her mouth with three fingers and felt the tears slide down her cheeks. She held in the sobs. "Was she pretty?"

"What? I—don't know. I suppose she was, but I told you, I had no feelings for her. She was just—a…"

"A what, Henry? A substitute?"

"In a way, I suppose. But I wasn't thinking straight. We were at a party. Everyone was drinking, and she came on to me. She'd been chasing me for some time, and I knew it, but I—I didn't discourage it like I should have."

"Didn't it matter to you that you were married and had a daughter at home?" Her voice climbed a few decibels.

"Yes, it mattered!" Their eyes met, his pleading, hers blurred with tears. "That's why I stopped talking to her after that night. I told her I was married and couldn't see her again."

"Did you keep a picture of her?"

"No, I most certainly did not! The last thing I wanted was a picture of her. Sheesh, I wanted to forget everything about her. I quit drinking after that night, Nora. I never went to another bar. She had a job at the commissary, so it wasn't easy to avoid her entirely, but she knew. She knew—by the time I left—there was nothing between us. I told her to never try to contact me because I saw her copying down my parents' address when I laid one of Dad's letters down at the commissary. She must have given that address to Helen Felton before she died, and that's how the woman was able to contact me. Something you've got to realize, Nora, is the girls over there want nothing more than to hook up with an American soldier. It is every girl's dream to come to America, and they'll do whatever it takes to land a soldier."

"Even get pregnant."

"I suppose so. But I swear, honey, I didn't know she was pregnant."

"And what if you had? Would you have stayed?"

"Stayed? In Japan? No way! I would have done the right thing though. I would have sent her money for our—for—"

Old-fashioned anger made its way to the surface. "Your son. Say it, Henry. You would have done right by your son."

"Yes. I would have."

They sat in silence for the next little while, cars passing on Wood Street. At one point, a police car flew by, its siren blaring. Neither glanced out the window. They sat there, eyes down, hers still brimming with tears. With the back of her hand, she wiped them, but the tears just came back until they spilled faster, dripping down her neck and stopping at the rounded collar of her sleeveless dress. He rose from the sofa and approached her, but she held out a flat palm. "Don't. Don't come any closer."

"Nora."

"I mean it, Henry. I don't want you touching me. I don't even want to look at you right now."

"But—we have things to discuss. I love you, Nora. Nothing about my feelings for you have changed." He stood over her, a couple feet away. "When I came home in forty-six, I realized as never before how much you mean to me. I can't take back what happened, but I can move forward from it—we all can. ..."

"What do you mean, we all can? Maybe *you* can, but I can't, and if you think we *all* can, meaning our family, your parents, my mother, our church, well, you—you just think again, *Reverend* Griffin! You just think again!" This she said with the fiercest anger and a voice to match.

He jolted and stepped back. "Screaming at me will get us nowhere, Nora."

"Oh, don't you dare patronize me, Henry. You've had nine years to ponder this—this sin in your life."

"And a little over a week to ponder the fact that I have another son. A motherless son, I might add."

That phrase, that single phrase—*a motherless son*—fell hard on her chest, like a cement block that she hadn't the strength to remove. What would that mean for them—as a family? A motherless son? Would he now become Henry's responsibility and *hers*? Must they take this child into their home? They could barely afford the two children they had. Perspiration beaded her brow as a hot flush crept up her neck and flooded her face, making her feel faint and prickly. He must have seen it, for he was gone and back in less than a few seconds, pressing a cool cloth to her forehead and handing her a glass of cold water. "Here, take a couple sips." She indeed took a couple swallows and regained her composure, then felt like a frail fool for allowing her emotions to get the better of her.

"Oh, God, oh, God, what a nightmare," she mumbled. "What a terrible nightmare."

NINE

The LORD is good, a strong hold in the day of trouble;
and he knoweth them that trust in him.
—Nahum 1:7 (KJV)

It was a nightmare all right, but Henry could not stop thinking about the little eight-year-old boy who'd just lost his mother. He was the one suffering the real nightmare right now, but he dared not tell Nora that lest she release another uproarious outburst. He wanted to say she'd reacted in less than a Christlike fashion, but he had a feeling that was about the last thing she wanted to hear. Could he blame her? His actions of nine years ago weren't Christlike either, never mind that he hadn't been much of a mature Christian at the time. They sat beside each other on the sofa now, but she kept her distance. She gave a couple of jerking sobs and took another swallow of water then set the glass down on a coaster. Never had he felt so helpless, so out of control. Folks normally considered him level-headed, a quick, capable thinker, even clever. It was something that served him well behind the pulpit. Now, however, clever was the last attribute he had to his name.

Minutes passed before he dared to speak. "How shall we tell the kids?"

She lifted her puffy face and gawked at him. "How shall *we* tell them? Don't you mean, how are *you* going to tell them? This is your problem, Henry, not mine. I can't imagine what you'll tell them, but it's not going to be easy, that much I know. Paul won't fully grasp the meaning, but Paige is old enough to know that babies don't just grow from a tree and fall off when they're good and ripe. I've talked to her a little bit about where babies come from, but we haven't had the actual *talk* yet. She'll have questions for certain, and there will be a sense of betrayal when it at last dawns on her what you did. She'll instinctively know it was wrong."

"And you're not even going to be there when I talk to them?"

"I don't know. I haven't thought that far."

More silence, as they both sat and pondered their own private thoughts, she staring into her lap at her clasped hands, he staring off across the room, not focusing on anything in specific.

"So—tell me what this Mrs. Felton has to do with anything?"

It was her first attempt to talk with any amount of rationale. He jumped at it, trying his best to maintain a sense of calm. "Ironically, I met Mrs. Felton while standing in line waiting for permission to board the ship that would take my regiment and several others back to the States. She was taking the same ship back to America to visit a family member, if I recall correctly. She told me she was a missionary, and we had a friendly conversation that only lasted a matter of minutes. It was Mrs. Felton's family mission that Rina—the boy's mother—went to shortly after—after she learned she was pregnant. Mrs. Felton helped her and has helped to raise the boy, as far as I can tell. Rina had no family."

Nora did nothing more than nod. "Hm. How did she die?"

"Mrs. Felton said cancer took her. You can read the letters if you like, so you'll know exactly as much as I know."

"Maybe later."

"That's fine."

"And so—what are your plans?"

"I—would hope that they can be *our* plans."

"Don't push it, Henry. Just tell me what lies ahead."

"I don't know what lies ahead, Nora. You will have to help me decide that, whether you like it or not. We're married, and so we're in this together."

"Well, where is the boy now?"

"His name is Emiko, and he's with Helen Felton. In Naperville, Illinois. She has legal custody of him now."

"Good. She can keep him then."

"It's not that easy. As I said, she's in her seventies. She said she is physically unable to keep him. She did say she could adopt him out to an American family affiliated with her mission. She has the legal wherewithal to do that."

For the first time, she looked up with a glimmer of hope in her eyes. "That's the answer then. Let him go to a well-deserving family. You know as well as I do that there are folks out there who would do anything for a little boy."

His heart sank to his toes, but he couldn't let her see his disappointment. It was, after all, a very natural reaction on her part. It had even been his first reaction. Give the boy away, don't talk about him to anyone, pretend it never happened, and go on with life as usual. It even seemed like the sensible thing to do. But could he do it—that was the question. Would his conscience allow it?

"It's the only way, Henry," Nora said, as if reading his mind. "You know what the church would say. You can't keep a child who was conceived out of wedlock. You committed a sin, and in the eyes of most, a quite unpardonable one."

"Unpardonable in your eyes, Nora? That's my question."

"Henry, don't ask me such a thing. What you did was terrible. You broke our sacred wedding vows. You've breached a precious trust. How do I know you haven't been unfaithful to me since then?"

"Nora, how can you ask such a thing? Of course, I've been faithful. I can't believe you could even suggest that I haven't."

"Well, think again, Henry. You've got me questioning everything we ever shared over the last fifteen years."

She had calmed down considerably, but now the part of her that was talking was not the Nora he knew. There was a hardness to her tone he wasn't accustomed to, and it made him queasy. In fact, it flat out scared him half to death. She sounded like a woman who wouldn't think twice about packing her clothes and the children's and leaving him tonight. Of course, her mother would take them in and not ask a single question just to have them under the same roof with her. No matter how hard he tried, he would never be good enough for the likes of Florence Harrison.

He folded his arms across his wide chest and studied his size twelve scuffed loafers, feet crossed at the ankles. "Mrs. Felton is driving over here on Wednesday from Hope College. She's bringing Emiko with her."

She jerked her head up, mouth sagging. "Here? In two days? To our home?"

"Well, she has Mom and Dad's address. If you'd rather she met me there, that's fine."

"So, you're meeting this boy even though I just said I think it's best you adopt him out?"

"If he was your son, wouldn't you want to meet him?"

"There are women who have babies out of wedlock who give them up at birth. It happens. You have to think about what's best for Paige and Paul—not you."

"And what about Emiko? What do you suppose is best for him?"

"I don't know, Henry. He's not my worry."

He paused before saying what was really on his mind, but in the end, decided to say it anyway. "You sound so harsh, Nora. I don't know this side of you."

"And I don't know this side of you!" she shrieked—enough to make him shrink back. She jumped up and looked down at him. "If you're looking for sympathy, Henry, you're not going to get it. You don't like this side of me? Well, I don't like it either, but then I've never been wronged like this before. Don't expect me to bounce back like some—some sinless saint. I'm human, and what you did to me was cruel and hurtful." She walked around him, taking care not to brush against his spread-out knees. "I'm going to our room, and I'm closing the door behind me. Don't even think about coming inside to ask me anything because I don't plan on talking." She got as far as the end of the hall before turning. "Oh, and, yes, if you must meet the boy, I think it's best you meet him at your parents' house, and before you ask, no, I do not wish to go with you. You can explain my absence to your parents in any way you choose."

For the next ten minutes, he sat in utter stillness listening to his jagged breathing. "God almighty," he at last said in a shaky whisper, "I have failed You so miserably. I've botched my life, my marriage, my family, my congregation—everything." He partially stood, then turned around and went down on one knee. Hands clasped, he wept into his closed fist, the tears spilling down his face as he poured out his heart to the One and only Person who understood everything—and loved him anyway.

A little after one o'clock, after making himself half of a peanut butter sandwich and downing a small glass of milk, Henry walked down the hallway to his bedroom. He bent down and pushed the two letters he'd received from Helen Felton under the door. After straightening, he stood there for a few moments, thinking he might hear some stirring. Figuring she must have fallen asleep, he walked away, then decided to go over to his office. Sunday's sermon loomed. Lord, did he even have a sermon in him? And if he did, what would be its content? *Lord God, guide me. I need a fresh renewal of my heart and spirit. I need—I need—God, I don't even know what I need.*

Outside, he passed quickly by the Mercy Tree. Overhead, gray, menacing clouds rolled by, as a fierce wind started to pick up. The tiniest ounce of peace washed over him despite all the unrest—for while he himself could not see into the future, the Lord could, and for now, that bit of knowledge was all he had.

Nora knew Henry had left the house, having heard the door open and close a while ago. Exhausted from crying what felt like the entire Muskegon River, she pushed the single blanket off, rolled out of bed, and walked to the window. Cars passed by, the drivers oblivious to the fact that someone's world had fallen apart inside the little red brick house. She glanced at the clock on the dresser. Two-thirty. At some point, she'd cried herself to sleep, but she couldn't have dozed more than twenty minutes. The remainder of the time, she'd tried to pray, but God felt oddly distant. Of course He did. She hadn't the wherewithal to forgive her husband, and as long as she harbored unforgiveness, her relationship with God would be fragmented. Hardly seemed fair, especially when she wished for nothing more than to stay angry, even deserved to, gosh darn it! And if she'd said gosh darn it as a girl, her mother would've washed her mouth out with soap. Florence Harrison was a Christian, but a rigid, rather unhappy one, and all of Nora's life, she'd worked hard not to mirror her. But here she was, playing the part of her mother, scoffing, filling with anger, and now letting out a horrendous howl of frustration! To accentuate her anger, she walked up to the wall and gave it a good hard kick, which only made her bend over with excruciating pain. Immediately, she dropped to the floor and hugged her foot. Good grief, had she broken her toe? She, the preacher's wife, known for her sweet and saintly ways, had just screamed so loud her lungs gave out, kicked the wall, left a black smudge mark there, and on top of that, hurt herself. She winced at the pain and rocked back and forth a few times.

In her rocking, she glanced across the room and saw the envelopes Henry had slipped under the door. She crawled to the letters, picked them up, and then gingerly stood, testing her foot. Deciding her toe was still intact, she limped to the bed and plopped down, fingering the two letters, one an airmail letter and the other a simple first class. She didn't really wish to read them, but she supposed it would help if she did. She lifted the flap on the airmail missive, unfolded the paper, and gave it a quick read. Then she read the second one. They were pretty much what she expected, matching what information Henry had given her, but they certainly didn't help to ease any of her anger.

And where was the photo that the first letter mentioned? Had Henry torn it up and thrown it away—or was it tucked into his wallet beside the photos of her and their children?

If he was your son, wouldn't you want to meet him? Henry's question to her hung in the air like a black storm cloud.

"Ugh!" she groaned, flopping back on the bed while she waited for a new batch of tears to come. When it was clear they weren't coming, she let out a quivery sigh and shuffled to the door, her big toe still throbbing. As long as Henry stayed away, she could go out to the kitchen and start fixing the children their after-school snack. Soon, they'd come flying through the door, full of giggles and chatter, and she'd have to put on a cheerful front. When Henry came home, though, she'd drop the façade. He was responsible for this tornado, and she'd be darned if he thought she was going to clean up his mess.

TEN

Have not I commanded thee? Be strong and of a good courage;
be not afraid, neither be thou dismayed:
for the LORD thy God is with thee whithersoever thou goest.
—Joshua 1:9 (KJV)

Henry watched the clock, and when the time drew near for Paige and Paul's return from school, he stood at his office window and waited. Right on time, he spotted the usual group of eight to ten neighborhood kids crossing the street, a sixth-grade crossing guard wearing his orange banner across his chest and giving them the go-ahead. He remembered the job of crossing guard and how it only went to the most responsible students who demonstrated good citizenship and proved to the principal that they were trustworthy. He'd been one of those students himself, and he suspected Paige and Paul would eventually take their turns serving in the role if they wanted it. They certainly held the necessary requirements.

At the end of the Griffins' driveway, the students parted, each going to his and her own home, some giving little farewell waves as they sauntered along. A deep sigh rolled out of Henry at what lay ahead for him. How was he going to tell his children they had a half-brother? How could he possibly make them understand the gravity of the matter without them turning against him? He could only surmise their emotions would be a mix of resentment, jealousy, anger, confusion, and who knew what else. "Lord, give me wisdom as I attempt to navigate these unknown waters."

He pulled himself away from the window, walked over to his desk, and straightened a few stacks of papers in neat piles. He had accomplished very little in his office today other than to pray, read his Bible, and seek forgiveness for the wrongs he'd committed. Oh, he'd sought forgiveness years ago and knew by God's grace he'd received it, but now, the wound of his past sin had broken open, making it seem fresh and raw again. With extreme heaviness, he gave the office one last glance, flipped off the light switch on the wall, and locked the door behind him.

He quietly entered by way of the front door and found the children in the kitchen sitting in the nook, each with a glass of milk and a couple of ginger cookies. They chattered faster than two hungry birds, Paul saying something about a science experiment they'd done in class that day in which the teacher had almost set the school on fire. Henry doubted it was quite that bad, but Paul made the story believable. Paige talked about the pop quiz they'd had in math class and how she and another girl were the only ones who achieved a perfect score. "We got ten extra minutes of recess with the sixth graders," she bragged.

"That's nice," Nora said in a flat tone, her back to them as she washed a few dishes. None of them were even aware he stood in the arched entry, arms crossed as he leaned against the doorframe. He wanted to freeze this moment, skip over all the junk that had to come out sooner or later, and turn the clock back to the way things were a little more than a week ago. If only…

At last, he cleared his throat. Both kids gave a little jolt. "Daddy!" Paige smiled and took another drink of milk, but in his usual fashion, Paul leaped off the banquette bench and ran to give him a big squeeze around his middle, nearly stealing his breath. Warmed clear through, Henry hugged him back then ruffled his blond head. "So, your teacher almost burned your school down today, huh?"

"You heard that part?" Paul walked back to the table and sat again.

"He exaggerates, Daddy," Paige offered, sliding off the bench and taking her dishes to her mother. Nora took them off her hands but failed to turn around and acknowledge Henry's presence. He wasn't surprised.

"I'm going to do my homework," Paige announced.

"How are you doing on those state capitals?" Henry asked.

"We're done studying that unit. I got a ninety-eight percent."

"Not a one hundred?" Henry teased her.

"I misspelled Juneau. Can you spell it, Daddy?"

"Is it J-u-n-o?" he asked, deliberately misspelling it.

"See? You can't spell it either!"

"What's Juneau?" Paul asked.

"The capital of Alaska, dummy," Paige said.

"Paige, apologize to your brother," Nora said. "You know better than to call each other names."

"Yeah, how would I know what the capital of Alaska is? What's a capital anyway?"

"You'll learn all that soon enough," said Henry, wishing only to keep the peace as long as possible.

"Paige?" Nora said, casting a disapproving look.

The girl gave a tiny eye-roll but told her brother, "I'm sorry." After thanking Nora for the milk and cookies, she skipped past Henry to go to her room.

Well, there went his chance to talk to the kids about their half-brother. It was probably best to bring it up after supper anyway.

Finishing his milk with two big gulps, Paul slid out from the table and carried his dishes to his mother. She took them and said not a word. If Paul noticed her lack of conversation, he didn't let on. It was more than obvious to Henry though, for normally, Nora was the talkative one, always eager to get the children conversing about their school days and doing her best to bring joy and laughter to the family. Not today, however.

"Daddy, when are we going to get a television?"

"I don't know, Paul. I haven't given it any thought."

"Well, did you know Jimmy Faber's dad bought them one last week?"

"No, I hadn't heard that. Good for them."

"All the neighbors are getting them."

"Are they now? Well, good thing we don't have to keep up with the neighbors, isn't it?"

"They get to watch the *Big Top* circus every Saturday morning."

"Really?"

"My teacher said her husband is buying them a set this weekend."

"I'm happy for your teacher."

Nora, finished puttering in the kitchen, reached under the sink where she kept her watering can, and filled it with water. Then without a word, she left the kitchen and stepped out onto the back patio. Henry didn't know why she felt the need to water the flowers when they'd gotten plenty of rain the last day and a half. He supposed she wanted nothing more than to escape his presence.

"We'll talk about that television later, all right, Son?"

"Really?"

"I didn't say we were getting one. I said we'd talk about it later. Now, why don't you go study your spelling words?"

"Our teacher didn't give us a new list this week."

"Well, that's lucky. How about you go read your library book?"

"I already read it three times."

"I'll give you a nickel if you go read it a fourth time."

His eyes widened. "You will? Will you take me to the Shop 'N Go tonight so I can spend it on a candy bar?"

"Maybe tomorrow. We'll see. Go read your book, sport."

"All right."

As soon as Paul left, Henry gathered his courage, walked across the linoleum floor, and stepped out the back door onto the brick patio, where he found Nora watering a few of her potted plants. Their neat little fenced-in backyard held a picnic table covered with a plastic red and white checkered tablecloth. On top of that were three petunia plants in colorful clay pots. Nora always kept them deadheaded and neatly trimmed. She also had a flowerbed that ran the length of the north side of the white picket fence. He could only identify a few of the plants in the array. At the far end of the backyard was the children's play equipment—a swing set and slide that Paige no longer used, which Paul only played on if his friends joined him. There were also a smattering of trucks and other toys lying about.

"You think it's done raining?" Henry asked Nora, stuffing his hands into his pants pockets.

She didn't turn. "I don't know, but it doesn't hurt to give my flowers a little drink anyway."

He cast a glance at the cloudy skies, then noted how quickly some of the trees had started to change colors just since last week. "Won't be long and there won't be any plants to water."

"I'll keep them alive as long as I can."

"You always do. You do love your flowers." It had been a long time since he'd had to grapple for ways to keep the conversation flowing with his wife. "I called Boyd's Uptown Service today to see about getting the Packard fixed. They're picking it up tomorrow."

"That's nice."

That's nice? That was it? She'd been after him for weeks to get their second car fixed. Granted, it was pretty much an old junker, but as far as he knew, it was worth fixing. He'd find out tomorrow. She emptied her watering can. Would she now go refill it? No, he supposed not, for she set it down next to the step and wiped her hands on her apron.

"Well, I suppose I'll go in and start supper. Before you ask, I'm fixing grilled cheese sandwiches and opening a couple cans of Campbell's Tomato Soup."

"Sounds delicious."

"Uh-huh."

She started up the step, but he grabbed hold of her arm. She flinched. "Don't, Henry."

"I think we need to talk."

"I'm not ready."

"When will you be?"

"I have no idea."

Frustrated, he shook his head. "I'll be talking to the kids after supper."

"Good. I hope you've figured out what you're going to tell them."

"Will you be there?"

"I don't know."

"I could use your moral support."

"If I'm there, it won't be for you, Henry."

She shook his hand off her and walked into the house, leaving behind an awful chill.

⌒

Supper was a quiet affair. Nora knew Henry was busy rehearsing in his head just what to say to the children about the brother they had no idea existed. She would feel sorry for him if she had it in her, but her heart was still too raw and broken to feel much of anything other than numbness. Perhaps it was coldhearted of her not to be filled with love and compassion at a time like this, but Henry had betrayed her in the worst possible way. Why, she even had biblical grounds for divorce if she wanted to go that far. She didn't, however, as much as she was hurting. She had no idea what tomorrow held—or the next day. So much hinged on what he decided to do about the boy. She'd made her wishes known: give him up for adoption. It was the right thing to do in her mind and would cause the least amount of grief for everyone—including the boy. Since he didn't know anything about his American father, what possible good could come from enlightening him? The child needed a fresh start with a new family. Just not *her* family.

The children were full of chatter, and it was all Nora could do to hold herself together. More than once, she had to force smiles and even a laugh or two. She didn't want them growing suspicious of her behavior, although she knew the hour of truth would soon be upon them. It came after the kids polished off their dessert of one brownie and a small scoop of vanilla ice cream, a treat they'd always reserved for Monday nights, a kind of way to kick off the new week. In fact, many were the Monday nights in the summer they'd pile into the car and drive north to Ludington to indulge in a tasty cone from the popular House of Flavors Ice Cream Parlor. Afterwards, they'd take their cones down to Lake Michigan and walk the shoreline, ice cream dripping down their wrists if they didn't eat fast enough.

"Can I go over to Jimmy Faber's house?" Paul asked after scraping the last of his ice cream off the bottom of his bowl. "He invited me to come over and watch *Kukla, Fran, and Ollie,* and he said it's funny. It's a puppet show. It starts at seven o'clock, but he wants me to come over sooner so he can show me the train set he got for his birthday.

"Not tonight, Son," said Henry.

"Why not?" Paul's voice rose to a high-pitched whine.

"Because I want to talk to you and Paige about—about something important."

"Like what?" Paige asked, eyes suddenly bright with excitement. "Are we going to go on vacation this summer? I want to go to California. I heard there's a new park opening soon called Disneyland. Maybe it's already open. Can we go there?"

"No, Paige, sorry, we are not traveling all the way to California. Good grief. You guys want the moon."

"Then what is it?"

"It's something quite serious, so I'll need your full attention."

"Oh, no, are we moving?" Paige asked. "I don't want to move. I like it here."

"Paige, let your father talk," Nora injected. She had decided to stay seated, not for Henry's sake, but for the children's. The table needed clearing and the dishes needed to be washed, but for tonight, that could all wait. Her heart pounded hard. To quell her nerves, she took a sip of water then folded her napkin in her lap and tightly clasped her hands atop it.

Henry also took a sip of water, then after setting down the glass, he cleared his throat. By now, the children had quieted, for they seemed to sense that something big was coming, though they couldn't possibly know its magnitude. If Nora prayed anything, it was that Henry had come to his senses and decided it best to tell Mrs. Felton not to come to Muskegon. She wondered if he had even spoken to her on the phone, though she supposed she'd find that out soon enough.

"What is it, Daddy?" Paige asked, a pleading sound in her voice.

"What I am about to tell you is something quite life-changing in that it involves our entire family. From this day forward, things will never be quite the same for us."

"What do you mean?" Paige and Paul threw each other wary glances, and Nora knew their little hearts had already filled with confusion. She wanted to shout across the table at Henry to get on with it, but she knew he was busy trying to find a way to express himself so that the children would understand, even though they wouldn't.

"There is—there is an eight-year-old boy named Emiko. He—he is your half-brother. He was born in Japan, and I am his father."

Both children sat wide-eyed and gawping, mouths hanging open. The first thing Paige did was whip her head in Nora's direction. Nora gave no reaction, just kept clasping her hands in her lap, unable even to utter a word of assurance to the ten-year-old. Instead, she trained her eyes on Henry to see how he would finish out his explanation.

"So, you and Mommy have another boy you never told us about?" asked Paul.

"He's our half-brother, Paul. That means he's only half related."

"What's that mean?" Paul asked.

Henry cleared his throat. "Well, he's fully related to you. He is your brother, but he's your half-brother."

"How can anybody be a half-brother?"

"It means he is your daddy's son, but not mine," Nora explained. She avoided looking at Henry, but heard the jagged sigh that came out of him.

"So, Mommy's not his mom, but you are his dad?" asked Paul.

"That's right."

"Why didn't you tell us about him before?" Paul asked.

"I—I didn't know about him. It's very complicated."

At that, Paul's brow scrunched, and Nora could almost see the questions forming in his head. Paige, on the other hand, looked flushed and confounded. Nora wondered how much she had put two and two together, or if her fifth-grade, ten-year-old mind truly had the knowledge necessary to come up with an accurate assumption. She supposed that tonight, when she tucked her daughter into bed, she would have to clear up matters for her without being too specific. She didn't want the girl to wind up hating her father for the mistake he'd made. He was, after all, her beloved daddy, and Nora despised the notion that she would think less of him, regardless that she herself did. Children should not have to deal with such hideous matters. The fact that they were even now sitting around their dinner table discussing such a thing enraged her to no end.

"What does he look like?" Paul asked.

"I'll show you his picture if you like." Henry reached into his pocket.

"No!" Nora said, stopping him midway.

Henry frowned at her. "Nora, the children have a right to see a picture of their brother."

He proceeded to take the picture from his wallet and hand it over to Paige first. Out of the corner of her eye, Nora got a glimpse of a dark-haired boy, sitting straight, the tiniest smile on his square-jawed face. That was all she needed to see. She tossed her napkin down on the table, pushed back her chair, and left the dining room, taking a few dishes with her on her way to the kitchen.

From there, she overheard more questions, questions Henry quietly and patiently answered. Questions like: "Are we going to meet him?" "Where is his mother?" "How did she die?" And comments like: "He must be sad." "He looks kind of like you, Daddy." "His eyes are smaller though." "Does Mommy like him?"

Nora made as much racket as she could washing, rinsing, and drying the dishes, especially after that last question. She had no idea how Henry planned to answer it, and she didn't want to know. She returned to the dining room just long enough to pick up more dishes—until at last, she'd gathered them all. She didn't miss Henry's eyes on her each time she returned, but she avoided even the tiniest glance his way. She didn't want to hear the discussion, didn't want to think about their children's sudden interest in a boy they'd just learned was their long-lost brother. As expected, Paul had asked most of the questions, but only because he was the more spontaneous and inquisitive of the two. Paige was more apt to internalize information first and ask questions later. Still, Paige clearly wasn't missing a word of the discussion.

Nora's heart bled with heartache, the sort of pain she could barely find a way to handle. She wished she could feel differently. She wished she felt full of Christian mercy and understanding, lenience and grace, but those emotions were not coming to her. Instead, anger bubbled up around her heart, making her feel cold and dry inside. *Lord, teach me how to react as You would have me.* But even as she let the prayer wash across her mind, it didn't quite reach her heart. How on earth was she going to get through the coming days? And what would she do if Henry went against her wishes and brought the boy home on Wednesday? *Oh, God, this is such a mess. I don't even know how to behave as Your child.*

ELEVEN

My grace suffices thee; for my power is perfected in weakness.
—2 Corinthians 12:9

Henry's stomach burned; it felt like a giant ulcer was eating at the sides of his gut. In a daze, he drove east on West Laketon Avenue, then once at the end, he took a sharp right turn onto Lakeshore Drive. His parents lived in a turn-of-the-century two-story house across the street from Muskegon Lake. In other words, they had a wonderful view of the water, but didn't have to pay the taxes of a lakeside home. It was in a great location—only a few miles from Pere Marquette Park on the sandy shores of Lake Michigan.

As a teenager, before he started dating Nora seriously, Henry and his friends used to cruise the Ovals, a drive that curved in a figure eight, while they looked for girls to honk at and follow. Sipping on their Cokes and hanging their heads out the open windows of their fathers' cars, they thought of themselves as the biggest hotshots in town. Of course, he was a preacher's kid, so his idea of being a hotshot differed a great deal from the *real deal*, but Henry tried his best to fit in. Still, his friends were pretty tame compared to those fellows who smoked and drank. In high school, he was more a goody two-shoes. That was how he eventually attracted the attention of the most beautiful blond he'd ever meet, Miss Nora Harrison.

He found his parents lounging on their covered front porch when he pulled into their driveway. Both were wearing fall sweaters and enjoying the brisk air that came with a late September evening. Dusk was upon them; across the street, between two houses, they could watch a slice of the golden sun falling on the horizon and painting the sky around it orange, red, and dusty purple. It had always been a peaceful place to spend an evening. Tonight, however, a sense of foreboding impinged on that peace, for he knew the conversation that lay ahead could either draw a line of division between them that could cause irreparable damage or draw a widening circle swathed in unconditional love and forgiveness. He hoped for the latter. Ever since childhood, the one thing Henry most regretted doing in life was disappointing the two people who had his greatest respect. He parked his car, climbed out, and stepped up onto the porch.

Lillian greeted him with her usual warm smile. "What in the world brings you here at this hour? Aren't you putting your kids to bed about this time?"

He dusted a couple of stray leaves off a webbed chair and plunked himself into it. "Wanted to come and talk to you about something."

"Hm. Sounds serious. Might this call for a cup of coffee or some hot tea?" she asked.

He looked from one to the other. "No, but thanks."

He had no idea where to start. He'd grown so weary of rehashing the story over and over in his head, thinking of all the different ways to present it. After talking to his parents, he'd be calling both of his brothers. Then tomorrow, he'd be calling Mrs. Felton. After that, he planned to call Morris Grayson, the chairman of Open Door's elders, to ask to meet with him. He'd also have to tell Marlene, his secretary, and then the congregation on Sunday. "Oh, God, what a monster has befallen me," he mumbled under his breath. Then, simultaneously, he thought about the innocent child named Emiko, *his son*, and could not help the fatherly instinct building up inside him. "Lord, You alone can turn around this awful situation and make it work for the good of our family. Please have mercy." Had it not been for his faith, where would he even be? Even now, he sensed an overwhelming undergirding that he could only attribute to his Savior, and he felt unworthy of such grace.

He tossed back his head and gulped down a large breath of evening air. But still he sat in silence trying to find the right words. "First of all," he started. "Thanks for preaching for me yesterday, Dad. I always hear such great things from people afterward. I get the feeling they wouldn't mind my taking off a few more Sundays."

"Nonsense. I'm happy to fill in, but they love you. Of that, I'm certain."

He gave a slow smile and simple nod, suddenly tongue-tied. This was almost as bad as confessing to Nora.

"What is it, Son?" his father asked, reaching across the three-foot expanse between their seats to rest a hand on his shoulder. "Are you having some financial struggles? Mother and I have some extra cash in our savings…"

"No, no, nothing like that."

His father withdrew his hand and gave a little shrug. "All right then. We'll just sit here and wait. We have the entire evening, and as you can see, we don't have a great deal going on in our lives." He cast an arm out in front of him and smiled.

"I have something to tell you—concerning my past."

Both took simultaneous sips of their hot drinks. Were they also experiencing a sudden case of nerves?

"We're all ears, honey," his mother whispered.

A neighbor walked by with her dog and gave a friendly wave, and Henry prayed she wouldn't stop to visit. Thankfully, her dog pulled her along, its leash stretched taut. He breathed a sigh of relief.

"I guess I'll come right out with it." He swallowed and let his eyes go from one parent to the other and hold for three seconds, looking them both dead on. "I just found out last week—after receiving that letter that came to your address—that I have an eight-year-old son I never knew existed."

A yellow leaf fell to the bottom porch step, and he swore he heard it hit the wood slat.

His mother took in a breath and simply stared wide-eyed. His father sat in silence, one gray eyebrow arched, his blue eyes wide, his bearded chin slightly tipped to the side.

Slowly and with careful deliberation, Henry spilled the entire sordid story, relaying it in much the same way he'd told Nora, though leaving out certain details. Not surprisingly, their reactions were completely different from hers. Where she'd been filled with anger, disbelief, and obvious betrayal mixed with tears, they lacked any kind of emotional response. Whatever it was they truly felt, he believed they'd reserve it for a private discussion later, perhaps before retiring for bed.

Lester rose, stood in front of Henry, and placing his hands firmly on his shoulders, pulled him up out of his chair. "Come here, Son," he said. And just like that, Henry fell into his father's embrace.

There was much for Lester and Lillian Griffin to digest, details they would question but would never fully know the answers to because Henry felt like some things needed to be reserved for Nora's ears only. But they knew as much as they needed, and probably *wanted*, to know. After a time, they went inside and allowed Henry the privacy he needed to make long-distance phone calls to each of his brothers. Both were understandably surprised to hear from him, but because of their close relationships, said little in the way of condemnation. He was certain they'd have plenty of that to toss around with their wives later, but for now, they both reacted in civil, if not loving, ways. He told them he would completely understand if they chose not to talk to him for a while. Both seemed to agree it would be best to give each other some time and space. They were scheduled for Thanksgiving visits, of course, but he hoped by then, they would be ready to forgive him and hopefully meet Emiko for the first time.

His oldest brother, David, who lived in Pittsburgh with his wife Peggy and their four children, asked if Emiko would be living with him. His answer had been the same one he'd given his parents. He had to discuss the matter further with Nora. Neither brother offered his opinion or advice, for which Henry was grateful, but there was that part of him that wanted to know what they would do if they'd been in his shoes.

By the time ten o'clock rolled around, he found himself physically, mentally, and emotionally exhausted, but there was the matter of another discussion with Nora. The trouble was, when he arrived home, the house was dark, the children soundly sleeping, having been put to bed long ago. There were no lights on in his bedroom, and Nora was still, lying on the far side of the bed, her figure under the covers barely visible by the light of the street lamp. He walked down the hallway to the bathroom, took care of his nightly ablutions, then reentered the dark bedroom. Quietly, he slipped out of his trousers and shirt, laid them on a nearby chair, and as he did every other night of his life, climbed under the covers in just his underwear. He pulled the sheet and blankets up to his chin and lay there in the dark, eyes wide open as he stared at the ceiling. Her breathing was measured and deep, but he couldn't tell if she was sleeping.

With cautious deliberateness, he gently put a hand on her arm. "Are you awake, Nora?"

In an instant, she withdrew. If she'd been pretending before, she certainly wasn't now. "I don't want to talk."

"But—we need to—"

"If you persist, one of us will have to go out to the sofa."

He turned his back to her. Without another word, he closed his eyes and gave his mind and heart over to prayer and meditation. Only God could fix the mess he'd gotten himself into. Only God.

~

Whereas Nora had barely slept more than a total of two hours, it seemed to her that Henry had snored the entire night away. How could he sleep with such abandon when so heavy a weight had fallen on their marriage? It made her all the madder when she tossed the scrambled eggs in the pan and flipped the bacon. No one had entered the kitchen yet, but when her children arrived, she'd have to put on a halfway pleasant front for them. Last night, Henry had spilled the news to his parents and while she was curious to know how they'd responded, the last thing she wanted to do was inquire. She just could not bring herself to talk to Henry even though tomorrow was the day he was scheduled to meet his son. She'd had a full day and all last night to let this whole matter sink into her mind, but it seemed like a mere blip in time considering he'd had more than a week to adjust. And the notion that he'd kept his affair secret for nine years and would no doubt have taken it to his grave gave her even more pause. What other secrets lay buried?

Just as she'd feared, Henry entered the kitchen ahead of Paige and Paul. He didn't come up behind her as he'd always done before, to wrap his arms around her and smother her neck with kisses. This morning, he knew better. The wall between them forbid even a decent conversation. He'd wanted to talk last night, but she'd had neither the will nor the energy. Perhaps today, after the children left for school, she'd find it in her.

"How did you sleep last night?" he asked, coming up beside her to take down four plates from the cupboard.

"Oh, just dandy," she answered, her words soaked in sarcasm.

He opened the drawer and removed four sets of silverware, then shuffled to the kitchen nook and set the table.

"Kids up?"

"Yes. They should be coming out any minute."

"Did you have a chance to talk to them about—you know—before they went to sleep?"

"They had a few questions, which I answered to the best of my ability."

"I see. Will you tell me what they asked?"

"Paul didn't have much to say, but Paige asked why you did that to me."

"She did? So, she understands more than we give her credit for I guess."

"Seems so."

"How did you answer her?"

"With the truth."

"Which was?"

"I told her I had absolutely no idea," Nora replied in a whispery hiss. "What did you want me to tell her, that you were in love with another woman?"

Henry gave a loud huff. "I did not love her, Nora, not by a long shot."

"So you say." She scooped the eggs and bacon onto a platter and brought them to the table, accidentally brushing against him as he made his way to the refrigerator. Neither reacted, although she swore a wave of electric current ran between them with that simple touch. She hated what had happened to them over the past twenty-four hours—and fixing it would be no easy feat. Henry had spilled his guts to his parents, so she supposed she'd have to call her mother today and invite her over. She fretted over Florence Harrison's reaction. She was a woman who thrived on her neat and tidy existence; anything that interrupted her perfect lifestyle put her in a state of turmoil. Any sort of blemish to the family reputation—and certainly an illegitimate child would qualify as a blemish—would offend her personally. Nora knew her mother would react as if she herself had been wronged. Marrying Henry right out of high school had enabled Nora to escape from her mother's clutches. Of course, she had loved Henry dearly, but had her mother not been so controlling, they might have waited a couple of years.

"Hm, bacon and eggs," Paul said, sweeping past her in his stocking feet, dapper trousers, and clean T-shirt. The boy had even wet down his head to tamp down his flyaway blond hair. Not bad for a second-grader.

Paige entered shortly afterward, dressed in a red pleated dress, white socks, and black Mary Jane shoes, hairbrush in hand.

"Good morning to you! Don't you look pretty?" Henry greeted. Nora could tell he was forcing cheerfulness.

"Thanks, Daddy. Mommy, I want you to braid my hair today." To Henry, she explained, "This is school picture day."

"No kidding. Do you have the money for them?"

"Mommy put it in two envelopes for Paul and me, and we put them in our lunch pails."

"Well, good for Mommy for remembering," Henry said.

"Good thing we have Mommy 'cause she don't forget anything," Paul chimed in.

"Yes, you are very blessed indeed," Henry said.

"Mommy is the best there is!" Paul added.

"All right, all right," Nora said, feeling a bit bewildered by all the gushing. She sat down next to Paige and across from Henry and Paul, took up her napkin and set it on her lap. "Let's say our morning prayer before we eat, shall we?"

"You want to pray this morning, Nora?" Henry whispered.

She gave a little shake of her head. "You say it."

"I'll say it," offered Paul, his voice eager.

"All right then," said Henry. "Go ahead."

Everyone bowed heads and folded hands.

"Dear Jesus," the boy prayed. "Thank You for our breakfast, and thank You for Mommy for fixing it. Help us to all love Mommy, and make Daddy love her most of all. And be with that boy who is ar' new brother, whatever his name is."

"It's Emiko," Paige inserted.

"Yeah, Emiko," he said. "And help ar' family to get along real good. Amen."

His prayer finished, everyone began to eat. Nora kept her eyes pointed downward and squirmed in her seat. What a prayer! You couldn't put much past children. When trouble brewed in their homes, they picked up on it.

Henry cleared his throat after swallowing his first bite. "Just so you know, kids, I do love your mother very much. I have never stopped, nor will I ever. You may sense a bit of tension going on, but I don't want you to concern yourselves. Things will work out, but that's for your mother and me to solve, not you. Understood?"

Slowly, both children nodded their heads.

"Now, eat your breakfast so you can finish getting ready for school. You have to leave in about twenty minutes."

For reasons Nora could not name, other than her emotions were riding some wild waves, tears welled up in her eyes. Of course, she knew Henry loved her. She'd never doubted that. But to hear him declare it in front of Paige and Paul made her instantly weepy. She set down her napkin, and walked to the cupboard to retrieve a cup and pour herself some coffee. Without looking up she asked, "You want some coffee, Henry?"

"No, thank you. My orange juice will do me for now."

Nora filled her cup and with her back to her family, she lifted the hem of her apron and dabbed at her tears. The last thing she wanted was for the kids to notice. The three of them continued their quiet conversation while she gained control of herself. Then with her coffee cup in hand, she returned to the table. She felt Henry's gaze on her, but she didn't return it. After a few minutes, she said, "Now then, Paige, we best hurry and get those braids done so you'll be ready for school pictures."

"Okay. I want the French kind."

"I think that will be perfect. Do you want ribbons?"

"Naw. That's for babies."

"Well, of course. What was I thinking?"

TWELVE

The LORD of hosts is with us; the God of Jacob is our refuge.
—Psalm 46:11 (KJV)

Oh, my goodness, Henry, how did Nora take the news?" Marlene exclaimed when he revealed his wicked secret to her. True concern was etched across his secretary's rather plain but kind face.

"Not well, I'm afraid."

Of all the people who attended Open Door, Marlene and her husband Tom were two of the finest, most caring individuals, always lending helping hands when needs arose, delivering casseroles to the sick, giving above and beyond financially if they got wind of someone in trouble, and loving without barriers. They had two married daughters, two sons in college, and one grandchild on the way. Henry was not only blessed by Marlene's careful attention to detail with regard to church office duties but also blessed to call her his friend.

Marlene shook her head. "I can only imagine how she's feeling. She needs time to let this news settle."

"Yes, she's deeply hurt, angry, sad, confused—everything rolled into one big emotional ball." He hung his head. "I did it to her, Marlene. I did it to my family, to my friends, and to my church. I have made this big mess, and now I have to clean it up."

"Henry, listen to me. You were much younger back then. You made a mistake, a terrible one to be sure, but good can come from it. Romans eight, twenty-eight tells us that God makes all things work together for good to those who love the Lord and are called according to His purpose. I believe that verse with all my heart. I support you and Nora, and I hope others in the church will do the same. However, these are difficult times, and I'll be honest, Henry, there are ill feelings towards the Japs right now. Not from me, mind you, but from a vast amount of people, probably some right here in our congregation. Don't be surprised if some turn against you. A few might even leave the church. They won't take kindly to you having committed adultery, and the boy will be a constant reminder. I'm just trying to be honest."

He nodded. It was a sobering statement. "I'm well aware. I met with Morris Grayson before coming into the office this morning. Since your Tom is also an elder, I'm sure you and he will have plenty to discuss over dinner tonight because Morris said he plans to call each elder today to inform them of the news. If need be, they'll get together later this week to discuss what he called 'the possible ramifications'. I don't know exactly what he meant by that, whether removing me as pastor or making me take a leave of absence—I don't know, Marlene."

She took a step forward and touched his arm. "But God knows, Henry, and for now, that is enough."

"You're right, I know. I told Morris I intend to divulge the story to the congregation this Sunday. If I don't, the news will leak, and that would make matters even worse. He agrees wholeheartedly and promised to pray for me as I prepare."

She gave a solemn nod. "While Tom and I might discuss your predicament tonight, we will not discuss it with anyone else, not even our immediate family. Instead, we will commit to praying and fasting over you and your loved ones—including that new little boy who's come into your life."

His chest pinched at the mention of his son. He still had no idea how to proceed regarding Emiko since he and Mrs. Felton had yet to speak on the phone. He needed something concrete from Nora before he could decide what to do, and that thought alone made him shudder. She had mentioned adoption, but his heart and mind couldn't quite come to terms with that. How could he live with himself knowing he'd rejected his own son?

"You have worry lines all across your face, Henry. Try not to be so hard on yourself. God has forgiven you."

"Are you sure about that? I'm having a difficult time believing it's possible."

"That's because you can't find peace in your home. When that comes, the rest will follow. It might take Nora a good long while. I'll be praying for your family."

"Thanks, Marlene. I knew you'd be understanding. I appreciate that more than you know."

"We all make mistakes, and because of God's grace, He forgives the vilest of sinners."

Her words were powerful, but he still had to say what was heaviest on his mind. "I'd understand completely if you decided to quit working for me. You may get some criticism otherwise."

She flicked her wrist. "Don't you worry about me. I can handle whatever comes my way. You just concentrate on your family and your church, and I'll take care of myself. Rather, the Lord will take care of me. And now—I believe you have a sermon to prepare, Pastor. You need some coffee?"

"Now that you mention it, I didn't have my usual morning cup. I'll take some, yes." She nodded and turned to leave. "And, Marlene..." She stopped in the doorway and looked at him. "Thank you—for everything."

She smiled, slipped out into the hallway, and closed the door behind her.

⌐⌐

"Mother, calm down."

"What do you mean, calm down? This is a travesty. If people find out my son-in-law has a Japanese son, I may have to withdraw my membership from the ladies' club."

Just as Nora had anticipated, her mother took the news of Henry's son as a personal insult.

"That's quite doubtful. You don't even have to tell anyone if you don't want to."

"Pfff, that won't be necessary, will it? Everyone will find out whether I tell them or not. News like that travels fast. Besides, there are a few ladies in the club who attend our church, Arletta being one of them. They'll know, and they'll surely want to tell others." Florence Harrison huffed a loud breath, took a handkerchief from her pocketbook, and dabbed at her brow. "Imagine a preacher of all people having an illegitimate child—and to think, he's kept it a secret all these years."

"No, he didn't keep it a secret. He just found out about the boy last week."

Her mother straightened her spine against her chair and wrung her hands in her lap. "Well, did he forget about the affair he'd had too? Did you know about that, Nora? And how do you know he hasn't had other women on the side? If he could keep that secret, what would keep him from—oh, good grief, maybe there are other children out there!"

"Oh, Mother, stop! Please." Nora bit down hard on her lip and stared down at the coffee cup she held tightly between her hands, trying to maintain her composure. Why couldn't her mother just sit and listen? Why did she have to interject scenarios that only made Nora more confused and distressed? Where was the parental support and compassion? It saddened her to think she'd mostly grown up without it, save for her beloved father, who in her eyes could do no wrong. God rest his soul.

Florence stood up from the chair and started pacing. "Wouldn't you think Henry's conscience would have dictated that he told you about the affair? Had you known, at least you could have been partially prepared for this—this boy. Good grief, I hope he's not going to live with you. That would be a disgrace. Talk about creating a scandal! It's bad enough that Henry will probably visit him from time to time. Oh, do you think he'll do that? Visit him, I mean?"

"I don't know." Her mind started spinning.

"Well, I should hope he'll go through with the adoption you mentioned and then never have to deal with the situation again. That of course would be the best all-around solution."

"For you and me perhaps—and the church, I suppose."

"What do you mean, you *suppose?* Of course, it's the best solution. It's the only solution in my mind."

"Mother, I merely told you so you could be informed ahead of everyone else. As I mentioned earlier, Henry's going to tell the congregation on Sunday. The final decision as to what to do about this young man will rest with Henry and me. You'll just have to accept that."

"Well!" Florence huffed and gave Nora a stern look, one eyebrow arched. "He's a Japanese boy, and that will not sit well with folks. Look what the Japs did to us at Pearl Harbor."

"That's in the past. We defeated Japan in World War II. Besides, you can hardly blame an eight-year-old boy for what happened at Pearl Harbor."

"You're defending him? Listen here, Nora, if you take that boy into your home, you may as well know right now, I'll never accept him as my grandson. I'm just making myself good and clear."

Nora felt the color leave her face. "So, are you saying you would purposely exclude him in the event I ask you to watch the children for a few hours—*if* he were to live with us, that is?"

Florence lifted her pointy chin and straightened her shoulders. "That is precisely what I'm saying. I can't believe you would even question me on that, Nora."

For some odd reason, Nora's hackles went up, not because she wished to defend Henry and his horrid mistake, but because they were talking about a little boy who was, after all, guiltless of any wrongdoing. And Nora's mother already hated him. Something about that realization tore a hole in Nora's heart. Was she also guilty of hating the child? She'd barely caught a glimpse of his photo, but from what little she saw, he bore a resemblance to Henry. If she were to take the boy into her home—and it was a stretch to even consider it—would she resent him for the rest of her days? *Oh, Lord, I can't let that happen.*

Her mother's blather continued. Nora took a sip of cold coffee and tuned her out.

"Well?"

"I'm sorry. What did you say?"

"I said, can you imagine what your father would say? Why, he would have detested the whole situation."

That caused a direct stab to Nora's heart, for her father had been nothing but kind to his very core. He would have accepted the child and loved him as if he were his own blood. But of course, she didn't share that thought with her mother. It would have sent her into an even wilder frenzy. Instead, she stood and walked to the kitchen, seething inside. "I'm just going to wash this cup, Mother. Is there anything I can get you? Would you like a muffin?"

"No, no, I must be going. I have errands to run. I only stopped on my way to the market because you asked me to come over. I must say, I'm disappointed you didn't have another reason for inviting me."

She didn't turn around at her mother's words, just let them linger there between them. There was no changing Florence Harrison's mind once she made it up. No, she was bound and determined to hate Emiko. A horrid thought that she might be turning into her mother gave her great pause. *Oh, Lord, give me a loving spirit. I cannot come to terms with this whole idea yet, but may I not grow bitter and hateful.*

THIRTEEN

O my God I am ashamed and blush to lift up my face to thee,
my God for our iniquities are increased over our head,
and our trespass is grown up to the heavens.
—Ezra 9:6

H enry slipped through the door at noon on the dot—ironically, just as Nora was preparing to walk out. They nearly ran smack into each other. "Oh!" they said in unison.

"I was just coming over to see you," she said.

"You were? I was coming home to grab a bite of lunch. I was hoping we might have a chance to talk?"

"I suppose it's time."

His heart jolted at the thought of them having a civil conversation. At least he hoped it might be so.

"I didn't fix you anything for lunch," she said. "I—I wasn't sure what your plans were."

"No worries. I see that your mother just left."

"You saw her car, did you?"

"I did. I'm afraid to ask what you talked about."

She gave only a hint of a smile, which he considered progress. "I'm sure you know."

He nodded. "How did she take the news?"

"Terribly. She ranted and raved and said some things that I won't bother repeating."

"I see."

They stood there awkwardly, neither moving. "Well," he said. "Did you happen to notice the auto shop came to tow away the Packard?"

"Yes, I saw them out the side window."

"When I explained the problem, they seemed to think it might need a new carburetor. At any rate, they'll give her a tune-up and then call to let me know what the issue was. Once they finish it, someone from the shop will deliver it to our driveway, maybe as early as tomorrow, but more likely by Thursday."

"It's nice that they provide that extra delivery service. I hope it won't be too expensive."

"Like I said, I've put the money aside. No need to worry. And—I've been thinking, Nora, if you do want to get a job, I wouldn't stop you. I am serious when I say we will manage fine on my salary, but if getting a job will help fulfill you…"

"Are you trying to appease me?"

"No. No! What I'm trying to do is see things from your point of view. I realize over the years, I've probably made too many family decisions without discussing them with you. If you want a job—then you have my blessing."

"That's nice, but—I suppose my getting a job is a bit up in the air now—considering our uncertain future."

He clenched his jaw and rubbed his hands together, unsure quite how to proceed. "I think I'll make a bologna sandwich."

"I'll make it for you." She always made his lunch.

"You don't need to."

"No—I will make one for myself as well. You can pour each of us a glass of milk."

"I'll do that."

They maneuvered around each other gingerly, to avoid touching. How awkward. Neither one was used to behaving this way, but then, he'd never dropped a bomb of such magnitude either. He deduced she deserved to act in any way she chose, especially after his talk with Marlene.

She wordlessly got out the bread and fixings for their sandwiches, while he poured them each a glass of milk and carried the glasses to the kitchen nook. He took an apple from the bowl in the center of the table. "Want to split an apple if I slice and peel?"

"Sure."

He passed her again on his way to the utensil drawer, where he with-drew a paring knife, then returned to the table. While he was peeling and slicing, she walked to the table and set down two small plates. He divvied up the apple slices and laid them on the plates next to the sand-wiches, then scooped up the peelings and tossed them in the kitchen wastebasket. Returning, they gave each other tiny glances before sit-ting down, two adults who'd lived together for years but had suddenly forgotten how to communicate. He was afraid she would misconstrue whatever he said, and for all he knew, she feared the same. Where to begin—that was the prominent question.

"I'll ask a quick blessing," he stated. She nodded and bowed her head so he quickly prayed. "Thank You, Lord, for this simple lunch. Bless it to the nourishment of our bodies. And Lord, be present in our discussion—whatever is said—that we may find wisdom beyond our abilities and discernment for how to move forward in a way that would be pleasing to You. In Your name I pray. Amen."

The prayer finished, they each took up their sandwiches and began to eat. *Give me the words, Lord.*

He chewed and swallowed, then ate an apple slice, and she did the same. After a couple of bites, he laid down his sandwich and took a sip of milk. He cleared his throat.

"I've been thinking that perhaps it's best I call Mrs. Felton and tell her not to come."

Her head jerked upward, and her eyes went round as the plates under their noses. "What? Why?"

"I've prayed about it, and it just seems to make the most sense for all of us. My wanting to meet him is purely selfish. I wasn't thinking about the child's best interest, just my own. I shouldn't disrupt his life any further. I mean, he lost his mother, so I imagine my suddenly coming into the picture would only create more confusion for him. I'm sure Mrs. Felton has already spoken to him about the probability of his being adopted by an American couple who are desperate for a child. He's probably already started processing that idea as well as can be expected." He did his darnedest not to let his emotions show. He could almost imagine the sense of relief rushing through Nora's veins, so it was important that he stay strong.

Rather than react with a show of great relief, she merely stared across the table at him, eyes having gone back to their normal size as she seemed to digest his words. She gave a tiny nod, but that was it in terms of reaction.

"I want to add something, Nora. I know this whole matter has caused you great stress and terrible sorrow. I can't even tell you how regretful I am for having brought this upon you and the kids. I'm especially sorry for the strain it's put on our marriage. I know it will take a long time to work through it, and I don't blame you for hating me, but I'm confident we will work this out because I know *us*. We are not about to throw away fifteen years of marriage, at least I'm not. I think, with time and patience, we'll come through this even stronger." He studied her face as he talked, but for a change, he couldn't quite discern her expression. It was sober, but unreadable. "I—still believe I should confess my wrongdoing to the congregation. If I am ever going to move forward in my ministry, then I need to be honest. I could use the philosophy that what they don't know can't hurt them, but I did that with you, and look where it got us. I'm not saying there won't be repercussions. I talked to Marlene this morning, and while she was understanding and compassionate about our situation, she was also honest. She believes this knowledge could do great harm to our church body, and I must agree with her. I just want to prepare you for—"

Nora put up her hand to halt him. "May I speak?"

He caught a nervous breath and looked at the ceiling. "Please."

"All right, first, I don't hate you, Henry. I'm deeply hurt, yes, and I hate what you did, but that is the extent of my hate. Second, I don't quite know what to make of your decision. I don't know if you are making it solely based on prayer, or if it comes from a sense of obligation to me because you want to keep the peace. I know I've been nothing but negative about the idea of welcoming this boy into our family, and for that, I do have some regrets. I mean, I'm not entirely coldhearted." She winced when she looked at him, as if it pained her to speak the words. "Because of something that Mother said today, I realize that I am partially responsible for this boy's future well-being. I don't want to be, but because you are my husband and Emiko is your son, I have to go outside of my own selfish desires."

He could hardly believe it. "Your mother actually said those words?"

She gave a snide little chuckle. "Hardly. She actually said just the opposite."

"Well, then I don't understand what you're saying."

Rather than continue just then, she picked up an apple slice and ate it then took another bite of her sandwich, chasing it down with a couple gulps of milk. He waited with all the patience he could muster. She took a deep breath and looked him straight on. "Mother said if we were to ever bring this boy into our home, she would never accept him as her grandchild. In fact, she said she would exclude him entirely if we ever asked her to watch the children. When she made that statement, it did something to me, Henry." She put a hand to her heart. "It made me question whether I am a replica of my mother. Oh, Henry, I don't want to be like her. She can be so harsh."

He heard the anguish in her voice and dared to reach across the table and lay a hand over hers. She allowed it for a few seconds before withdrawing and putting her hands in her lap. "You're not your mother, Nora. You have your father's heart."

"And that's another thing. She dared say Daddy would have detested everything about this situation. She's wrong, of course. Daddy was a forgiving, loving, godly man. He would have…" She stopped, took up her napkin, and dabbed at her eyes. "Sorry, just talking about Daddy gets me emotional."

He didn't dare reach out to her, much as he wanted to. "I understand that."

She regained her composure. "Anyway, after she left, I was bound and determined to tell you the very last thing we could do is bring this boy into our home because I am certain Mother would make life miserable for him, but—but—"

He held his breath when she stopped talking.

"But I'm thinking that you must at least meet him tomorrow. I think your telling Mrs. Felton not to come would be wrong. I know you said you prayed about the matter, but I do think your decision came from a place of wanting to please me. I don't want this to be about me, Henry. That would not be what Jesus would want either. I realized when Mother was talking about how much she already dislikes this child—that, well, here is this little boy who has no idea what life holds for him. And he's innocent, Henry." Now she allowed the tears to drip unchecked down her cheeks, and she gave him a pleading look. "He's innocent." Her voice trembled as she uttered the words. "As much as I am still so mad at you, Henry, that little boy had nothing to do with *your* mistake."

His emotions went raw as the moisture started collecting in his own eyes. He gave them a swipe with the back of his hand. "You're right about that," he said in a jagged voice. "I'm filled with so many regrets."

"I know you are." She bit down on her lower lip and paused before continuing. "My mother said that folks will not take kindly to Emiko's Japanese heritage, that people still hold a grudge against the Japs for what they did at Pearl Harbor. She thinks taking the boy into our home would be disgraceful, even scandalous. I don't know. Maybe in some ways she's right, but I cannot allow her rude, callous, and opinionated remarks to continue to influence my decisions. She's been doing that my whole life."

That much was true, but Henry had learned many years ago not to echo Nora's sentiments about Florence lest she grow defensive. Oddly, she could voice her views about her mother all she wanted, but if Henry were to complain about something Florence said or did, she quickly took offense. Some days, it was just plain confusing, not to mention a little comical, so he'd learned in matters concerning Nora's mother to remain quiet and merely nod his head in agreement.

"So, what exactly are you saying?" he asked, too afraid to think she might be hinting at inviting Emiko to live with them.

She shrunk back a bit. "I'm not exactly sure myself, Henry."

A thought came to him, whether directly from the Lord or from the commonsense head the Lord had given him. "How about we do this? How about I tell Mrs. Felton to bring Emiko to Muskegon tomorrow? We could meet at my parents' house if that would make you feel better. I'll tell her not to tell Emiko I'm his father. I can simply meet him, and see how things go. Then she can take him back home with her tomorrow. After that, you and I can do some praying, and we can see how God leads."

She gave a slight nod. "We don't even have room for a third child—unless we put bunkbeds in Paul's room."

He couldn't even believe her suggestion. It was the very thing he'd been thinking but hadn't expressed. "Do you think Paul would object? I mean, is his room even big enough?"

"We could rearrange the furniture a bit. Paul has outgrown some clothes that I can donate to a charity. I'm sure we could manage to free up a couple of drawers for the child. And while Paul's closet is small, with a bit of organization, we could make it work. Paul would have to learn to share, and there is the potential for problems. We can't guarantee they'll even get along."

Henry's heart thumped hard against his chest wall, and suddenly, his mind started spinning with all manner of crazy notions. "If we thought Paul and Paige argued a lot, what will happen when we throw a third child into the mix?"

"Exactly. And where is the money going to come from for this extra child? We always said your preacher salary is best suited for a small family—two children was our limit—yet I can't fathom taking on a job either. The timing just isn't right."

"God has always provided our every need, Nora."

"But adding another person to the household is no small thing."

"Could God be telling us to trust Him? Could He be saying He knew all along that we'd be facing this difficult situation?"

"You think God endorses that you had an affair?"

That remark caught his attention—and his ire. "Nora, you know that is not what I meant. This morning, Marlene reminded me of Romans eight, twenty-eight, which clearly promises that God can take our hopeless mistakes and turn them around for good in our lives if we love and serve Him. Do you believe that?"

She gave a quiet nod. "I do. Marlene is a wise person."

They both resumed eating their lunches, neither speaking for the next five minutes, chewing on their food and their thoughts. After a time, Nora collected the dishes and utensils except for his glass and walked to the sink. While rinsing the dishes, she said. "I think you should give Mrs. Felton directions to *our* house, not your parents'."

"Seriously?" He picked up his glass and quickly gulped the rest of it, then slid off the bench and walked up next to her, placing the glass in the sink. She kept her eyes on her task of rinsing.

"It only makes sense that I meet him too," she said.

Were his ears deceiving him? With no forethought, he put an arm around her shoulder, but she quickly flinched. "Don't." He dropped it back to his side. "I'm not doing this for you, Henry. I'm doing it for Emiko. He deserves a chance."

She did not say *he* deserved a chance, just that his son did. And by gum, he would have to be happy with that—at least for now.

⌒

Florence Harrison walked into her three-bedroom home on Sheridan Drive in North Muskegon, shrugged out of her lightweight coat, and hung it in her hallway closet. Sighing to herself, she walked to the kitchen, filled the teapot with water from the sink, and put it on the stove, turning the burner to its highest setting. She stood there staring at it for a moment before snatching a teabag from the metal box on the counter and dropping it inside a teacup she selected from the shelf over the stove.

What a terrible mess her son-in-law had created for his family, not to mention his church. Disgraceful, that's what it was—and disgusting. So hideous, in fact, that it stirred the worst memories in her mind and made her chest constrict. She clutched her pounding heart and waited for a pinch of pain…but none came. Oh, how she detested such mortal sins. They always put her in such a dark and angry mood.

Ever since Nora had broken the news to her about Henry having this other son, she'd been recalling those days when he'd first come back from Japan. She'd thought back then that he hadn't been himself. Perhaps morose and gloomy best described him. Nora and the others called it war fatigue, or some such term. Florence now knew it was guilt and maybe even a bit of lovesickness for the woman he'd left behind. When he should have been elated at reuniting with his wife and meeting his daughter for the first time, he'd seemed distracted and inattentive. Now she knew why. After all these years, she finally understood it. He had left behind a lover—a *pregnant* one at that. While Nora labored over birthing their daughter, he'd been in Japan making a son with another woman. She made a tsking sound with the roof of her mouth and tongue. How dare he hurt her daughter like this? She knew Nora, perhaps better than she knew herself. Oh, Nora liked to give the appearance that everything was well and good, but Florence Harrison wasn't easily fooled. She knew better than anyone how putting on appearances looked!

The teakettle whistled, indicating the water was ready. She filled the cup to the brim and breathed in the piping hot steam, boiling internally like the teakettle itself. And this story about him not knowing he had a son until now? Pfff. Hogwash. He knew alright. He just hadn't been forced to spill the truth till now.

"I never have liked him much," she muttered to herself. "And now I know why. He's a cheat. And he has no business standing behind a pulpit every week. No business." She seethed a bit while she leaned against the kitchen counter and sipped on her tea. "Just wait till I tell Arletta. She will be irate, and she'll know what to do. She knows just which elders to speak with to see to it that this matter is handled in an appropriate fashion. If that means my son-in-law loses his pastoral position, then so be it. Hmph. I should've suggested Nora and the children come and stay with me. She has every right to leave him after what he did."

She let that thought ruminate until she remembered the few sacks of groceries still sitting in the car. She put down her cup and left the kitchen, her mind still awash with bitter thoughts.

FOURTEEN

But we do know that all things work together for good to those who love
God, to those who are called according to purpose.
—Romans 8:28

Wednesday arrived before Nora was ready for it, but that's usually the case when it comes to situations one would just as soon avoid. Still, she had come to grips with what she was facing, and she was as prepared as anyone could be to meet a boy who wasn't her own but belonged to her husband. To say her heart had begun to mend would be untruthful, but she had at least accepted the boy's innocence in all of it.

Mrs. Felton and the lad arrived around one in the afternoon. When Henry opened the door to invite them in, Nora pasted a smile on her face despite her heart's resistance. At first glance, there was no denying Henry had fathered the boy, and that fact alone caused a tiny ball of resentment to form in her chest. From his straight nose and smooth-lined jaw to that little indentation in his left cheek, he had all the marks of being a Griffin. His eyes, though a rich brown like Henry's, were distinctly Asian. His hair too was darker than Henry's, bordering on black, and hanging straight in a cute little bowl cut. To be sure, he was a handsome young man, rather tall for an eight-year-old, and with a lean frame. He bore no likeness to Paul and Paige, who seemed to favor her more in facial features, skin tone, and hair color. Everyone had always commented on how much Paige especially resembled her, and she'd sometimes bemoaned the fact that folks never remarked on how much they looked like Henry. Well, that would not be the case with Emiko, even though one could notice his Japanese heritage. She could not help but immediately imagine their home with Emiko squeezed into it. Oh, there would be trials. Of that, she was certain. But she was also quite certain a bond would form between the three children, if for no other reason than the blood relation.

When Henry introduced Mrs. Felton to Nora, she forced herself to extend her hand, and to her surprise, she found Mrs. Felton's handshake warm and her demeanor friendly. She didn't know why she'd prepared herself for someone stern and austere. Perhaps she'd been expecting a replica of her mother.

Mrs. Felton's genuine smile reached all the way to her hazel eyes. "So lovely to meet you, Mrs. Griffin. I was quite delighted to learn that Henry is a minister. I'm sure he told you about our chance meeting while waiting in a long line to board a ship to America back in forty-six."

"Yes, he did mention that."

The woman still held her hand in a soft squeeze, her smile lingering, her kind eyes resting intently on Nora's face. Might she be pondering whether Emiko would ever find a place in Nora's heart? Nora glanced down at the boy, and Mrs. Felton let go of Nora's hand. "Oh! Let me introduce you to my young friend. This is Emiko. Emiko, I want you to meet Reverend Henry Griffin and his wife, Mrs. Nora Griffin. I met Mr. Griffin when he was a soldier many years ago—before you were born."

The young boy's eyes brightened, and he extended a hand to Nora first. "How do you do, ma'am?"

A bit flustered, Nora took his hand and noted his firm little grip. My, he had good manners. She wondered if he'd learned them from his mother, and for an instant, a pang pinched her heart for the boy's terrible loss. "It is very nice to meet you."

The boy smiled, dropped her hand, and then turned to Henry and did the same, extended his hand. "Hello, sir," he said.

She couldn't help but notice the expression of wonder on Henry's face as he studied the boy from head to toe. Goodness, what must be going through his head? Surely, his heart was full. Did he see glimmers of the boy's mother when looking in his eyes? The very notion chewed a hole in her side. Oh, but she didn't want him seeing that woman every time he addressed the boy. A painful lump made its way to her throat.

Henry smiled down at Emiko and cupped his other hand on top of their handshake. "It is indeed an honor to meet you, young man. I'm— very sorry for the loss of your mother."

The boy's smile vanished. "Thank you." His eyes trailed to the older woman. "At least I have Helen. For now, anyway. She says I'm getting adopted."

"I see." Henry's eyes flitted to Nora's for the briefest moment, then back to the boy and Mrs. Felton. "Well, what say we all sit down for a visit, shall we?"

"Yes, please do," Nora put in. "I'll get some lemonade and a plate of cookies for us." She hurried off to the kitchen while the three of them found places to sit in the living room and continued their conversation.

Once in the kitchen, Nora gripped the handle of the refrigerator door and pressed her forehead against it, catching a much-needed calming breath before pulling it open. Once her wits were gathered, she took out the pitcher of lemonade and proceeded to fill four of her best glasses. She set them on a wooden tray, along with a plate of sugar cookies she had just baked that morning. Snagging one more breath, she lifted the tray by the two end handles and walked through the dining room and into the living room.

"What do you think of America?" Henry was asking.

Sitting on the sofa beside Mrs. Felton, Emiko gave a little shrug. "It's different. There's way more cars here. In my country, most people ride their bikes everywhere."

He speaks such clear English, Nora thought. Granted, he had a definite accent, but no one would have a hard time understanding him.

"Do they have bikes in America?" Emiko asked.

"Of course," Henry told the boy. "Both our kids have their own bicycles. They didn't get them new, mind you, but they serve them well. Paul just learned to ride this past spring."

"What are your children's names?" Mrs. Felton asked.

Nora set the tray down on the coffee table. "Paige and Paul," she answered. She handed out the glasses of lemonade and then sat on the sofa on the other side of Mrs. Felton. "Paige is ten and Paul is seven. Please, help yourself to some cookies."

She couldn't help but picture Paul scooting up and snatching a cookie, maybe two, off the plate before being invited to do so. Emiko, on the other hand, sat politely with his hands in his lap waiting for Mrs. Felton to give the word. When she nodded, he slid forward and took one while also taking care not to spill his drink. His mother had done a fine job.

"What grade are you in, Emiko?" Nora asked.

"Grade three, ma'am." He took a single bite of cookie and a tiny sip of lemonade then set the glass down on the pine table.

"He reads at a much higher level though," Mrs. Felton said. "Of course, he is bilingual, which is a great advantage. His mother saw to it."

"That's wonderful, a very important skill," Nora said.

"I don't know any Japanese kids in America though, so Mrs. Felton said I might forget how to speak it after a while."

"That would be a shame," she said.

He shrugged. "I guess I could re-learn it when I get older, but I might not ever go back to Japan, so it might not matter."

"What sort of games do you like to play?" Henry asked, changing the subject.

Another shrug. "Mostly, I enjoy reading." He turned his head and looked beyond Mrs. Felton at Nora's grand piano. "I used to take piano lessons in Japan. Mrs. Kiyama was my teacher."

"Really?" Nora asked. "My own children take lessons from me. Do you have any pieces memorized?"

"My teacher taught me to read the notes, but then to also memorize what I'd learned. My mama loved to hear me play."

"Would you like to play something for us?" Nora asked, hopeful.

Another shrug.

Mrs. Felton caught Emiko's eye. "Why don't you play for us, Emiko? Your mother would be so proud of you if you did."

He hesitated for a few seconds, then slid off the couch and walked to the piano. While he situated himself on the bench, Mrs. Felton said, "He also takes cello lessons. We had to ship his instrument, but it hasn't arrived yet. We were told it could take a month or more to get here."

"Really?" Henry asked. "Isn't he rather young to—?" But he stopped short because the boy had started playing "Minuet in G major" by Bach, clearly an intermediate piece that the average eight-year-old probably wouldn't be playing yet. Of course, Nora had played the piece at a young age too, but few children could play with the precision that Emiko now displayed. Even ten-year-old Paige wasn't playing the piece yet because, sadly, she didn't take piano as seriously as Nora had as a girl.

Henry had joked that the kids had probably inherited his musical gene, which was, in a word, nonexistent, but Nora didn't quite buy that. After all, both Paige and Paul could sing fairly well.

When Emiko finished, the three adults clapped. He slid off the piano bench and gave a little bow, as if he'd just performed for a large audience, then walked back to his place on the sofa.

They continued their conversation, the adults talking some and Emiko politely listening, speaking only when asked a question. He was so polite and reserved that Nora began to wonder if he even had the potential to be a rascal. Had his entire life thus far been spent around adults? Surely, he'd had school friends. Or had he been the type who interacted with his peers during brief recess periods, but then went straight home to his piano and cello? So many questions stirred in her head.

After an hour or so, Henry asked Emiko if he would like to go outside and explore their backyard. The boy shrugged his shoulders in what seemed to be his usual response, which made it difficult to know what he really wanted. "If you want me to," he said.

Henry looked at Mrs. Felton then back to the boy. "Or you're welcome to go to Paul's bedroom and look over his books and toys if you like."

He tipped his head in thought, as if the decision were a fierce one. "I guess I'll go outside."

"Fabulous. There's a swing set out there."

He picked up his shoulders and then dropped them again. "Okay."

Henry stood with the boy. "Come, I'll show you. Later, if you like, you can come back in and check out Paul's room."

"Okay."

Nora knew Henry's thinking. He wanted to speak with Mrs. Felton, perhaps ask questions, without the boy listening in. It made sense. She too had questions.

⌒

Henry led his son out through the back door, pointing out the play equipment, the sandbox, which even Paul had pretty much outgrown, and the trucks and various other toys lying on the ground by the swings. The week's laundry hung on the clothesline on the south side of the yard.

"Play with whatever you like, Emiko. If you get bored, just come back in the house and I'll show you to Paul's room. Nora and I would like to visit a little bit with Mrs. Felton, and I just sort of figured you wouldn't be very interested in our conversation."

"I don't mind listening to adults."

Henry smiled and put his hand on the boy's shoulder. It was narrow and rather bony. He'd been tall and lanky himself as a boy, not really filling out until he engaged in sports in his early teen years. "Oh! I nearly forgot. We do have a basketball hoop in the driveway. It's nothing fancy, just a metal circle really. But it's good for practicing."

Emiko shook his head. "I never shot a basketball before."

"Really?" Henry wanted to tell him that would change eventually but he also didn't want to presume anything yet. He and Nora still had a lot to discuss, even though she had opened the door to the possibilities yesterday. He looked down at Emiko, his hand still on his shoulder. "Well, do you like to swing?"

"We had three swings at my school, but we had lots of kids so I hardly ever got a turn."

"I see, well, you have the whole backyard to yourself now."

"Yes, sir."

"Okay, I'll leave you then."

"All right."

He was a boy of few words, this son of his.

The women were engaged in conversation when he reentered the room, but as far as he could tell, they were not discussing Emiko. He supposed Nora wanted to reserve that for his return. Spying his glass of lemonade, he realized he was suddenly thirsty. He took up his glass and drank a few good swallows.

"Emiko seems like a very bright boy, if not a little shy," Henry said after setting down his glass.

"He's not shy once you get to know him," Mrs. Felton said. "And, yes, he's very intelligent, perhaps because much of his life has been spent with adults. He excels in everything he tries."

"I'm not surprised to hear that," Nora said. "I play the piano myself, so I recognize talent. He's quite exceptional."

"I would hope he would be challenged to continue—by whomever adopts him. He's quite accomplished with the cello as well, for one so young. It would be nice if he could continue that."

Henry didn't recall Rina ever saying anything about having musical talent, but with her rather underprivileged upbringing, perhaps she'd never had the opportunity to pursue it. Thinking back, he remembered very little about her, only that she'd been pretty. Truly, he'd never had a substantial conversation with her. He would like to ask Mrs. Felton about her, but he worried how Nora would feel about that. The last thing he wanted was for her to think he'd clung to any long-lost thoughts about Rina.

"How did you or his mother discover his talents?" Nora asked.

"Well, she had quite a lovely singing voice. She started singing in our church services at the mission. She came to us when she was pregnant. I don't know how much Henry has told you."

"He—hasn't told me much, but only because I—well, I haven't been willing to talk."

"I understand. It must have come as quite a shock to you, all of this. I'm sorry for the trouble I've caused."

"No, no, it wasn't your fault," Nora said. Nora turned to Henry, her face gone pale.

He quickly jumped in. "When your letter came, I was so thrown by the news that I'm afraid I kept it from Nora until just a couple of days ago. I just didn't know how to tell her. It's been very difficult for all of us, our children included."

"I can only imagine," Mrs. Felton said, her hands folded in her lap, her forehead crimped. "It wasn't an easy letter for me to write either. Rina had become a very good friend, and it was heartbreaking for me and the others at the mission when she got the cancer diagnosis. There was nothing the doctors could do, as it was quite advanced. I will say, though, that she had come to love Jesus, and she wanted only the best for

Emiko. It was her desire that I keep him, and so she went through the legal process so that I could assume guardianship of him. But toward the end of her life, she gave me permission to adopt him out—or to inform his father. She gave me your father's address, which she had kept hidden in a safe place all these years."

Henry pursed his lips and shot Nora a quick glance before turning his eyes back on Mrs. Felton. "Why didn't she ever tell me about Emiko?"

"I believe she wanted to, but she told me you had given her strict orders not to contact you. Truly, though, I believe what she most feared was that if you found out about him, you would come to Japan and take him back to America with you, making it impossible for her to ever see him again. That thought terrified her."

"Hm. I did sort of wonder if that might have been her reasoning." Again, he glanced at Nora, but she sat rather stiffly.

A bit of silence hung between the three of them. "I need to get back to the college in Holland, as my son will be wanting to make the trip back to Naperville. May I ask you how I should proceed? You mentioned that you needed some time to consider all the ramifications."

"And you mentioned that you have an American couple interested in adopting?" Henry asked. He wanted to know exactly what Mrs. Felton had done to move forward on the chance that things did not work out for Nora and him to take Emiko into their home.

She lifted her glass and took a couple swallows of lemonade, then held the glass in her hands and brought it to her lap. "Yes, there are a couple of families, one who lives in California and another in Texas. Both have sponsored our mission financially for several years and know all about Rina and Emiko. I don't know how I will choose when the time comes, I mean if you…"

Nora gave a little cough. "Henry and I have discussed it, though not in detail. Truly, it was only yesterday that we started talking about keeping him. We—talked about getting bunkbeds for Paul's room and having the boys share the space."

Mrs. Felton's face brightened. "I'm glad to hear you're giving it some thought anyway. Emiko has been through so much. I worry about him. He is brave beyond his years, but he's slow to show his emotions. For one so young, he can be quite stoic. I've tried to get him to talk about his sadness over losing his mother, but he's got it in his head he must be strong."

That tugged greatly at Henry's heartstrings. Oh, how he wanted to make everything right for Emiko. At the same time, he wanted Nora to be just as anxious as he. Nora merely nodded at the older woman but didn't comment. Mind-reading abilities would come in handy right about now.

"We'll have an answer for you soon," Henry said. "I'm sure the quicker a decision is made, the better it will be for all concerned."

Mrs. Felton nodded. "Yes, I believe you are right, although I don't wish to rush you either. This is a very big decision."

"Oh! I almost forgot." Mrs. Felton said, reaching into her purse and withdrawing a couple pieces of paper. She handed them across the coffee table to Henry, and he started perusing them. "It's Emiko's birth registration form and passport information. What you're looking at is an English version, of course. I have all his original papers in Japanese, but shortly after his birth, Rina took everything to the Citizens' Affairs Department at Tokyo City Hall to have English copies made. I suppose she thought it a necessary thing to do since he had an American father. Naturally, I'll have to take everything back when we leave. Once he is legally adopted, the process of U.S. citizenship can proceed."

"Yes, that makes sense." Henry hungrily scanned the papers, looking for his name. When his eyes landed upon it, he had to fight back tears. There was no denying it. This made it official. The boy was his.

He lowered the papers and gazed up at Nora for all of three seconds.

"May I see the certificates?" she asked, her voice low and reserved.

"Of course!" He stood and handed them to her, then sat back down.

She began looking over everything just as he'd done, probably also looking for his name. However, she did a more thorough scan than he had done, seeming to read each line. Once done, she licked her lips and closed them tightly before giving several sober nods and handing the papers back to Mrs. Felton.

They all sat there for a few wordless moments. Nora spoke first. "Thank you for all you've done for Emiko—and his mother." Henry detected a catch in her voice. "We appreciate it more than you know. I hope you will be patient with us for the next few days."

The woman placed a hand over Nora's. "Of course, dear. I understand how difficult this must be for you. This is no small matter."

Just then, the back door squeaked open, and shortly thereafter, Emiko appeared in the arched entry to the living room. "Am I allowed to come in yet?"

Henry's heart wrenched at the sight of him, and he realized in an instant how much he loved this boy. "Yes, come in. We were just having an adult conversation. Did you enjoy yourself?"

"Yes, thank you."

Mrs. Felton stood. "Well, now that you've come in, we must be on our way, Emiko." Nora and Henry hurried to stand as well.

Henry longed to wrap his boy in a hug, but instead he extended his hand. "It was nice meeting you, Emiko. I hope we meet again."

"I hope we do too." He withdrew his hand and turned to Nora. "Nice meeting you too, ma'am." He tipped his head at her, and she smiled and did the same.

"It was quite lovely," Nora said. "I'm quite sure we'll see you again."

Henry's eyes went wide for the span of a heartbeat. Had he heard right?

At the door, they said their goodbyes, then Nora and Henry stood watching them climb into their car. He was quite impressed that Mrs. Felton had driven clear from Holland to Muskegon. He couldn't envision his mother doing the same. In fact, she almost always relied on his father to take her places.

After they drove away, Henry quietly closed the door, his mind a whirl of thoughts, but his tongue tied.

"He's a lovely boy, Henry."

"Yes. He is something."

"So talented."

"Very."

He studied her face, trying to determine what she might be thinking.

"For now, let's commit to praying about where God would have us go from here," she suggested.

"Yes, yes, that's a good idea."

She glanced at her watch. "The children will be home in an hour. I'm going to go take the clothes off the line."

"Do you want some help?"

She lifted her brows and gave an exaggerated blink. "When have you ever helped me with the laundry?"

He didn't have an answer. She gave a brief smile. "Go back to the church, Henry. You have a sermon to prepare, remember?" And just like that, she disappeared into the kitchen. When he heard the back door open and close, he went out the front door and made his way to his office.

FIFTEEN

Beloved, let us love one another; because love is of God, and every one that loves has been begotten of God, and knows God.
—1 John 4:7

Over the next few days, Henry and Nora said little regarding Mrs. Felton and Emiko's visit. Henry stayed overtime in his office preparing for his Sunday message, and Nora went about her normal household chores, praying as she worked, and continuing with her personal Bible study. She called one of her girlfriends, Veronica Hardy, and the two agreed to meet for lunch at the restaurant inside the Occidental Hotel. It would be quiet and private there, and she could pour out her heart and soul with no fear of judgment or a breach of confidentiality. She and Veronica had been friends since elementary school, but lost contact after Nora married Henry, and they moved away. A couple of years after they returned to Muskegon, Veronica, her husband Leon, and their children started attending Church of the Open Door, and that's when the longtime friends reconnected. She now considered Veronica her best friend, although there were other ladies in the church she considered friends too, including Sarah Samson and Rosemary Hewitt, with whom she had formed a vocal trio. In fact, they were scheduled to sing this Sunday, but because of the sermon Henry planned to preach this week, she rescheduled their choral number for a later date.

There had been no physical touch between her and Henry since last weekend, but only because she could not bring herself to allow it. They slept in the same bed, but she kept to her side and he kept to his, she generally going to bed ahead of him and he joining her a half hour later. The only talking they did concerned Emiko and how they would go about welcoming him into their home. Much to Henry's joy, she had come to terms with having him join their family, but she had not come to terms with Henry's betrayal. She wanted to...but every time she tried, a new surge of resentment roiled up. It would take time, she kept telling herself, but how long, she couldn't say.

They had yet to tell the children about Emiko living with them, but she supposed they would sit them down before Sunday's sermon. They certainly deserved to know before the congregation learned about it. She had already begun reorganizing Paul's bedroom while he was at school, sorting through his clothes and cleaning out his small closet. And Henry had told her he'd found a nice bunkbed, which included the mattresses, at a secondhand store. Ken Parker had a truck and had gladly volunteered to go pick up the bed at the store and then help Henry carry it into the house. Henry and Mrs. Felton had spoken on the phone and arranged for Henry to drive to Naperville on Wednesday to get Emiko. Both had decided it would be best if she were the one to break the news to Emiko about his father's identity so that when Henry arrived, he would be at least partially adjusted to the notion that he wasn't entirely an orphan. Nora couldn't imagine being eight years old, losing her mother, leaving her country, and then moving into a home with a family of strangers. Surely, Emiko's young heart was full of varied emotions, not to mention heartache. She only hoped she had it in her to give him the care and attention he would need.

Nora's mother had called her several times over the past few days, wanting to know the status of "this Japanese boy." Surely they had reached the conclusion that he must go to another deserving family. During one of Florence's rants, she had said, "How disgraceful that Henry wants to tell the congregation that he fathered a child out of wedlock—while married to *you*, of all things! Why, he and his entire family would be the talk of the town, and Open Door would lose members. Certainly, that's a big concern for Henry, isn't it? And if it's not, then what kind of preacher is he? Good heavens, he might even lose his pastorate."

Florence had even invited Nora and the kids to come live with her because after all, Henry had committed adultery while married to her, so she had a sound biblical reason for leaving him.

"Mother, I can't believe you would encourage divorce."

"I'm not encouraging it, dear. I'm presenting it as a viable option. The Bible talks about divorce as a sin, yes, but it also states that in cases of adultery, it is acceptable."

"That topic has not come up, and I don't expect it to, but thank you for the offer anyway." Nora had had to bite her tongue to keep from snapping a few harsh words at her mother.

During Florence's last call, Nora finally dropped the bomb. "I'm afraid you're not going to like this, Mom, but Henry and I have talked, and we've decided it's best to invite Emiko to live with us. We will face whatever consequences come our way as a result."

"What? After everything I've told you? But this is preposterous." Nora had had to hold the receiver at arm's length due to Florence Harrison's overloud reaction. She had heard a click—meaning someone had eavesdropped on the party line—but at this point, she no longer cared. It would become public knowledge in two short days anyway.

"Perhaps, Mother, but the decision's been made. Henry plans to tell the congregation this Sunday."

"Oh, for heaven's sake! That's one service I will not be attending."

"You do whatever you have to do."

"I won't be able to face my club ladies at our next monthly meeting."

"I don't know what business it will be of theirs."

Her mother prattled on until Nora begged off with the excuse that she had several things to do.

Nora stood in front of the bathroom mirror now, staring at her reflection. She swore two new wrinkles had etched themselves into her forehead over the past week from all the frowning, crying, and moping she'd done. She gave a heavy sigh and applied some light pink lipstick then picked up a hairbrush and ran it through her wavy blond hair a few times. As for applying any other makeup, she chose not to bother, knowing she'd surely shed more tears while sitting at the table with Veronica and sharing her woeful tale. How would her best friend react to the news that the pastor, a man she'd trusted for years now, was not the person she'd thought him to be? Would it make Leon and Veronica consider leaving the church? As much as she hated the thought, she knew she couldn't blame them. Others would probably consider it as well.

She drew in another breath and walked out to the hall closet to get a lightweight jacket since it was a chilly, cloudy day. She retrieved the old Packard's keys from the hallway table, thankful the repair shop had fixed it for a minimal cost, and stepped outside.

She found Veronica standing just inside the door of the Occidental Hotel in downtown Muskegon. They gave each other quick embraces, and then Veronica's dark blue eyes narrowed as she perused Nora's face. "You're not looking quite yourself, honey. Is something going on that I should know about?"

Nora sighed. "You know me so well, Vernie."

A dapper-looking host, dressed in a suit and tie, greeted them in the lobby. "Here for lunch in the dining room, ladies?"

"Yes, please."

He nodded. "Follow me, please." He picked up a couple of menus and ushered them to a table back in a quiet corner, a perfect location for spilling her doleful story.

After they each ordered a salad and had gotten the small talk out of the way, Veronica prodded Nora to tell her what was on her heart. Then the story and tears all spilled out. Veronica listened intently, minus any judgment in her eyes, and at one point reached a hand across the table and placed it on Nora's arm. "Cry on, dear. This is good for your soul." And so, she did, Veronica's understanding tone further coaxing out her deepest, darkest emotions.

"There are t-times that I hate him, Vernie."

"I can imagine you do. I am certain I'd feel the same way if Leon told me something similar."

"H-he has made a few advances toward me this week, but I—I can't. Just his touch makes me want to cringe. I k-keep envisioning him with that other woman."

"Yes, I'm sure you do."

"I-I don't know when, or even *if*, it will ever be the same between us. And I'm afraid that when the boy comes to live with us, I'll—I'll come to resent him, and I don't want that to happen. The child is completely blameless. I—I don't feel like much of a preacher's wife right now, full of love, forgiveness, and benevolence."

"Just because you're a preacher's wife doesn't make you immune to hurt and angry feelings, honey. You're simply human, experiencing the normal feelings any woman would have if faced with the same situation."

"But—as a Christian, I'm supposed to be sanctified, pure, set apart, and holy in my thoughts and heart."

"We are all called to seek out holiness, sweetie, but as I said, you're a human being—with emotions that sway like a tree in the wind. No matter how strong you think you are, without the strength that Christ gives, we are just a blink away from falling flat on our faces in our Christian walk. Besides, I don't believe sanctification is a one-time experience as so many think it is. It's a day-to-day commitment that's as necessary to our spiritual lives as eating is to our bodies. The beauty of Christ in us is that He sees our flaws and failures and yet loves us despite them. As we seek to know Him better, He daily renews our hearts and minds. He does not expect perfection in us; He seeks our surrendered hearts. That surrender is what gives Him leeway to work through us."

Nora nodded, released several jagged sighs, and then blew her nose and wiped her swollen eyes with the hankie she had tucked into her purse that morning, knowing full well she'd need it later. She gave her friend a weak smile. "*You* sound like a preacher's wife."

A waiter came up to their table just then and refilled their water glasses without a word. Surely, he'd seen her crying. Fortunately, the other diners sat at a distance and seemed quite immersed in their own conversations.

Veronica removed her hand from atop Nora's arm and took a sip of water. After setting the glass back down, she asked, "You say that Henry will be confessing his sin in his message on Sunday?"

Nora nodded. "Yes. I don't know how he'll go about it."

"Leon and I will be praying for him."

Nora looked her friend full on. "I have not brought myself to do that—yet—but I will. I'm sure he's in a lot of anguish."

"We'll be praying for both of you."

Silence hung between them. Nora took a few bites of the salad she'd barely touched. A quick glance across the table revealed who'd done all the talking. Not much salad remained on Veronica's plate. Nora took another bite, but sadly, she had little appetite. That's when she realized she'd eaten like a bird the whole week, making nightly meals for the family, but barely eating more than a few bites herself.

"Do you hate him, Veronica?"

"Hate Henry? Hardly. Yes, he sinned, and he's hurt you terribly. That part I despise. But I don't hate him. We've all sinned, Nora, and we've all fallen short of God's glory, but by God's grace, we are redeemed, purchased by Christ's blood sacrifice on the cross. I can't hate sinners if Jesus Himself doesn't."

More tears rolled down Nora's cheeks. "You're too good a friend for the likes of me."

This brought on a spurt of giggles from Veronica. "Do you know how many times I have thought the same about you? How can the preacher's wife consider silly, old, imperfect me her best friend? I don't deserve her."

"Oh, please," Nora scoffed. "Now, you're being a tad ridiculous."

Their conversation lightened, and Nora forced down a few more bites of salad before pushing the plate to the side. She drank a little more water. They talked about their children and how they were all doing in school. Veronica and Leon had two girls, ages eight and six, and a boy who was four. Whenever they joined Nora and Henry for summer barbeques, they joked about their stairstep children, all two years apart. Now Emiko would join the mix, the thought of which sobered Nora. Somehow, she would come to love him, she knew, but how and when remained the mystery.

"Listen, Nora." Veronica leaned forward. "Don't work too hard at this. Leave it to the Lord. Your job is simply to trust Him. If you do that, He'll do His work. I see the torment in your face. I can almost read your mind. You're trying to picture how all of this is going to pan out—how Emiko is going to fit into your family, how you're going to move forward with Henry, how you're going to put on a happy face for the congregation, how you're going to show love and compassion to Henry when he's hurt you so deeply and, finally—hmmm. How are you going to deal with your mother in the middle of everything else?"

A tired sigh rolled out of Nora. "Oh, Vernie, that is no joke! How do you know all this?"

Veronica sat back in her chair and crossed her arms over her ample chest. She was a larger woman than Nora, but pretty and very well put together, with light brown hair and dark blue eyes. She flashed Nora a lovely smile. "Humph. I've known you since first grade, remember? I've learned how you tick."

Nora clasped her hands into a loose fist and rested her chin atop them, giving a slow nod. "And I'm grateful for it. Thank you for today, my friend. You've helped put things into perspective for me. I needed this talk."

"Don't bottle things up, honey. You know you can call me anytime."

"I know. That's the beauty of friendship."

"You can say that again."

Florence picked up her phone and dialed her best friend Arletta Morehead's number. It was past time for cluing her in on what to expect at Church of the Open Door this Sunday. She wouldn't tell her everything. No, she would let her lovely son-in-law do that. But her friend did at least deserve a heads-up. Arletta picked up on the third ring. "I just wanted you to know I'm not coming to church on Sunday," Florence said after their initial greetings and a bit of small talk.

"No? Why not?" Arletta asked. "Feeling under the weather?"

"Ha! You might say so. No, it's a bit more serious than a little bug."

Her friend gave a gasp on the other end of the line. "Florence Harrison, do you have a deadly disease that you've been keeping from me? Are you dying?"

"No, nothing quite that catastrophic, though I'll let you be the judge of how cataclysmic the news is after you've heard it."

"Well, now you have me grasping for reasons for this call. What exactly are you trying to tell me?"

"You'll find out at church on Sunday. I am not attending church because I don't want to be present when our dear, beloved Reverend Henry makes the announcement."

"Whatever are you talking about, Flo? You must tell me now."

"I can't. I just wanted to warn you to come prepared for a big blow, something that could affect the future of our church."

"No! Really? Has someone been embezzling money from the offering plates? Are the police involved? This is terrible."

"No, no, it's not a crime. Well, it is a crime in a way, but not the sort for which the police will get involved. You'll find out soon enough, and when you do, so will everyone else in the congregation. Then the news will fly from church to church and town to town. It could be quite disastrous."

"You're making no sense whatsoever, Flo. Tell me what it is so I'll be prepared to handle it when I hear it on Sunday."

"No, I really can't tell you—although I really want to because I'm dying to get some things off my chest. Besides, I don't want anyone eavesdropping on the party line. We'll talk again on Sunday afternoon. I'll want to know how the congregation took the news."

"Oh, for pity's sake."

"That's all I can say for now, Letta, except—pray for me."

"Pray for you? Are you involved in some sort of scandal?"

"Not me personally, but perhaps in a roundabout way, I am. It's most disturbing."

A wave of silence fell between them while Arletta tried to guess the secret and Florence did her best not to spill any more than was appropriate. "I must go. I'll talk to you Sunday."

"You've got me hanging by a thread, Flo Harrison."

"We'll talk later."

Florence replaced the receiver and stared off across the living room, rays of late sunlight casting long shadows on the floor.

SIXTEEN

He that goeth about talebearing revealeth secrets; but he that is of a faith-
ful spirit concealeth the matter.
—Proverbs 11:13

Henry had spent so much time on his knees during the past several days, he was sure they'd started to form calluses. Marlene had typed up his sermon notes, then delivered them sober-faced to his desk at the end of the day. "This is a fine sermon, Henry. I can tell you've put a lot of careful thought into it. I've been praying for you all week and won't stop until you give the final amen on Sunday morning."

"Don't stop there," he'd told her. "It's folks' reactions afterwards that I'm most concerned about. How they receive the information I present to them will be the true test."

"Have a little faith in the congregation. I think you'll find they are a forgiving, loving bunch of folks. Like I said earlier, there will be a few naysayers, but the majority will embrace you. I'm feeling confident."

"They've never had their pastor confess to such a hideous sin though. And what of the fact that Emiko will be joining us for church next Sunday morning—and all the Sundays to come? My own mother-in-law has declared she won't claim him as one of her grandchildren, and she told Nora she won't attend church on Sunday due to the shame my sermon will bring upon our family."

Marlene scowled. "Do not gauge the rest of the people's reactions on Florence's behavior. You know how dramatic she is."

To that, he'd given a little snicker. "Oh, do I!"

She had stood in the entry to his office, biting her lower lip for all of three seconds. "How has Nora been handling everything?"

Nora. Throughout their fifteen years of marriage, she'd always been consistent and loyal, loving and supportive, ready to defend him at every turn. But...this time was different. He must have worn a pained expression, for she quickly took back her question, begging his forgiveness for even asking.

"No, no, it's fine, Marlene. I was just sitting here trying to figure out how to answer you because, to be truthful, I'm not sure what's going on in her head. Yes, she wants to bring Emiko into the family, not because she wants to satisfy me, but because she thinks it's only right that a boy who recently lost his mother should live with his natural father."

"Well, that's good then," Marlene said.

"Yes, but—she can't seem to find it in her heart to forgive me for my betrayal of trust. I don't blame her, mind you. These things take time. I just—I just wonder how much time, you know?"

Her eyes shone with sympathy and perhaps a little dampness around the edges. She had crossed her arms and leaned against the doorframe. "Hm. I think you hit upon the key word, Henry. Time. I've been praying for Nora as well. She is caught in the middle of this scenario, and so it will be a difficult adjustment, but be patient with her. Above all, be patient."

"Yes, you're right, I know. It's just—I miss her. We live under the same roof, but she has become almost like a stranger, speaking to me only when necessary. Good grief, she can't stand it if I even accidentally touch her."

"That can't last forever, Henry. Like I said, patience. I envision Emiko's entry to the family as being something extra positive. Everyone will have to learn to come together, and I just see the Lord working in marvelous ways for the good of your family. You just wait and see."

He appreciated her wisdom and concern. "Well, enough about me for a while. Tell me, did you print up the Sunday bulletin on your new Bruning Copyflex Copying Machine?"

A smile brightened her face as she straightened. "Oh! You bet I did! I'm in love with that machine."

"I know you are. It's a bit embarrassing to walk past your office on Tuesday mornings and see you draped across it, hugging it with all your might."

"Oh, you've never caught me doing that. Have you? I mean, I've tried to be discreet."

He couldn't help the laugh that exploded out of him, nor ignore how good it felt. One of their members, Howard VanHook, who owned an office supply store in downtown Muskegon, had donated the machine to the church. Marlene was so enamored with it, it was comical, and he got a charge out of teasing her.

They had chatted a few more minutes, and then she bade him goodbye for the day.

Now, as he sat here reflecting on his week and his conversation with Marlene, he realized how short was the time remaining before his Sunday sermon. His stomach lurched at the thought. He uttered another quick prayer, then giving his sermon notes one last look, he stacked the pages neatly, glanced at the clock on the wall, and stood. He took in a good-sized breath and walked out of his office, locking the church door behind him. Tonight, during supper, he would talk to the children about bringing Emiko into their home. "Lord, be present in the conversation. Bless it, I pray."

As was often the case when he walked into the house, he found Nora in the kitchen. She glanced up at him, but did not greet him, merely offered a weak smile. "How was your day?" he asked, wishing he could approach her and plant a kiss on her neck like old times.

"Just fine. I met Veronica at the Occidental Hotel. We had lunch."

"Really? That's nice. I imagine you talked to her about—everything that's happened."

"Naturally. She's my best friend."

"I know she is. I'm glad you had the chance to talk."

She was stirring something, so he stepped closer to have a look. "Hmm, beef stew. Looks and smells delicious. Are the kids in their rooms?"

"Yes, they were arguing about foolish things so I sent them there."

"I see." Tensions were high everywhere—had been for the past week. The children sensed it and found ways to act out. "I was thinking we'd tell them tonight—about Emiko coming to live with us."

She didn't look up. "Yes, that would be good."

"Do you want me to do the talking?"

"Whatever you wish."

"How about I start, and if the children have questions, I'll answer them to the best of my ability, but you feel free to jump in if you have a better answer?"

"I'm sure your answers will be sufficient. There's really nothing more I can add."

He stood there for a moment gazing at her stiff frame. If he thought she was going to give an inch, he was woefully mistaken. He sighed and left the kitchen, loosening his tie on the way down the hall to their bedroom. It was going to be another long night.

"Our brother is going to live with us?" Paige asked later over supper, nearly choking on her spoonful of stew. She set down her spoon, coughed into her napkin, and then took a quick drink. She let her gaze trail from Henry to Nora and back to Henry. "Where's he gonna stay?"

"He'll share Paul's room," Henry said.

"Huh?" Now Paul's eyes went wide. "I don't got room for him."

"I bought a set of bunkbeds. We're bringing them home on Monday."

"Bunkbeds? I always wanted bunkbeds, but only so I could have a friend stay overnight. I didn't think I'd be having somebody stay overnight with me every night. Why can't he sleep somewhere else?"

"Where would you suggest?" Henry asked, not up for a fight with his children.

"The couch," Paul said.

"You haven't even met him yet, and you're already relegating him to the couch?"

"What's real-ah-gatin' mean? Never mind. I never asked for a brother," Paul groused. "Why can't he stay in Paige's room?"

"Paige is a girl, and she needs her own room."

"Her room is bigger than mine."

"He's not staying with me," Paige put in.

"Don't worry, he's sharing with Paul," said Henry.

"What if we fight all the time?" Paige asked. "Don't Paul and me fight enough as it is?"

"I am not promising you that everything is going to be perfect between you," said Henry. "But I would appreciate it if you tried to give him a chance. Maybe you and Paul could try to get along a little better for the sake of setting a good example. Emiko's never had a brother or sister, so this will be a new experience for him."

Both kids grew quiet as they sullenly slurped their stew.

"You might be surprised at how fun it can be to have an extra sibling." He glanced at Nora who, so far, had been no help. A bit of ire flared up in him. Just how long would she punish him? It had only been a week, but it felt more like a year. He focused on the kids again. "Things will work out, you'll see."

"Did you say he's coming on Wednesday?" Paige asked.

"Yes, I've arranged to travel to Naperville, Illinois, where he's currently living with his guardian, Mrs. Felton. It's probably going to take me the better share of the day to get there, visit for a bit, and then drive back, and that's not counting our having to stop for gas and stop along the way to eat. I'll probably pack a few sandwiches and put them on ice as well as take a big jug of water."

"Can we go along?" Paul asked.

"No, you two have school."

"Is Mommy going with you?" Paul asked.

She raised her head at that. "It's best your daddy takes this trip alone." She dabbed her mouth with her napkin, taking great care to look only at the children.

Henry hadn't had a chance to discuss with Nora whether she'd like to accompany him, but there was his answer. He supposed there'd be time for her to get to know Emiko in the days to come, and perhaps she was right. It was best if he went alone.

They all took a few more bites of their supper. "I guess it's okay if I share my room with Emiko. I want the top bunk though."

"All right," Henry said.

"You'll take the bottom bunk," Nora quickly put in. "Emiko is older than you. He's less likely to fall out of bed."

"That's not fair," the boy whined. "It's my room. I should be able to decide which bed I want."

Nora and Henry made eye contact. "He is right about that," Henry said.

She squared her shoulders. "Maybe when he's older they can switch places. I'm not comfortable having a seven-year-old on the top bunk."

He could see she wasn't about to budge. He looked at his frowning son and shrugged. "Mom is probably right, sport."

"Can I get some bunkbeds for my room too?"

"We'll see," Henry said.

"Maybe sometime in the future," Nora tacked on.

"Well, that's better than absolutely not," she said. "Can we get a puppy?"

"That's a definite no," Nora answered.

Not wanting to close the door entirely on the subject, Henry directed his gaze at Nora. "Maybe once we all get settled in and Emiko feels like a member of the family, we can entertain the notion. The kids have been asking for a good year."

Nora started gathering up the dishes, then with her hands full, she stood. "I don't know. We'll see."

"Huh?" Paul asked.

Henry looked at the children and winked. "That's better than absolutely not."

Later that night while lying in bed, Henry seized the opportunity to speak into the stillness. He knew Nora wasn't sleeping, for while she hadn't spoken to him, she had turned over when he crawled under the covers.

"Can you tell me what's on your mind?"

"I'd rather not."

He rolled his eyes, wishing she'd get beyond this silent treatment. She had talked more to him when they were deciding whether or not Emiko should join their family. It was even she who had said he should direct Helen to drive to their address rather than his parents'. She had been just as anxious to meet Emiko as he had been. Why had she resumed the silent treatment? "Did Veronica give you any advice today?"

"No, she just listened."

"Is she madder than blazes at me?"

"I wouldn't say that."

"What did she say about the whole situation?"

"I told you, she mostly just listened."

She made no move to turn back around and face him so they could have an actual conversation. He began to wonder if the day would ever come. Just how long did she plan to hold his mistake over his head? Another week, a month? A year, for heaven's sake? Lord, have mercy! He didn't know how long he could handle her snubbing without exploding.

He wasn't accustomed to not being able to talk to her about everything. He decided to come out with it. "How long, Nora?"

"I don't know, Henry. Don't ask me."

"But I need to know. We can't go on like this. The kids know something is up between us. Shoot, when I tucked Paul into bed tonight, he asked me if you were mad at me. I told him he shouldn't worry over adult matters. I assured him everything would be fine, but—I'm beginning to wonder."

"I don't know what to tell you."

"Do you think you could turn over? I'd like you to face me."

As if he'd asked for a new Cadillac, she heaved a sigh and rolled her body over. It was dark, but her silhouette showed in the moonlight. He even got a little glimpse of her solemn expression. He longed to reach out and snag a few strands of her hair to massage between his fingertips, but he dared not.

"I wish I could make you understand how sorry I am about the affair, Nora. I—"

"Oh, so now it's an affair. You told me before it wasn't an affair, that you'd only been with her one time."

"That's true. It was just a slip of the tongue."

"You also said we never should have gotten married when we did. That we were too young."

"Well, we *were* young."

"Perhaps had we waited, we never would've married, and you would have then been free to marry—*her.*"

"What? I didn't want her. I wanted you."

"Pfff, yeah, you wanted me so badly that while I was back home dutifully taking care of our little girl, you were in bed with someone else. That's how much you wanted me."

"Nora…"

"It's always been my fault we married young. You know that, right? I accept the responsibility. I wanted to escape my mother's clutches, and so I suggested we marry as soon as I graduated. Oh, you had already asked me to marry you, but I am the one who set the date."

"I don't think you were. It was a mutual decision."

"You say that now, but many times afterward, before the Army drafted you, you would comment that we shouldn't have married so young."

"Somehow, you have twisted this thing around. We married young, yes, but it was a mutual decision. We were very much in love."

"But obviously not enough for you to honor your wedding vows."

He felt like they were in the middle of an argument he couldn't possibly win. "I hate this, Nora. I'm preaching Sunday morning, and I don't feel prepared for it because you and I are not at peace."

"What do you expect? You want me to smile and act like nothing is wrong?"

"No, I didn't say that."

"I'm sure there are some wives who would put on that happy face, but that's not me. Yes, I know I'm supposed to play the role of submissive, dutiful preacher's wife, but when it comes to my husband having had an affair that resulted in a child, well, I just can't play that role. Something happened to my sense of trust in you, Henry. It went out the window, and I can't just call it back on a whim."

That shattered him to the core of his being, for it was the second time she'd brought it up. "What have I done to cause you to distrust me? Tell me."

"I don't know, Henry, but that's where the rub comes in. I didn't know about this woman until a week ago. Would you tell me if you had another affair with someone? I think not. Not unless another child cropped up you don't know about."

"What?" This he shrieked so loud that the bed vibrated.

"Mother told me you might have other children out there that you don't know about. She also told me I have biblical grounds to divorce you, and that the kids and I could move in with her if it came to that. Of course, I turned her down."

He whipped the covers off him and sat up, red hot fury boiling in his blood. "Your mother said all that? Nora, I try my best to be civil to your mother, you know I do. I have always kept my opinions to myself because I don't want to offend either one of you, but I have to tell you she was way out of line by suggesting such a thing. She has never liked me, that's obvious. I don't know why, but I do know from the very beginning she didn't consider me good enough for you. And now she wants us to divorce, and she even suggested you and the kids come live with her? That is *not* going to happen, Nora Griffin. First, this whole fiasco is *our* business to handle, not hers." His voice had jumped to a high decibel, but doggone it, he couldn't remember the last time he'd been so angry. "So, now, because your mother suggested the possibility of my having other children out there *somewhere*"—he spread his arms out wide— "you're going to buy into that notion? Tell me, when in our marriage have you ever suspected me of having an affair?"

"Pipe down, will you?"

"Pipe down? After what your mother is trying to pull? I'm about ready to jump in my car right now and go give her a piece of my mind!"

"Shh, you'll do no such thing. And I never said I *believed* her, Henry. I'm just trying to be honest with you about my—doubts. I don't know. Can't you try to understand my side of things? We have your son coming to live with us, and—and I'm working hard to mentally prepare myself for that. I don't blame this child for any of this. Believe me on that. And I will do my best to make things work in the family, but as for you and me, well, I am somewhat of a tangled emotional mess right now."

He took several calming breaths to gain control of his anger. "I get that."

"No, you don't. You want me to get over this thing and bring everything back to normal. My doubts are something I have to contend with and work through. You don't understand because you've never had to wonder whether *I've* been faithful." Now *her* voice had raised several pitches!

He was about to say something more when their bedroom door swung open, and Paige stood in the entryway, her slender body a shadowy figure. "Why are you fighting so loud? I bet the neighbors can hear you." Her voice shook with sobs.

Quicker than a flash, Nora jumped out of bed, snagged her housecoat off a chair, and wrapped it around herself as she made her way to the door. "I'm sorry, honey."

Because he had nothing on but his boxer shorts, Henry crawled back under the covers. "I'm sorry too, Paige. Your mom and I just got a little carried away, that's all."

"I don't want Emiko coming to live with us after all," Paige wailed. "Ever since you told us about him, nothing's been the same around here. I just want him to go back to Japan!" Her sobs increased, and Henry worried that Paul would come bounding out of his room next. Thankfully, he was a heavier sleeper than his sister.

"This doesn't concern Emiko—or you, Paige," Nora said. "And, no, he is not going back to Japan. Emiko is an innocent party. You must remember that if you remember nothing else. Your daddy and I are going through a rough patch right now."

"How long is it going to last? Are you going to get a divorce?"

"No," they both answered in unison.

"I heard Daddy say the word divorce when he was yelling," she said between loud sobs.

"Shh, Daddy and I are not getting a divorce. Let's go back to your room. I'll tuck you in again." Nora nudged Paige out of the room and closed the door behind her.

It was a good long while before she returned. In fact, he'd begun to think she was going to snuggle into Paige's bed to comfort her and wind up sleeping there.

"Is she all right?" he asked when she finally crawled back under the covers.

"She'll be fine. I was able to calm her down and pray with her." She immediately put her back to him.

"Thank you for doing that."

"Good night, Henry."

Clearly, she did not wish to talk anymore, and frankly, he was glad. He would stew about his mother-in-law and her ridiculous inferences in silence. "Good night, Nora."

It may have been hours before he fell into a fitful sleep during which the slightest movement from her side of the bed roused him. *Lord, help us get beyond this. And in the waiting, help me find a way to be patient and kind. Please, Lord…no more of these loud battles that solve nothing. Help us to resolve this thing. I want my wife back, Lord. But—I don't know how to go about it.*

That was his hushed prayer before he at last drifted off to sleep.

SEVENTEEN

Let us approach therefore with boldness to the throne of grace, that we may receive mercy, and find grace for seasonable help.
—Hebrews 4:16

Almost as if the congregation sensed that something big was coming, folks started filing into the sanctuary in record numbers that Sunday morning. To be fair, summer was over, and attendance had been up the past few Sundays, meaning families were falling back into their regular routines. Living just miles from the sandy shores of beautiful Lake Michigan pulled many regular attendees away from church during the summer—either to go on weekend camping trips, picnics, or long vacations. But come September, folks returned to their normal schedules and duties, and church attendance always climbed back to normal. Nora sat at the piano and played a lively set of memorized hymns, glancing out at the growing number of incoming folks as her fingers effortlessly danced across the keyboard. She missed Iva Herman on the organ today, but she had sprained her ankle and would be out of commission for a few weeks. There were no other accomplished organists in the congregation, so Nora's piano playing would have to suffice until Iva's return.

Nora's stomach had been in knots all morning, but she still managed to put on her usual smile whenever someone familiar caught her eye. She casually looked for her mother but didn't see her in her customary pew. Perhaps she would indeed be a no-show, which was fine by her. Poor Mother and her wounded self-image. She caught the attention of Paige and Paul sitting in the second row next to her in-laws. Paul waved, and she smiled at him. She generally joined them when finished accompanying the congregational hymns, and today would be no different, except that she had very little enthusiasm for hanging around. In fact, she'd very much like to escape out the side door, race across the lawn to her house, and jump back into bed for the remainder of the day. Veronica and Leon and their youngsters entered and sat on the piano side, directly behind where Shirley Roberts and her four children usually sat. Shirley wasn't there, however, which caused Nora a bit of concern, but with her own angst to deal with, she dared not dwell too much on Shirley's absence. Veronica gave her a reassuring smile, which helped to calm her. She gazed over the top of the piano at Henry, who had made his way to the platform to seat himself in one of the ornamental high-back chairs. Herb VanOordt, the song leader, came and sat next to Henry. She and Herb had discussed this morning's song choices yesterday over the phone, and she had gone solely with his suggestions—"When Morning Gilds the Sky," "Blessed Assurance," and "Oh, for a Thousand Tongues to Sing"—because she had no idea what to tell him about Henry's sermon topic, nor the specific Scripture passage he'd be using. Guilt, if not Holy Spirit conviction settled around her heart, and she'd be lying if she said she was going into this morning's worship service with a pure and penitent heart. If anything, she was the greatest sinner in attendance. Why, she had barely uttered a prayer in the past week, so angry and out of sorts had she been. And yet, here she was, sitting at the piano, playing with all her might, like she'd done on many previous Sundays. Perhaps Shirley Roberts' husband Fred had been right after all when he'd said the church was full of hypocrites.

Yesterday, Henry had met with the seven-member board of elders. After the meeting, he had arrived home rather sullen-faced. She had asked him how it went, and he'd said it went as well as could be expected. Most of the men were reserved in their remarks, probably needing more time to process the correct thing to do regarding the situation. They hadn't mentioned anything about him losing his position as pastor, but one of them did say much would depend upon how his Sunday announcement was received by the congregation. They would prayerfully take everything into consideration and trust the Lord for wisdom and guidance as they moved forward.

Rather than rub salt into his wound, she'd merely nodded and remained quiet. What was there to say anyway? He'd dug his grave, she feared. Next, they'd be voting about whether to force his resignation. Henry had been a big drawing card for Church of the Open Door. His sermons were current, challenging, inspiring, and biblically based, and his personality was charismatic. Was life at Open Door about to drastically change? As if it weren't enough that they were taking in a new family member, would they also be embracing a move to a new town— or, worse, would Henry need to seek a new profession?

She continued to play as the clock ticked down to the eleventh hour. When Herb approached the podium, hymnal in hand, she brought her playing to a close, allowing for Herb to give his Sunday morning greeting, make a few announcements about the upcoming week, and then invite folks to stand and open their hymnals to the correct page number for their first song. He was a good musician, perhaps even a perfectionist, always concerned that they select the proper music, and that the special music for that specific Sunday went off without a hitch. In fact, when folks performed a special number, he insisted on being present at the final rehearsal to ensure it met with his approval. At times, he made suggestions to the singers to enunciate better or to slow down or speed up the rhythm. Generally, when Nora's ladies' trio sang, they practiced at her house so Herb wouldn't impose himself. They often joked about their sneakiness. This morning, there was no special music because she'd postponed their performance, and Herb hadn't assigned anyone to fill in for them. Good. She wanted off this platform, and the sooner the better.

At the close of the song service, Nora slid off the piano bench, then stepped down from the platform and quietly tiptoed down the side aisle and out the door to head to the ladies' room. She could not bring herself to sit quite yet. She entered the restroom, used the facilities, and then washed her hands and stood at the mirror for a bit to assess her appearance. She looked pale despite the makeup she'd applied that morning, and her lipstick had mostly worn off. "Lord, I am a big failure," she muttered. "Help me."

The door opened, and there stood Veronica. "Are you alright?"

How could she lie to her best friend? "No."

"Just as I thought. Tell me what's going on."

"I don't know if I can sit in there and listen to Henry's confession."

"Why?"

Nora gaped at her friend. "Would you be able to?"

"It would be hard, but I'm quite sure I'd do it, if for no other reason than to show my support. Like it or not, Nora Griffin, you are the pastor's wife."

"But I—"

"I know. You're deeply hurt. You feel betrayed, heartsick, angry—every emotion imaginable. But he's still your husband, Nora, and you have children sitting in there with their grandparents. Would you make them sit through his confession without you?"

"You're right, of course. I'll go back in."

"Let me pray for you and for Henry. He's got to be a bundle of nerves himself right now."

Guilt for not having asked him how he felt that morning rippled through her veins. What kind of Christian was she, no matter that she was the one who'd been wronged? Henry was hurting too, even though she hadn't truly stopped to think about his feelings.

Veronica said a prayer that somehow soothed Nora's splintered heart. When she finished, Nora hugged her. "Thank you, Vernie. What would I do without you?"

"You'd survive."

"Just barely."

Together they walked back down the hall and quietly reentered the sanctuary, Veronica sliding into her family pew, and Nora tiptoeing past other congregants until she reached the Griffin pew toward the front. "Where were you?" Paul murmured loudly when she sat down next to him.

"Shh," she said, putting a finger to her lips to shush him. "I went to the restroom," she whispered.

"Do you got some gum?"

She opened her pocketbook and retrieved a pack of Black Jack. He snagged hold of it, and there transpired a little tussle between Paige and him for the gum. Good grief. She grabbed it back, gave each of them one stick and tucked it back into her purse, throwing them both a scolding scowl. Her mother-in-law glanced her way and smiled. Lillian understood what was really going on. All three of them were on edge, and it showed. After Lillian whispered into Paige's ear, the girl stood and moved to sit between her grandparents. Nora made a mental note to thank Lillian later for taking matters into her own hands.

Henry's sermon was about God's grace, saying it is one of the most important concepts taught in the Bible. "Though we do not deserve His grace, and can't do anything to earn it, God is good and kind and wants the best for us, so He freely gives it," he said. "Simply put, grace is the unearned, unmerited favor and love of God, and it is by this grace that we experience forgiveness and are then able to extend forgiveness to others." Around the room, amens ascended, and Nora braced herself, for she knew it wouldn't be long before Henry's hideous confession. What would become of the amens then?

It was one of Henry's better sermons. He had bathed it in prayer, and it showed. Truth was, he'd labored over it all week, searching out the right words and phrases to get his points across, all of which led to a pivotal moment twenty minutes into his message where he paused and looked carefully out over the congregation. "All of us have sinned and fallen far short of God's glory," he was saying. Nora's heart commenced to pounding out of her chest. Out of the corner of her eye, she watched Lillian sit a little straighter. She couldn't see Paige, but Paul sat blessedly oblivious, loudly chewing his gum and using a pencil his grandma had given him to draw a picture on a blank space on the back of the church bulletin.

"I myself am a sinner," Henry said, "But I am a sinner saved by grace. My salvation is complete—there is no question about that—but does that make me perfect? Not by a long shot. Unfortunately, I continue this faith journey as an imperfect, damaged, sadly lacking human, but I continue with perseverance, striving always to walk by faith and in obedience to Christ. Every day, my prayer is, 'Lord, make me more like You.'"

He stopped there for just the briefest moment and caught Nora's eye. Her heart surely stopped for she gave a quick gasp. Henry, too, visibly sucked in a deep breath. "I'm going to be brutally honest with you dear folks. The last two weeks have been a true test of my faith. They've been heart wrenching. They've brought me to tears and to my knees." He stopped again, took out his handkerchief and blew his nose, then took a big gulp of water from his glass at the pulpit. By now, one could have easily heard a pin drop on the tile floor. Clearly, the majority did not have any notion of what was coming. Nora took great care not to move her head one way or the other, sitting staunch as steel. *He is still your husband, Nora.* Veronica's words echoed in her head. *You need to show your support.*

Help him, Jesus, she prayed. *Thy will be done.*

"Two weeks ago today, I learned something very startling, very life-changing, and perhaps some would say very scandalous. Approximately nine years ago, while serving in the United States Army during World War II, I was not living for the Lord in the way that I should have been. Nora and I were married, and she and Paige, then a baby, were back home awaiting my return to the States. Unfortunately, I picked up some bad habits, imbibing in alcohol for one. This led me down another road that would result in the terrible sin of adultery."

Something like a hot hush sizzled through the room, and Nora swore she could cut the air with a knife. She still didn't glance around, but she didn't need to. The hair stood up on the back of her neck as she imagined a hundred or more pairs of eyes seeking her out to appraise her reaction. Paul must have sensed a change in the atmosphere, for he stopped what he was doing and looked up at her, but was thankfully silent. On the other side of Lillian, she did get a peripheral glimpse of Paige wiggling in her seat. The poor child had been forced to learn more than Nora had ever known as a ten-year-old.

After only a short pause, Henry continued. "I sought the Lord's forgiveness after ending the tryst, and He graciously forgave me. After returning to the States, I fully recommitted my life to the Lord and obeyed His calling into the ministry, putting away the sin of my past. I figured if God could cast my forgiven sin into His sea of forgetfulness, I ought to be able to do the same. In fact, I forgot it so well that I failed even to mention it to Nora. Why would I? What possible good could come from her knowing? I was thousands of miles away from Japan and reasonably certain I would never see or hear from that woman again. And my thinking was correct. I did not see or hear from her.

"However, just two weeks ago, I received an airmail letter from a woman whose name I didn't recognize, and the return address indicated the letter had come from Japan."

At this point, Henry stopped, picked up his glass, and took a good, long swallow. A wave of sympathy came over Nora for the torment he was suffering, but it didn't last much longer than a few seconds for she knew this was something he'd brought upon himself, and dealing with it was something he had to do on his own. It was *his* story, not hers. In the audience, there came a nervous rustling and a few coughs, as folks braced themselves for what was to come.

"The moment I opened that letter and began to read its contents is a moment that will stand out in time for me until the day I breathe my last." He paused again and bit his lip, allowing his gaze to peruse the congregation from one side of the sanctuary to the other. "I learned in that letter, dear people, that I have an eight-year-old son I didn't know existed."

Several gasps sounded around the church, but certainly no amens! He had done it. Henry had confessed his iniquity, his horrendous lapse in judgment. Now would come the next blow. She held her breath, strangely proud of her husband for his uncanny courage.

"I can't imagine what all of you are thinking and won't even try to guess, but as you know, my sermon this morning was about grace, receiving it for ourselves in the form of forgiveness, even when we don't deserve it. I would hope that in the days to come, while I don't deserve it, you would find enough grace in your hearts to forgive—not to forget, but to forgive.

"One thing I would add is that this eight-year-old boy named Emiko lost his mother some four months ago to cancer. He is here in the States now with his legal guardian, an American missionary from Tokyo who is in her seventies. She will be handing over her guardianship to Nora and me, so we'll be increasing our family starting this week."

In that moment, Henry turned his gaze on Nora. She longed to turn from it, but she couldn't bring herself to do it. She bit back tears, but they fell anyway, stinging her eyes as they slipped down her cheeks.

"As you can imagine, this has been difficult for everyone, but particularly for my beloved wife. We would appreciate your prayers.

"And now—I'm going to step off the platform and kneel at the altar because I am a sinner, but a sinner saved by grace, and I want to acknowledge my guilt again, but also my gratitude for the gift of salvation. If anyone would like to join me to acknowledge a certain sin or weight of guilt that has plagued you, please feel free to come now. You can bring your burdens and leave them here at the altar, then go home changed and free."

And just like that, he concluded his sermon and stepped down from the platform, kneeling at the altar.

One by one, others moved forward, some crying, others simply walking purposefully and kneeling when they reached the altar. Nora's heart beat wildly as folks moved forward one after the other. Sensing God's leading, she stepped out from her pew and walked forward, finding a spot next to Henry and wedging in beside him.

She instinctively looped her hand through the crook of his arm and took his hand. He gave it a squeeze, while he sniffed and swiped at his eyes with his handkerchief. He whispered for her ears only, "Thank you for coming forward, Nora."

"Of course," she said back.

At the close of the service, Nora stood next to Henry at the door. Most stepped up to them and shook their hands. While they had little to say in the way of encouragement because most were in shock, they at least acknowledged that they would pray for their family. "This must be hard for you, Nora," one woman said in low tones. "I'll be praying." She nodded and gave a quiet thank you. Then there were those who purposely avoided looking at them and simply walked out the doors. They would have to take time to process matters, and it was quite understandable in Nora's eyes. Perhaps they were the ones who would decide to stop attending Church of the Open Door. They would move on to a church where the one in leadership had not committed such a heinous sin.

Ila Flood, one of the older women in the congregation who was ever warm and generous with her heart, wrapped Nora in a hug. "I'm here for you if you ever need to talk," she whispered.

"Thank you, Ila," Nora said, her eyes misting over.

Leon Hardy gave Henry a hearty handshake while Veronica took her best friend's two hands in hers and squeezed them gently. "I'm proud of you, honey. You're going to get through this."

Church elder Tom Bunyan tipped his head to Nora and then shook Henry's hand. "You're a fine man, Henry. Don't let anyone convince you otherwise. We serve a God of grace and goodness. I think you demonstrated that very well this morning. Great message. If anyone gives you any trouble, you come to me, hear?"

"I appreciate that, Tom."

Tom moved along, making way for others to approach. Ken and Sandra Parker were next in line. "We're anxious to meet that young man. We'll be sure to have you over for Sunday dinner once he settles in."

"We appreciate it," Henry said.

While Henry talked to another parishioner, Bill and Sue Wittmyer, who owned a local grocery store, approached Nora. "This comes as a surprise and you will probably need to give folks time to adjust," Bill said, "but we promise to pray for your family."

Nora nodded. "Thank you very much."

After they left, who should appear but Arletta Morehead? The woman always dressed to the hilt, and today was no exception with her navy-blue suit, floral blouse ensemble, and beige feather pillbox derby hat with a half veil that reached the tip of her nose. Her red lips pursed, causing deep wrinkles at the corners of her mouth. "Well, if this isn't a shock," she muttered in a low voice while moving close. "Your mother told me to brace myself, but I couldn't possibly have predicted this. Good grief, now I see why Florence stayed home today."

To that, Nora had no words. So her mother had warned Arletta of impending doom? She wasn't surprised. They were best friends, two peas in a pod as the saying went. How lovely of her mother to forewarn the church busybody! She forced a smile for the woman and wished her a good week, but Arletta didn't budge, just kept her eyes starkly fastened on her. The last thing Nora wanted to do was ruffle her pretty little feathers. She carried weight with several church members, her mother being one of them, and she had no doubt Arletta had the potential to cause harm to their congregation.

Arletta wrung her hands, her short-handled blue purse draped over her arm. She leaned in closer yet. "I feel it is my duty to consult with the board of elders, Morris Grayson in particular, since he is the chairman."

"Why would you do that?"

"Well," she huffed. "You don't think Reverend Griffin will get off without some form of discipline, do you? Something of this magnitude requires more than a simple apology."

"G'morning, Arletta," Henry said, finally free after a lengthy conversation with another parishioner. Good. Let Henry deal with Arletta.

"Well, Reverend," Arletta said with a sniff, "that was a very nice sermon—until you reached the part about your transgression. I can appreciate your apology, but, well, it seems to me…"

"Now, now, Sister." Edgar Warner, one of Open Door's longstanding members and also one of the church elders, stepped forward. "Let he who is without sin cast the first stone. John, chapter eight, verse seven, I believe."

Arletta turned to face the man. "Sometimes we are made to pay penance for the sins we commit—even after God forgives. Remember when Zacchaeus stood up and said, Lord, here and now I give half of my possessions to the poor, and if I have cheated anybody out of anything, I will pay back four times what I owe them. Luke, chapter nineteen, verse eight, I believe."

"I'm impressed that you recalled that verse from memory, but Zacchaeus was referring to those he may have harmed," said Edgar. His wife Rose stood dutifully at his side, neither nodding her head nor shaking it. "In the reverend's case, he is repaying the wrong he did by seeing to the needs of his son. He did not wrong *you*, ma'am."

"Perhaps not personally, but the church holds a preacher to a higher standard. And should word get out to the public about this—this transgression, no telling what could happen to our congregation."

"You are indeed right about that, Sister," Henry interjected. "I am happy to go with whatever the board of elders thinks is appropriate, and since Edgar here is one of our elders, he was made aware of the situation before today. They will be taking all matters into consideration. Isn't that right, Edgar?"

Edgar nodded at Henry and then almost glared at Arletta. "And since Reverend Henry is willing to leave this matter in our hands, perhaps you should do the same, Sister Arletta."

The woman gave another huff of disdain. "Well, we shall see. Good day." And with that, she straightened her spine, marched to the door, pushed it open, and stepped outside.

"Goodness gracious," someone murmured after the door closed.

"Well, that was not appropriate," said another.

"I'm sorry you had to listen to that, Reverend," said Edgar.

Henry, ever the diplomat, shook his head. "No, don't be sorry. Everyone is entitled to his and her opinion. What she said is entirely true."

"But did she have to voice her opinion for everyone to hear?" asked another longtime member. Nora took a quick look around. She had not known so many had been eavesdropping on the exchange. By now, most of the congregation had already filed out, but about a dozen remained. Nora had no idea what to say or think, so she did what any good preacher's wife would do and stayed quiet.

"She's simply outspoken," said Rose. Turning to Henry, she added, "I hope you won't take her words to heart."

"Oh, but I do. I do take them to heart—as I should," Henry replied. "I appreciate any words of support, but I certainly don't expect them. Everyone will react differently, and I expect that." He looked around at the lingering few in the narthex. They were all ears when he spoke. "She is right about the matter of restitution—when she mentioned Zacchaeus, the tax collector. He was a traitor to his own people, and I imagine Arletta feels betrayed. I don't blame her, and I don't blame any of you if you share her feelings. We will see where my confession goes from here. The last thing I wish to do is cause strife among the good people of Open Door. None of you deserves that."

"I don't feel betrayed," came a quiet voice. "I feel encouraged."

Nora turned about, for she recognized that voice. "Shirley! I didn't think you were here today. I didn't see you in your usual pew."

Shirley Roberts gave a shy smile. "I, er, we sat in the back as we were a bit late. My—my husband Fred also attended."

Nora sucked in a loud breath and looked from Shirley to Henry then back to Shirley. "I'm happy to hear that, but—of all Sundays for him to attend."

Shirley gave a little sigh. "Fred had nothing to say to me following the service, as he promptly left to go to the car, but I hope he recognized Reverend Griffin's sermon as admirable. My husband has always said the church is full of hypocrites, but today, he witnessed a Christian man, the preacher of all people, admit his sin and weakness. I pray your honesty will soften hearts, including my husband's."

"Thank you, Shirley," Henry said. "I'll make a point to call on Fred one of these days soon. I hope he won't mind my dropping in sometime."

She smiled. "I can't guarantee his openness, but I sure do appreciate your willingness to try."

"We'll pray the Lord softens his heart," Rose told Shirley. "Perhaps today will be a catalyst by which your husband will see that we all make mistakes, and yet by God's grace, we can receive forgiveness and move on."

"Agreed," said Edgar. "You can count on us to pray."

Others also chimed in with their promises.

"Well, thank you, everyone, and now I must be going," Shirley said.

After she left, others started moseying toward the door and saying their goodbyes.

Soon, it was just Henry and Nora remaining, the children having gone outside with the rest of the youngsters.

"Well, I'll go pick up whatever bulletins were left behind and see to it that all the hymnals are put in the proper place," Henry said. He started to turn.

"Henry."

He paused to look at her. He was so handsome in his black suit, white shirt, and striped tie. He arched his dark brows. "Yes?"

"I am very proud of you. We will deal with whatever comes our way."

He didn't close the short distance between them, and frankly, she didn't expect him to, but it did feel good to be talking again, if only just a few words. He smiled. "Yes, we will. It won't be easy, but we'll get through it."

"I believe you're right."

For a long minute, all they did was stare at each other. Finally, he said, "Why don't you take the kids on home? I think I'd like a little time to myself."

"Yes, yes, I understand. We're having a simple dinner today, spaghetti and salad."

He nodded and smiled. "I'll be home shortly."

And just like that, they parted. There were still problems aplenty between them, mountains to climb no doubt, but as she pushed through the church's big door and stepped out into September's sunshine, her heart felt a little lighter.

⌇

"Well, for mercy sakes, I wasn't expecting that!" Arletta shrieked across the phone lines on Sunday afternoon. "You might have given me a bit of a hint. I didn't know the scandalous activity you alluded to would involve our pastor—your son-in-law—of all people. You poor thing, you must be so devastated."

"Indeed I am. There are just no words. It's plain disgraceful, thinking of him carrying on with a Japanese woman while my Nora was back here doing her wifely and motherly duties and faithfully awaiting his return."

"Unconscionable."

"How did he go about telling folks? And how did they react when he made the announcement?"

"You haven't talked to Nora about it yet?'

"No, not yet. How did she seem to you at the service?"

"Stronger than I would've been, that's for sure. After Henry's confession, if that's what you call it, he had an altar service whereby he invited folks to come forward and pray if they wished. He led the way and Nora went up and knelt beside him. It was quite touching in a way. I just hope it wasn't all for show. Do you think he's truly repentant?"

"I couldn't say. I haven't talked to him about it on a personal level. Frankly, I'm too put off by what he did to have the wherewithal to talk to him. He knows where I stand on the matter."

"How do you know that?"

"I think my silence speaks volumes. Besides, I'm sure Nora told him my reaction when I heard the news."

"Hm, yes, I suppose you're right."

"It's a terrible thing, Letta, him thinking he can hold on to his pastorate after committing such a sin. I don't care if it happened nine years ago. It's something he's kept hidden all these years, and when someone you trust betrays you in that way, he doesn't deserve immediate forgiveness. I told Nora she has grounds for divorcing him. It's in the Bible, you know."

"Yes, I know. When my husband cheated on me, I would have divorced him, but times were different then. I had no way to support myself. What exactly do you think will happen—I mean with Nora and him, and with this Japanese boy, and then with Henry's pastorate? I am of the opinion the board of elders needs to suspend him."

"Well, he certainly needs to do more than apologize in front of the congregation and then go kneel at an altar as a show of penitence."

"Yes, yes, you are so right. But this is your daughter's husband we're talking about. Surely, you wouldn't want anything to happen that will affect her or your grandchildren in any way."

"It's a bit late to worry about that. She's already been deeply affected. I saw the hurt in her eyes, you know. A mother detects these things."

"Of course."

Moments of silence passed between them before Arletta spoke again. "I plan to approach Morris Grayson. Surely, he will be in favor of taking disciplinary action."

"I don't know. He is a big fan of my son-in-law."

"Yes, but he's also a stickler about making sure the church bylaws are carefully adhered to. This matter of your son-in-law's moral misconduct can't possibly set well with him. Henry's been here for nigh onto five years, and most pastors don't stay at the same church much beyond that. Perhaps it's time Mr. Grayson nudged him on his way."

"Perhaps, but I don't want my daughter and grandchildren to leave Muskegon either."

"Do you think their marriage will last?"

"She loves him a great deal, but an act such as the one he committed is not easily forgiven or forgotten. I certainly wouldn't fault her if she left him. As I said before, she has biblical grounds."

"Of course she does," said Arletta. "She and the children could stay with you, and Henry and that son of his could go elsewhere."

After a bit, their conversation wound down. "Well, keep me abreast if you hear anything," said Florence.

"I will, and you likewise."

When they hung up, a nipping, nagging twinge chewed at Florence's conscience. Oh, she'd done nothing wrong herself—that was all Henry's doing—but the fact that she hadn't gone to church to support her daughter hadn't been the smartest move on her part. She just couldn't do it. She couldn't sit there and listen to him confess his adultery without reliving some of the worst moments of her life. It was all just too much for her. Too much. And here she thought she'd put it all to bed a long, long time ago.

EIGHTEEN

Forgetting the things behind, and stretching out to the things before,
I pursue, looking towards the goal,
for the prize of the calling on high of God in Christ Jesus.
—Philippians 3:13–14

With Ken Parker's offer of both his 1950 Ford truck and his muscle, he and Henry picked up the bunkbed on Monday afternoon and once in the driveway, they carried it piece by piece into the house. Ken hung around afterward and helped Henry put it back together. Paul danced all around the house with glee at the thought of bunkbeds, having resigned himself to sleeping on the bottom bunk after Henry told him he would build some railings to alleviate any worry of either of them falling off the higher bed. He assured Paul that the boys could trade places after six months, if they so desired.

While Henry studied in his office, Nora spent Tuesday making last-minute changes to Paul's room, taking a few of his toys down to the basement and freeing up space for Emiko's toys—if he had any, that is. They also didn't know what to expect as far as clothing went, but they decided they could return to the secondhand store for some clothes if necessary. Emiko would be starting school on Monday morning, so they wanted to be prepared.

Much had to be done on the business side as well, including a visit to the county courthouse to make Emiko's adoption legal. Even though Henry was Emiko's father, Helen Felton had been named his guardian some months ago—and in Japan, no less. No doubt there would be some red tape to cut through before getting to that finish line. Henry didn't care. It would be worth it. Over the past weeks, his parental instincts regarding this eight-year-old boy had truly set a flame under him, and he could only hope and pray that Nora would soon catch up. Yes, they had started talking again, so things were much easier between them, but most of their conversations revolved only around the children and all the necessary adjustments that needed to be conquered.

As for the romance side of their marriage, it wasn't there, but he had faith it would return. They had discussed his sermon on Sunday afternoon, and she had told him she was proud of the way he had carried it off. She could tell the Holy Spirit had guided him as he spoke, she had said, and that except for Arletta Morehead, most folks seemed to take the news of his illegitimate son as well as could be expected. Still, the question remained of whether, after giving the matter serious thought, some members might choose to leave Open Door in hopes of finding a more unblemished pastor. He wouldn't blame them if they did. He only hoped Arletta wouldn't be the one to cause the division. Few things were more detrimental to a church body than busybodies stirring up quarrels and animosity. Arletta certainly had the power to do that at Open Door if given the chance. He wondered how he would handle the situation if she started a firebomb. And what would happen if the woman's blather succeeded in influencing the elders to turn against him? Perhaps he needed to call on his friend Reverend Samuel from Lake Drive Methodist. Ever since meeting up with him a couple of weeks ago to discuss a problem in the reverend's congregation, he had felt the need to confess his own transgression. All in due time, he told himself.

On Wednesday morning, directly after sending the children off to school, Henry made final preparations for his long drive to Naperville. He had put written instructions in his car's glovebox to refer to once he reached the city limits, and he had carefully studied his Michigan and

Illinois maps to obtain correct highway directions. It would be a long drive, roughly five hours, but he would pass the time with much prayer and gas stops along the way. Nora had been kind enough to pack him a lunch for the road, as well as another meal for him and Emiko on their way back to Muskegon. Henry had also filled their gallon-sized insulated thermos with water and ice cubes and packed some paper plates and cups. Perhaps he and Emiko would find a roadside picnic table along the way to eat their supper. If all went well, he estimated he'd return home by ten o'clock that night.

"Do you have everything you need?" Nora asked.

"Yep, I've put all the necessities in the car and checked to make sure my jack and spare tire are in the trunk should I need them. Pray I don't have any delays along the way."

"I will do that. We'll all be anxious for you to get back."

He lingered in the doorway and gave her a slow perusal, wishing she'd elaborate on her statement. "So, you're saying you're going to miss me?" he asked with a hopeful tone and a tilt of his head.

"The kids and I are anxious to welcome Emiko into the family," was her brief reply, as she brushed right over his question. He wondered what she'd do if he stepped toward her and kissed her on the lips. But he decided not to find out because he'd told himself the ball was in her court. She would have to give him a sign that she wanted to be touched, and so far, that hadn't happened. Once again, he wondered how long he'd have to wait. Did she still not trust him? And if she didn't, what could he possibly do to regain her confidence?

He glanced at his Timex. "Well, I guess I'll be going now."

She hadn't budged, just stood there a good five or six feet from him, donning her apron and still holding the kitchen towel with which she'd dried the breakfast dishes. "Drive carefully," she said. "I'm sure the children will balk at going to bed before you get home."

"Let them stay up then. In fact, maybe we can allow them to stay home tomorrow."

Nora's eyes widened. "You mean skip school?"

"Yes, one day couldn't hurt. Then on Friday, I'll take Emiko into school and get him registered, but tell them he won't be starting until Monday."

She bit her lower lip. "I suppose that would be alright, their missing school for one day, providing Paige doesn't have any tests."

"If she does, she can retake them. Don't tell them quite yet though. I want to be here when you let them know."

She smiled. "They'll be excited. I hope it turns out to be a nice day so the children can play outside."

"So do I." He thought a moment before asking his next question. "Have you talked to your mother this week?"

She gave a tired sigh. "Yes, and she told me she's spoken to Arletta."

He nodded. "I wondered about that. Arletta and Florence are good friends."

"The best. I'm worried the two of them might try to hatch a plan."

"I can't imagine your mother going along with something that could potentially cause you pain."

"One would hope, but Mother tends to put herself above God and others. Sorry to say that about my own mother, but you know it's true."

"I don't want to say anything negative about her."

"I know you don't. You are a kind man, Henry Griffin." They stared at one another a few seconds longer. "And now you best be going."

He put his hand on the doorknob and nodded. "Yes, I best. You have a good day."

"And you as well."

And with that, he stepped out onto the porch and closed the door behind him. In just five hours, give or take, he'd be laying eyes on his son. Excitement rustled up in his chest. Still, he would have been a little more excited if Nora had approached him for a kiss. *Lord, may it come soon.*

Nora completed a long list of chores around the house, including sweeping floors and doing some laundry, then drove to the bank, the post office, and Plumbs Supermarket for some milk, bread, and a few other essentials. Her final stop was the gas station, where she asked Burt, the Sunoco attendant, to fill the Packard to the brim. She had hoped to stop at the S&H Green Stamps redemption center with her stamp books to purchase the hand mixer she'd been eyeing for a few months, but she ran out of time and didn't want the children to arrive home before she did.

All day, she'd thought about Henry, praying for his safety along the roadways and praying too for his reunion with Emiko. She knew he had wanted a kiss goodbye that morning, and perhaps she should have granted it, but she couldn't bring herself to allow it just yet. For some reason, although she told herself she had forgiven him, her heart had not quite caught up to that reality, and though she tried to forget the sense of betrayal she felt, it still lingered in the deepest part of her soul. *Lord, I know it is wrong of me to harbor resentment, but I can't seem to get beyond what Henry did to me nine years ago. Help me find a resolution, so that our marriage can return to a healthy place.* This was the prayer foremost on her mind and heart since Sunday's message and Henry's churchwide confession, and yet she felt stalled, as if sitting in the middle of a train track, fastened with chains to the railroad ties, unable to move despite the approaching locomotive. What would it take to unleash her sadness, to relinquish her resentment and anger solely to God? *Lord, give me strength.*

While she was putting the groceries away, the phone rang, and to her delight, it was Shirley. "I don't want to keep you," Shirley said. "I just wanted to let you know I've been praying for you."

"Thank you. I've been praying for you as well. Henry left this morning to go pick up his son in Illinois. Starting tonight, our household will never be the same."

"You are right about that, Nora, but try to imagine it being better rather than worse."

"I like your attitude. By the way, what did Fred have to say about Henry's announcement on Sunday?"

"That's one reason I called. Fred has been a grump and a sourpuss. I don't know why I put up with him other than it is my wifely duty. He had very little to say after church so I don't know his thoughts. All I can do is pray for him, as I'm sure you do for your husband. I didn't tell you this before, but Fred has a drinking problem. He is able to work every day, but at night, after the kids go to bed, all he does is drink one beer after another while watching that stupid black and white television he bought six months ago. When he gets to drinking heavy, I have to leave him be because he can get mean, so that's what I've been doing."

"I'm sorry, Shirley. I will continue praying for Fred and his salvation and also that God will soften his heart toward Him."

"And I will pray that your family situation and any feelings of hurt or disappointment you may be suffering will come to a head and you'll be able to work everything out for everyone's best interest."

"You're very kind, Shirley. I always enjoy talking to you. Thank you for calling."

At the supper table that night, the children were keyed up with extra amounts of energy and enthusiasm. They talked nonstop about what it would be like to see their brother for the first time and asked constant questions about him, questions that she and Henry had already answered to the best of their knowledge. Still, they continued to repeat them. How tall is he? What's his favorite school subject? When's his birthday? What games does he like to play? What is his middle name? Nora did her best, but found she didn't have all the answers. "You can ask him yourself when he gets here," she said finally.

"When are they gettin' home?" Paul asked.

"Daddy thought he'd make it back around ten tonight."

"I bet Emiko will be tired."

"I bet we'll all be tired," Nora said.

"Not me," Paul answered. "I could stay up all night if you'd let me."

"No, you couldn't," Paige said. "Remember when Mom said you could stay awake on New Year's Eve, but you fell asleep two minutes before midnight?"

"No, I didn't. I was awake the whole time."

"No, you weren't."

"Was too."

"Don't argue," Nora told them. "Help me clear the table. It's almost six o'clock. We can listen to *Our Miss Brooks* on the radio if we hurry."

They scurried to clean up, Nora rinsing the dishes and stacking them in preparation for washing later, Paige taking the wet cloth Nora handed her and wiping the kitchen table clean, and Paul getting the broom and sweeping up any crumbs. "If we had a dog, we wouldn't have to sweep under the table," he said.

"Yes, well, in the meantime, we use the broom."

"In the meantime?" Paige said. "Does that mean we'll be getting a puppy sometime soon?"

"How did you jump to that conclusion?"

"Because you said in the meantime. That usually means you're waitin' for something to happen."

"Does it? Hm. I learn something new from you every day."

The telephone sounded two short rings. "I'll get it!" Paul announced.

"Use your best telephone manners," Nora told him as he raced out of the kitchen.

Nora listened carefully when he said hello. "Oh, hi, Grandma," Paul said. "Yeah. Uh-huh. Nope. Yup. Just a minute." Then as loud as if he were calling a cow home from some distant field, he called, "Mom-my!"

She wiped her hand on a towel and looked at Paige. "Go turn on the radio so you don't miss the start of the show. You know how to find the station. Keep the volume low till I'm off the phone."

"Which grandma?" Nora mouthed to Paul.

"Your mom," he answered, giving her the receiver.

Just as she'd feared. Florence Harrison was the last person she wanted to talk to right now. "Hello, Mother."

"Hello, dear. So, tell me, did Henry go to Naperville to pick up that boy?"

"Yes, I told you yesterday he was going."

"I know, but I had hoped he would come to his senses before he made that long trip. Good grief, have you two even talked about this?"

"Well, of course we have. He wouldn't have gone to get him if I hadn't agreed."

"But surely you felt obligated to do it for Henry's sake."

"No, not really. I've been thinking what was best for Emiko and reached the conclusion that he needs to be with his father. You and I have talked about this already, Mom."

She tried keeping her voice down, glad the radio was on the other side of the living room. The children pulled dining room chairs close to the radio box so they could hear. As a family, they normally sat themselves in a semi-circle to listen and laugh together. She really cherished these times, and now her mother was interrupting with her disgruntled chatter. "You know, I've been talking to Arletta."

"I know, you told me yesterday."

"Did I? Sometimes I don't remember who I've talked to. Did I tell you Arletta is quite upset about the whole matter of this Japanese boy moving into your home? Neither of us think Henry truly considered all the complications that can result from this disaster. These are uncertain times in our society. You know, just because the war is over doesn't mean folks have forgotten. Japan did a terrible thing in—"

It was the same old thing. Her mother just couldn't let it rest. "Yes, Pearl Harbor was a terrible thing, but there is a time for moving on and letting go of the past."

"Does that mean you have fully let go of the past as well? After what Henry did to you?"

Nora sucked in a deep breath and looked at the ceiling. A quick glance at the children told her they had immersed themselves in the radio show. For that, she was grateful. "Mom, you'll have to let Henry and me work things out on our own. I don't wish to discuss that now."

"Well." She huffed across the airwaves. "I wouldn't expect you to confide in me. You never do, you know. You talk more to Lillian about private matters than you do to me."

"I do not. In fact, I haven't talked privately to Henry's mom about any of this. She is very sensitive about matters such as these, not wishing to interfere."

"Oh, so now you are accusing me of being insensitive and interfering. All I was doing was trying to tell you I didn't think you and Henry had given this matter enough thought."

Nora blotted her forehead with her apron. "Mom, I'm sorry if you took what I said the wrong way. I'll call you tomorrow and let you know how things went tonight. If all goes well, I expect Henry and Emiko to arrive home around ten. Please do me a favor and stop talking to Arletta. I believe she wants to stir up trouble at Open Door."

"You're asking me to stop talking to my best friend? Well, do I ask you to stop talking to your friends?"

Nora gave her head several shakes and rolled her eyes.

Across the room, the children laughed. "Mommy, you're missing the funny parts. Miss Brooks' student just put a piece of gum in the middle of Susie Lambert's braid, and now it's stuck," Paul said.

"I'm sorry, Mom, I must hang up. I'll call you tomorrow." Before Florence had a chance to argue, Nora said goodbye and quietly replaced the receiver. Then she pushed up from the telephone table and joined the children in front of the radio.

NINETEEN

*Be to one another kind, compassionate, forgiving one another,
so as God also in Christ has forgiven you.*
—Ephesians 4:32

It had been a long drive back home, Emiko sitting quietly on the
front seat next to the passenger door and staring out the window
while Henry tried to make conversation, eager to answer any questions
he might have. He'd been friendlier on his visit a week ago; today, he
was shy and withdrawn. Emiko and Helen had shed a few tears, and
he'd clung to her before getting into Henry's car. Poor kid had to have so
many emotions roiling around inside—from losing his mother, leaving
his country, learning a new culture, finding out he had a father, saying
goodbye to Helen, adjusting to using English exclusively... Yes, he was
well-spoken, but it had to be strange realizing he'd probably never con-
verse again in his native tongue. Henry's heart hurt for the youngster
who sat with his hands clasped and legs crossed at the ankles. He looked
so small and pensive. When they passed a road sign that read, "Picnic
Area Ahead," Henry decided this would be a good place to stop for the
supper Nora had prepared for them.

"Are you getting hungry yet, Emiko?"

The boy gave a shrug and a quiet reply. "A little."

"I plan to stop up ahead. We can get out and stretch and have a little supper. How does that sound?"

"Fine."

"And we can talk a little more. If you feel like it, that is."

"Okay."

When the roadside park came into view, Henry slowed his Ford Mainline and pulled into the small picnic area. There were a couple of picnic tables, a small wooden building with restrooms, and a large waste bin that appeared to be overflowing. At present, they were the only visitors there, but that could change as folks were always seeking out these little spots along the two-lane highway.

They walked to one of the tables and Emiko sat down then swung his legs over the bench. Henry sat across from him, but chose to straddle the bench instead. He opened the picnic basket. "Well, let's see what Nora packed us, shall we?"

The boy sat mute while Henry investigated the contents. His thoughtful wife had packed a clean floral tablecloth on top, so he spread it on the dirty table surface. Then he withdrew a couple of sandwiches wrapped in waxed paper, an apple for each of them, and two bunches of grapes. Nora had also packed a jar of dill pickles and a couple of cookies for each of them. "You like pickles?" he asked.

The boy shook his head and made a sour face. Henry laughed. "That's alright. Paul doesn't like them either, but Paige does. Everyone's tastes are different."

"I don't like too many American foods, but I'll get used to it."

"I imagine it is a big adjustment for you. Maybe Nora can find a Japanese cookbook at the library and copy down a few recipes of foods you especially like."

"Does she have rice in her cupboard?"

"Rice? I'm sure we do. You like rice?"

"We eat that every day."

"Well, we'll make sure to have rice for you then."

Henry unwrapped his sandwich and inspected it. "I hope you like bologna."

The boy shrugged. "It's okay."

Henry said a mealtime prayer, then afterward, poured each of them a cup of water from the thermos jug, and soon they commenced to eating.

After a few bites, Henry ventured onto the sensitive topic that loomed over them like a vulture. "So, Emiko, can you tell me what you thought when Mrs. Felton told you I am your father?"

Emiko studied his sandwich. "I was surprised." His voice was little more than a murmur.

Henry waited, hoping the boy would say more. When he didn't, he continued. "I can only imagine the shock you felt. You probably wondered why I didn't tell you last week when you came to visit. Nora and I had much to discuss first. We didn't wish to do or say anything that could hurt you. We wanted to be certain the time was right. Does that make sense to you?"

"I guess."

"Do you have any questions for me?"

Emiko took a bite of sandwich, broke off a couple of grapes, and then drank a few swallows of water. Rather than use the napkin Nora had provided, he wiped his hands on his pants. "How come you never came to visit me?"

"Didn't your mother ever tell you that I didn't know about you?"

"No. She only told me that my father lived in America. She never wanted to tell me anything else about you, and if I asked too much questions, she got sad, so I tried not to ask her."

"I see. Well, Son, I didn't know about you, but if I had, I would have tried to contact you. Maybe we could have exchanged letters. I'm sorry if you ever felt abandoned."

"I didn't."

"That's good. You were a good son to your mother. Mrs. Felton told me that. She said your mother was very proud of you."

The boy nodded, remaining staunchly solemn as he ate, eyes gazing down at his food.

"How did you come to speak such good English?"

"My mama made me speak it."

"Did she speak it well?"

"I guess. We always talked in English whenever we went to the mission or to the laundry service where she worked, which was most every day. Besides doing the laundry, Mama swept floors at the mission and dished up supper for people who didn't have any food. Mrs. Felton was sort of like my grandmother and my mother's ma. Mrs. Felton cried when my mama died."

That pulled on Henry's heartstrings. "It sounds like they had a very special friendship."

"Yep."

They both finished their sandwiches then worked on their fruit. The boy started chomping his apple. "Anything else you'd like to ask me?"

Emiko thought a moment, looked overhead at the swaying trees as they dropped a few stray, orange leaves. "How much longer do we have to ride before we get to your house?"

"It shouldn't be too much longer." Henry looked at his wristwatch, glad Chicago's traffic had not been nearly as heavy as he'd expected it to be. "We've made pretty good time. We should arrive home around 9:30. I'm sure the family is eager for us to get there. How about we both go into the men's room over there, and afterwards, we can start out again?"

"Sure." Emiko stood, though not with any degree of enthusiasm. He stepped over the picnic bench, picked up his leftover trash, and threw it in the outdoor waste receptacle.

The restroom was relatively clean, with four stalls, and once they were finished using the facilities, they meandered back to the car.

On the way home, Henry tried everything he could think of to draw his son out of his shell, but all the child did was answer his questions in as concise a manner as possible. It wasn't until they pulled into his driveway on Wood Street that the boy sat up straight and looked over the dashboard, the car's headlamps lighting up the area in front of them. "There's the basketball hoop," he stated.

"Indeed, it is. The kids and I will teach you how to shoot some hoops, maybe play a game of Around the World."

"I'm no good at basketball."

"Don't say that till you've given it the old college try."

"Huh?" He looked at Henry as if he'd just lost his last marble.

Henry laughed, shut off the engine, and dropped the keys into his front shirt pocket. "Come on, let's go in."

⌒

"They're here!" Paul squealed from the front window, loud enough to start the neighborhood dogs barking. It was a mild night considering it was almost October, so the three of them stepped out onto the porch without jackets after Nora switched on the outdoor light. Her eyes first searched out Henry, who gave a little wave after closing his car door. Next, her eyes traveled to the boy who climbed out from the passenger side. He looked especially small standing there next to the big fifty-two Ford. Nora hoped he wasn't frightened. She wouldn't blame him if he were. Paige and Paul stood like two statues, gawking and suddenly shy, their mouths gaping. She nudged Paige in the center of her back. "Go say hello." When she still didn't move, Nora stepped down from the porch, and the kids followed her. She and Henry exchanged smiles. "I hope your drive went well."

"Very uneventful."

"Good." Then she extended her hand to Emiko. "Nice to see you again, Emiko. Welcome home."

Very slowly, not at all like their first meeting, he stuck out his hand for a brief handshake. It only lasted a moment for she wanted to make introductions. "Emiko, this is Paige and Paul, your sister and brother. I'm sure Henry, er, your *father*, told you all about them."

All three children gaped at each other—and no one said a word. Well, good grief, Nora couldn't remember when she'd ever witnessed such outright shyness from Paige and Paul. She chose not to make an issue of it, knowing they would all come around with time.

By now, Henry had collected Emiko's suitcase from the trunk of the car. "Well, we're glad to be home," he said. "At least I am. Shall we go inside?"

They all moved toward the house, Paige and Paul leading the way with Emiko walking behind them, while she and Henry brought up the rear. Every once in a while, as he carried the unwieldy old suitcase, they brushed arms...and she didn't even flinch. To be honest, she was delighted to see him. For the first time in ten or more days, she could truthfully admit to herself that she'd missed him. She wanted to tell him about her earlier phone conversation with her mother, but that would have to wait. For now, they had to focus on the children.

Henry walked in last, closing the door and locking it behind him. "You kids must be very tired. Paul, how about you show Emiko to your room?"

"Okay." The two boys eyed each other from head to toe. They were curious about each other, of that Nora was certain.

Paige wore a half smile, equally interested but perhaps a little more confident. "Come on, Emiko. Your room is down here."

"*Our* room," Paul corrected, as the three of them set off toward the hallway. "We're sharing a room. Did Daddy tell you?"

"Yeah," came Emiko's quiet reply. How strange to hear Paul refer to Henry as Daddy when speaking to Emiko. How long would it take for the boy to feel comfortable enough to do the same? Which begged the question: how should he address *her*? If he called her Nora, that might sound strange to her own children. Such a dilemma, although probably a minor one considering all that lay ahead for their family.

The children left Nora and Henry alone as they walked down the hallway and then disappeared into the boys' room.

"Well," Nora said. "Shall we bring in the rest of Emiko's luggage?"

Henry put the suitcase down. "This is it. He doesn't have much, and Helen said it's mostly clothes. She told me they had to leave a lot behind, although he didn't really own anything of value."

"Well, then I suppose he'll fit right in with Paige and Paul. Was there any mention of his cello and when that will get here?"

"Helen said she hadn't received any word as to its whereabouts, but she expected it to arrive in Naperville in a couple of weeks. She mentioned we could meet somewhere halfway when it did get here, saving both of us a bit of time, not to mention gas money."

"That's very generous of her. What was your visit like this time?"

"Very pleasant, although somewhat strained. It was obvious that she and Emiko are very fond of one another, and he's going to miss her. I told her she could visit anytime, but she thought it best to give him time to settle in with us first so that he wouldn't beg to go back with her. Perhaps in a few months, she said. I told her to feel free to call him, but she said she thought exchanging letters at first might be best for him. She truly wants him to adjust to the idea of this being his new home."

"That makes sense. Was he talkative on the way home?"

"Not at all. He's overwhelmed at the present."

"That's understandable."

"In fact, most every word he spoke was in response to a question I asked. I think he's downright scared. I asked him if he had any questions for me, and his one question was, 'Why didn't you ever visit me?' Apparently, his mother failed to tell him that I didn't know about him."

"That hardly seems fair."

"You're right, but I'll do what I can to make it up to him."

"I know you will."

The children's voices carried from Paul's room. "Sounds like they've found something to talk about," Henry said. Soon, Paige's high-pitched giggle erupted.

"Shall we go see what's so funny?"

"I think we should, but first..." He snagged hold of her arm as she started to walk toward the hallway. She stopped and looked up. "Thank you," he whispered.

"For what?"

He gave a brief shrug. "I don't know. For being willing to give this thing a try, I guess."

"We could hardly leave the child stranded."

"But—there was the viable option of giving him up for adoption."

Nora gazed up into his deep brown eyes. "It would have eaten you alive."

"Yes, you're right."

"Come on then." She set off down the hallway, and he followed behind.

TWENTY

Be strong and of a good courage, fear not, nor be afraid of them:
for the LORD thy God, he it is that doth go with thee;
he will not fail thee, nor forsake thee.
—Deuteronomy 31:6 (KJV)

October had arrived on a frosty morn, the trees changing their colors a little more each day—from dullish green to bright oranges, reds, and golds. Over the past two weeks, Emiko had seemed to be settling in, although he wasn't one to show much emotion, nor did he have much to say. He only seemed to laugh when Paul humored him, and even then, he generally covered his mouth to hold it back. It was as if he viewed having fun as a sin. Henry wondered if Emiko carried some sort of guilt that prevented him from laughing. Surely his mother would have wanted him to be happy. He knew Helen certainly didn't begrudge him. Emiko hadn't even touched the piano, even though Nora had encouraged him several times to sit down and share his talent with his new siblings. She continued to give weekly lessons to Paige and Paul, but for some reason, Emiko turned down her every offer for a lesson. Somehow, they had to find a way to break through the walls he'd erected that kept anyone from getting too close.

Henry's parents had purposely stayed away, reasoning that Emiko needed to adjust to his new family before meeting his grandparents. They believed seeing him at church would suffice for now, but told Henry that an invitation to Sunday dinner would be forthcoming. "That sounds great, Mom," he had said last Sunday after the morning service, ever thankful for her easygoing, pleasant, and agreeable personality.

Florence was another matter entirely. As much as she'd balked at the idea of welcoming Emiko into the family, she'd certainly wasted no time on Thursday, showing up unexpectedly on their doorstep. Henry had gone to the office extra early to study for his upcoming sermon, then arrived home at noon, deciding to take off the rest of the day to spend with the children. Paige and Paul were ecstatic when they'd learned they didn't have to go to school that day, and Henry wanted to take the kids to Lake Michigan and then over to Deer Park in Whitehall. Florence's interruption at 12:30 p.m. put a damper on their plans. She entered the house without being invited inside and pushed her way past Henry and Nora, demanding to meet "the boy," neither referring to him as her grandson nor using his name. It took all of Henry's sense of restraint to keep from telling her to go back home because they weren't quite ready to introduce Emiko to anyone. The children were in their rooms getting their jackets, when Florence started down the hall.

"Mother, we're getting ready to go out," Nora said. "Now is not a good time to visit."

"Oh, pooh. Anytime is a good time for a grandmother to drop in."

Just then the three children emerged from their rooms. "Grandma!" Paul said. "I didn't know you was coming with us."

"She's not," Nora put in. "She merely came to say hello—and to meet Emiko."

"Oh! Well, then, Grandma, this is Emiko. He's ar' new brother. Emiko, this is Grandma."

Paige dutifully approached her grandmother and gave her a hug, and Florence, not one to show much affection, wrapped her in a tighter than usual embrace, looking over Paige's head at Emiko. "Hello there, young man."

"Hello, ma'am."

"You may call me Florence—or Mrs. Harrison," she stated none too warmly. "Now then, thank you for the invitation to tag along with you, Paul, but I have several errands to run. I just wanted to stop by for a minute."

Henry hadn't recalled anyone inviting her to join them, but he kept his mouth shut. He was still out of sorts over the things she had said to Nora about a possible divorce and having her and the kids move in.

"Children, go jump in the car," Nora said. "We'll join you in a minute."

"Yes, go on now," Henry said.

Once the children had run out the door, Florence sent them both a scalding look. "Well. He looks very—um—Japanese."

"What did you expect?" Nora asked.

"I suppose I had hoped he'd look more, you know, American. He doesn't appear very friendly. I thought you told me he was highly intelligent and talkative, even talented."

"He is all of those things, Florence," Henry said. "He's just been very shy since getting here last night."

"I see." She shifted her weight and let her eyes travel from one to the other. "Have you heard anything from the elders?"

An uncomfortable chill skittered up Henry's spine. "No. Why do you ask?"

"Well, I should think one of them would've approached you by now."

"About what?"

She rolled her eyes upward. "This whole debacle. What else?"

"Mother, now is not the time for discussing such matters," said Nora, shifting impatiently.

But Florence had him curious. "Do you know something I don't know, Florence? Should I expect a call from Morris Grayson?"

She took the handkerchief she'd been holding and dabbed at her nose, lightly blowing. "I don't know what the discussion has been exactly, only that Arletta is most upset. She has been in conversation with several of the elders about this disgraceful situation, the boy being a Jap and all."

Henry's dander shot up to a dangerous level. "Emiko is a fine young man."

"Perhaps so, but he's a Jap, nonetheless, and what you did with that woman, well—it's unconscionable."

"I can't argue with you there, Florence. But since I can't take back the past, I'm choosing to move forward. As your only son-in-law, I would like your blessing."

She laughed. "I can hardly promise that. It will take me a good long while to adjust—just as it's taken my daughter."

"Enough, Mother. I am dealing with things as best I can, and like Henry said, it would be nice to have your blessing. Please don't waste time gossiping or allowing Arletta Morehead to influence your thinking."

Florence left in a huff, no doubt more annoyed than when she'd first arrived. Seldom did Nora stand up to Florence Harrison, but that day was an exception.

Except for Florence's spontaneous visit, the family's Thursday outing went well. Emiko thrilled at the sight of Lake Michigan and was enthralled by their visit to Deer Park, a small animal-petting farm that also included a few children's rides. Of course, what excited all three children the most were the deer that freely roamed the large parcel of land. The small herd was tame enough to walk right up to the children and nibble at the treats Henry had purchased at the park entrance. On the way home, they stopped at Drelles's Restaurant in downtown Muskegon for hamburgers and chocolate milkshakes. Emiko's eyes lit up at the first sip of his milkshake. He proclaimed he'd never had anything like it before. They all giggled at his enthusiasm.

He and Nora drove the three children to school on Friday and registered Emiko for third grade. Although the legal papers were still incomplete, Principal Ben Peters said it was no problem to have Emiko start class on Monday, giving Henry time to visit the county courthouse to complete matters. Thankfully, the principal, a rather stout, black-haired man in his mid-thirties, was pleasant and happy to register a new student, no matter what his background. Henry wanted Emiko to have the best possible experience in his new school without any fears of being ridiculed for his mixed race, and he had been praying to that end. When he privately mentioned his concerns, Mr. Peters assured him he would do his best to ward off any possible bullying or teasing from the other students. He also promised to speak to the third-grade teacher, Mrs. Ellen Stipe, to be on the lookout for any problems with Emiko adjusting to his new environment. Everything had been handled very professionally; the principal did not even ask how Emiko came to live with the Griffins. Henry was grateful for that. He already had enough on his hands with his congregation without having to answer to the staff at Moon Elementary.

Mid-October rolled in with a harsh wind and cooler temperatures. Henry had spent a good share of the day studying in his office and listening to the wind gusts rattle through the church rafters. While he studied, he prayed, ever conscious of each word that came from his mouth when presenting his sermons. Although he had sinned, he wanted his congregation to know that no one is perfect, not even the Reverend Griffin, but a perfect plan of salvation is within reach for all who lay their sins at the foot of the cross, seek forgiveness, and repent of their sins.

A rap came to his office door. "Come in," he called.

To his surprise and delight, Reverend Samuel from Lake Drive Methodist stood in the doorway, wearing a tweed gray herringbone jacket over his dress shirt and tie, his dark gray homburg hat in hand. Henry quickly pushed his chair back and rose, extending a hand across his desk as a means for welcoming him inside.

"Well, glory be, if it isn't Brother Samuel. You know I've been thinking about you a lot lately, thinking how I ought to pay you a visit."

"Have you now?" the elderly gentleman said. He looked to be nearing retirement age with his thinning white hair, rather slumped shoulders, and wrinkled hands. He was a well-respected, deeply loved pastor whose church would be hard put to hire a replacement when the time came. Henry for one hoped he'd stay around for a long time to come, as he considered Reverend Samuel to be a wise mentor. "Well, that's a wonder because I've been thinking about you too, pondering if there's anything I can do for you. I should tell you I've heard some talk."

They ended their handshake, and Henry invited him to sit in one of the two leather accent chairs on the other side of his desk. "I wondered how long it would take for news to travel. I'm not surprised you heard. It wasn't my place to ask my congregation to keep anything a secret. These things are bound to come out when you inform a whole church body."

The fellow situated himself on the chair, set his hat on the edge of Henry's desk, and crossed his legs. "Tell me, how long have you known you had this bonus son?"

"I just found out last month. It's been a whirlwind of events and has caused quite a stir between my wife and me. I confess I had just found out the night before I paid you a visit. I'm sorry I was quite distracted that day. By the way, have you managed to meet with the man and woman in your congregation who are having the affair?"

"That's another story. Goodness, it does seem like things creep up on us when we least expect them. Yes, I called them both into my office at different times and asked them to explain. I invited one of my board members to sit in on the meetings, not to speak necessarily, but to act as witness. Both parties assured me they had ended the affair and were making every effort to work on their marriages. Now I shall wait and see if they follow through. I read Scripture to them, and then I prayed over them. I certainly did sense God's presence in our midst on both occasions. Oh, how our enemy Satan enjoys stirring up trouble in the hearts and lives of believers. We must put on our spiritual armor every morning to be assured of thwarting his evil darts."

"Yes, Reverend, I've learned that over the years—and now more than ever. I am this minute in the throes of trying to save my own marriage. My short-lived tryst nine years ago in Tokyo has caused tremendous hurt to Nora. Not only did the news shatter her trust in me, but I sometimes wonder if she still loves me. Not a mention of love has come off her tongue, and to be honest, it's made me hesitant to express how much I love her. The fear of her not returning my love really eats at me." Henry picked up a pencil out of the jar on his desk and started turning it in his hands while shaking his head. "I don't know if I'll ever fully forgive myself, even though I'm fully confident God has extended me His grace and forgiving mercy."

Reverend Samuel gave a quiet nod and tipped his head to one side while seeming to consider his next words. "I believe things will work out between you. She needs time and patience. I wouldn't expect too much from her. I know you want everything to go back to normal, but, brother, I can tell you that's not going to happen. This unexpected addition to your family will impact you for the remainder of your lives, but I don't say that to be negative. I'm viewing it as a positive. Remember, God works everything out for the good of those who love the Lord and are called according to His plan."

"You can't imagine how many times I've recited Romans eight, verse twenty-eight these past several days. Maybe a hundred."

The older preacher smiled. "How has your congregation handled the matter thus far? Have they welcomed the lad?"

"I believe many have, but there are those who can't seem to accept our decision to make him part of our family. I would say about five families in total have written letters explaining their need to search for another church. I am hurt by it, but I also quite understand their reasons."

"Were they longstanding members?"

"No, and none of them were regular church-goers either, so for that, I'm thankful. I can't say more won't leave in the future though. It's in God's hands, that's all I know."

"That's the right attitude to take, my friend."

"There is a woman in our church who wouldn't dream of leaving Open Door, but she'd sure like nothing better than for *me* to resign. She's approached various members of the elders board in her attempt to persuade them. Unfortunately, my mother-in-law is one of her closest friends."

"Ah, yes, you have mentioned in times past how difficult Nora's mother can be. And what of your board of elders? What is their position?"

"Surprisingly, they all reached a unanimous agreement that at least for now, things should go on as usual. They want to work toward healing and restoration, and they feel that removing me from the pulpit for a sin committed nine years ago, even for short time, could do more harm than good, particularly since I repented of my sin and made a public statement. The elders held a special meeting to give church members a chance to speak their minds and ask questions. Nora and I were not invited, of course. After the meeting, the elders reconvened and reached a unanimous decision that I should remain as pastor of Church of the Open Door. From what I understand, there were a few dissenters among the attendees." A pinch of worry snagged a nerve in his stomach. "But I can only pray for them and for the elders' decision—that it was the right one, and that those who are discontent can either accept the decision or make the choice to move on to a different church. I regret having to say that because I don't want to be the cause of anyone leaving, but I also don't wish to continually preach to a group of people who disapprove of everything about me."

Reverend Samuel listened intently, as he was inclined to do anyway, soaking up Henry's words as if each one held great importance. He never had been one to make fast judgments; rather, in wisdom, he took his time in responding and then always weighed his words with care. "I'm glad they reached that conclusion. Had I been on the board, I would most certainly have voted in favor of your staying. God bless you as you deal with those people who wish to remove you from the pulpit and may the message of God's love and healing tug at their hearts. I believe good things can come from this if you allow the Holy Spirit to do His work. How is that young man, Emiko, settling in?"

"Ah, Emiko. I'd appreciate prayer for him. He is a fine boy, but he's bottling up a great deal, so it's hard to determine how he's really doing. He's still trying to find his place in the family."

"That's understandable. Allow me to pray for him."

Right then, the reverend bowed his head and offered a prayer of thankfulness, first, for bringing Emiko into the Griffin home and, then, asking the Lord to soothe his young mind and grant him assurance and peace. He also asked for wisdom, an open spirit, and a heart of love on Nora's part so that their marriage could wholly heal and their family grow stronger than ever. He mentioned a few more areas of concern before offering a final amen.

After that, they visited for the next ten minutes or so to talk about a variety of other topics until Reverend Samuel stood. "I best be on my way. I only stopped by because I wanted to see how you were doing. I shall be praying that all turns out well and that God's hand will rest upon you as you navigate the days ahead."

Henry pushed his chair back and stood. "Thank you for that, my friend. And thanks for stopping by. It is always a pleasure seeing you."

"I feel the same. You ever need a listening ear, you know where to find me."

"I appreciate that—more than you know."

They shook hands again over Henry's desk, and the preacher set his hat back on his head then gave a warm smile. Just as he turned to leave, a loud crash sounded from somewhere in the church. "What in tarnation was that?" Reverend Samuel asked.

"I don't know, but I'm about to find out."

Both hustled out of Henry's office and down the short hallway toward the sanctuary. "Nothing seems amiss," Henry said. "But with the wind gusting as it is, I wouldn't be surprised if a big branch fell on the roof."

"Let's check inside the sanctuary," Reverend Samuel suggested. They approached the doors leading into the vast room and pushed one of them open. They immediately noticed that one of the beautiful, stained-glass windows was lying on the tile floor, no doubt shattered, although the frame and casing were still intact.

Henry's heart dropped. "Oh, no! One of our prized windows. Do you think it was the wind?"

"Most likely a tree branch," Reverend Samuel said. Together, they walked down the center aisle, around one of the floor-to-ceiling beams, then wended their way between two rows of pews to reach the window. "One of our congregants, Frank Sheen, is an excellent, skilled crafts- man. His specialty is stained glass, and he made every one of these win- dows then donated them to the church." Henry walked a little closer to study the damage. Amid the pieces of colored glass, he spotted a large rock with a paper attached by means of a rubber band.

"What's this?" he asked, a sickening feeling coming over him. He bent at the waist, picked up the rock, and removed the paper. Unfolding it, he read aloud, "Men like you ought not to be standing behind a pulpit. You're supposed to set the example. Or did you forget? Get out of town, preacher—and take your little half-breed with you."

Wheels squealed, alerting both men. They moved to the open hole where the window had once been and got only a tiny glimpse of a dark car, perhaps navy or black, spinning out of the parking lot. "What kind of car was that?" Reverend Samuel asked.

"I didn't get a good look at it," Henry admitted sadly.

"Do you think you'd recognize it if you saw it parked in your lot on a Sunday?"

Henry shook his head. "I wouldn't have a clue. A lot of folks own dark cars—black, navy, dark gray...Who would do such a thing?" He reread the note while Reverend Samuel looked over his shoulder.

"Well, one thing's certain," the older pastor pointed out. "He typed it so no one could identify his handwriting."

Henry mulled that thought. "Yes...or *she*."

"Are you referring to that church busybody you mentioned earlier?"

"You read my mind."

TWENTY-ONE

*I leave peace with you; I give my peace to you: not as the world gives do
I give to you. Let not your heart be troubled, neither let it fear.*
—John 14:27

The children were talkative at the supper table that night. In fact, they had been full of conversation ever since Emiko joined their family. Although Emiko seemed to have little to say, he was taking a few small steps toward becoming a full-fledged Griffin, and Nora had to give much of the credit to Paige and Paul for their abounding efforts to draw him out of his little tortoise shell. The legal process had been set in motion with Henry's visit to the county courthouse, and it had seemed like things were moving quite smoothly—until today's incident at the church.

Nora scooped up another forkful of green beans while Paul droned on about how he wanted to be Davy Crockett for Halloween, and Paige talked about the autumn leaves they'd pressed between waxed paper that day in class. Nora and Henry exchanged looks. She knew him well enough to recognize when he carried a weight of concern, and there was no getting around the fact that today's criminal activity affected him. The police had been called, of course, and had already opened an investigation. Law enforcement had knocked on doors in the neighborhood to see if anyone had spotted anything suspicious—or witnessed anyone squealing their wheels while exiting the church parking lot at approximately two o'clock that afternoon. But no one came forward with any helpful information. Without that witness, police said they'd be hard-pressed to find the perpetrator.

Nora and Henry had decided not to say a word to the children about the incident, but come Sunday, they'd find out right along with everyone else when they saw the boarded-up window. Frank Sheen had promised to produce a new one, but said it would have to wait until he completed his current stained-glass project. Sam Cordelle, the church janitor, had covered up the window space and swept up the debris. He also set aside the larger pieces of colored glass for Frank in case they were still useable. Outside, a storm raged with driving rain, thunder, and lightning, a carryover from the afternoon's strong winds. It seemed to add to the morose mood hanging between Henry and Nora.

"What's for dessert today, Mommy?" Paul asked.

"I made some cupcakes. Are we ready for them?"

"I am!" Paige said.

"Me too!" said Paul.

She glanced around the table and noted almost everyone was finished with supper...except for Emiko, who was still trying to adjust to American food. She'd been making rice for him every night, which he almost always devoured, but he merely picked at the rest of the food on his plate. She didn't want the boy starving under her watch. Maybe they'd have to take another trip to Drelles's Restaurant for another chocolate shake. Anything to fatten him up a little.

Just as Nora rose to begin collecting the supper dishes, thunder vibrated the house and a simultaneous streak of lightning caused the lights to flicker. Nora's body gave such a jolt that she sat back down. More thunder and lightning followed—and then there was a tremendous, tumultuous boom and cracking sound. Paige screamed.

"Whoa!" Henry said above the noise. "Something's been hit!"

Nora's heart thumped hard, especially after Paige's scream. "What was it?"

Paul jumped up first and ran out of the dining room. "It's the Mercy Tree!" he squealed from around the corner.

Everyone pushed their chairs back and stood, then hurried to the side window overlooking the church. Across the yard lay a gigantic section that had fallen away from the big maple. Rain came down in torrents, soaking the ground like a small lake, making it hard to even see the church, and the wind whipped ferociously as the storm raged on.

"Is it going to hit the house next?" asked Emiko, worry lining his voice.

"I doubt it, Son," answered Henry. "It's just a bad storm, but it'll pass over before you know it."

"It sounded like a—a bomb," he said.

Nora and Henry just looked at each other, realizing the boy must be relating the storm to wartime in Tokyo. Who knew what sort of fears he'd experienced in his little neighborhood? Although the war had ended before his birth, he had surely heard stories that would curl his hair. Henry put a hand on the boy's shoulder and pulled him close to his side. "It's just a storm that will soon pass over. Nothing more than that."

"But the tree," he said. "Is it dead?"

"The tree will survive. I'm sure of it. Mr. Cordelle will call the men of the church, and they'll come out to help clean it up. By Sunday, you'll hardly know anything happened to the old Mercy Tree."

"Why's it called the Mercy Tree?" Emiko asked, gazing up at Henry.

"I can answer that!" said Paul, ever the helpful one. "When folks ask Jesus to forgive their sins, then Daddy tells them they can go carve their name in the tree. There's lots of names there. Did you ask Jesus into your heart, Emiko?"

The boy nodded. "Yes, I did that before my mama died."

It was the first time Nora could recall him offering a word about his mother's passing. "That means you can carve yer name in the tree," said Paul.

"I don't know how to."

"Daddy will help you. He helped me an' Paige 'cause it's a sharp knife, an' no kids can do it without help." He paused and cast a curious eye at Nora. "Did you ever carve your name in the tree, Mommy?"

"Me? No, I never have."

"Why not?"

"I don't know. I suppose I thought it was intended for new converts."

"What's converts?" asked Paul.

"People who have just become born-again believers," she said.

"Daddy said it don't matter when you did it, you can carve your name, right, Daddy?"

"That's right, sport." Henry ruffled Paul's hair and issued him a fond smile, even as he held his other son close to his side. "But enough about the Mercy Tree. What say I go turn on the radio and see if we can get some information about the weather?"

"If we had a television set, we could find out that way," said Paige.

"Yeah, a TV would be faster," said Paul.

"Oh, goodness, when will you children quit talking about getting a television?" Nora asked, urging everyone to move away from the window.

"Not till we get one, I suspect," said Henry, a slight grin tickling at the corners of his mouth, as he led everyone out of the room. "Go sit down while Mommy gets each of you a cupcake, and I'll turn the radio to WMHG to see if I can get a weather update." Another streak of lightning and clap of thunder rattled the house. Paige shrieked.

"It's alright," Nora quickly said. "It's just a little autumn storm. We get them all the time." But when the lights flickered again, and then went out altogether, she realized it was more than just a little storm.

The children hurriedly ate their cupcakes, all aflutter about the lack of electricity, while Nora and Henry gathered candles from a kitchen drawer, then lit them and placed them strategically around the house. Henry also took a couple of flashlights down from a shelf in the broom closet and put them on the kitchen counter. Dusk was upon them, so getting as much done as they could with the remaining daylight was paramount. While Henry went around the house securing all the doors and windows, Paige and Nora washed and dried the supper dishes. The rain came down hard amid bursts of thunder. Paul skipped around the house declaring it exciting not to have any lights. "Let's see if you feel that way when it grows completely dark, and you have to walk down the hall to the bathroom," Henry said.

"I don't need a light to go to the bathroom. I can do it blindfolded."

"Ewww," Paige said. "Don't talk about junk like that."

Nora glanced at Emiko and saw a tiny grin playing on his lips. It reminded her of Henry's, and it struck her again the strong resemblance he had to his father. Some unknown emotion tugged at her heart. When would she fully accept that Henry had a son that wasn't also hers?

Lacking proper light, bedtime came a bit earlier than usual. Nora read stories to the children by flashlight, then Henry read a short Scripture passage, and they said prayers together as a family. Afterward, he tucked the boys in while Nora tucked in Paige.

When it came time for them to get ready for bed, she was unusually flustered, perhaps even nervous, though she didn't know why. Somehow, the loss of electricity had made her uneasy, even vulnerable in Henry's presence. She had always looked to him to take care of matters when emergencies arose, for his strong, confident nature put her at ease. But because of the constant tension between them and the wall she'd erected around herself, her nerves stood on end. When they bumped against each other in the bedroom between the closet and the bed, she gave a tiny gasp.

"You alright?" he asked.

"Yes," she replied, but she couldn't help but wonder if he picked up on her guardedness. "It's just a bit difficult to see what I'm doing—with no electricity. Why didn't you bring the flashlights in here?"

"I put one in the boys' room and gave the other to Paige. They might have to use the bathroom in the middle of the night."

"Or they'll play with them or read with them when they're supposed to be sleeping," she said. "We don't even have the streetlight to see by."

"I can walk down the hall with you if you like."

"No, I'll manage. Besides, I already brushed my teeth and washed my face. Do you think it will take the electric company very long to fix whatever the problem is?"

"I don't know, but I'm sure there are men working on it even now. These things are hard to predict." Outside, the storm raged on—matching her inner turmoil.

"Yes, I know."

In one fluid movement, she stepped out of her clothing, then just as quickly, tossed a nightgown over her head and made for the bed. In the dark, she tossed her clothes onto a chair and then pulled back the covers on her side of the bed and crawled under them, relishing the warm, secure comfort of their cotton softness. She had just ironed the sheets that day and changed the bedding, so the lingering smell of Fab laundry detergent wafted off them.

Once Henry crawled into bed, they both lay still in the darkness. Nora stared at the ceiling and assumed Henry did the same. When would she feel fully comfortable in his presence again?

"What do you think of Emiko's adjustment so far?" Henry asked.

"I think he's starting to get a little more relaxed with us, but it'll take time."

"That's what the Reverend Samuel said today."

"I'm glad that you have found a friend in him."

"Yes, he's a fine person, gentle spoken and wise."

"Every young pastor should have a mentor like him."

"Most definitely."

She heard him turn on his side and face her. She lay still, eyes still trained on the darkness above her.

"How—um?" He paused, as if unsure how to finish his sentence.

"What?"

"I was just wondering how you've been feeling lately—about *us*, I mean."

"Oh." She left the question dangling while she tried to form a clear answer. Hadn't she just been pondering that exact question, with no clear answer? How was she to respond if she couldn't yet come to grips with it? "I suppose I would have to say—nothing has changed much."

"Really?" He released a wobbly sigh, and she imagined him twisting his face into a frown.

"Yes, really, Henry."

"But when—I mean, what can I do to help you?"

"Nothing, Henry. Don't ask, okay?"

"Don't I have a right to know?"

"I don't know what to tell you because I'm not feeling it."

"You're not feeling what?"

"You know."

"No, Nora, I don't know. I am trying to understand."

"Well, so am I, Henry, but I am not the one who cheated. You are, and until you can explain to me why you—why you did that, I will continue to struggle letting it go."

"I don't know why I did it, Nora. It was nine years ago, for pity's sake. I barely remember it."

"That's convenient for you. But not for me."

He heaved a loud breath. "Boy, I'm glad God doesn't look at our sins in the same way—unable to let them go, unwilling to forgive and forget."

That got up her dander. She bit down hard on her lip before replying, then just let the words come out anyway. "I am not sovereign, Henry James Griffin. Sorry to have to break it to you."

"I never said you were, but we are supposed to strive to be as Christlike as possible."

"Are you saying I'm not trying?"

"I don't know what I'm saying." His voice came out on a hoarse hiss, cutting the air between them. Not only did she sense his frustration, she heard his anger. "I am doing everything I can to make this thing right, Nora, but I've reached the point where I don't know what I can do or say that won't come off all wrong to you."

"Well, I'm sorry, but there is nothing more I can offer you at this point—and maybe you should stop trying to say or do the right thing and simply let things play out as they will."

"Well, what's that supposed to mean? I shouldn't fight for you? I should just let our marriage and our communication continue to deteriorate? If I do that, it won't be long before there's nothing left of us."

"That's a bit of an exaggeration."

He pulled the covers back and sat up. She heard him swing his legs over the side of the bed and plunk his feet on the floor. "Doggone, Nora, it's not an exaggeration, and you know it. At the rate we're going, I'm not even sure you want to make our marriage work."

"Don't say that." Her own irritation started to boil over.

"I thought that one Sunday you knelt at the altar with me would be a turning point."

"That was more a starting point than a turning point, Henry."

She heard him run his fingers through his thick, dark hair and could envision the persistent scowl swathed across his fine-looking face. In times past, she would have sat up, drawn close to him, and massaged his back to bring comfort. But not tonight. She wanted to assure him that everything would be alright, but her mouth could not form the words… because her heart could not wrap itself around the conviction. What was she to do? Fake her feelings, pretend her shattered emotions didn't exist? She was at a loss for words, so she said nothing. Another clap of thunder splintered the air. He stood up and shuffled across the room.

"What are you doing?" she asked.

He pulled open a dresser drawer, a scraping sound against the worn glider squeaking in protest.

"Grabbing some socks. My feet are cold. I'm going out to sleep on the couch."

"What? Why?"

"Why shouldn't I, Nora? It's clear you don't want me near you."

"I never said that."

"Pfff. You didn't have to."

"What if the children find out?"

"They won't. I always get up before they do."

He came back to the bed, snatched up his pillow, and marched to the door. When he opened it, a faint light from some distant place seeped into the room. Tears crowded her eyes and rolled in silence down her cheek. When he stepped out and closed the door with a bit of punctuation, it gave her body a tiny jolt.

"Oh, Lord, what am I to do?" she cried into her pillow. "Help me. Help *us*."

TWENTY-TWO

There is then now no condemnation to those in Christ Jesus.
For the law of the Spirit of life in Christ Jesus has
set me free from the law of sin and of death.
—Romans 8:1–2

The next morning dawned without a trace of electricity, only the beginnings of daylight. Henry awoke achy and cranky. He had probably overreacted by moving to the living room couch to sleep, but criminy, he'd been exasperated by Nora's behavior. Would he never regain her trust? What did he have to do to earn it? Perhaps it was time he sought wisdom from his dad. In the meantime, he had a Sunday sermon to prepare, not to mention a congregation to convince that his marriage and family were safely intact. His desperation only worsened when he recalled the problem of the broken window and the message that had been attached to a rock. Clearly, someone was out to get him, and he had a feeling his mother-in-law might be privy to some information, which only increased his anxiety. "Lord, give me strength," he pleaded aloud as he stood and stretched, then haphazardly folded the afghan and tossed it over the back of the sofa. He needed a hot cup of brew—but the realization struck that no electricity meant no coffee. He moaned and pawed through his scraggly hair with both hands, then padded down the hall to grab the flashlight off the top of Paige's dresser and prepared to take a shower. It would be a cold one, but perhaps that was just what he needed. Even deserved.

After his shower, he stepped into the bedroom, towel wrapped around his waist, thankful that Nora still slept. Using the flashlight, he found a pair of slacks, a shirt, and a vest, then carefully closed the closet door. He grabbed a clean pair of underwear and socks from his dresser drawer, then in the dark, slipped into his apparel. Good grief, how did people exist in pioneer times? He squinted at his watch in the dark but had to use the flashlight to read it. It was just past 5:30, a full hour before the rest of the house would awaken. He decided to take his Bible out to the dining room to read by candlelight. He tiptoed out, closed the door behind him, and headed down the hallway.

Outside, the storm had subsided, but a portion of the Mercy Tree, branches, and debris lay strewn across the yard. He had his work cut out for him today while the kids were at school—unless Sam managed to gather some men of the church to help with the cleanup. Henry wondered when he would find time to visit his father.

He situated himself at the table and opened his Bible to the book of Romans, which he'd been studying. He'd underlined several passages that stood out to him and by the light of the candle, he reread all that he'd underscored, along with his notes in the margins. For a short while, he lost himself in the Scriptures, praying as he studied and sought God's wisdom. *Rest in Me*, a voice seemed to whisper. *I have everything under control.* A certain peace came over Henry even as he read and reread the first two verses of Romans eight: *"There is then now no condemnation to those in Christ Jesus. For the law of the Spirit of life in Christ Jesus has set me free from the law of sin and of death."*

He pressed his back against the chair and let out a long, slow breath. What assurance to know that the sins of his past—and even those of his future—were forgiven by the shed blood of Jesus. Yes, others condemned him, and they had every right, but Christ Himself did not hold any sins over him. He'd been freed of them because of the work that Jesus did on the cross. What a blissful thought, knowing the most important person, God Himself, did not condemn him. For now, he had to let that be enough. He had to release his selfish desires, his wants and wishes concerning his beloved wife, and give her all the time she needed to build back her trust. "Lord, may it be so," he prayed. "May that day come when she will love me unreservedly. In the meantime, may my faith and trust in You grow to new heights."

And as if God longed to impress on Him the importance of trust, the dining room light suddenly flickered to life as did the lamp in the living room and a light down the hall. Outside, the streetlights set to glowing, and in the distance, a dog barked, as if to announce the good news. Henry blew out the candle he'd been using and smiled to himself. "Thank You, Lord, for the light of Your Word, and for light restored."

After lunch that day, Nora called her mother. Florence picked up on the first ring.

"Hello, Mom. How are you this morning?"

"Oh, I suppose I'm doing alright, considering."

"Considering what?"

"You know, all the things that have been happening in our family and in our church. Of course, my arthritis is always acting up."

"I'm sorry about your arthritis. Where is the pain this time?"

"Mostly in my back and across my shoulders. Doctor said there's not much I can do about it except take aspirin. Thank goodness for that, as it does help a little—unless I take it in excess. Then it burns my stomach, which forces me to take antacids."

"Well, try not to overdo it."

"I do, but it's a losing game. I dislike this aging thing. Someday, you'll know what I'm talking about."

"Ha! There are already days I feel about as weary as an eighty-year-old."

"Of course you do. Just look at what you've been through for more than a month now. How are things going, by the way?"

"I'd say about the same."

"And by that you mean not that great, I suppose."

"I didn't say that."

"Well, you don't sound too chipper, dear. Is that boy settling in?"

"Emiko, you mean?"

"Who else would I mean?"

"You can call him by his name, Mom."

"I prefer not to just yet."

"I see. Well, since you ask, he's adjusting, but very slowly. He's a very talented pianist, but so far, I haven't been able to convince him to touch it. It's almost like he's afraid he'll make a mistake, and I'll be upset with him. I'm not sure what his reasons are."

"Hm. Well, if he's as talented as you say, I suppose the day will come when he'll sit down and surprise you all."

"I hope so."

"You sound tired, dear."

"Do I? Well, I did say there are days I feel about as weary as an old lady."

"Yes, you did. I would guess you and Henry had a good spat."

"You could say that. In fact, he slept on the couch last night."

"Good. That's exactly where he should be. What woman wouldn't be devastated to know her husband did unthinkable things with another woman?"

Nora gave a painful sigh. "I really didn't call you so that we could discuss the state of my marriage, Mom. I just wanted to see how you fared in last night's storm—and to ask you something."

"Okay, for starters, I slept like a baby. Aside from my back pain that is."

"I'm glad to hear it. No damage to any of your trees?"

"Not at all, but I did notice several twigs and leaves on the ground this morning. The boy next door, Kenny Brown, is coming over after school to clean up my yard for me. He already called me to see if I needed help. Of course, he knows I'll pay him for his efforts."

"It's kind of him to offer and nice that you have someone to look after you. He's lent a hand to you more than once."

"Yes, he's a fine boy. How about you? Did you survive the storm?"

"We lost a huge limb off that giant maple in the church yard, the one they call the Mercy Tree. It's lying sprawled across both yards. But Mr. Cordelle called several men of the church, and they've been working out there all morning to clean it up. A couple men brought saws and another fellow brought a truck to hall away the debris." Even now, the screeching noise echoed through the neighborhood.

"Oh, for goodness' sake. I've been saying for years the church needs to cut down that monstrosity. Arletta's brought it up several times at church meetings too. Some agree with her, but no one ever seems to do anything about it."

"It's a beautiful tree. It would take a lot of convincing to get the people's vote to cut it down. It's very sentimental to a good number of folks."

"Yes, yes, I know. All that silly name carving in the trunk—as if having one's name etched into the bark will assure them of a spot in heaven. Good grief."

"I don't think that's the idea behind the tree. It's more a gesture than anything. I myself haven't carved my name in it, but you never know. The day might come that I will."

"Pfff. It's just plain silly if you ask me. Anything else new?"

The hair on the back of Nora's neck stood up. It almost seemed as if her mother was "fishing" for something.

"Yes, we lost our electricity last evening during the supper hour."

"Goodness, didn't it come back on yet?"

"Yes, it returned before breakfast this morning."

"Well, that's good. At least you got to sleep through most of it."

Nora thought about that. Yes, she'd slept, but not that well, especially after Henry had left their bed to sleep on the couch. She knew he was nearing the boiling point with her. It almost made her wonder if she *should* stay at her mother's place for a couple of weeks after all until she and Henry sorted things out. But of course, she wouldn't speak a word about it to her mother, not unless it came down to that. At least then Henry wouldn't feel obligated to sleep on the couch. Her stomach twisted into a knot at the very idea of breaking up her family—but then she wasn't the one who'd committed the heinous sin either.

"You mentioned wanting to ask me something," Florence said.

"Yes, yes, I do. Did you happen to hear anything about someone throwing a rock through one of the church windows?"

"Indeed, I did! I was wondering if you were going to bring that up."

"Well, why didn't you say something if you'd heard?"

"I didn't know if it was my place. Arletta called me first thing this morning."

"Of course, she did. How did she find out about it?"

"Well, I wouldn't know. I suppose someone from the church called her. I understand the police stopped by. News travels fast when officers of the law show up at a church building on a weekday."

Nora bit down on her lip before continuing. "You wouldn't happen to know anything about it, would you, Mother? I mean, do you have any idea who would do such a thing?"

"Good gravy! Why would I know anything about it?"

"I didn't mean to upset you. It was just a simple question."

"Well, I'm quite put out that you should think I'd have any information about it."

How convenient of her mother not to give a direct answer. Nora decided not to belabor the issue. After all, would she *really* want to know if her mother was involved? That would feel like the ultimate betrayal— her mother deliberately bringing shame upon her husband, which would in turn affect Nora and the children.

"What exactly did the note say?" Florence asked.

"The note? Did I mention anything about a note?"

"You didn't have to. Arletta told me about it."

"Who informed her?"

"How should I know? Goodness, Nora, you're touchy this morning. Perhaps you need to get away for a while. Come over here and take a nice little nap. It might do you good to simply get a change of scenery. I'll make you a hot cup of tea and..."

"No, I can't. I have several things to do today, and the children will be home in a little over three hours."

"All right then, but don't say I didn't offer. So, back to the business of that note. What did it say?"

Nora fidgeted with a loose thread on the hem of her apron. "I didn't personally read it, but Henry told me it said something to the effect that he had no business standing behind a pulpit and that he should get out of town and take his half-breed son with him."

"Hm. Well, I don't condone violence, but I can certainly appreciate that someone would be angry enough with Henry to do such a thing."

"Are you serious, Mom?"

"I said I don't condone violence."

"But you also said you understand the hateful act."

"Don't put words into my mouth, Nora. I didn't mean it in the way you think."

Nora shook her head and pushed a hand through her hair, then pressed her palm to her forehead to tamp down a looming headache. "I better hang up, Mom. I must finish hanging some wet clothes. I'm glad you didn't suffer any damage to your property in the storm."

"As am I. Call me if you hear anything more about who broke the church window."

"I'll see you at church Sunday," she said, ignoring her request. They said their goodbyes, and after hanging up the phone, Nora walked across the room and plopped into the sofa. If she was weary before, she was more so now. The very idea that her mother and Arletta may have been in cahoots with the vandal who threw the rock put her on edge. She wouldn't put it past Arletta, but her mother? Surely, she wouldn't be involved, would she?

Outside, the chainsaw whirred. She stood back up and walked to the window to watch the men cut sections from the massive fallen limb, which they then hauled to the back of a pickup truck. Others busied themselves with rakes, picking up debris and stacking it into piles. There must have been at least eight volunteers, Henry right there in the midst of them. He was a good man, hardworking, kindhearted, passionate, and a lover of God's Word. Her chest pinched. There had been a constant ache there ever since she'd learned about his shocking betrayal. Try as she might, she could not rid herself of it. Neither of them had spoken much to each other that morning other than to comment about how glad they were for the workers who'd spent the night working on the electric lines. Of course, they'd put on a cheerful façade for the children and wished them all a good day as they scooted out the door to walk with the neighborhood kids to Moon School. But once they left, the silence between them mounted, and soon afterward, Henry left to go to his office.

All morning—until calling her mother—she'd busied herself by doing laundry, vacuuming the carpet, mopping the kitchen and bathroom floors, and dusting. It was amazing how adding just one extra member to the family also added to the workload. Not that it bothered her, but she'd noticed the subtle change.

She took a deep breath, recalling that she still had wet clothes in a basket in the kitchen. Thank goodness for a return of sunshine and a nice breeze for drying clothes. Now if only she could reclaim a sense of personal joy and gladness to go along with the sunny weather.

⌣

"I believe she's suspicious I had something to do with it," Florence told Arletta on the phone later that day. "Can you imagine your own daughter thinking ill of you?"

"No, I can't imagine. Of course, I only have daughters-in-law, but even they would not be so brutal."

"I didn't say she was brutal. I just said she seemed suspicious of me."

"Well, did you give her reason to be?"

"Heavens no. Why would I?"

"You wouldn't. At least, I don't think you would. Did she mention if the police have any leads? Do you think your son-in-law would ever bring up either of our names to them?"

"If he did, that would be reason enough for me to leave the church."

"You wouldn't leave Open Door, not with Nora and your grandchildren there."

"Perhaps I could convince her to come with me."

"I don't see how you'd do that. She'd never leave Henry."

"I'm not so sure. They're not getting along well."

"What makes you say that?"

"For one thing, he slept on the couch last night."

"Haw! Did Nora kick him out of the bed?"

"I have no idea. She didn't elaborated on their argument. She has grounds for leaving him, you know—biblical grounds."

"Heavens. Do you think she ever would?"

"Perhaps—if things got bad enough."

"I don't see how they could get any worse."

"Not unless she learned about another affair besides the one in Tokyo."

"What? Your son-in-law has had more than one affair? Flo, why didn't you tell me?"

"Because I didn't know about it."

"Well, when did it happen, and with whom?"

"Oh, I didn't say he had one—none that I'm aware of anyway. But you know as well as I that once a man is unfaithful, he can never again be trusted." Her heart skipped a beat at that admission, for she knew the utter truth behind the words.

"Please. Don't remind me," said Arletta. "Unfortunately, Harv had more than one woman on the side. I never told anyone, but I was plain glad when his heart gave out on him, and he passed on. I know that's a horrid thing to say, but I was good and tired of covering up for him."

"I'll never understand why you made excuses for him, Letta. You should have left him. There he was, a deacon in the church, a seemingly upstanding citizen, yet living a double life."

"Women stand by their men—through thick and thin. At least, that's what I was taught as a girl. He's been gone ten years now. Perhaps had it been now, I wouldn't have been so forgiving. At least, I got his life insurance, never mind that he spent some of our life savings on supporting some woman who quickly sold her little house and moved to Florida right after he died."

"Yes, she didn't want you laying claim to it, although had you hired an attorney, you might have been able to recoup some of that money he invested in her. After all, it was your money too."

"That would've been too disgraceful."

"I suppose. But this is the fifties. Women are at least beginning to stand up for themselves a bit more, getting out into the workforce, even going to college rather than jumping immediately into marriage like my Nora did. I always did think she was far too young. Now look at her, barely scraping by on a preacher's salary. It's just not any kind of life."

Arletta gave a yawn on the other end of the line. "Well, I certainly hope you're wrong about Henry, but you are right about one thing. Men don't often stop at just one affair. It gets in their blood, you know."

Yes, I know. I know all too well. "My father wasn't one to stay around home much. He put my mother and all my siblings through the wringer."

"Yes, you've mentioned that before. You had a difficult childhood."

"You can say that again. Church was not even in my family's vocabulary. The only place my parents faithfully attended was the corner tavern." At that, she gave an icy chuckle. "I better hang up. I must go pay the neighbor boy for cleaning my yard."

"I'll talk to you tomorrow."

"Yes, we'll talk then."

TWENTY-THREE

Let not your heart be troubled; ye believe on God, believe also on me.
—John 14:1

As the days passed, Nora and Henry slipped into a dangerous sort of passivity, neither speaking much to the other except to discuss the weather, the children's progress in school, the Sunday services, and Emiko's first real friend, a boy named Randy Gentry who lived two streets over and was also in the third grade. Henry had walked with Emiko over to the boy's house on a Saturday to meet the Gentrys and to make sure it was safe for Emiko to visit for a few hours. They were nice folks, and Randy's mother had promised Henry they would walk him back home at five o'clock. When Emiko returned, he had a rare wide smile and a carefree attitude.

The Monday after that, Emiko's cello finally arrived, giving him even more reason to smile. Rather than meeting Henry halfway to deliver it, Helen Felton had paid to have it shipped straight to his door. Henry had called to thank her, and they had talked a great deal about Emiko's adjustment. "It's coming slow but sure, Helen. We just had parent-teacher conferences last week, and his teacher told us she is thrilled with how well he's doing. We were very pleased. He excels in all his subjects, just as our other two do. The one thing she mentioned is his extreme shyness, but she is very kind and supportive and said she's been working to draw him out as much as possible." Helen had been gratified to hear it, and mentioned she was planning a trip back to Tokyo in early December to visit friends and of course her one son and his wife who had taken over the mission there. It had been pleasant talking to her again.

Everyone gathered around as Emiko and Henry unpacked the cello. Pairs of eyes gawked at its splendor when Henry at last lifted it out of its secure packaging.

"What a big guitar!" Paul exclaimed.

"It's not a guitar, dodo bird. It's a cello," Paige said.

"Well, how do ya play it?" he'd wanted to know. "It looks too big and heavy to pick up."

Henry himself wondered at how Emiko's fingers could be big enough to stretch around the bar and form the chords. But stretch they did when Emiko sat down, placed the shiny wood instrument between his spread legs, picked up the accompanying bow, and began to play a mesmerizing tune. They all listened in awe. When Henry and Nora locked eyes, he was certain he caught a glimpse of pride in her expression. It wasn't the same size cello that an average adult would play, but a smaller one to fit Emiko's age, height, and arm length. In his future, Henry envisioned taking several trips to Beerman's Music House to measure him for the next size up. The boy played well, and clearly, with his level of talent, he would continue his musical journey.

After he played a classical tune from memory, the family clapped for him. He blushed, but it was evident that the attention pleased him. "Now play us a song on the piano," Paige said.

His mouth dropped as his face flashed with pink. "I can't play the piano very well."

"What do you mean? Mommy and Daddy said you're extra good," Paige said. "I bet you play worlds better than me."

"I hear you play when you take lessons from your mom. You're good. And so is Paul. And your mom, she's better than good," Emiko said.

"Yeah, ar' mom is good. That's 'cause she took lessons when she was a little kid," said Paul. "I take lessons too, but I can't play half as good as Paige, and I don't think I play as good as Mom did when she was my age. I don't got that much talent."

"Paul Griffin, you're full of talent. But I'll admit you'd be more proficient if you practiced," Nora said.

"Maybe, but I'd rather shoot baskets."

Henry chuckled because he understood that. He'd never been musically inclined himself, and there were times he wondered if Nora wasn't almost too determined to make a pianist out of Paul. It could well be the boy took more after Henry than he did Nora when it came to musical ability.

"Come on, play us a song," Paul coaxed his half-brother.

"Yeah, play something," said Paige.

Emiko set his cello aside and wiped his palms on his pants. He turned his head and set his eyes on the piano, then let them fall to Henry. Henry gave him a reassuring nod. "No one wants to force you, Son, but we'd all like to hear you play."

Emiko looked at his lap. "I—I sometimes get sad when I play because I—I see my mother in my mind." His young voice cracked.

A hush fell over the room. Even Paul seemed to pick up on Emiko's dilemma about playing.

Nora walked over to Emiko and put her hand on his shoulder. "You know, Emiko, it's alright to think about your mom and even talk about her. I wouldn't want you to ever forget her. I happened to see a picture of her under your pillow the other day when I made your bed. I could put it in a frame for you if you'd like so it doesn't get damaged. Is that the only picture you have of her?"

"Yes. Helen might have more, but I only got one. I—I guess I would like to frame it, but can I still keep it under my pillow?"

"How about your daddy makes a shelf and fastens it to the wall right next to your pillow so you can look at it last thing before you turn off the light and first thing in the morning? Because picture frames have glass in them. I wouldn't want it to break under your pillow."

"Oh."

"That is a very good idea, Nora," said Henry, thrilled that she'd come up with the idea. "I'll build a little shelf this weekend."

"And I'll pick up a frame."

Emiko looked from Nora to Henry. "Thanks." Then to Paige and Paul, he said, "I guess I could play a song on the piano."

Paige clapped her hands. "Yay! Let's all sit down like we're at a concert."

Everyone took her advice while Emiko situated himself on the edge of the piano bench so his foot could reach the sustain pedal. Henry wondered if he might play the same number he'd performed when they first met.

Emiko placed his hands on the keyboard, swallowed once, seemed to ponder just where and how to start, and then without further hesitation, launched into a lively tune, his little fingers flying across the keys. Henry knew his mouth sagged, but it couldn't be helped. How his son could be so accomplished at this young age stumped him, and when he caught a glimpse at Nora, he knew innately she had the same thoughts. He didn't recognize the musical piece, only that it was some classical number that Nora no doubt recognized. With her glistening eyes fastened on the boy's flying fingers, Nora shook her head in wonder. As for Paul and Paige, they sat watching with wide eyes, looking thunderstruck. When Emiko finished, he promptly put his hands in his lap and hung his head. The room fell silent for all of three seconds before Paige woke everybody from their stupor with mad clapping—after which the rest joined in. At that, Emiko lifted his head and presented them with a small smile. "Thanks," he said.

"Wow, you know how to play the piano about as good as Mommy!" exclaimed Paul. Then to Nora he said as serious as an owl, "I'm quitting piano. I'd rather play basketball."

"No!" cried Emiko. "Don't quit because of me. If you quit, then I'll quit too."

"Oh, my goodness, nobody's quitting anything," said Nora. "This is not a quitting family." Her eyes lit on Henry. "Isn't that right, Henry?"

He came to life, hoping her statement held a double meaning. "You're righter than rain, Nora Griffin. Nobody under this roof quits."

⌢

A few days later, Nora walked out to get the mail. Looking over it on her walk back from the mailbox, her eyes landed on a typewritten envelope addressed to her. It wasn't her birthday, nor was she expecting any personal mail, so the envelope intrigued her, especially since its sender typed her address but included no return address. Out of habit, she glanced at the church and Henry's office window facing the road. She wondered if he'd seen her go out to the mailbox. If he had, there was no indication. There'd been a time when if he'd seen her, he would have knocked on the window to get her attention, then blown her a kiss. Not today though.

Things between them had become so strained, they hardly knew how to act around each other. It pained her, but she didn't know how to fix it. She could easily say, "I forgive you. Let's move on and forget about everything," but that was easier said than done because she *couldn't* forget about his betrayal. She wanted to, but her heart wouldn't allow it. She supposed she'd forgiven him—as best as she knew how to forgive—but she couldn't forget. And that was the problem. Because of that, there'd been no intimacy, not even a kiss, and while she longed for it, the idea didn't set well. How could it when all she ever saw were visions of him being intimate with Emiko's mother? Oh, he'd told her more than once that it had been a short-lived affair. In fact, he refused even to call it an affair, excusing his actions by blaming them on being drunk one night.

"Just one night, Nora!" he had told her. "One terrible night that I can barely remember."

But she didn't entirely believe him—and why should she? His actions had produced a child, and she could hardly believe the woman's pregnancy resulted after just one intimate rendezvous. That seldom happened.

All around her was an array of color, both in the trees and on the ground. It was about time she dragged the rake out of the back of the garage and started picking up leaves. Perhaps they would make it a family event this weekend with everyone chipping in. She stepped into her freshly cleaned house and walked to the kitchen, where she set the mail on the counter...all but the letter addressed to her. She studied it with a certain degree of angst. She immediately thought of the typed message attached to a rock that flew through the church window. Would this envelope contain a similar message? And did it come from the same individual who'd broken the window?

She gulped and slowly opened the sealed envelope, then removed a folded piece of paper. Upon unfolding it, her heart tripped. This was not a typed message, nor was it handwritten. No, this was something far more puzzling, if not fear-provoking. Someone had composed a cryptic message using words cut from a magazine and carelessly pasted to a piece of white paper.

Dear Preacher's Wife,

Don't for a minute believe your husband has only had one affair. Once a cheater, always a cheater. I'm proof! *Remember that.*

Someone who knows...

She tossed the letter down, as if holding it a second too long would scald her fingers. What did it mean, especially the sign-off? Had one of Henry's jilted lovers composed the bizarre note? And if so, what was her motive? Did she want Henry back? How long ago had he had this so-called affair? Was it with someone she knew? Oh, Lord, did the woman attend Church of the Open Door? She stared at the underlined words, "I'm proof." Nora's stomach roiled, and her face went hot, so much so that she had to go to the faucet and splash water on it.

Her mind flew in every which direction as she weighed the possibilities. She traveled back in time to past church events such as potlucks and programs where Henry had visited with any number of women. Granted their husbands were there, but perhaps they too were too naïve and trusting. Should she have kept a more watchful eye on Henry? Had he been plotting ways to get alone with various women off and on? In all their married life, she'd never been suspicious of him having an affair, but that was all before Emiko. Then there were the supposed visits Henry made to church families. What if on those nights he said he was calling on this person or that, he was really meeting up with his lover? She had never once thought to ask for proof of where he'd been—or ever asked anyone how their home visits with her husband had gone. He never invited her to go with him on those calls. Was it because he had ulterior motives? "Oh, Lord, oh, Lord," she cried.

Her chest hurt so badly that she had to clutch it with both hands. "Jesus, what shall I do? How shall I handle this? Should I show this note to Henry? Should I tell Mother about it? Should I share it with Veronica?" A dreadful notion that Veronica might know something about Henry's other affairs crept stealthily into her mind like a hideous spider. Not that Nora would ever accuse Veronica of adultery—no, never—but she might know of some other woman in Henry's life. Heaven knew he was a sight to behold, and over the years, more than one woman had commented on his good looks. She wouldn't be a bit surprised if there were women out there who envied her. Perusing the message again made her suspicious that even now something could be going on. Oh, how she detested such a repugnant thought, and yet something told her she'd been far too trusting. Hadn't she heard it said that the faithful, dutiful housewife is often the last to learn about her husband's guileful affairs because she is too busy taking care of the children and tending to the house?

"Yoo-hoo!" came the familiar voice of her mother at the front door. Florence never had been one to wait for an invitation to enter. She just gave a rap at the door, and in she walked.

"Mother!" Nora picked up the mysterious note, moved quickly around the kitchen, and nervously sought the best place to hide it. In haste, she opened the silverware drawer, which was closest, and placed it there, then, just as her mother entered the kitchen, she pushed the drawer shut and turned around, her back shoved up against it. "What brings you here?"

Florence entered, took a gander around the room, as if to search for anything out of place, and smiled as she walked to the kitchen nook and sat down. "Does a mother have to have a reason to drop in on her daughter?" She folded her hands and put them under her chin.

"No, I suppose not. It's just that the children will be home soon, and I'll be getting their after-school snack ready."

Florence quickly jumped to attention. "Well, then, I shall help you. What did you have prepared for them?"

"Nothing—yet."

While Florence advanced to the refrigerator and opened it, Nora stayed planted in front of the drawer. "Let's see here." She withdrew a container of grapes. "This will serve nicely." She opened the lid. "Are these washed?"

"Of course."

"Now then, do you have any cheese?" She bent and perused the refrigerator shelves until her eyes lit on a brick of American cheese. "I'll need to slice this." She set the cheese down next to the grapes. "Where's your cutting board, dear?"

Nora pointed at the double doors under the sink. Florence walked to the sink and retrieved the board, then returned and set it on the counter, then laid the cheese atop it. "And what about some soda crackers? Oh, I do so love soda crackers." She began opening one cupboard door after another.

"Crackers are next to the cereal boxes, Mother. Over the oven."

"Well, that's a rather high shelf," Florence complained, standing on tiptoe to open the door and snatch the box from its home. She returned to stand next to Nora. Only then did she give her a glance. "Nora, what is it? You look as pale as a summer cloud. Are you ill?"

"What? No, I'm fine. It's just that I—I wasn't expecting you."

"And my being here has given you reason to feel contrary?"

"No, not that." She relaxed her stiff shoulders.

"Then what?"

"Nothing, nothing at all." She remained planted.

"All right then, you go sit down and allow me to fix the snacks. What time will they come through the door?"

The question didn't immediately register. "What?"

"The children. When do they get home?"

Nora gave a quick glance at the teapot-shaped wall clock. "Um, they'll be home around three-thirty."

"Good. Go sit down then."

Nora stood frozen in place. "You don't have to help, Mom. I can do it. Why don't you go sit down?"

"Nonsense." She pushed her to the side and began to pull open the silverware drawer. Nora shoved it closed again. "They won't require spoons or forks."

"Goodness, aren't we touchy? Where is your cheese slicer?"

She pointed with her tipped head across the kitchen. "In the top drawer next to the stove."

From there, the women worked side by side, Nora placing crackers on a small platter, her mother slicing the cheese and laying the cut pieces next to the crackers. While they worked, Florence hummed, something Nora rarely heard her do. In fact, Florence had been a brusque and rather cold mother when Nora was a child—nothing like the easygoing, happy, and genial mothers that so many of her friends had.

"How have things been going between you and Henry?"

"The same."

"Still the same? I should think by now you two would have made up."

"It's not that simple. This is so much more than a little argument."

"Oh, I know that. A disaster is what it is, but do you see yourself moving past it?"

"I don't know. I certainly hope so."

"Well, if you need to get away for a while—to think about things— as I said before, you are certainly welcome to move in with me. The children too, of course, except for—"

Nora couldn't help her eye roll. "Emiko belongs with us, Mom, and that's that. And, again, I thank you for the offer, but I can't see myself ever leaving Henry unless—" She left the sentence unfinished.

"Unless what?"

"Well, I mean, if he ever had another affair, I'd have to think twice."

Florence put a hand on her arm. "Are you suspicious?"

"Not—not really."

"You hesitated a bit."

Should she show her the note? No, what would it accomplish except to turn her against Henry even more?

"Is everything alright? Do you worry that Henry may have been unfaithful to you on any other occasion?"

"I—have never had a reason to think so until—all this happened."

"Humph. I'll say this. You can never be too careful."

Nora's head jerked up. "What do you mean?"

Florence flicked her wrist. "Oh, nothing. Absolutely nothing. I'm sure everything is fine, and you will get through this horrid mess."

Before she could say anything else, the front door flew open, and the sounds of shoes being kicked off, jackets being hung, and excited chatter filled the house. "Is Grandma here?" asked Paul from the front door.

"I certainly am! Come and give your grandmother a hug."

All three of them walked through the arched opening, Paul and Paige leading the way, Emiko following slowly behind. Florence opened her arms wide, and Paige and Paul went in for a hug. Again, Emiko stayed back, and Nora noticed the way her mother deliberately failed to acknowledge him. She quickly moved to him and touched his arm. "How was your day today, Emiko?"

"Fine." She wanted to hug him, but that still felt awkward—almost like a privilege she had yet to earn from him.

"I'm glad. Did you make any new friends today?"

"No, just the same ones. I played with Randy at all three recesses."

"That's lovely. I'm glad you've made such a good friend. How nice it is that he lives just around the corner."

By now, Paige and Paul had wrangled out of their grandmother's possessive embrace. "What's for our snack?" Paul asked.

"You'll be happy to know I prepared it for you," Florence said. "Take the platters to the table, and I'll get your drinks. Would you like milk, water, or juice?"

"Do we got apple juice?" Paul asked, walking to the kitchen nook.

"You mean, 'Do we *have* apple juice,'" Florence corrected, scurrying to the refrigerator. "And the answer is yes, you do." She snatched the bottle from the shelf. "Now then, glasses."

"Next to the oven, upper cabinet, Mom." Nora said, crossing her arms while she watched with curiosity as Florence took this sudden interest in the children's after-school time. She took down two glasses and set them on the counter next to the juice. "Mother, you need three glasses, not two."

Florence paused as if to consider her words. "Oh! Yes, I seem to have forgotten."

A quick glance at Emiko told her he hadn't caught the deliberate oversight, and she gave a sigh of relief. What had happened to Florence Harrison to make her so cruel at times?

Just then, a childhood memory crossed her mind. Once, Nora had had a friend come over after school. She was a little seven-year-old black girl named Carlita Jones who wore her hair in two tight braids, with pink ribbons tied to the ends. She had quick brown eyes, a pretty round face, and a big toothy smile. When they walked through the door that early spring day, her mother looked horrified. She immediately told Carlita, "We don't usually have little girls like *you* in the house. Why don't the two of you go outside to play?"

Before Nora had had a chance to ask her mother why, Carlita had grabbed her hand and pulled her outside onto the porch. "Have you got a backyard?" she had asked as cheery as could be.

"Yeah, with swings and a playhouse and a ladder that goes up our apple tree."

Carlita's eyes had gone round and bright. "Who wants to play in the house anyway?"

"But I wanted to show you my doll collection."

"It's okay. Maybe some other time."

Later, Nora would learn the meaning of the word *prejudice* when she overheard her mother tell her father, "Those people should not be allowed to live in white neighborhoods. It causes nothing but strife and dissention, not to mention the ruination of otherwise lovely communities." Her father, bless his soul, had argued that God created all people equally, but that did nothing to persuade her mother to think otherwise.

Once the kids seated themselves, Florence served them their juice glasses, Emiko included, then looked at Nora. "Come, dear, rest your feet and come sit with your children."

"Thanks, Mother, but I think I'll—"

"Come on, Mommy, sit by me," said Paige, patting the seat next to her.

How could she say no to that? She gave the drawer she'd been guarding a quick glimpse and walked to the table to join the others, quite confident no one would have reason to open it.

TWENTY-FOUR

Be still, and know that I am God.
—Psalm 46:10

Henry closed his Bible and set his freshly typed sermon notes in a neat stack at the corner of his desk. He'd always been particular about straightening his office at the end of the day so it would be fresh for the following morning. He looked at his watch. It was earlier than usual for his leave-taking, but he felt confident of Sunday's sermon, and knew that with a bit more study and prayer tomorrow, he'd be set for the weekend.

He sucked in a deep breath and expelled it in one loud gush of air. Lately, he'd been doing a lot of that, taking deep breaths that came out loud and shaky. Things at home were not good, and he hadn't the slightest idea how to fix them. His father had said just yesterday that Henry needed to give the matter more time and dedicate himself to prayer and fasting. "God hears the cries of our anxious hearts, Son. Trust me on this. I've experienced His faithfulness over and over. He will work this thing out for you, and in the end, your marriage will be stronger than ever."

"I hope you're right, Dad. I'll admit I'm getting downright scared. I've taken to sleeping on the couch."

"At Nora's request?" he had asked.

"No, not really. I just don't feel like she wants me near her. I haven't even kissed her in weeks."

"Perhaps you need to do a little romancing—as in your dating days."

"Romancing? I hadn't thought of that. She might think it's corny and reject me all the more for my feeble attempts."

"You won't know till you try, right?"

"I guess you're right."

So after he had paid a visit to church members Frank and Lois Sheen, Henry had stopped at the corner flower shop, where he bought a vase filled with colorful fall flowers. He now picked it up off his desk and headed out the door, wishing Marlene a good weekend, since he wouldn't see her on Friday. "You have a lovely weekend too, Henry, and do as your father said, take your wife on a date."

"I intend to do just that, that is, if I can find a babysitter."

"Give Veronica Hardy a call. She'll gladly watch your youngsters, or at least give you the names of some trustworthy teen girls who'd like to make fifty cents."

"Good idea. I'll do that first thing in the morning. See you Sunday morning."

"You bet. I'll be praying for you."

"Thank you. I need it."

He left her then and headed for the side door. When he pushed it open, he stopped in his tracks. Great. Florence's car was in the driveway. He really couldn't stomach seeing her right now, but he could hardly go back to his office after already wishing Marlene a good weekend. What excuse would he give her for returning?

He gave his head an irritated shake and proceeded on his way. It was *his* house, and he would not allow his mother-in-law to dictate his comings and goings. If she said something contrary to him, he would just buck up and pray for divine patience. *Lord, give me strength.*

He entered by way of the side door, took two steps up, and walked into the kitchen, bouquet in hand. Swallowing hard, he donned a smile. "Hello, everyone."

"Daddy!" shrieked Paige, jumping up and running to him. "You brought flowers. Are those for Mommy?"

"Yes they are, sweet thing, but they're for everyone to enjoy."

Florence, who'd been sitting with her back to him, whirled around. "Well. Flowers. Look, Nora, isn't that lovely? What's the occasion?"

He gritted his teeth and cast Nora a glance, hoping he might earn a smile from her or a simple thank you. Instead, she gave a quiet nod and a half-smile that lacked expression.

"The flowers are beautiful, aren't they, Mommy?" said Paige, who undoubtedly sensed the tension in the room. "Where should we put them, Mommy?"

Nora shrugged. "I don't know, honey. You pick the spot."

"How about right on the kitchen nook where the sunlight will catch all the colors?" She took the vase of red, yellow, and orange chrysanthemums, pansies, and black-eyed Susans from Henry and walked to the table, then set them in the middle. Then she took a step back. "There. Isn't that perfect?"

"Yes. Quite perfect," said Florence. She gave a pained smile then looked at her watch. "Well, look at that. I must get a move on. Arletta has invited me over for supper."

"That's nice, Mother. You two enjoy yourselves."

"Oh, we always do." She stood and gave a little stretch.

Paige left Henry's side and walked to the refrigerator, then withdrew a container from the shelf. "I'm going to have some of that Jell-O Mommy made last night." She swiveled on her heel to open the silverware drawer.

"Paige, no!" Nora said, leaping off her seat and making it to Paige just as she was withdrawing a piece of paper.

"What's this?" the girl asked.

Nora snatched the paper away and hid it behind her back, then hastily turned around to face everyone.

"Good heavens, what is the ruckus?" Florence asked.

"Nothing, Mother. I thought you had to get to Arletta's house."

"I do, but what is that you're holding behind your back?"

"Yes, Nora, what is it?" Henry asked.

The boys didn't leave their seats at the table, but they looked as curious as everyone else.

"It was a note that started with 'Dear Preacher's Wife,'" said Paige. "That's all I saw, except the words were weird."

"Dear preacher's wife? Gracious, what else does it say?" asked Florence. "Read it to us."

Nora bit down on her lip, her face a picture of worry the way it went red as a berry.

Henry advanced on her and held out his hand. "Give it to me."

"No, not here."

"Fine. Somewhere else then." He looked at the children. "Your mother and I need some privacy. Paige, go ahead and dish out some Jell-O for the three of you. I know it's almost suppertime, but I think I'll be taking you out for burgers tonight so Mommy doesn't have to cook."

"Yay!" all three kids cheered.

He turned to Florence, who stood in the archway. "I think it would be best if you went home now, Florence. This is between Nora and me."

Her jaw dropped. "Well, I never!" Then to Nora, she said, "Call me tomorrow, dear." Rather than linger, she turned and marched through the living room and straight out the door, letting it bump hard against its frame on her way out.

Henry snagged Nora's arm and pulled her out of the room and down the hallway to their bedroom. Once there, he closed the door behind him and leaned against it to prevent her escape, then extended his hand, palm up. "Now then, give it to me."

"You don't have to be so bossy," she said, lifting her chin.

There went his patience again. Lord, but it was hard to keep it in tow these days. "I'm not playing games, Nora. Just give me the blasted note."

Ever so slowly, she brought her hand out and placed the note in his hand.

He began to read the thing aloud. "Dear preacher's wife, don't for a minute think…" The rest he read to himself—and as he read and reread, his anger bubbled till it reached the boiling point. "What in the name of all things holy is this?" He lifted his eyes to Nora. "Did this come in the mail?"

"Yes."

"Was there a return address?"

"What do *you* think? Is someone going to write a note like that and then be so kind as to give me her address?"

He scratched his head, his stomach starting to twist like it had when he'd read that first letter from Helen telling him he had a son. He looked at the note again. "Who would write such a thing?"

"You tell me, Henry Griffin." Her back went as straight as a pole, her chin jutting forward.

"What? You think I have a clue? What are you saying, Nora Griffin?"

She raised her blond eyebrows. "I don't know exactly, but it seems as if someone knows something."

If he'd still been in the Army, a few choice words would've flown out of his mouth. But he knew unleashing them would solve nothing. "You actually believe this ridiculous note inferring that I've had more than one affair?"

As sober as a judge, she said, "For all I know, you could be having one right now."

He put his hands on her shoulders and squeezed, tempted to shake her but refraining. "Would you listen to yourself? Look at me." She kept her eyes pointed downward. "Nora, look at me." Slowly, she lifted her head. "Would you just think back to early September, before any of this stuff happened, before Emiko? Didn't it seem to you that we had a near perfect marriage, one that others might even have envied? Did it appear to you then that I was having an affair? Don't you think if I were, there would've been some telltale signs?"

She shook her head. "I don't know, Henry. I don't know what to think. These past six weeks or so have been hard for me. First, the church window, and now this. Someone appears to know something."

"Or they're just plain tortured by the fact I had that little affair with Emiko's mother, and there's no getting past it, so they're determined to make me pay."

"It wasn't a little affair. You made a child."

"I didn't mean it the way it came out. I've told you before I didn't consider it an affair. It was more a—"

She ducked out of his clasped hands and moved away from him. "I know what you said, and I don't need you repeating it." She lowered her head and buried her face in her hands. "I'm tired of all of it, Henry. Tired. What's going to happen next? Is someone going to throw a rock through one of *our* windows? Are there going to be more notes? What and who are we dealing with?"

He went to her, and while she might not have wanted it, he wrapped her in an embrace, tucking her head under his chin. Her body began to shake, so he held her tighter. "I love you, Nora. I will never love anyone else," he whispered into her hair. "I don't know who is behind these evil events, but with God's help, we'll get through it. I know you're having a hard time, honey, and I'm sorry, but it's going to be okay. I promise you."

Tears started to soak the front of his shirt as little shudders wracked her body. He ran his hand up and down her spine, kissing the top of her head, and holding her like he would a precious jewel. "It's alright," he whispered again. He instinctively planted little kisses across her forehead and then both cheeks, then lowered his mouth to hers until their lips melded—but only briefly because she put her hands on his chest and pushed him back.

Still weeping, she tipped her head at him. "Why don't you ever invite me with you on your pastoral visits?"

"What?" Her off-the-wall question threw him a bit. "I suppose because you have to stay with the kids."

"But you could do some visits during the school day."

"Yes, I could, and I usually do, especially with the older folks who prefer I visit during the day. Why the sudden interest?"

"How do I know you're really visiting parishioners? You could be out somewhere with a woman."

"What? Are you kidding me, Nora?" He took a step back. "Who is putting these ideas into your head? Is it your mother?"

"I can think for myself, Henry Griffin. I don't need someone putting thoughts into my head."

He held the cryptic note directly in front of her. "This right here. This is an example of someone putting thoughts into your head. Ugly ones. Lies, Nora." He swept his fingers through his hair. "Do you want to go with me on my church calls? Is that it? You're welcome to if that's going to ease your mind. Today, I visited Frank and Lois Sheen. Do you want to call and ask them if that's true?"

She turned as if to walk away, but he snagged hold of her wrist. "What do you want from me, Nora? What more can I do to make you trust me?"

"Stop yelling. The children will hear."

He gritted his teeth, put his face close to hers, and lowered his voice. "I'm asking you a very sensible question."

"I. Don't. Know," she said, emphasizing each word. "All I can say is time."

"How much time? Because that is your standard answer. I'm beginning to think I need to give you a time limit."

"Or what?"

He raked his hands through his hair again. "I don't know. You tell me," he hissed.

"Again, I don't know. Just—just let me digest all this please. I just got this strange message right before Mom came over, and I haven't had time to think about it."

"What's to think about, Nora? Whoever wrote that is trying to stir up trouble. If they think they have any dirt on me, they are dead wrong. I have done nothing. There has been no other affair, not even an inkling of one. Criminy, Nora, when would I have time for an affair?" This he said in jest, but he wanted to make it extra clear. "I don't know what else I can say to you to convince you."

"I don't either."

"I'm going to pay a call on Bob and Thelma Ormston out at their farm tomorrow if you want to come along."

She bit her lip. "I don't know. Maybe."

Now Henry was just plain annoyed. So much for the whole notion of taking his wife on a date this weekend.

"I'll take the kids out for hamburgers. Do you want to come?"

"I guess I'll stay home."

"Of course you will."

"Henry, don't speak to me as if I have no reason to be upset. Can't you understand that I'm leery right now? I don't know who or what to believe anymore."

He leaned in, anger poking at his insides. "You could believe *me* for a change. Now, there's a thought."

"I would like nothing more." She still had a few tears seeping out of her eyes, and her voice trembled when she spoke, but there was nothing he could say to ease her tortured emotions.

He felt helpless, baffled—and truth was, exhausted. His shoulders raised and dropped with his deep breath. "I'll see you later then." He turned and left her standing in the middle of the room.

⌒

"She got a mystery message from someone?" asked Arletta. "What did it say?"

"I didn't see it. My son-in-law made me leave the house before I had a chance. Can you imagine?" Florence answered, still seething over Henry's dismissal of her, as if she didn't have a right to stay with her daughter. "This is between Nora and me," she said, making her voice deep to repeat his very words in a mocking tone.

"Is that what he said? In that tone?" Arletta asked.

"You bet he did. He made it sound as if I were one of his children."

"Good grief, Flo, you shouldn't have to take that."

"I know, it's disgraceful. My daughter was visibly upset and needed her mother, but, oh no, he wasn't having any of it."

"Did you at least get a peek at the note?"

"Not really, but I don't think it was handwritten."

Arletta's brow scrunched. "What makes you say that?"

"Because Paige said the words looked weird. Don't worry, I'll ask Nora to show it to me the next time I see her. From a distance, I only got a glimpse of it."

"Hm. How strange. Did they ever get a lead on who threw that rock through the window?"

"Not that I've heard. Nora and I didn't talk about that. I imagine there's a link between the two incidents though."

"Like the same person being involved in both cases, you mean?"

"Wouldn't you think so?"

"I suppose I would. With nothing to go on and no witnesses, I imagine the police have stopped looking for the rock thrower. I wonder if either of them will report this mystery message to the police."

"Oh, I rather doubt it. It's too personal, don't you think?"

"Ah, yes, wouldn't want the police thinking the reverend is up to something suspicious," said Arletta. "I don't think they'll get involved until the next public incident takes place."

"Do you think something else will happen?"

Arletta raised her eyebrows. "Of course it will, Flo. You should know that."

Florence squirmed under her friend's scrutiny. She picked up her water glass and took a few nervous sips. "The pork chops are quite scrumptious, Letta."

Arletta sipped too, her blue-green eyes fixed on Florence, the crinkles around them accented by her purple eye shadow. She set the glass down. "I'm glad you are enjoying the meal. Next week, your house, correct?"

"Absolutely. I think I'll have baked chicken and mashed potatoes."

"Aren't you little Miss Plan-Ahead? Perhaps we'll have even more tidbits of information to share, right?"

Florence picked up her napkin and nervously dabbed at her mouth. "Yes, perhaps."

TWENTY-FIVE

I have strength for all things in him that gives me power.
—Philippians 4:13

Nora rearranged her music on the church piano, attaching paperclips to the hymns they were singing that morning, dragging the trio number she and two other ladies were singing just before the message off to the side, and adjusting the piano bench so that it was a comfortable distance from both the written music and the foot pedals. Folks moseyed from the narthex into the sanctuary, and she started to play a rousing song to get everyone in the Sunday morning spirit. Too bad she had not found herself in a Sunday morning spirit for several weeks now. Fine example she set for the folks of Open Door. Living the life of a pastor's wife could be a lonely one because she didn't feel safe bearing her soul for fear of exposing too much. You never knew who to fully trust. There were exceptions, of course. Her best friend Veronica knew and understood Nora's need for a confidante, having grown up a preacher's kid and remembering her mother's sense of loneliness. Oh, folks were always plenty friendly to the preacher's wife, but for some reason, they set her on a pedestal and expected perfection. The preacher's family had to set the example for good, clean, and upright living. That included ensuring the children all behaved in a proper manner, which could sometimes be a challenge with Paul. Now, with the addition of Emiko, Nora knew all eyes were on her—and they were watching closely.

She tried to get in the right frame of mind as she looked across the platform at Iva Herman. Iva's sprained ankle still bothered her, but the woman was determined to play her beloved organ, so she'd practiced at home using her one good foot, making it literally fly from one end of the floor pedals to the other in the most magical way. Oh, what joy it brought Nora to have Iva back on that organ bench! Nora caught the woman's eye now, nodded her head in three/four time, and then launched into their first pre-service hymn of praise, "I Sing the Mighty Power of God." While playing, Nora gazed out at the incoming church attendees as they looked for their favorite seats. Shirley Roberts and her four children made their way to their usual pew on the piano side, meaning Fred had not accompanied them, as he preferred to sit in the back. Henry, bless his heart, had invited Fred to coffee last week, but he declined, saying he was busy that day. More likely, he wasn't ready for meeting the pastor one on one, particularly when church attendance was a rarity for him. Nora remembered Shirley's telling her about his excessive drinking and had mentioned it to Henry. He had said he would continue trying to meet with him, but there was only so much he could do.

As usual, the three Griffin children situated themselves next to their Grandma and Grandpa Griffin. Her mother sat on the opposite side of the church next to Arletta. Lately, the two were nearly inseparable, making Nora wonder if they were up to something. She prayed not.

They moved into the second verse and then the third. People were still seating themselves, visiting with other congregants, and waving or smiling at friends. It did warm Nora's heart at how the majority of folks accepted Emiko. A few had even introduced themselves to him. There was also that faction of folks who walked past him as if he didn't exist. She prayed this was because they simply had no idea what to say to him rather than some animosity on their part. A few people had given him little gifts, such as toy cars, storybooks, a winter hat and scarf set, and a new pair of socks. Emiko always put his hands together and gave a little bow of his head when he said thank you. People often commented on his good manners and handsome features, often also mentioning how much he resembled Henry. One Sunday after church, a woman had an awkward slip of the tongue when she remarked that Emiko's mother must have been a beautiful woman. When she discovered Nora standing immediately behind her in the narthex, she blushed, then tried to cover her blunder by changing the subject. Soon afterward, she made her exit to the parking lot.

They finished out the rousing hymn just as Herb VanOordt stepped up to the podium. He made a few announcements, then drew special attention to the lovely new stained glass window Frank Sheen had crafted and installed just that week. Folks applauded for Frank's generosity in replacing it. The mention of the new window served as a reminder to Nora—and no doubt to everyone else—of the yet-unsolved vandalism. She cast a quick look over top of the piano at Henry. His eyes were fastened on his shoes, but then he looked up once the applause finished. He had to be awash with confusing thoughts and emotions. Her own insecurity and inability to move forward didn't help, she knew. What sort of wife was she anyway? Certainly not a supportive one—at least not on the inside. The way she appeared to others was another story. She was quite certain folks thoroughly believed she'd forgiven and forgotten, and if she could, then certainly so could they.

Herb announced the first congregational hymn, "Come Thou Fount of Every Blessing," and invited the congregation to stand. They did so, and the morning service on the second Sunday of November commenced.

⁓

"Fine message today, Son," Lester Griffin told Henry after dinner that day. They had just finished dessert, and Lillian had sent the three kids outside to play while she and Nora went to the kitchen to wash and dry the dishes. The men left the dining room and moved down the hall to the first door on the right, Lester's office. They seated themselves in two occasional chairs.

"Thanks, Dad, but every Sunday, I feel a little less confident than I felt the week before. I don't know if it shows or not."

"You're a fine preacher, and you're always very prepared. I don't think most people would notice your feelings of uncertainty. God is on your side, Henry. He continues to use you even as you experience unwanted trials."

Henry smirked. "Hmm, now if I could just get my wife on my side, everything would be great." He immediately regretted his sarcastic remark. He didn't really want to hash things out with his dad about matters concerning his marriage. He'd already done that, and nothing had changed. "Before you ask, I did buy her flowers, but things went sour after that, so the time never felt right for asking if she wanted to go on a little date. It's to the point now where I don't know what we'd even talk about."

Lester gave his head a little shake, his eyes glistening with what looked like sympathy, something Henry neither needed nor wanted. "Don't lose hope. You have a strong marriage."

"I'm glad you think so."

They sat in a few moments of silence. "Emiko seems to be adjusting," Lester said finally.

It felt good to switch topics. A smile formed. "I see evidence of progress, Dad. We finally got him to play the piano and his cello for us. He's been sitting down at the piano almost every day now. It's amazing to hear him play, Dad. Sometimes, I can't believe he's my son. I don't know where he acquired such talent."

"Perhaps his mother was musically inclined."

"I don't know. If she was, she never mentioned it to me."

Lester glanced down at his trousers and picked at a piece of lint, then lifted his head and tilted it to one side while studying Henry with particular interest. "Did you think about Emiko's mother much when you came back to the States?"

The question was unexpected. The last person Henry wanted to talk about was Rina, and the last person he thought would encourage it was his dad.

"I'm sorry to be nosy, Son. I can almost read your mind. But it's something I'm curious about because as I recall, when you returned from Japan, you seemed quite changed to me. Almost distant, resolute, closed off. I blamed it on the war, but now I wonder if part of you wasn't thinking about her."

"I understand why you want to know. It was a long time ago, and mostly I've put it all behind me. Buried it, I suppose."

"Don't you think talking about it is necessary if you ever want to mend things with your wife? I mean, if you want to fix your marriage, you have to fix yourself first."

"That's true, but I feel like when I repented of my sins to the Lord, He forgave me, I was done with the whole affair, and I could move on. During that time of repentance and renewal, God called me into the ministry. I obeyed, and here I am. Did I think about Rina when I got home? Of course, but my feelings were ones of remorse for what I'd done with her. To her. Never feelings of love or longing."

"And you never once thought to bring any of this up with Nora?"

"No, Dad. It wouldn't have accomplished anything. It would have killed her."

"More than it's killing her now?"

Henry ran his hand down his face, feeling the beginnings of beard growth even though he'd shaved that morning. After a moment of reflection, he said, "Truthfully, I don't know. I've gone over this a million times, wondering why I didn't tell her. I guess I always hoped I'd never have to, but that was before I found out about Emiko. Our sins do have a way of finding us out, don't they?"

Lester gave a tiny, knowing grin. "That's what God's Word tells us."

Nora and Lillian had a very easy relationship, vastly different from the one Nora had with her own mother. Her mother-in-law put no expectations upon her, didn't force her to prove anything, or make her follow a particular set of rules in order to gain her approval. Truth was, from the time Henry had first introduced her to his parents, she'd known she and Lillian would be fast friends. She simply had a way of making Nora feel comfortable and accepted. So when Lillian asked her how things were going between her and Henry while they stood next to each other at the sink, Lillian washing, Nora drying, the words tumbled out of her with hardly any hesitation.

"Not the best, Mom. I'm sorry to have to say that. I can't get past my terrible hurt, and Henry can't get over the fact that I'm stuck in what I'm sure he thinks is self-pity. He wants everything back to normal, and he wants it now. I do too actually, but I can't just flip a switch and pretend. He wants intimacy in the worst way, and I do not."

Lillian nodded her head. "Everyone is different in the way they react to these situations, but I must say I think I'd feel like you do. My son is foolish to think you should be eager to jump right back into an intimate relationship—if indeed those are his thoughts. I love my son very much, but I'm very disappointed in him for what he did. The one positive from all of it is Emiko."

"Yes, Emiko is a fine boy, and I care very much for him."

"You don't resent him then?"

"Emiko? Heavens no. I've thought from the start that he is not responsible for any of it. To begin with, I wasn't excited about meeting him, much less bringing him into our home, but when it came right down to it, I knew it was the only answer."

"Yes, it was the best thing you could have done for him, and I commend you for it."

"I thought the extra child would significantly change our budget, but it hasn't. Paul is probably the most affected because he has to share his room, but so far, the three children have gotten along well with only a few little snares here and there."

"That's a relief."

They finished the dishes, and Nora hung up the towel. "I'll go wipe off the table, Mom." She took the dishcloth in hand and walked to the dining room. Lifting the vase of fresh cut roses in the middle of the table, she gave a sweep of the wet cloth under it, then set it back in place. "I've apologized to her till I'm blue in the face, Dad. What more can I do?" Her hand froze in place as her ears sharpened. "You have to be patient, Son."

She should have instantly returned to the kitchen, but instead, she moved closer to her father-in-law's office, where the two men were conversing. The office door was ajar, so their voices carried.

"I'm sure she wants nothing more than to live in harmony with you," Lester said.

"Sometimes I wonder if she doesn't enjoy holding this thing over my head. It puts her in control."

Was *that* what he thought? Ire rose as she bit down on her lip. Good grief. She was not the type to hold a grudge for the sake of it, or to make somebody suffer while she took her sweet time forgiving their wrongdoing. She swallowed hard, wishing she could tie up all the answers into a pretty bow, but knowing it wasn't that easy. Why couldn't he see her side of things?

"I'm sure that's not the case," said Lester.

"Seems to me it is."

"Are you still sleeping on the couch?"

"Darned tootin'."

"At her request?"

"Of course."

That did it. Nora had never once requested that. She stepped closer, pushed the door open, and stood in the entryway. "I beg your pardon! When did I demand you go sleep on the sofa? You chose that solution all on your own, Henry James Griffin!"

Henry whirled around at the sound of her voice. "You've been eavesdropping?"

"The door was open partway, and you were pretty loud. Don't you think your voices carried? Now tell your dad the truth. It was your idea to move to the living room."

"You wanted it."

"I *never* told you that. I don't think your sleeping on the couch is going to fix anything."

Both spoke in frenzied tones.

"Now, listen…" Lester said.

"Well, how is my sleeping in the same bed with you going to fix anything when you won't even let me touch you?"

That downright embarrassed her. How dare he shout at her in her father-in-law's presence—and about such a personal matter? Yes, she and Lillian had talked about it, but she didn't want her father-in-law knowing such details.

"What's going on?" Lillian asked from behind.

Without turning, Nora fixed her eyes on Henry while answering. "Your son is spewing untruths."

Henry stood, his face red with anger. "I am doing no such thing."

"Yes, you are, and you know it!"

Just then, the front door burst open. "He hit me! Emiko hit me," they heard Paul wail.

"No, I didn't!"

"Did so!"

Lillian made it to the front door first, followed quickly by the others. For now, the dispute between Nora and Henry was over.

"Alright now, who can tell me what happened?" Lillian asked upon reaching the youngsters.

"I was swinging on the rope when Emiko pulled me off. He said it was his turn, but I only just got on 'cause Paige was taking too long."

"No, I wasn't."

"Were too. After I fell off, Emiko hit me."

"After *you* threw dirt in my face," said Emiko.

"I didn't throw dirt in your face. At least not on purpose."

"I saw you pick it up."

"But I didn't mean to hit you with it. I was throwing it at the tree," said Emiko.

"What tree?" asked Paul.

"Now, now," said Lillian, "This kind of arguing will get us nowhere."

"Yeah, you sound like Mommy and Daddy," said Paige.

Nora gave a little gasp as her throat clogged. The very notion that the children had overheard Henry and her bickering put a weight of shame on her shoulders. She stole a glance at Henry and their gazes locked for a brief instant.

"I'm sorry you overheard us. It's true, Mommy and I have had a few quarrels lately."

Nora sucked in a breath and straightened her shoulders, guilt for the part she'd played weighing heavily on her heart.

"We're working on some issues that are just between us," Henry said.

"Yeah, and they're about me," said Emiko.

"No, they're not," said Nora, wanting to reassure him.

The boy hung his head. "I shouldn't have come to live with you."

"What? No, we're glad you did, Son," said Henry.

"And so are Grandpa and me," Lillian chimed.

"Now then, how about you three apologize to each other?" said Nora.

"We don't really got anything to apologize for," Paul said with a smile. "We heard you guys fightin', so we decided to fake ar' own fight so you'd see how silly you sound."

All three children burst out into big grins. Emiko lifted his head and let out a tiny giggle.

"We played a trick on ya," said Paul, his hazel eyes sparkling with merriment.

"What?" Nora said. Her brows snapped together. "You didn't."

"Yes, we did," said Paige.

"Well, I'll be," said Lester. "Aren't you the little connivers?"

The youngsters giggled, as if they were the cleverest people. Nora shook her head at them and put her hands on her waist. She and Henry locked gazes again, he with lifted brows and she with a tiny smile.

"I think it's you two who should apologize," said Paige.

"Yeah," said Paul. "Right here and now." Sometimes the words that came out of his seven-year-old mouth were more than either Nora or Henry could handle.

"Now, now," said Lester, butting in much to Nora's relief. "One can't force apologies. They have to come from the heart."

"Grandpa's right," said Lillian.

The children went quiet, but their eyes said it all as they roved from one parent to the other. "Alright, alright, I agree with you kids. Mommy and Daddy have been less than considerate of each other." He trained his eyes on Nora, and her heart stood still. "I'm sorry, Nora. I'm sorry for all of it."

She gave a slow nod. "I'm sorry as well, Henry."

"But did you mean it with your heart?" Paul asked.

Nora's face went as hot as her first cup of morning coffee. She gave a nod of her head. "I'm sorry that—there—has been so much fighting."

"There now," Lillian hastened, giving a little clap of her hands. "Isn't that better, children? They have both said their apologies, and now it is time for you to stop all your worrying."

"Grandma's right," said Lester. He winked and crouched down to their levels. "And grandmas are always right." He gave all three of them a gentle poke on the tips of their noses. "Now, who wants a lollypop? I bought one for each of you when I went to the hardware yesterday."

"Me!!!" they all squealed, as they followed their grandpa to the kitchen pantry, where Henry's parents always kept some sort of treat for special occasions.

Lillian gave both Henry and Nora two uplifted brows, her eyes a scrutinizing three-second stare with no words needed, then turned and left them both standing there alone.

Henry looked down at Nora, and she dared look up. In that single moment, an unexpected flicker of something washed over her, something odd and strangely revealing. She began to recognize the hurt in his eyes for what it really was—not a façade or a pretense, but something deep and genuine. From the furthest part of her soul, she asked the Lord to renew her love for her husband, for she realized then that it had waned some, and the very notion of it terrified her. No words passed between them because she didn't dare utter any.

"We should probably go home now," he said. "I have to get things ready for church tonight."

Within the hour, the family piled into the car and hit the road, the children's moods lighter and Nora's heart beginning to see a glimmer of something hopeful just over the horizon.

TWENTY-SIX

Forbearing one another, and forgiving one another, if any should have a
complaint against any; even as the Christ has forgiven you, so also do ye.
And to all these add love, which is the bond of perfectness.
—Colossians 3:13–14

Sunday night's church attendance was higher than it had been in weeks past. There were of course the faithful few who wouldn't think of missing: Edgar and Rose Warner, Herb and Marie VanOordt, Louis and Ila Flood, Richard and Dorothy Baker, and Bill and Sue Wittmyer. They were longstanding members of Open Door—in fact, they comprised the first congregation in the former church building, an old one-room schoolhouse. Herb VanOordt had been instrumental in raising the necessary funds to build the church where they now worshipped. While he was the church's song leader, he also made it his duty to get involved in matters of maintenance and upkeep. At times, he rubbed folks the wrong way with his somewhat bossy nature. It seemed like he always wanted to undermine Morris Grayson's decisions as the chairman of the church elders. For that reason, Henry had been forced to remove Herb from the board a year ago.

Among others in attendance were the Parkers and their four boys, Henry's parents, Nora's mother, and Arletta, who rarely missed services despite her many complaints. Henry smiled and nodded at Florence, who sat in her usual pew with a fraught-filled face, no doubt looking for something with which to find fault. He took pride in the fact that most of what she did and said rolled off his back. Even the accusation she'd made to Nora earlier of him possibly having other affairs had eventually fallen from his shoulders. It did no good to harbor resentment where she was concerned. She was who she was, and he supposed she would never change. To his surprise, Fred and Shirley Roberts slipped into the back pew with their four youngsters at about the midway point of his sermon, but then slipped out before he gave his final amen. He was almost sure no one else had seen them, as they'd been as quiet as mice coming and going. Even the children hadn't made a peep. It was a mystery to him why they'd shown up at all, but he didn't have much time to consider it.

Usually, his evening sermons were a continuation of that morning's message, although shorter in length. He usually took the key points of the previous message and elaborated, supporting his main ideas with additional Scripture and illustrations. Folks often commented how his evening sermons brought more clarity and understanding to the specific topic at hand. He had titled that morning's message "The Rewards of Faith," and listed several blessings that come from living a faith-filled life. The evening message concentrated on Hebrews eleven, which highlighted several men and women of the Bible who had great faith. It seemed to be a topic that resonated with folks if the comments he got after the service were an indication.

That night, Nora actually suggested Henry stop sleeping on the couch, so without arguing, he returned to their bed. There was no touching, but neither was there any additional arguing. They even had a decent conversation, discussing the evening service and the brief appearance by the Roberts family.

The two had also talked about their time at his parents' house that day and even shared a laugh about how the children had faked their spat in hopes of making an important point to them. "Good little actors, they are," said Henry.

"The craftiest," said Nora. "They did get our attention though. We must be more mindful of the children when in the middle of an argument."

"Or we could just agree to stop fighting altogether," he said, giving her a tiny nudge in the arm.

She giggled. "Forever? That sounds like a pipe dream."

"It doesn't have to be."

They both quieted for a full minute, then soon resumed chatting about more superficial topics. Henry didn't mind. At least it was a start in the right direction. After a time, they said goodnight, and turned on their sides, backs to each other. He didn't drift off to sleep until he heard her breathing fall into a slow, steady rhythm. *Lord, please continue Your healing work in our marriage.*

In the middle of the night, Henry awakened to the squeal and screech of tires as a vehicle hurried up Wood Street. He instinctively threw off the covers and sat on the edge of the bed to assess his surroundings. Yes, he was in his own bed and not on the couch, and, yes, the sound of squealing tires had awakened him. He stood up and walked to the window, pulling back the curtain to peer outside, first at his own front yard and then over at the church yard. From where he stood, and from what he could see in the moonlight and with the glow of the streetlamp, nothing appeared out of order.

"What are you doing, Henry?" Nora asked in a groggy voice.

He turned. "Oh, I heard a noise. It woke me, so I decided to get up and check. I guess I'm being paranoid, but I think I'll take a walk outside just to make sure everything is fine."

"What sort of noise did you hear?"

"Squealing tires."

"Oh, no. I hope nothing's happened."

"It was probably some careless teenage driver. The cemetery is across the road, and you know how the kids like to hang out at the back of the property and smoke cigarettes and do whatever else that fascinates them."

"Hm." She lay her head back against the pillow, and a streak of moonlight washed across her face, making her the prettiest sight he'd ever seen. He wanted to tell her, but right now, that shriek of tires had him curious. He hastened into a pair of pants, donned a long-sleeved shirt, then stepped into some loafers and shuffled out of the room and down the hallway, picking up a flashlight from the table next to the door.

Once outside, he hugged himself against the sudden blast of cold air. It wouldn't be long before the first snowfall. He shuddered at the thought and crossed the yard in the direction of the church, his feet striding through a mound of fresh-fallen leaves. Just two days ago, he and some volunteers had raked all the leaves into a pile, and then had a bonfire, but now he was wading through a mountain more of them. As he walked, he remained alert and glanced around. It was a still night, with no sounds except for the crunching of dead leaves under his feet and a couple of barking dogs. Now and then a car whizzed by, but aside from that, there wasn't much happening. A full moon and a trillion and one stars glistened in a clear, coal-black sky. Mindlessly, he flashed his light around the churchyard. Seeing nothing, he started to turn—until something caught his eye. Some sort of movement in a bush tucked up against the front of the church. What was it? He shivered from head to toe. "Who's there?" he called. "I don't want any trouble. I'm the minister of this church. If you have need of something, come on out. Maybe I can help."

Of all things, a raccoon emerged and sauntered across the yard toward Wood Street. Henry felt like a fool for having talked to the scavenger. He glanced up at the church's steeple, then moved closer to the big, red-brick church. Its five white pillars connecting the veranda to the peaked overhang glowed in the moonlight. He shined his light up the five cement steps and on to the veranda. Although the overhang cast shadows, he could see some dark splotches on the white double front doors. What in the name of heaven? A dark feeling of dread rushed over him. More vandalism? He quickly mounted the steps and stepped up to the doors with his flashlight. His heart dropped, and he fell to his knees as he read the ill-shaped words smeared on with black paint:

CAUTION!!! A fornicator preaches here!

⌒

Two officers of the law parked their cars in front of the church, their intense red warning lights flashing, and talked to Henry in the parking lot. Nora stayed in the house and watched from the window, her nerves jumping with angst. It was three-fifteen in the morning, and yet a few house lights came on as neighbors peered out of their windows or stood outside their front doors to see if they could figure out what was happening at Church of the Open Door. Nora wanted answers too, but as she stood in her dark living room with only one table lamp on the other side of the room dimly glowing, staring out her picture window, she realized she hadn't a clue. Who would be sending mysterious notes, casting rocks through church windows, and now painting hideous messages across the church doors? Although they hadn't notified the police about the cryptic message Nora had received in the mail, Henry told her before calling the police that he needed to show it to them. Agreeing, she had gone to her dresser and retrieved it from the top drawer, then walked back to the living room and handed it to him. "This is getting out of hand, Henry, and no telling what might happen next."

"I know, honey." Worry lines etched his face as he spoke in low tones. "I can't bear the thought of anything happening to you or the kids."

"Don't worry," she had said. "God will take care of us." She had wanted to fall into his arms then and there, as fear started wrapping itself around her chest, but she resisted the urge. She had to keep her head about her in case one, or all, of the kids came out of their rooms to see what all the commotion was about.

Now, she stood there praying for God's protection and asking Him to give Henry a special sense of His presence in the middle of the turmoil. The police had been there for at least a half hour or more, writing notes in their pads, then traversing all around the churchyard with bright flashlights. She really didn't think any harm would come to her or the children, as most of the anger behind these incidents seemed to be aimed at Henry. "Keep him, safe, Lord. What would I do without him?"

The question pounded hard against her. What *would* she do without him? He had always been their rock, even in difficult times, and yet in this time of personal upheaval, she had shut him out, keeping her distance as she sorted through her myriad feelings, and resisted allowing him to get too close. Now she wondered what she would ever do if something happened to him. Wasn't it time to give him her full support? Yes, the hurt of what he'd done early in their marriage still taunted her, and the fact he'd had years to contemplate his wrongdoing while she'd had mere weeks still exasperated her, but at some point, she would have to let go and let God take control. How many times had she asked God to direct her path, yet continued hanging on to her sin of unforgiveness? Yes, he'd wronged her, but he'd also pleaded with her to give him a chance to make things right. Good grief, how could she expect God to work in her life if she wasn't willing to surrender everything into His loving, caring hands? Hadn't He forgiven her, washed her own sinful slate clean as a young teen? It seemed the least she could do was settle matters with Henry so they could make a fresh start.

Tears of remorse dripped down her cheeks, tears she hadn't expected to come, not tonight when there were policemen standing out in the church parking lot, not now when she still had no answers regarding the strange message inferring that Henry had had other affairs, and not now when she still had hurt feelings flowing through her veins for what he'd done some nine years ago with a young Japanese woman named Rina. But there it was—all in front of her, and the more she thought about it, the more the hurt and betrayal began to wash away—like a refreshing rain really. "Lord, please forgive me for my stubbornness. I'm sorry, Lord." She looked upward at the dimly lit ceiling where shadows flitted from that single glowing lamp—and gave thanks.

When at last Henry came back through the door, all she did was stand there at the window and stare at him. The piano and a chair stood between them. "The police have no answers, of course," he said, kicking off his shoes in the entryway and closing the door. "But then I didn't expect them to." His voice carried a tinge of discouragement. "They searched all around looking for clues, but a lot of good it did them. Too bad the raccoon didn't hang around to put in his two cents. He probably saw the whole thing."

"What are you talking about?"

He gave a weak laugh. "Just a little critter that happened to be in the area when I went over there. Anyway, when the police left, I saw the guy who lives in that two-story brick home at the corner flag them down, so they pulled over and talked to him. I have no idea what he had to say. For all I know, it was completely unrelated because they didn't bother to come back and tell me what he said." He breathed deep and shook his head, his shoulders slightly sagging. "I don't know what to make of all this, Nora. It's got me fairly concerned, even though I know God's in control. What really bothers me is that I am the one who brought all this on our family and our church. If only I had…" He didn't finish, just scrunched his face until his eyes welled up, the lamp's glow revealing a sparkle of dampness on his cheek. That did it. She walked around the chair and came face to face with him, taking both his hands in hers. He didn't resist, just looked down at her with shiny eyes.

"I don't know how you intended to finish that sentence, Henry, but I don't want to hear it. What's done is done, and, best of all, we have Emiko."

His jaw went slack. "Do you really mean that?"

She squeezed his roughened hands. "Yes, I really mean it. He's a fine boy. He is making a good adjustment, I think, and the kids are getting along. I recognize it's still the honeymoon period, and any day now, things could go a little haywire. After all, they are siblings. But we'll deal with their spats when they come."

"You have always been naturally generous and caring where others are concerned. You amaze me, Nora."

"Oh, Henry, there is nothing amazing about me. In fact, let's drop that part of the conversation. I'm just glad you're alright."

"Me? I'm not worried about myself. It's everyone else."

"The rest of us, including the church folks, will be fine. It's you I'm concerned about. These threats are no laughing matter, and what you said earlier—about not knowing what you'd do if anything happened to me or the kids, well, it got me to thinking."

"About what?" A muscle in his jaw twitched when she looked up at him, her hands still squeezing his, and her heart pittering as if she were a teenager.

"The truth is, I'm the one who wouldn't know what to do without *you*. You've always been there for me and the kids, Henry."

He bent and kissed her forehead. "It's my job."

"And it's my job to support you—for better or for worse. I think I forgot that vow for a bit there."

He frowned. "I forgot the most important vow of all, remember? And for that, I'm thoroughly ashamed and full of regret."

She withdrew one hand and put two fingers to his lips. "While you were outside, I asked the Lord to forgive me my stubbornness. I held on to my anger a bit too long."

"No, you were entitled to it. You've been deeply hurt."

"And I'm letting that go. As of tonight, it's over and done, Henry. I'm letting go—and letting God." She said this with a shaky whisper, her own eyes beginning to tear up. "There will still be times I'll think about it."

"I wouldn't blame you for that."

"But I have forgiven you. I want you to be assured of that. And something else. I know you've been faithful to me over the years, except for your one night of drunkenness in Japan. I always knew that. I don't know why I allowed any doubts to seep in."

"Someone wants you to believe the lies, and it seems they'll go to any length to do it."

"Well, they can try all they want. I'm determined to ignore their attempts. I am serious, Henry. I've made up my mind. Our enemy Satan wants to kill and destroy our marriage, and it seems he is putting someone to work in hopes of doing just that. He, or *she*, also wants to kill our church community, where we have always mutually loved, encouraged, blessed, and nurtured each other. But First John, chapter one, verse seven says if we walk in the light as He is in the light, we have fellowship with one another, and the blood of Jesus, His Son, purifies us from all sin. The enemy wants us, Henry, but if we stay true to our Lord and Savior, God will thwart his evil attempts."

Henry blinked twice and stood braced and steady, then placed both hands on her shoulders, giving them a gentle squeeze. "I love it when you preach to me, Nora."

She reached up and gently cupped one side of his whiskered jaw. He instinctively leaned into it. Her lower lip trembled, as emotion spilled out of her. "I do love you, Henry. With all my heart. I want you to know that."

He lowered his head till their lips nearly touched, then he whispered back, his warm breath caressing her face. "I love you more than you know, Nora Griffin." They slipped into a rather tenuous embrace, holding each other loosely at first because of the tumult of emotions that had gathered in their hearts and souls these past two months. The loneliness she had felt, the grief, the rage, the deep pain, all melded together like cloud to cloud, then drifted off. When he touched his lips to hers, it began like a slow dance where neither dared make a misstep. But soon afterward, their embrace became a sort of desperate reclaiming of what each had lost. She wrapped her arms around his neck, and he drew the full length of her up close to him. They kissed with the passion of teens, breathless and unceasing, yet still questioning. She made a tiny sound in her throat, and he tightened his embrace, kissing her now with an urgency that came about as a result of weeks of self-denial. After a time, they withdrew for no other reason than to take in some much-needed air.

"Oh, Henry, I love you so much, and I missed you. Truly, I did."

"I love you too. Tell me again if you don't mind."

"I love you—and I will until forever."

He hugged her so tightly that her feet left the floor. "I was beginning to think you were never going to say it again."

"I suppose I had to sort things out, but earlier today at your parents' house, after the kids' charade, and then your dad taking them off to the kitchen, and your mom leaving us standing there alone, I sensed the Holy Spirit's prodding that it was time to let go of my anger. When I inwardly confessed it was time, it just started rolling off me, Henry. And then tonight—tonight—watching you stand out there with the police and that news reporter from the *Muskegon Chronicle* and I guess answering question after question, oh dear, it broke my heart. I know how concerned you are about what's happened in our marriage and what could potentially happen to our church family, and I want you to know I realize now just how important it is that I support you through it all. Oh, honey, I never want to have another fight like this one. Never."

He smiled. "I promise you we won't."

They kissed again—unreservedly and deep. After a minute, they pulled back and let their eyes rove over the other's face.

"What did the news reporter ask you out there? I saw him taking notes."

He shook his head. "Just the usual questions. He wanted to know if we had any idea who would do such a thing, why they would paint the note across the door, what may have led up to it. I told him I had little to offer him because I didn't want to dredge up the whole sordid story. The police told him they had no real leads. Both the police and the reporter took photos of the message on the door, so I suspect that will be in the paper tomorrow."

"Oh, Henry. I'm so sorry."

"It's in God's hands, honey. There's no point in worrying about the outcome because it's out of our control. All I can do is admit my wrong when asked, share the gospel, and talk about God's redemptive power and forgiveness."

She smiled up at him. "I'm so proud of you." She stood on tiptoe and kissed him square on the mouth. He reciprocated in full, his arms tightly wrapped, his hands splayed across her back.

"Shall we go back to bed?" he murmured.

Her heart thumped so hard she felt its pulse race in her neck. "I think it's time we do."

"Come here then." Grinning, he picked her up and carried her, one strong arm around her body, the other around her legs.

"Henry!" She looped her arms around his neck. "Don't drop me," she said, giggling.

"Have a little faith, my darling."

Down the hall they went. At the bedroom doorway, he paused. "I forgot to turn off the lamp in the living room."

"Put me down and go do it."

He chuckled. "I won't argue." He took her to the bed and lowered her, then used his pointer finger when he spoke. "Don't move."

She giggled again despite her quaking heart. "I won't." He started to walk away. "And, Henry," she said.

He stopped and turned. "Yes?"

"Hurry back."

TWENTY-SEVEN

Let the wicked forsake his way, and the unrighteous man his thoughts:
and let him return unto the Lord, and he will have mercy upon him;
and to our God, for he will abundantly pardon.
—Isaiah 55:7 (KJV)

Last night, the police had given Henry permission to repaint the front doors, so he set to work on it at first light. Fortunately, the church's utility closet contained brushes and pails of paint for touch-ups. The way news traveled, though, he may as well have waited. One by one, folks stopped by the church to verify the rumor they'd heard and view the damage. He'd called Morris Grayson as early as he could and the church elders' chairman had notified the rest of the board. They no doubt told their wives, who probably started a chain of phone calls that buzzed through the congregation.

Henry sat on the front steps, reading his Bible while waiting for the first coat of paint to dry, when Florence showed up. No surprise there. Naturally, she had to inspect the damage and make the comment that none of this would've happened had he not created such a scandal.

Nora had gone to run some errands, and thankfully, no one else was at the church, so Henry felt free to speak his mind. "Florence, tell me something, would you?" He set his Bible aside and stood to his full height, which was several inches taller than his mother-in-law. Weighing his words before speaking, he asked, "What is it I did to make you hate me so?"

Her mouth dropped. "Why! Whatever gave you the idea I hate you? I don't hate anyone."

He didn't give her an immediate response, just tilted his face at her and shifted the bulk of his six-foot-two frame to the other foot.

She gave a loud sniff. "I suppose I—have given you the impression—over the years."

He tilted his head the other way now, waiting for more from her.

"I think you're a fine man, Henry."

"But?" By gum, he was not going to let her off the hook. He'd done that enough over the past fifteen years.

She took to wringing her hands. He'd put her in an awkward position, but blast it all, he wanted answers.

"I don't know why you keep staring at me," she said, tipping her chin up in her usual stubborn manner and pretending his scrutiny didn't affect her.

"Because I want some answers, Florence, and now seems as good a time as any to get them. You told Nora she should divorce me and that she and the kids should move in with you. Why would you encourage divorce when you know it's not scriptural?"

"I said no such thing."

"Are you calling your daughter a liar?"

"No, I mean—alright, I did tell her she was welcome to move in with me. I sensed how troubled she was."

"And you didn't mention the word divorce to her?"

She hemmed. "If you must know, I told her she had biblical grounds—because of your adultery. And I wasn't wrong about that."

"I see. Okay, explain to me why you told her I'd probably had other affairs, and heaven forbid, other children I don't know about. Have I ever given you reason to think that?"

"Most men do—have other affairs."

"I'm not most men. I love Nora very, very much."

She gave a little huffing sound and started to turn, but he was brave enough to take hold of her arm and stop her. His grip was not tight, just firm enough that it got her attention. She looked down at his hand then up at him. "Drop my arm, Henry Griffin."

He immediately let it go, regretful that he'd chosen to touch her. "I just want some answers, Florence, that's all." He forced a calm tone, even though a certain desperation clutched him right at the core. His brows drew together as he leaned a bit forward. "Did someone hurt you?" When he asked the question, he saw an immediate flicker cross her expression. "Did something happen to you, Florence, maybe when you were much younger?"

"Good grief, what?" Her eyes went wide as the church doors he was painting, and her mouth fell open. In that instant, a sparkle of dampness showed in the corners of her eyes, but she quickly turned her head and blinked it away. She thought he hadn't seen it, but he had. He had a keen sense about people, and he knew immediately he had hit upon something. He thought how he might rephrase his question. "Florence, could you for a moment just think of me as your pastor and not as your son-in-law?"

She sneaked a suspicious peek at him and gave a slow, distrustful shrug. He saw the wariness in her hazel-colored eyes, the crinkles around them deeply creased from age. "What do you mean?" Her voice held a definite quake, and he'd never seen her looking so insecure.

"I mean, could you—for just a minute—talk to me as a parishioner to her pastor? By that I mean could you tell me what it is that has you so angry a good share of the time? I'm not trying to be judgmental; I'm just trying to understand. I realize, and I blame myself as much as anyone, that in all the fifteen plus years I've known you, we have never had a heart-to-heart conversation. I've tried to engage you, but you don't appear to be interested in what I have to say. As your pastor, could you tell me what it is about your son-in-law that rubs you wrong?"

She studied her brown, sensible shoes with the thick, one-inch heels for a few seconds. "Well, this is a little awkward."

"I'm sorry."

She gave her throat a good clearing. "I'll just say this. It's hard for me to trust men. It's just—difficult. I felt I understood Nora's dilemma, and I wanted to help her. I suppose I do become a little pushy at times."

"It's normal that as her mother, you would want to protect her." He was trying to be diplomatic. "If you don't mind, what happened to make you so distrustful of men?"

She shook her head several times and waved her hand around as if batting at a fly. "I've already said too much!"

"Florence, I'm your son-in-law, yes, but I'm also your pastor. I don't divulge anything to anyone when people confide in me. I wouldn't even say anything to Nora. Do you think you can trust me at least once in your life?"

Never in all his days since knowing her had they ever gotten this far in an intimate conversation. He hated to see it end there—even though he had a door to paint. Whether it was the Holy Spirit's direct guidance or his simple intuition, he had decided to delve into a subject he never would have dreamed he'd do with Florence Harrison. "Bruce was a wonderful father-in-law to me—and Nora loved him more than words can say, but—tell me something, Florence. Were things always good with you and Bruce?" He held his breath after blurting out the question because he knew it was one of those questions he could never retract.

She stared at him for all of a minute, then looked at her shoes. "Alright, alright, neither Bruce nor I were Christians when we married."

"I think I knew that much."

"Like Nora, I married him very young. My parents were alcoholics and did a terrible job of raising us kids. I was barely seventeen when I ran off with Bruce. He was twenty and very, shall we say, worldly? I know you weren't like Bruce, Henry, but I still feared Nora might make the same mistakes I made."

"But you and Bruce, I've always been led to believe you had a great marriage."

"We did—but that was later." She covered her face with both hands and mumbled into them. "It would shatter Nora's world to learn the truth."

Now she'd truly piqued his interest, but as her son-in-law, he wasn't sure he felt comfortable pushing her further. *God, please take the lead.*

"Oh, fumble foot, I've gone this far! I may as well spill it. Bruce had three affairs before he and I ever stepped through any church doors. He just couldn't mind his p's and q's around women." She shot him a straightforward look. "There. I've said it."

"And I don't think any less of you, Florence. Keep talking if you feel comfortable."

"I was never enough for Bruce. But after a neighbor invited us to go to church, Bruce accepted, and for the first time, we learned about God's love. It wasn't long before he turned his life over to Christ and became a different man. It took me much longer than he to come around though, maybe five years. For a long time, he went to church by himself, even became a member and a deacon. No matter what he said or did, though, I couldn't trust him. That's why we waited so long to have Nora. I was sure he was going to fall back into his old ways."

"And did he?"

She lowered her head, shivered, and then hugged herself when a gust of wind picked up. "Yes, just once. He swore it wasn't physical but might have turned into that if we hadn't left that church when we did. He had begun a close friendship with one of the church ladies whose husband had died. He was doing some repair work for her. I'd say Nora was about ten at the time. We left that church and went to a small congregation called Grace Fellowship in North Muskegon. Then once you and Nora started dating years later, we switched again to your father's church, and that's where Bruce truly started growing stronger in his faith. It's also when he developed the serious lung disease that took his life." She looked up at the sky. "I've talked too much."

"No, Florence, I'm glad you shared that with me. It's helped me understand some things."

"About why I'm such a battle-ax, you mean?"

He ignored that. "Betrayal does things to people. I can better see now why you were leery of me. And then when you learned what I'd done in Tokyo, it stirred up some hurtful memories for you. Have you ever told Arletta?"

"About Bruce? No, I've never told anyone—except for you just now."

"Well, you can be sure I won't betray your trust."

Her forehead creased. "I've thought about telling Nora over the years, but she had put her daddy on such a high pedestal, I'd hate to be the one to tear it down." She glanced down at her watch. "Goodness, I've got to run. I have my ladies' club meeting today."

She turned and headed down the steps, taking each one with careful precision. At the bottom of the stairs, she turned. "I'm sorry, Henry—about the door I mean."

Never to his recollection had she ever uttered those two words to him. "Thanks. Do you have any idea who would've done such a thing?"

"Are you accusing me?"

"Heavens no, Florence. I just thought you might have heard something." He wanted to kick himself for having asked the question—and right after she'd confessed her deepest secret.

"You're inferring I'm as much a busybody as Arletta?"

"Not at all. Please, just forget I asked such a ridiculous question. I've just been grasping at straws, searching for answers. Thanks for stopping by, Florence—and thank you for talking to me. Every word you said to me is sealed and safe!"

She gave a little wave and walked slowly to her car, her arthritis probably giving her problems. She opened her car door, and rather than turn to give him one last glance, she climbed into her shiny, dark blue '54 Plymouth, started the engine, and backed out of her parking space.

When she drove away, he took in a long breath, then picked up his paintbrush and resumed his job.

⁓

Florence could barely believe she'd confessed her long-held secret to Henry—her son-in-law, for pity's sake! What on earth had possessed her to do it? Gone was that shield she'd always raised in front of her when it came to Henry. Perhaps he wasn't quite the ogre she'd made him out to be all these years. Yes, he'd had that hideous affair, and with a Japanese woman of all things, but he'd pretty much succeeded in convincing her that was his one and only moral discrepancy. Could it be— was it possible—had she been wrong about him from the beginning? She entered the women's center in downtown Muskegon, where several women had started to gather, teacups in hand as they sipped and chatted with each other, everyone dressed in her finest, including Arletta, whom she spotted from a distance. Arletta glanced across the room and practically ran up to her.

"It's all over town now, Flo. Someone said they read about it in the early edition of the *Chronicle*, even saw a picture of the church door printed with the article. Goodness gracious, this is the worst thing to happen to Open Door since—well, I don't think anything this shocking has ever happened. Henry is to blame for all of it, of course. Something must be done."

Florence barely had a chance to take a breath before someone interrupted. "Hello, ladies." It was Margaret Bakker, president of the women's club. Holding her fancy teacup and saucer in both hands, she lifted the cup to her lips and sipped, her little finger jutting out prettily as she held the dainty handle. "We're about to get started with our meeting, so we'll be seating ourselves shortly." She directed her attention to Florence. "I understand there is quite a stir with your minister at Church of the Open Door. Arletta was just informing a group of us."

"He's a bit more than just the minister, Margaret. He is also Flo's son-in-law," Arletta hastened to add. "And it's a trifle more than a stir

I'd say. Him bringing his illegitimate child into the congregation—a Japanese boy at that."

"Well, I'm sure worse things have happened," Margaret said. Florence appreciated that.

"Not in a church, I would hope."

Margaret tossed back her head and gave a hearty laugh. "I have yet to find a perfect church. I'm a church-goer myself, although I would venture to guess perhaps half of the ladies here are not. Therefore, this is not a place for discussing religious topics—nor for spreading gossip. We are a charitable organization, if you'll recall. Today's subject matter is raising money for the Muskegon Rescue Mission. Our lovely guest speaker, Mrs. Rita Hollings, will be discussing the homeless men of Muskegon and some of their immediate needs for basic items like winter scarves, hats, socks, coats, sweaters, and so on. Her husband runs the mission, so she has a wealth of information." She looked at her watch. "Well, we'll be starting in about five minutes. Excuse me while I go spread the word to the others present. Isn't it nice to have such a large group today? Looks to be about a hundred ladies."

"Yes, yes indeed," said Arletta, rather sullen-faced. After Margaret walked away, Arletta groused, "Well, I would call that a put-down, wouldn't you? I thought Margaret was rather rude to me."

Florence sniffed. "You mean because she didn't wish to engage you in talk about Henry? I can see her point. The women's club is no place for chin wagging."

"Chin wagging? What Reverend Griffin did is not gossip, Flo. It's news. That's what it is, news. Why, as soon as I get home, I'm going to see if the *Chronicle* is on my doorstep so I can go in search of that article. To think Open Door is the subject of such controversy is downright unnerving. If the rock thrown through the church window wasn't enough, this vulgar message painted on the church door will certainly put a black mark on our name, that is for certain."

Florence gave a slow nod, recalling her brief discussion with Henry earlier, along with her confession. "Yes, I suppose."

"You suppose?" Arletta tipped her head at Florence. "What's happened? You seem so different."

"What do you mean?"

"I don't know. You just don't seem to have quite the fight in you that you once did."

"Nothing's different," she said, not wishing to get into it with Arletta. "Come, let's find a table. It looks like the luncheon is about to start."

They walked to one of the many round tables decorated with white linen tablecloths, pretty centerpieces, and fine china. Finding two empty place settings, they pulled back the white chairs and seated themselves for their monthly gathering.

TWENTY-EIGHT

Rejoice always; pray unceasingly; in everything give thanks,
for this is the will of God in Christ Jesus towards you.
—1 Thessalonians 5:16–18

All day, despite the nasty message on the church doors, the visit from the police, the newspaper article, and the gray cloud looming over Church of the Open Door, Nora's heart sang a jubilant tune, for at last, she and Henry were on speaking terms again. The wall she'd carefully erected around herself had shattered to pieces. Last night, in the wee hours before dawn, they had let down their defenses and allowed the passion between them to soar. Now, her joy swelled as all the doubts and fears of the past weeks sweetly drained out of her, leaving nothing but love and forgiveness in their purest form. It was what she had longed for but couldn't achieve until she'd given God full control. Once that happened, a heavy weight of bitterness fell away, and God set to working on her heart to bring about a fresh love for Henry and a new sense of trust.

Poor Henry had had visitors throughout the morning while she'd been out running errands, folks stopping by to see the vandalism, who were disappointed to see he'd already painted over it. Why would folks want to see such a hideous message, especially when it concerned their much-loved pastor? She feared the photo published in the *Chronicle* and the article accompanying it would paint Henry in a poor light, and she wished more than anything to proclaim from the mountaintops his fine character and loving attributes. Yes, nine years ago, he'd made a huge mistake, but much had happened since then to grow him into a man of great faith and integrity. He had led people to Christ, counseled the downtrodden, assisted the poor, and lent help to the needy. Surely, folks would eventually see beyond his past, just as she had learned to do, and recognize him for the fine Christian man God had made him to be.

When Henry came home for lunch that day, she'd greeted him with a ravenous kiss and a tight embrace, after which he'd threatened to pull her down the hall and have his way with her again if she didn't behave. "Alright," she'd said with a teasing snicker, challenging him with yet another kiss and then another. And he might have followed through on his threat if it hadn't been for the phone's two short rings that brought them both back to earth. Henry had answered and talked to the caller for a few minutes. It was another reporter from the *Chronicle*, not the one who had interviewed him the night before. This one wanted to set up another interview with Henry to talk about the various mysterious incidents. Henry had welcomed the opportunity, telling Nora afterward that this fellow seemed pleasant and genuinely interested in helping to bring the truth to light. "I'll be a little less rattled the second time around," he had said.

They conversed throughout lunch. Henry eyed her across the table. "I didn't tell you that one of the parishioners who stopped by today was your mother."

"Well, of course it was. She can't bear to miss anything newsworthy," Nora had said, using her napkin to swipe at a sandwich crumb on the corner of her mouth. "I suppose she had a couple of vile things to say about the instance, ultimately blaming you for all of it. Lately, my patience with Mom has grown exceedingly thin."

"At first, she was quite accusatory," Henry admitted

"What do you mean, at first?"

"Surprisingly, your mom and I had quite a civil conversation. In the end, she told me she was sorry."

"She apologized?"

"Well, let's not go to extremes." There was a twinkle in his eye. "She said she was sorry that someone would do such a thing. Regretfully, I asked her if she had any idea who could be responsible, which of course, I should have known better than to ask."

"Because she took offense. She thought you were in some round-about way accusing her of playing a part."

"You know her very well."

"I've had years of experience."

Nora picked up Henry's plate, set it and the silverware atop her own and then stood and carried it all to the sink. Henry finished off his water, then rose and walked the few steps it took to reach the kitchen and set his glass on the counter next to Nora. She turned on the faucet and rinsed their two plates, then switched it back off and pointed her gaze at him. "Do you think she did? Play a part in any of these mysterious incidents?"

"Oh, I don't think so. Good grief, do you?"

"I don't know what to think anymore."

They'd both ruminated over their words until Henry bent to kiss her cheek. "I've got to get back to the office," he told her. "We'll talk some more tonight, honey. I love you."

She had spent the rest of the afternoon organizing some drawers in their bedroom and cleaning the closet.

A few minutes before the children arrived home from school, she started fixing their afternoon snack of crackers and peanut butter with a glass of milk. Thankfully, supper was prepared. She had put a roast, potatoes, and carrots in the oven, and the wonderful smells were already wafting through the house. Tonight was Paige's piano lesson, and tomorrow was Paul's. She had gone to Beerman's Music House just today to purchase some advanced music for Emiko and hoped he'd be excited about delving into it. Since playing for the family, he had started sitting down at the piano more, but only when he felt like it. She hadn't wanted to push him on the off chance it would backfire. Instead, she wanted him to play for his own pleasure without coercion. With Paige and Paul, she had more control because they were accustomed to being told to come to the piano at five o'clock on such and such a night. They expected it and looked forward to it. With Emiko, she was still trying to find her way. One thing that delighted her was his eagerness to play the cello. She would often sit at the piano and plunk out some accompaniment while he played a memorized piece, and together, they could make pretty good music. She aimed to play a duet in church with him one day soon.

The children arrived home at their usual time, but with a different sort of energy. "Leave me alone!" were Paige's first words. "No! I said stop it!" she shrieked. "Mom!"

Nora hurried to the living room, where she found the three of them stepping out of their shoes at the door and methodically hanging their coats on hooks. Paige gave one of her shoes an extra hard kick, making it smack against the wall.

"What is all the racket? What's happened?"

"Paige got in a fight today," Paul said.

"I did not, you creep."

"Did too! That's what Stevie Evans said on our walk home."

"Well, Stevie Evans doesn't know anything."

Emiko stood there with a helpless expression, his shoes off and neatly pushed against the wall where they belonged, his coat on a hook.

"Paige, what is this talk about a fight? Tell me what happened."

She stomped her stockinged foot and put her hands on her waist. "I hate school. I'm not going back."

"You're not?"

"No. I quit today."

"Can I quit too?" asked Paul.

"Just—just tell me what it is that's upset you," Nora said, ignoring Paul's remark.

"Alright then. Francine Atkins said my dad is a bad guy, that he's a cheater."

"Haw! Did Daddy cheat on a test?" Paul asked.

"No, he cheated in another way, doofus!" Paige said. She narrowed her eyes and shook her head from side to side. "And somebody else said they saw words on the church doors this morning when their mom drove them to school. It was somethin' nasty. How come you didn't tell us about that before we went to school today?"

"Oh, Paige—kids—I'm sorry."

"Why are you sorry, Mom? You didn't do anything. Ar' daddy did."

Nora put three fingers to her forehead and pressed, as she tried to think of the right words to calm the storm. "Everybody sit down please."

"No, I don't wanna sit down," Paige shrieked. "What I want is for my family to be what it used to be before—before—" She paused, then looked Emiko straight on. "Before *he* came to live with us!" Her words came out harsh and hurtful.

"Paige, you don't mean that."

Emiko started to cry—and not quietly. Jerky sobs wrenched his lean frame, and tears rushed down his cheeks. He scrambled to wipe his face with his sleeve.

"Yes, I do. He doesn't like us anyway."

"What do you mean? Of course he does." She stepped closer to Emiko whose sobs had not lessened and drew him close to her side. "I know it's been hard for you kids, but we have to stick together."

"Why should we? You and Daddy don't," said Paige.

"Daddy and I are done fighting. We made that decision last night."

"I want to go back to live with Helen!" Emiko declared with a shaky sigh.

Somehow, Nora had to regain control. She thought fast and whispered a quick prayer. "Listen, please, just come into the living room, and sit down. We all need to talk."

"I just wanna go back to Helen's," Emiko repeated. "I don't belong here."

"You do belong here, honey. We're a family. I know you miss Helen. I know you miss your mommy. But it's here that you belong. With us."

"How can you say that when you're not his real mom?" asked Paige, her tone sharp.

"Because I love him." Just saying the words struck her full force. She *did* love him, this little boy from another mother. She bent and kissed the top of his head. "I'm his stepmom, and that should count for something." She directed everyone to the living room, giving each of them a gentle push. They reached the sofa. "Now then, all of you sit." Without further argument, they sat, Paige in the middle, her back straight and her arms crossed, the boys on either side of her. Emiko kept up his sniffling, and for a change, Paul was the quiet one.

Nora considered her words carefully. "First, yes, someone did come in the middle of the night and paint some unkind words on the church doors. Daddy painted over them this morning. Because vandalism is a crime, Daddy called the police, and they came to investigate. Of course, you already know about the rock that someone threw at the church window, and you know that someone sent me a rather mysterious message in the mail. The police know about all these incidents, and they are trying to put all the pieces together. Someone definitely wants to cause trouble for your dad. We must pray for that individual because he or she is holding on to lots of bitterness and hateful feelings, which, in turn, makes them very sad on the inside. The news reporters know too, and today, there was an article printed in the paper about our church.

"As for Emiko, none of this is his fault. Anyone who tries to make fun of you at school, or says cruel things about your family, or your daddy in particular, should be ignored. It's hard to ignore someone who's hurting you, I know, but that is the best way to handle it. Of course, if it gets bad, you must tell your teacher or the principal, and then of course Daddy or me. Don't hide your feelings or keep secrets because that will make things even worse for you."

She fidgeted with the hem of her apron while looking from one to the other. "Any questions?"

They all sat pretty motionless until Paige gave a nervous little cough, then swiveled to look at her half-brother. "Sorry, Emiko. I really didn't mean to hurt your feelings, and—and I don't want you to leave. I—I like having two brothers."

He looked down at his folded hands, his slender shoulders drooping. "I—I like living here," he said in a tiny voice. "And—I like having a brother and sister."

"So you're happy with staying here after all?" Nora asked.

He nodded. "But I do miss my mom and Helen."

"Of course you do. Would you like to talk to Helen on the phone tonight?"

He nodded. "But I just talked to her a couple of days ago."

"I know, but we can call her again if you'd like."

He shrugged his narrow shoulders. "Maybe I'll write her a letter instead."

"That would be wonderful. She would love that."

They were all quiet for a few moments.

"I'd miss my mom too if something happened to her," Paul said into the silence.

"Me too," said Paige.

In that moment, the front door swung open, and Henry stepped inside. "Ah, you're all sitting exactly where I wanted you to sit." He wore a mischievous grin on his face. "I'll need all of you to close your eyes."

"What?" Nora gaped at him.

He lifted his brow at her. "You included, my dear. Close your eyes."

"Well, really!" A tickly excitement stirred in her stomach. He was up to something, that was for sure.

The kids all squeezed their eyes shut, so Nora did the same, tempted to peek, but deciding to go along with him.

"No looking now. I've brought Ken Parker with me to lend a hand. Don't peek."

"We won't," said Paul.

"Right this way, Ken." Nora heard the two men shuffle past her.

"Promise not to look," said Henry.

"We promise," said Paige. "What's you got, Daddy?"

"You'll see. Okay, that's good, Ken. Right here is good."

There was a plunking sound, like something being set on the floor. "Can we look yet?" asked Paul.

"One, two, three—open your eyes!"

Squeals and shouts filled up the room. "It's a television! Daddy! You got us a TV!" Paul was the first to leap from the couch and make a bee-line across the room to look at the tall, dark wood furniture piece, with the television screen and round knobs. It was lovely to look at, but all Nora saw through her wide eyes were dollar signs. She remained seated while the other children jumped up and ran to join their brother.

"I think this will be a nice place for it. We'll need an antenna, but Ken says we should be able to get channels three and eight without one, although they will be fuzzy." He took a step back to admire the thing. "What do you think, everyone?"

"It's nifty, Dad," said Paul, flying around the box and running his hands across it. The others did the same, all making oohing sounds and gazing in wonder. Just a few minutes ago, they had been crying about all of life's troubles and woes, and now they were laughing with glee. My, how quickly moods could change when a TV entered the picture! Nora, on the other hand, had yet to move a muscle. Henry caught her eye from across the room. "What do you think, honey?"

She blinked. "Uh..." She hesitated to say much with Ken Parker standing there, but gee whiskers, why hadn't he consulted her before making a purchase of this magnitude?

"Don't look so worried, honey. The television is a gift."

"A—gift? Who—?"

"We'll talk later." He looked at Ken and shook his hand. "Thanks, my friend."

"You are most welcome. You enjoy it now, alright?"

"I'm sure we will."

When Ken walked out, closing the door behind him, Henry walked over to Nora, reached down, and took her hands. Pulling her out of the chair, he said, "Come and see this new piece of furniture that you'll be dusting."

"But—who—where—?"

He dragged her across the room. Like the kids, she ran a hand across the top of it. "It is lovely, I'll admit."

"Plug it in, Daddy. Let's see how it works."

"Okay."

"But first—where did it come from? Who gave it to you?" asked Nora.

While he bent to plug in the set, he pulled something out of his back pocket and handed it to her. With a wink, he said, "Here. Read this."

She unfolded the paper, went back to her chair, and sat down to silently read the note to herself.

Dear Reverend Griffin,

These have been difficult times for you. You sinned, it's true, and it was the worst of betrayals for any wife to endure. Ila and I have been praying for your family, and we believe God is going to work through Nora's and your situation and make it turn out for good. He does that, you know, takes bad situations, and turns them around for our good when we trust Him (Romans 8:28). We believe you have amply repented for this sin from nine years ago, and that our gracious Lord has forgiven you. If God can forgive you, then so can Ila and I. God has blessed us, and we in turn take great pleasure in blessing others. That said, I believe your family might need a bit of an uplift, especially after the day you've had today. Thus, Ila and I would like to do something for your family. We heard through the grapevine that your children have been begging for a TV set, and so we'd like to make that possible by giving you one today. You will find the one-year warranty taped to the back of the set, but if you have a problem with it, be sure to call me first so that I can handle the matter. The owner of the store from where I purchased it is a good friend, and he has promised he will guarantee the sale. Please enjoy it but keep our identity confidential. When possible, we like to give in secret. If someone asks, you can simply tell them it was a gift.

We look forward to seeing you behind the pulpit on Sunday.

With our deepest respect,
Louie and Ila Flood

Nora swiped at a stray tear. Such a lovely gesture from a dear couple and longtime members of Open Door. Truly, there were plenty of good people left in the world, people with hearts big enough for second chances.

"Mommy, look! It's working!" cried Paul. "Come and look."

She laughed. "I see it from here." It wasn't much to see with all the lines running through the screen, making the images difficult to discern, but the sound was good. Yes, the sound was very good—almost as good as their radio.

TWENTY-NINE

The LORD is good to all: and his tender mercies are over all his works.
—Psalm 145:9 (KJV)

That next Sunday's service went well, better than Henry had expected when considering the recent vandalism and then the articles in the *Muskegon Chronicle*. The second reporter had interviewed Henry, and his article gave a clearer picture of all that had transpired to trigger the acts of vandalism. Also, the second article had mentioned Emiko. Henry had wanted to avoid bringing his son into the story but realized midway through the interview that Emiko indeed played an important part, and so he answered each question about him with great care. In the end, the reporter painted Emiko in a very positive light, telling about his brilliant musical abilities and his bright personality, while also depicting him as strong, smart, and determined despite all that he'd suffered in his young life. The article highlighted the vandalism and asked people to call police if they had any leads regarding the culprit. In all, Henry and Nora had been pleased and called the reporter on the day the article appeared to thank him for a job well done.

Nora had told Henry all about the children's recent squabble, but since then, the kids had been getting along very well. Nora had called the principal the next day, and Mr. Peters promised to speak with Paige's teacher regarding the girl who had teased her. Henry was unaware of any further incidents, and Paige seemed to be back to her normal, happy self. It bothered Henry to no end that his children had to carry some of the burden for his past mistake, but there wasn't much he could do about it, except pray they would have the strength and courage to stand strong in the months and years to come.

Emiko had seemed to relax even more around the house, smiling and laughing more frequently and even playing some new piano music that Nora had bought for him. Henry loved watching Nora's joy at the boy's accomplishments and loved even more the way she had taken to him. He himself had been spending as much time as he could with Emiko to assure him they loved him and wanted him with them. However, he had to be careful to spend equal amounts of time with the other two kids so they wouldn't feel neglected. At times, it was like walking a tightrope to maintain that total sense of fairness. He had purchased an antenna last week and hired someone to install it, enabling the television to produce a clearer picture, and since then, his family had been sitting down together each night to watch one or two programs. Even Nora was showing signs of enjoying it, especially when they happened upon the right comedy—like *The Honeymooners, Father Knows Best, Leave It to Beaver,* or *The Danny Thomas Show.*

It was Monday, and this coming Thursday was Thanksgiving. At breakfast, the kids expressed their excitement at having a shorter school week, and Henry expressed his own excitement at seeing his brothers and their families when they all gathered at his parents' house for dinner. "It'll be the first time they get to meet Emiko."

Emiko scrunched up his face. "I hope they like me," he had said.

"Are you kidding? They will love you!" Nora returned. "I'll warn you though, they are a rowdy bunch!"

Once the kids left for school, Henry told Nora he was going to call on Fred and Shirley Roberts. "I thought about calling ahead, but I think Fred might turn me down for coffee. I often pay parishioners impromptu visits anyway, but never stay long. Would you like to come with me?" he asked Nora.

"Yes, I'd love to! Just let me go put on some lipstick."

"I don't know why you do that. You look beautiful just the way you are."

"Oh, you know. I'd feel better if I look my best."

No, he didn't know, but he shrugged his shoulders and smiled as she disappeared down the hallway. Henry's nerves rattled on the drive to the Roberts' house, so he and Nora prayed for the Lord's peace, wisdom, and direction on how to handle their visit. Fred worked second shift at Shaw-Walker Factory in Muskegon, so chances were good they'd catch the couple at home.

Nora had gotten the Roberts' address on one of the occasions that she'd spoken to Shirley. Henry easily found their small Cape Cod style home on East Isabella Street, pulled into the driveway behind a late model, navy blue Buick, and cut the engine. A medium-sized black dog came running toward their car, barking a friendly greeting, his tail wagging. Henry opened his door and climbed out, gave the dog a couple of pats on the head, then walked around to Nora's side and opened her door. She climbed out and the dog ran to greet her too.

As they started to approach the house, the front door opened, and lo and behold, Fred stepped out onto the small front stoop with the black wrought iron railing. "Well, would you look at that?!" he exclaimed. "The preacher and his wife are here! What brings you?"

"Good morning, Fred. Thought we'd pay a short visit. I hope it's not a bad time."

"Well now, I can't hardly tell the preacher it's a bad time, can I?"

Fred was a large man with thick, wavy red hair, a bushy mustache, and pudgy cheeks. His belly hung over the belt that held up a loose pair of beige trousers. His short-sleeved blue cotton shirt was partially tucked in. He also appeared to be wearing a pair of slippers. Shirley came up behind Fred, her eyes gone round as two saucers. "Oh, my heavens, it's the Griffins! Come in, come in!"

As if he'd been invited, the bouncy black dog ran up the stairs and tried to brush past Fred, but Fred let out a holler and blocked him with his leg. "Midnight, you ol' coot, you go lay y'rself down and wait till I give you permission." As if he understood, the dog dropped his head, turned around, and descended the porch steps, then found a spot under a tree to make himself comfortable.

"You drive a nice tank there, Reverend," Fred said, looking over Henry's car. "What is that, a fifty-three Ford Mainline?"

"Thanks, it's a fifty-two. I bought it at a good price last year. We drove our Packard into the ground. That serves as a second car now, but we don't dare drive it much further than twenty miles round-trip."

Fred nodded. "Your Ford a V-eight or six cylinders?"

"It's a six. I was admiring your Buick when I pulled in."

Fred hooked his thumbs in his belt and grinned. "I'm a Buick man. Always will be. I ain't got much use for Chevys or Fords, no offense."

Henry chuckled. "None taken."

"Y'r lucky to have two cars. We just got the one, and I am the sole driver. Shirley here used to drive on occasion, but she ain't the best of drivers. She backed herself right into a brick wall this past summer. Did some damage to the rear bumper. Wasn't a cheap fix neither."

"I didn't see the wall," Shirley said. "Come in, Reverend, come in Nora. We have coffee on the stove."

"Oh, we can only stay a minute."

"Just the same, come in."

Nora went ahead of Henry, so Shirley took Fred by the arm and pulled him inside, making way for their passage. Henry found the home's interior pleasant looking, certainly tidy and clean as a whistle. Somehow, he wanted to get to know Fred, find out what made him tick. If the fellow did indeed see the church as full of hypocrites, what had brought him to that decision? He glanced around the living room after Shirley pointed them to the sofa. She hurried to the blaring RCA Victor TV set, which was playing some morning show, shut it off, and closed the doors on the console to hide the screen, then disappeared into the kitchen.

"I think I'll go in the kitchen with Shirley if you two don't mind," Nora said.

"Go ahead, honey," Henry said.

Henry sat on the couch while Fred situated himself on an over-stuffed chair. The chair arms were worn and frayed. Henry imagined no one else ever occupied the chair when Fred was home.

"This is a very nice house, Fred."

"Thank you. We enjoy it. It's kind of crowded with four kids, but we manage fine."

"How old are your children?"

"Well, let's see here. We got Eddie who's thirteen, Marcia who's twelve, Billy who's nine, and then Francie who's seven."

Henry smiled and nodded. "You have a fine family. I've often noticed how well-behaved your kids are in church. You and Shirley are doing a good job."

"Yeah, well, they better be good. They know what'll happen if I hear otherwise. Kids ought to mind their manners when in public."

Henry nodded again, thinking about Paul and how restless he often got in church, and usually right in the middle of his sermons. So far, Emiko's fine manners had not done much to influence his brother.

"I s'pose yer kids is pretty perfect, seeing as they're preacher's kids."

He laughed now. "A far cry from that, I'm afraid."

"Oh yeah? Well, ain't that somethin'? Here I thought you'd make them toe the line."

"Nora and I try, but they're pretty normal kids."

"What about that newest kid you got—he behaving?"

"Emiko. Yes, he's adjusting well and is a very good boy."

"Humph." Fred quirked his brow and slanted his head just so. Henry braced himself, preparing for what might come next. "That was quite the shock, wasn't it, finding out you had another kid? I know I was surprised when you stood up there at that pulpit and told the story of how you'd committed adultery while in the Army. Took me aback, I'll admit. I always thought preachers stood on pedestals. Guess I was wrong."

Henry shifted a bit, seeking a more comfortable position. He didn't wish to talk about that particular Sunday, but perhaps today was as good as any other. "I wasn't a preacher at the time, not that that excuses what I did, nor did I have much of a relationship with the Lord. That said, preachers are far from perfect, and if they try to be, they'll disappoint others and themselves every time. We make mistakes like everybody else."

Shirley and Nora reentered the living room, carrying a tray with two cups of coffee and a plate of muffins. Shirley set the tray down on the coffee table in front of Henry. "Would you like cream or sugar, Reverend?"

"No, ma'am. Black is fine. Thank you very much." He lifted the cup and saucer from the tray and proceeded to take a sip.

"Help yourself to a cinnamon muffin too."

"Thank you." He wasn't hungry, but taking one was the polite thing to do. He lifted it off the tray and set it on the edge of his saucer. Shirley then turned and offered the same to Fred. He declined the muffin but took the coffee. She then set the tray back on the coffee table and helped herself to a chair across from Henry, spreading out her pleated skirt.

"The reverend here was just telling me about that new boy of his."

Her lashes flew up. "Oh! Well, I hope he's doing well. Nora was just telling me in the kitchen how fond she is of him."

"Ain't that somethin'?" said Fred. He gazed at Nora. "A person would think you not being the mother an' all would make you dislike the boy."

"You would, wouldn't you?" said Nora. "At first, I wondered if that was going to be a problem for me, but I was determined from the start not to blame him."

"Humph, would you be that kindhearted, Shirley?" He looked at his wife and gave a short laugh.

Poor Shirley went pink in the cheeks. "I—"

Fred let go a thunderous burst of laughter. "Good thing you don't have to worry about it. Unlike the reverend here, I been faithful to you throughout our marriage."

Shirley played at the pleats in her skirt.

"That's very commendable, Fred," Henry said, just dogged enough not to let the man's subtle pokes get under his skin.

Then to Shirley, Fred said, "I was just commenting to the reverend how shocked I was when he made the announcement that Sunday I came with you to church. Didn't I tell you I was confounded by the whole thing, Shirley?"

"Yes, yes, you did, but we don't need to talk about—"

Fred looked at Henry head on. "Here I been telling Shirley all along that the church is made up of a bunch of hypocrites, and then you go and declare to the whole world that you had an affair. You. The preacher!"

"Fred," Shirley said. "It is not necessary to—"

"No, I don't mean that in a bad way," Fred said. He turned his eyes on Henry. "You came forward with the truth. You were repentant. A true hypocrite would've made excuses—or even lied about the boy, and then kept hidin' it and gettin' up there Sunday after Sunday, actin' like he did nothin' wrong."

"I appreciate that."

"Now, me, I'm no hypocrite. I don't pretend to be something I'm not. I say it like it is, you know? I'm just not the church-going type. I ain't opposed to driving Shirley and the kids though. I think that's fine."

"That's generous of you, Fred."

"I got no need for God."

"No?"

"Nah. I got everything I want and could possibly need. Far as I'm concerned, folks who claim to need God are nothin' but weaklings."

"Everyone is certainly entitled to think whatever thoughts they choose. But what brought you to the conclusion that Christianity is for weaklings?"

"Nothin' in particular, just a hunch."

"So, I'm a weakling, Fred?" Shirley asked, suddenly sitting straighter.

"Now, don't go gettin' mad at me."

She gave no signs of caving. "I think it takes a pretty strong person to give up control of one's life and hand it over to God. It's a matter of surrender, and it's not for weaklings."

"Yeah, yeah."

"She has a point there, Fred," Henry said.

"'Course you'd say that. See, I got too many things in my life I'd have to give up."

"Now we're getting to the crux of the matter," Henry said with a smile. "You're pretty sure if you gave your heart to the Lord, God would hand you a list of dos and don'ts."

"He likes his smokes and his beers," said Shirley.

"Now, Shirley, don't go spillin' all my vices to the preacher here."

"I'm not an innocent man, Fred. I did my fair share of livin' in my Army days. I have to say though that living for Christ is not a death sentence. It's a new lease on life. When you make the choice to live for Him, He doesn't ask you to do anything that He won't give you the strength to do. I mean, if you've got some bad habits, He can help you with those. I'm not saying everything happens at once, or that you won't have trials. I'm not even saying He'll lay any immediate convictions on your heart. Too many people get caught up in the do's and don'ts of Christianity when, really, it's not about that. It's about living in freedom and forgiveness. Whenever God asks us to do something, you can be sure He also gives us the desire and the will. You say you don't need God, but if you take the time to think about it, I bet you'll find you need Him a lot more than you think. I'm not trying to push you. I'd never do that. But the day might come when you'll say, 'Hm. I think I know what the preacher meant when he said that.' When and if that day comes, I hope you'll keep an open mind and an open heart."

Henry drank some of his coffee and then took a couple bites of his muffin.

Fred went quiet. "Well, preacher, I thank you for takin' the time. I'll give it some thought, but I ain't sayin' I'm about to change. Can't see the need for it."

"That's fair, Fred. You just let me know if you ever want to talk. I'll drop everything."

"You'd do that, huh?"

"You bet I would." He finished off his muffin and looked at Nora, who'd been sitting dutifully at his side hardly saying a word. He knew she'd been praying. "Well, I'm sorry to eat and run, but we best be on our way. I've got a sermon to prepare for. Maybe I'll see you next Sunday, Fred?"

"Ha! Don't count on it." At that, they all stood, and Henry moseyed toward the door.

"It was wonderful of you to stop by, Reverend—and Nora, of course," said Shirley. "We're honored, isn't that right, Fred?"

"Indeed we are, Shirley," Fred said, looping a lazy arm around his wife's shoulders. "You come again now."

On the way back to the church, Henry and Nora talked about the visit. "I have no idea if what I said made an ounce of sense to him."

"Don't worry about it, honey. God can untangle any thoughts and reservations Fred may have about serving Him and bring him to a point of desire and need, however that may play out. You planted the seed, and now it's God's job to grow it."

⌒

Before going off to sleep that night, Henry and Nora lay in each other's arms, two spent and satisfied lovers, talking about their day. They talked again about their visit with Fred and Shirley, the luncheon he'd attended, and the topic he'd chosen for his upcoming sermon. She, in turn, told him about her day, laundry, paying some bills, baking two loaves of bread, going to the grocery store, and talking to her mother.

"Mom seems somehow different to me, although I can't quite decide what it is."

"Maybe God is working on her heart."

"Maybe. She doesn't seem as agitated as she once was, even commented that she might take all three kids to the zoo after Thanksgiving. I said to her, 'What did you say? Did you say all three kids?' and she just sort of laughed and said, 'My heart is not entirely made of ice. I've had some time to think. It would be cruel of me to leave out Henry's son.' She still didn't call him by his given name, but, well, I mean, I was stunned."

"Hm. God is in the miracle-working business."

She had snuggled in closer to him, loving their intimacy and thanking God for emotional healing. "Indeed He is."

In the middle of the night, Nora awoke and sat upright. "Henry!" she whispered. He didn't budge. "Henry!"

"Hm-m? W-What is it?"

"Listen. Do you hear that?"

"I don't hear anything."

She shoved the covers off and swung her feet over the edge of the bed.

"What are you doing?"

"I'm going to go look out the window."

"Not without me."

Together they walked down the hall and peered out the picture window, but they saw nothing. "I know I heard something," she whispered.

She walked to the side window, and that's when she saw a dark colored car parked in the church parking lot and the figure of a man doing something to Henry's car. "Who is that?" she whispered urgently. "What's he doing to your car?"

Just as Henry stepped up beside her, the fellow took off on a run across the yard in the direction of his parked car.

"What in the—?" Henry rushed to the door and quickly unlocked it, then stepped out on the porch. Nora followed him. "Hey!" he yelled across the yard. "Hey, what are you doing?" The fellow slammed his door shut, started his car, and buzzed out of the parking lot.

Henry ran down the steps to have a look at his car. "Oh, yuck."

"What is it?" she called out.

"I need to get the hose. There is egg all over my car."

"Egg? Why would somebody...? Oh, Henry, it's another sinister prank."

Standing next to his car, he looked back at Nora. "I'm afraid you're right." He stood in a moment of silence. "I may have recognized that car, Nora, and now that I think about it, I'm afraid it may well be the same car that someone drove away in after throwing the rock through the church window."

"Really? Any idea whose car it may have been?"

He stood there in the dark, wearing only his underwear. She might have laughed if the situation hadn't been so serious. "If I had to guess, I'd say it was Fred Roberts' car."

"Fred Roberts? Are you sure?"

"I gave his car a good looking over when we pulled into their drive-way today. Looked to me to be the same car, Nora."

"Oh, no, that's heartbreaking. Are you going to call the police?"

He looked at his car. "No damage was done. I'll be able to rinse these eggs off before they dry and ruin the finish. Let's keep this incident to ourselves. I don't want the media getting wind of yet another incident."

"I'm in complete agreement."

"I'll get the hose."

She raised a finger. "Um, you might want to put on some pants first."

He glanced down. "Oh, yeah, good idea. Besides, it's freezing out here."

She giggled in spite of herself.

THIRTY

Be not conformed to this world, but be transformed by the renewing of
your mind, that ye may prove what is the good and acceptable
and perfect will of God.
—Romans 12:2

Thanksgiving Day brought a thin layer of snow, an early intro-
duction to winter. Lillian and Lester Griffin's house buzzed
with happy chatter, laughter, and lots of bodies, including a houseful of
children, exactly what Lillian loved—all her family under one roof. As
was usually the case, she refused any cooking or baking help from her
daughters-in-law or even Florence, whom they always included in the
festivities. Lillian enjoyed the chance to use her culinary skills, along
with her gift of hospitality. Nevertheless, all the ladies convened in the
kitchen to talk and do what they could to help with any last-minute
chores. Lillian had prepared most of the food the day before, including
a variety of pies and cakes. Then that morning, she'd risen early to put
a giant turkey and a couple casseroles in the oven. Mashed potatoes sat
ready and whipped on the stove, and all that was necessary was to put
it in two big bowls. The gravy was on the stove and the cooked turkey
sat on a long platter, ready for Lester's skillful slicing. As for setting the
tables, one for the adults and one for the children, Lillian had done that

the night before. By the time everyone arrived around one o'clock, there was very little for anyone else to do.

"Mom, we girls will clean the kitchen and wash and dry the dishes," said Peggy, Nora's sister-in-law.

"Yes," agreed Nora. "That's the least we can do."

Lillian refused to acquiesce. "Well, we'll see, girls. I want you all to enjoy yourselves and have a lovely visit."

"Mom, women are quite talented when it comes to washing dishes and conversing simultaneously. We've had years of experience." This came from Charlotte, another sister-in-law. To that, everyone laughingly agreed. Nora enjoyed visiting with Henry's brothers, their wives, and their children. She was always sad when their visits ended, and they went back to their homes in Minneapolis and Pittsburgh. This was their one big family holiday this year, as Henry's brothers would spend that Christmas with their wives' parents.

While Lillian took the rolls out of the oven and Florence arranged them on a large platter, the sisters-in-law found things to chat about.

"Emiko is a lovely boy," said Charlotte. "So handsome."

"How have Paige and Paul adjusted to having another brother?" asked Peggy.

"They're all getting along much better than we ever anticipated," said Nora, sneaking a peek at her mother to see if she would interject anything. Thankfully, she had taken up conversing with Lillian over by the stove.

"I understand he's very musically talented," said Charlotte. "Frank said Henry told him that in one of their phone conversations."

"Yes, he's very gifted. Mrs. Felton, the woman who brought Emiko home, told us his mother had a lovely singing voice."

"Has this whole thing been—difficult for you?" Peggy asked in a low voice.

"Uh, you could say that. I felt terribly betrayed at first. Henry and I had a very rocky go of it for a couple of months, but God has brought us through it, and it's been so much better."

"Is Emiko doing well in school?" Charlotte asked.

"Exceptionally well. We're so thankful."

The ladies talked for a few more minutes until Lillian called from the other side of the kitchen, "Peggy, honey, will you call in Lester and tell him his turkey slicing duties are needed?"

Lillian finally gave Nora and Charlotte a task, so they were soon filling water pitchers to put on the tables.

After a lovely prayer by Lester, the grand dinner commenced with nine children seated at the kids' table in the living room and nine adults at the formal dining room table. There were so many individual conversations going on, Nora hardly knew which one to engage in. Every once in a while, she glanced in the adjoining room to see how Emiko was doing and was tickled to see him adapting well to all the commotion. There was one thing the Griffins were not, and that was quiet. Getting the three brothers together made for comical stories, boisterous laughter, and immense joking. And Nora hung on to every ounce of the fun, so thankful to have the bitterness of the past several weeks behind her.

It was a miracle—a miracle that only God could have orchestrated—and Romans, chapter eight, verse twenty-eight came back to remind her of God's goodness in all things. Even her mother, who was sitting between her and Peggy, seemed different, less angry, more accepting, and pleasanter. Even now, as she engaged in conversation with Peggy, Florence was actually laughing heartily. Laughter had never come easily to her mother—and yet something had happened to bring about some sort of newfound joy in her. Nora realized that in itself was yet another miracle.

That night, while lying in bed after a long and full day of fun, food, and family, the children fast asleep in their rooms, Nora asked Henry, "Did you enjoy seeing your brothers again?"

"We had the best time." He had drawn her close to him, his arm around her shoulders, and her head resting on his chest. "It's always fun reminiscing about old times. 'Course, we had time for some serious talk too. We went outside to look at Frank's new Dodge Coronet. Boy, that's a beaut. Anyway, they wanted to know all about Emiko, how he's doing, what the family thinks of him, how you're handling all of it, those sort of things."

"Hm. I hope you told them I'm handling things much better now than I did at the beginning."

He kissed the top of her head in a tender way. "I told them things were rough in the beginning, but that we're finding our way through the maze. They were very understanding of your position, calling you a saint."

"Pfff, I'm far from that."

"Not in my eyes you're not. I thank God every day for you."

"Hm. I do the same."

They lay there lazily, both exhaling long sighs of contentment. They kissed a couple of times, spoke a few more minutes, then lazily turned on their sleeping sides and drifted into sweet slumber.

⌒

"I'm really sick, Flo," Arletta said around noon the next day. "I don't know if I ate something bad yesterday at my son Thomas's house, or if I've caught some kind of virus. I've even wondered if my daughter-in-law tried to poison me."

"Oh, for goodness sake, Letta, she doesn't dislike you that much."

"Yeah, probably not enough to kill me. Anyway, I can't keep anything down."

"Oh, dear," Florence said. "I happen to have some turkey noodle soup on hand. Lillian gave me some leftover turkey, so this morning I cooked some noodles, added some seasoning and the turkey, and made a delicious soup. I can bring you over a jar of it that you can heat up later when you feel like having some."

"Oh, you don't have to bother. I don't want you getting sick too."

"Don't worry about me. I'm a tough old bird. I'll be over soon."

They said their goodbyes, and Florence hung up the receiver. Fifteen minutes later, she was rapping at Arletta's door and letting herself inside.

"I'm here, Letta," she called. "I'm putting the soup in the refrigerator. You can heat it up on the stove when you're ready to try some."

"Thanks," her friend said in a small voice.

"How are you?" She approached her friend's bedroom after closing the refrigerator and walking around the kitchen wastebasket that stood in the middle of the room. At Arletta's door, she paused to peruse her from afar. Her color looked good. "Doesn't look like you're dying."

"Not this minute. I make no promises for tomorrow."

Florence chuckled. "Do you want some water?"

She motioned at the full glass next to her. "Just got some ten minutes ago. Thanks for the soup. I'll probably have some later."

"You're welcome. Anything I can do for you before I leave?"

"Hm. If you want to dust and vacuum, that'd be nice. Oh, and you can take out my trash, check my mailbox, and then wash all my windows."

Florence gave a little gasp, and Arletta waved her hand. "I'm joshing you. I did all that two days ago. Except for the trash and the windows. You can do those if you want."

"I'll pass on the windows. I haven't even washed my own. When you get well, we'll arrange for a window-washing day, and we'll take on both houses together. I will take out your trash though."

"Thanks. I was going to do that earlier, but grew too weak to stand. You're a good friend, Florence Harrison."

"I know. The best. I'll call you this evening."

"Thanks."

She left Arletta's doorway and made her way back to the kitchen. It was clear Arletta had attempted to take out the trash, the way the container overflowed. Florence picked up the container, but stopped when something caught her eye—an open magazine lying at the top of the rubble. The front cover of *Better Homes and Gardens* had rectangles cut out where there were once words. She quickly thumbed through the rest of the magazine and found several other pages missing letters and words. A sinking feeling rose briefly in her chest and then dropped to her stomach. She set the magazine on the counter, picked up the waste basket, and carried it out to the trash barrel in the backyard. After dumping the trash and replacing the lid on the barrel, she stood there for a moment pondering how she might handle her discovery with her sick friend. She said a silent prayer.

Florence wasn't the best at praying, but lately, she'd been brushing up on the long-neglected practice. God had been dealing with her heart lately, and she had reached the conclusion that she needed to set things right with Henry and Nora. She had been a terrible mother in-law, but if it wasn't too late, she wanted to make amends. This latest finding— the magazine with the cut-out words and letters—gave her pause. Was Arletta responsible for the cryptic message that went to Nora? And if she was, had she also committed the vandalism around the church? She could hardly believe Arletta would do all that, but then, like Florence, she'd been plenty miffed at Henry for his vulgar act with that Japanese woman.

She reentered the house by way of the back door, replaced the waste basket in its proper place, behind the doors under the kitchen sink, then turned around and leaned against the counter, taking up the magazine one more time.

"You're still here?"

Florence's head jerked up and she hastened to lay the magazine back down unnoticed, but it was too late. Arletta stood in the doorway, her face as pale as a cloud, and not from her ailment. Florence decided to tackle the issue head-on. "Did you forget that I'd see this lying on the top of your trash, Letta?" She held the magazine up. "Nora showed me that hideous message she got in the mail. It was constructed with cutout letters and words from a magazine."

The Mercy Tree 301

Arletta's shoulders slumped. "I was going to throw that magazine away a few weeks ago, but I forgot."

"So—you are the one who sent it then?"

She put her face in her hands. "I was just so mad, Flo. You know that."

"And did you throw the rock through the church window too?"

She lifted her head, her face drawn and crinkly. "No! I only sent that one ugly message. I know it was wrong of me. I've felt guilty ever since."

Arletta trudged heavy-footed into the living room and sat down. Florence followed and sat adjacent to her. "Will you forgive me, Flo? I didn't mean to hurt you."

"You didn't hurt me, Letta. You hurt Nora. But I understand why you did it. After all, I was tempted to do something similar myself. Thankfully, I resisted. I've decided I'm done being angry though. It doesn't get me—or *you*—anywhere, Letta. I don't want to participate in anymore hateful talk about Henry. He's my son-in-law, and it's time I started behaving myself."

Arletta's forehead puckered, and she made a swipe at her disheveled hair. She gave a slow nod while looking at her lap. "I know you're right."

"I'll go with you to talk to Henry and Nora."

Arletta's forehead creased. "What?"

"You have to confess, Letta. Otherwise, you'll never find peace. You did the deed. Now you have to make amends."

Even though sick, Arletta's eyes went round as marbles. "I have to do that?"

Florence gave a weak smile and slowly nodded. "Yes, you have to. But not until you feel better."

Arletta shook her head back and forth several times. "Alright. I'll do it. I'm mortified by the whole thing though." She suddenly gasped. "Oh, Lordy, do I have to go to the police?"

"We'll leave that up to Henry."

Minutes passed. "What a mess I've made."

"Don't worry so much about it, Letta. Nora and Henry are good kids. They'll forgive you. But you need to handle this matter sooner than later. If you wait too long, you'll run out of courage."

"I know you're right. Are you still my best friend?"

"Nothing has changed in that department. And now, you go back to bed. I'll let myself out."

She left her friend sitting there to ponder her sin, but while driving back to her house, she realized she was no less guilty. She'd thought about doing something similar. Arletta had just carried it out. *Lord, forgive me. Make me a better person.* A sense of peace came over her as she turned into her driveway. From this day forward, and with God's help, she was turning a new page.

THIRTY-ONE

*The God of all grace who has called you to his eternal glory in Christ
Jesus, when ye have suffered for a little while, himself shall make perfect.*
—1 Peter 5:10

There had been no more incidents of vandalism, and every day,
while Nora held her breath awaiting the next prank, she hoped
whoever was responsible had lost his or her desire to do any further
harm. No good could come from it, and nothing would be accomplished.
It was the first week of December, and with Christmas in the not too
distant future, she longed to go into the holiday free of worry about
what might lie in wait just around the next bend.

Last night after the evening church service, the police had stopped
by the house to tell Henry they were still on the case. In fact, they had
set their sights on someone in particular and had started following him.
Henry asked who the individual was, but they said they couldn't divulge
anything—not yet anyway. They assured Henry he'd be the first to
know as they got closer to making an arrest. In some ways, Henry and
Nora were relieved to learn the police hadn't forgotten about them, but
it was still unnerving, for it made the whole thing a sad reality.

The phone rang at 2:30 p.m., just as Nora was putting her broom
and dustpan in the closet. On her way to the phone, she gave an admiring

glance at the Christmas tree in front of the picture window. The family had decorated it two nights prior, and its twinkling lights and wafting pine smells put a soothing warmth in the center of her chest. She picked up the phone's receiver on the second ring. "It's me, honey," Henry said. "I'm at the church, of course. I just got an emergency call from Tom Baskin. He said Fred and Shirley Roberts' house is on fire."

An instant tight knot replaced that warm spot in her chest. "Oh no! How—What—? Is everyone okay?"

"I don't have any details, honey. Their kids should all be in school. I'm on my way over there right now to see if there's anything I can do."

"Oh dear, this is awful."

"I know. I don't know when I'll be home, but I'll try not to be too late. If I'm not home for supper, you'll know where I am."

"Alright. Be careful."

She hung up the phone and immediately called her friend Veronica to ask her to pray.

⌒

By the time Henry reached the Roberts' house, the fire department had contained the flames, but much of the structure had burned, and the roof had collapsed. His heart broke at the sight. He parked his car on the street behind two fire trucks and climbed out. Several people, probably neighbors, gathered in clusters in the front yard to look at the parched spectacle, a skeleton, really, of what it had been, black smoke still rising from the house in great stormy puffs and burning the eyes. He gave a frantic search of those gathered and at last spotted Fred and Shirley, standing arm in arm on the west side of the yard. He stepped over a fire hose and approached.

Shirley spotted him first and called out to him. "Oh, Reverend. It's gone. Our house is gone."

He gave a slow nod. "I see that, and I'm so sorry. Are both of you alright?"

"Yes, yes, we're fine, but we fear we've lost everything inside. One of the firemen told us he thinks he found the origin of the fire down in the crawl space under the house where we have some electrical wires. He said some of the wires were frayed."

"We were going to have all new electrical installed next month. Can you believe the irony of that?" Fred murmured with a long, glum face. "We had already put it on our calendar."

Henry set a hand on Fred's shoulder. "I'm sorry about this, friend. These things are hard to understand."

"God protected us, and that's the important thing," said Shirley. "I've been trying to tell Fred that, but he doesn't want to listen. What if the fire had started in the middle of the night when our whole family was fast asleep? We might well have all perished."

They stood silent for a moment, staring at the debris. "I can't believe I'm standing here looking at my charred house with nothin' to our names but the clothes on our backs," Fred muttered.

"At least we have those, Fred," Shirley pointed out.

"And your lives," Henry added. "Thank God no one perished."

Fred nodded. "I know. I guess I'm just mulling stuff in my head."

"Of course you are. I'd be doing the same thing were I in your shoes. What can I do to help you? Can I pick your kids up for you at their school and take them somewhere? Do you have any family living nearby?"

"Thank you, Reverend, that's very kind of you," Shirley said. "Our neighbor already offered to pick them up when she picks up her fourth grader. I have an aunt and uncle who live up in Fremont, but they don't have much room in their house, certainly not enough room for four kids. Our neighbor will bring the kids here."

"We haven't thought too far yet," said Fred. "I have to call my insurance company and find out what they can do for us. One fireman told us we'll have to tear the rest of the house down and rebuild."

"That's a shame, but your insurance should cover it. They can't replace precious things like photographs and other memorabilia, though, and I'm sure you must be mourning that."

"Everything we had is replaceable," said Shirley, standing closer to Fred, his arm still positioned around her shoulder. "As for photos, we'll have to rely on our memories and start right now making new ones. I'm not going to worry about it. God has all of this under control."

Henry couldn't help but think about how tragedies like this often pulled people closer together. "Well, listen, I'm going to go back to the office and make some phone calls," he told the couple. "I don't want you worrying about a thing. Our church is full of good people. We are going to see to it you're taken care of, you can count on it. I'm confident that by the end of today, you'll have a whole lot more answers than you have right now. The important thing is that you take care of your family, Fred, and let me see what I can do from my end."

Fred looked over at him, his eyes betraying his concern. "That's awful generous of you, Reverend, but I can't imagine how all of this is going to work out. The church folks don't even know me."

"Doesn't matter. We've got you covered, and best of all, God knows all about your struggles, the new ones, the old ones, and even the future ones. Shirley is right. He is in control. Just trust Him and watch how He works through this."

Henry was on the phone the rest of the afternoon, finding volunteers for various roles, someone to oversee helping the Roberts' family pick through the debris in search of anything salvageable, looking for someone else to find temporary housing for the family until a new house could be built, locating another person to arrange for clothes to be dropped off at the church, and someone else to see to food donations. By the end of the day, Church of the Open Door had covered all the bases, and by dusk, the Roberts family was settled into a nicely furnished house just a mile from their homesite. The owners had already moved out and were preparing to put the house up for sale, but when they heard about the Roberts' need for housing, they agreed to postpone selling it in lieu of renting it to them for as long as they needed. As for food, the ladies of Open Door delivered boxes full of groceries to the new house—enough food to last at least two weeks. Clothes of all sizes arrived by the boxful, enough that Shirley said they now had more clothes than they'd had before the fire.

"You led well today, Reverend Griffin," Nora told him that evening while they sat at the kitchen nook, sipping on cups of coffee, house lights dimmed, the children all in bed. All was quiet save for the pitter-patter of a steady rain.

"Thank you. It's been quite a day, hasn't it?" Henry said. "Fred got a front row seat to see the church at work today. I hope it made a positive impact on him."

"I'm certain it did. This is the way the church should operate, recognizing needs and then setting out to meet them. I'm proud of our people. If Fred is indeed the one who committed the acts of vandalism, I hope he's filled with second thoughts about his actions."

"Me too, honey. Changing the subject, how is that piano/cello duet with Emiko coming along? Will you be ready to perform it in church soon?"

"Yes indeed. We're having such fun practicing the piece. I found a piano/strings arrangement of 'How Great Thou Art' at Hage's Christian Supply. He's so accomplished for one so young. I wouldn't be surprised if he made a career of his music someday, either as a performer or an instructor. Who knows? Perhaps he'll even conduct an orchestra. The sky is the limit."

Henry reached across the table and took her hand, their eyes meeting. "Thank you, Nora."

"For what?"

"For being the loving, generous, grace-filled person that you are. I love you more than you know."

She smiled and put her other hand on top of his. "And I love you."

"I don't think you fully understand how humbled I am to have you as my wife. God knows I don't deserve you."

"Oh, phooey! I'm no one special. I'm the one who's so blessed."

He lifted her hand to his lips and kissed the top of it. "Let's call it a tie."

"It's a deal."

In the middle of the night, Henry awoke with a start, a certain kind of urgency to pray crowding his heart and mind. He sat up and walked to the window. Nothing was amiss that he could see. He tried to listen intently, but the only sounds he heard were the humming of the refrigerator and the occasional creaking of the house itself. It was too dark to see the time, and he had no sense of how long he'd been sleeping.

He found his trousers where he'd left them on the back of a chair, along with his long-sleeved shirt, so he slipped into them. Nora's breathing was slow and rhythmic. Good. He didn't wish to waken her. He slipped into his shoes, and pushed the door open, and stepped out into the hallway, then headed toward the living room in search of his Bible. He intended to read and pray, read and pray—until he felt a sense of peace that he could return to bed.

He switched on the table lamp next to the sofa, thinking he'd find his Bible there. That was always where he sat early in the morning. When he didn't find it in its usual spot, it occurred to him that in all the hubbub to help the Roberts family, he'd no doubt left it in his office. That's when he glanced at his watch. It was 3:00 a.m. It was awfully early for rising, but there was that urgency to open God's Word, so he took the church key off the hook next to the front door, found his coat in the closet, and slipped into it, then quietly opened the door and headed across the yard to his office.

There was a single car parked in the lot, a dark car—a Buick to be exact. Had Fred driven to the church? And if he had, for what purpose? Was he up to no good? He approached the car and peered inside, the streetlamp giving off enough light to see the car was empty. *Fred, what are you doing?* The church was locked up tight, so he couldn't be inside unless—unless he'd broken a window and climbed in. Henry's chest tightened. Without taking time to ponder his decision, he slowly advanced, remembering vividly the last time he'd done this—and the painted words he'd found on the door. Was Fred Roberts painting another message? He moved around to the front of the church but saw nothing. He gave a little sigh of relief. He then walked around to the other side of the church, and that's when he saw a couple of policemen climbing out of their patrol cars. Upon spotting him, both officers pulled their pistols out.

"Stop where you are," one of them demanded.

He stopped in a jolt, and then raised his hands in the air. "I'm Henry Griffin, the pastor here."

They zeroed in on him and lowered their guns. "What are you doing here?" one asked in a hushed voice.

"I—I was just coming over to retrieve my Bible from my office," Henry answered in an equally quiet voice. "But then I noticed somebody's car parked in the parking lot, one of our parishioners, I believe— rather, a *part-time* parishioner. I decided to come over and investigate. Why are you here?"

"We're answering a call from a neighbor who saw some mysterious activity. Who is the parishioner to whom the car belongs?"

"His name is Fred Roberts. I wanted to ask him what he's doing here."

"We're relatively sure the owner of that car is not Fred Roberts. Why don't you go on back home, Reverend? We'll send an officer over later to talk to you."

"I—alright then." Somehow he knew asking if he could go inside to retrieve his Bible first would be futile, so he made his way back home, his mind a whirl of questions. If it wasn't Fred Roberts inside the church, then who in tarnation was it?

THIRTY-TWO

Be to one another kind, compassionate, forgiving one another,
so as God also in Christ has forgiven you.
—Ephesians 4:32

A police officer came to their house around 5:00 a.m. to report they'd arrested Herb VanOordt after catching him in the act of ransacking Henry's office.

"He made mighty fast work of damaging the church," the officer said. "He ripped up several hymnals, knocked over a candelabra, tipped over the communion table, tore down a painting at the front of the church, and threw various papers all around. We also found that he'd run into the church offices and dumped all the drawers' contents on the floor. All told, he made a mess of things."

"That's crazy!" exclaimed Henry.

"Unbelievable!" Nora said, her eyes wide.

"But why?" Henry asked, running his fingers through his hair. "What was his purpose? He's our church song leader. I've always considered him a loyal member of the church—if not a bit of an oddball. I did have to dismiss him from the elder board last year because of his desire to control everything."

The officer shrugged. "Well, might be that's part of the answer, Reverend. Near as either Officer Brant or I can tell, he has a definite bone to pick with you. He was mad as all get out that we caught him in your office, not because we arrested him, but because he wasn't done doing the damage he wanted to do. He claimed he intended to set your office on fire next."

"What? That would've been ironic seeing as we already had one house fire in our congregation today. Thank God he didn't get that far." Both Henry and Nora shook their heads in disbelief. What on earth had possessed Herb VanOordt? Unfortunately, the officer didn't have the answers, and Henry wasn't sure if he'd ever fully understand. "What about the other acts of vandalism?" he asked.

"We can now connect him to the broken stained glass window and the painted message on the church door," the officer said. "We have witnesses to that, thanks to a few of your watchdog neighbors. The neighbor up the street saw his car pull out of the church parking lot the day the rock went through the church window. He had just pulled into his driveway when the squealing wheels caught his attention, and he was able to get his license number. He did not see him throw the rock, however, so he didn't report him to the police. The night of the painted message on the church door, someone else from the other direction saw the suspect's car spin out of the parking lot. He flagged down the police after he saw them leave your house. He said he hadn't been able to sleep so he'd been sitting on his porch. He figured the fellow was up to no good, so he was extra alert about looking at the car, and even though it was dark he managed to identify a couple of the numbers on the license plate. Those three numbers matched the license we had on file from the previous incident. He also didn't catch him in the act of painting on the door, so our hands were pretty tied. We needed something more concrete to pin on him, and tonight sealed it. Yet another of your neighbors who lives across the road saw a man break the lock on the church's side door and walk inside. He had stepped outside to smoke a cigarette when he witnessed it. He went back inside and called us right away. Mr. VanOordt managed to do a fair amount of damage in the few minutes it took us to get there. He'll be sitting in the county jail until his arraignment. After that, it's in the judge's hands."

Henry and Nora did not go back to bed after the officer left. Instead, they walked over to the church to see the damage for themselves. It was a terrible mess inside, but thankfully, nothing they and a few volunteers couldn't clean up. Marlene would be in for a shock when she arrived for work in the morning.

In Henry's office, he shuffled through a few of his papers to see if Herb had destroyed anything of value. Most everything was intact, including his upcoming sermon notes—dispersed across the floor in a haphazard manner. Henry surmised Herb must have just gotten started in his office before the police came upon him. "Henry, look," Nora said.

He looked up. She was holding a framed picture of Emiko, which Henry had placed on a wall shelf between the framed school pictures of Paul and Paige. Herb had broken the glass on the frame then across Emiko's face had scrawled a vulgar word. He shook his head as sorrow overwhelmed him, not at the loss of the photo—photos could be replaced—but at the depth of hatred a person was capable of achieving. "God woke me up for a reason this morning, honey. He wanted me to pray for the vandal, and now it's very clear to me who I need to bring before our very loving and forgiving God."

"Let's pray together for him," said Nora.

And so they knelt right there in Henry's office and asked God to soften Herb's heart.

They arrived back home in plenty of time for Nora to prepare breakfast for the children. Although it was highly unlikely that news would leak out at school about the criminal charges against Herb VanOordt since reporters from the *Chronicle* had arrived late on the scene, they decided it best to give the kids a brief account of last night's events.

"The police arrested Herb VanOordt," he said after telling them at the breakfast table what had happened inside the church.

"Isn't he the song leader?" Paige asked.

"Yes, he is," Henry said.

"Well, not anymore, he ain't," said Paul. "He's fired."

That gave Henry a little chuckle. He reached across the table and ruffled the boy's blond head. "Yes, I'm afraid he is."

"He's not a very good Christian if he did all that bad stuff to the church—and then sent that bad message to Mommy too," Paige said.

"Well, we're not sure he sent the message, but you're right. He's not a very good example of a true Christian. Mommy and I have been praying for him, and you three can do the same."

"Why did he do all those bad things?" Emiko asked in a small voice. "Was it about me again?"

That brought Henry up short. "No, Son, it was all meant to try to hurt me. You are not to blame for any of the ugly things that have happened at our church. You are perfect in God's sight and mine."

"And mine," added Nora.

"You ain't perfect in my sight," said Paul. "You got the top bunk, and I wanted it."

Emiko stared gape-mouthed at Paul. "You can have it."

"I'm just kiddin' ya!" Paul said, laughing.

"Hey, why don't you trade bunks on New Year's Eve?" suggested Paige.

Both boys' faces lit up. "Good idea, Paige," said Emiko.

"Once in a while she comes up with a good one," said Paul.

That lightened everyone's moods, and the kids finished their breakfast.

At nine o'clock, Henry opened the church door for Marlene.

"Morning, Henry. It isn't every day you greet me at the door with a smile. Where's my coffee?"

"Ha! No coffee—yet. I wanted to catch you before you got to your office."

Her smile vanished. "Uh-oh, something's happened. What now?" It was so sad that lately, she and so many others had started to expect the next bad thing to hit.

"Brace yourself, Marlene. Your office and mine are a sight to behold."

"What do you mean?"

"I'll explain everything. Follow me."

⌒

While Nora swept and vacuumed her floors, she prayed for Herb. And then she prayed for the Roberts family. When she washed the windows facing the backyard, she prayed for them again. Then she prayed some more when she got down on her knees to scrub the kitchen linoleum. Then she switched to praying for her mother while she took the broom to the front porch and shook out a couple of rugs. Then she prayed for Arletta and anyone else God happened to bring to her mind. All morning, she prayed, and in between praying for parishioners and family members, she prayed for Henry—that God would give him wisdom and discernment as he dealt with various issues concerning the church and its people. "Lord, please don't allow this recent arrest of Herb VanOordt to create an even bigger stir within the congregation than the one that happened when Henry announced his sin of adultery. Work on the hearts and souls of Your people, Lord—and if need be, let Your work begin in me. Whatever You ask of me, Lord, may I be Your willing servant."

The hours ticked away. Henry came home for lunch, soup and a sandwich, stayed just thirty minutes, and then returned to the church. He had been busy all morning, he'd said, helping Sam Cordelle, whom they'd called in on his day off, bring the church back to rights. Marlene had notified Morris Grayson and the elders' chairman left his bank job to come right over. Henry also called his father, who dropped everything to come over to see what he could do to help. Things were abuzz at the church, and so Nora figured it best to inform her mother about what had happened—if Arletta hadn't already done the deed. Rather than call her, though, she jumped into the Packard and drove to her house. It wasn't often that she dropped in on her uninvited. They didn't have that sort of relationship. But today was an exception.

She found her mother outside hosing off the driveway. When Nora pulled in, she quickly turned off the faucet at the house and walked over to greet her. It was a cold December day, so both women wore heavy jackets. "Glory be! What brings you here?" Florence asked Nora.

"Hi, Mom. Just thought I'd stop by. What are you doing?"

"Just trying to get the oil stains out of the driveway. Your father used to be so particular about the house's appearance. I try to do what I know would make him happy."

"That's nice that you keep up with it. Dad would be proud. Don't overdo it though. You know how your arthritis acts up."

Florence waved a hand. "I'm not concerned. Come in the house, dear, and we'll have some tea and cookies."

"I can't stay long. The kids will be home before I know it."

Inside, her mother busied herself at the stove, bringing down some teacups and putting the burner on high for the teakettle. She set some teabags on the counter, then opened the cookie jar and brought it to the round table by the kitchen window. Nora's parents had bought the house after she graduated from high school. She and Paige had lived in it for eighteen months while Henry served in the Army. It had been a few years old when they bought it and was showing some need for updates, but Nora doubted Florence would ever change anything about it. It had Bruce Harrison's touches written all over it.

In a few minutes, Florence delivered two cups of piping hot tea, then pulled up a chair and sat down. "Now then, I know you didn't just drop in for a casual visit. What brings you here?"

"We had a break-in at the church last night."

Her mother gasped. "Are you serious?"

"You didn't know? I figured Arletta would surely have found out and called you with all the details."

"Arletta and I currently aren't speaking."

"What?" That news came as a shock. "I have never known you two to squabble. I hope it wasn't over anything too serious."

"It's fairly serious, but I can't really discuss it, not yet anyway."

"Oh, that's fine. I wouldn't expect you to talk about something private. I'm sure you'll make up soon."

"Tell me about this break-in."

Nora gave her mother all the details, including how Henry had been awakened in the night with a strong urgency to pray, decided to walk over to the church in the wee hours of the morning to get his Bible, and found the police officers in the church parking lot. At long last, she named the perpetrator.

"Herb VanOordt? Well, I always have considered him a rather odd duck. You've mentioned his idiosyncrasies over the years and the problems dealing with him when it comes to Sunday's worship music."

"Yes, he's always been set in his ways, but I've always managed to work with him. I would like to know how his wife is coping with all of this. I tried to reach out to her today—just to be supportive—but she didn't pick up the phone."

"Well, that was mighty generous of you."

"She is innocent of all this."

"I would certainly hope she is."

"Henry has extended a special invitation to our members, asking them to attend tomorrow night's prayer meeting. He and Marlene and a few volunteers put in phone calls to everyone today. He wants to bring everyone together so he can enlighten them about Herb VanOordt. Most will already be aware, but Henry wants to allow for a question and answer time and also have a season of prayer for Herb as well as the Roberts family."

"Ah, the Roberts family. I hope they are doing alright."

"As do I." Something was different about Florence Harrison. Nora had thought it the last time they'd talked on the phone, but seeing her mother today convinced her that something had definitely changed. "Mom, may I ask you something?"

"Of course, dear."

"What's different, if I may be so blunt? You're—I don't know—not as—" she hesitated to use the word ornery, so she fished for something less accusatory. "Um—"

"Severe? Harsh? Judgmental? Snappish?" Florence supplied with a little laugh. Even that came off gentler. Goodness, who was this woman? "I *am* different, honey, by God's grace. I am learning to let go of some things that have long made me bitter. And I'm learning to let God have control of my life. I fear I've been a bit of a bear over the years. I won't go into all the details because the past is in the past—right where it should be—but I will say I've committed my future into God's hands, and I'm frankly quite excited about what that holds for me."

"Mom! I'm so happy to hear that!" She'd never seen her mother appear so contented or peaceful. "What has brought on this change in you?"

"Oh, goodness, I suppose a lot of things. As you know, for some time, I had ill feelings for Henry, and I can't even fully explain why. Perhaps I resented that he'd taken you away from me at such a young age, when I wasn't ready to let go. Then his announcement to the church about his unfaithfulness only cemented my misgivings about him, and I felt almost proud of myself for having hung on to them all those years. Then after the vandalism done to the church door, I drove over to see it for myself and found Henry painting over the vulgar message. That chance meeting resulted in the two of us talking about some very important things. It gave me a clearer understanding of him, and I think he of me. I don't know. From that day forward, I've been consciously drawing closer to God through prayer and Bible study, and I have sensed God working on my heart."

"Oh, Mom." Tears came to the surface, and Nora pushed her chair back, stood, and walked around to the other side of the table. She put her arms around Florence and the two hugged for a solid minute. "I love you, Mom."

Florence held on tighter. "And I love you, my darling daughter."

After a few moments, they released their hold, each dabbing at their eyes. "And I do intend to take the children to the zoo. How does this Saturday sound?"

"All three of them?"

"Of course, all three of them. It's time I started loving on that bonus grandchild Henry gave me, don't you think?"

THIRTY-THREE

Blessed be the God and Father of our Lord Jesus Christ...in whom we have redemption through his blood, the forgiveness of offences, according to the riches of his grace; which he has caused to abound towards us.
—Ephesians 1:3, 7–8

Florence seated herself in her usual pew—the fifth one from the front on the left side of the sanctuary facing the platform. It was strange not seeing Herb on the platform with Henry, but Edgar Warner was every bit as capable of leading the hymns. Florence had never seen so many people show up for Wednesday night prayer meeting, but the extended invitation to attend had sparked a lot of interest, if not blatant curiosity, among folks. Florence prayed the service would go off as God willed—without any undo tension, bitter feelings, or unkind words spoken. She prayed that any questions that folks still had about Henry and Nora or Herb VanOordt's acts of vandalism might come to a head tonight so that full healing could take place and new life take root. She knew that had been her prayer for herself, and she had begun to see God's fruit abound in her own life. Now if only Arletta would experience the same. To date, she had not approached Henry or Nora to ask forgiveness for having written the devious message to Nora. For that reason alone, Florence had distanced herself from Arletta. She missed her friend—and was sure Arletta missed her too—but Florence could not stand by while Arletta continued her charade of innocence after admitting her guilt to Florence.

On the platform next to the piano sat a chair and a youth-sized cello. Nora had told her she and Emiko were planning to play a piano/cello duet on Sunday morning, but they'd obviously decided to change their performance date to Wednesday's special prayer service. She hadn't heard the boy play yet, so she was especially excited.

Over on the other side of the church, she noted the arrival of the whole Roberts family. They seated themselves in the third row. Just two days ago, their house had burned, and from what she'd read in the paper, they had lost everything. Fortunately, Open Door supplied a good share of their needs, which was also mentioned in the article, and with what funds their insurance company provided, they would be able to rebuild. Even so, house fires were always a traumatic event, and Florence applauded them for coming out tonight.

At seven o'clock on the dot, Edgar approached the podium and invited the congregation to stand and open their hymnals to "All Hail the Power of Jesus' Name." Nora and Iva Hermann filled the room with a magnificent piano/organ duet, which in turn encouraged folks to sing at the top of their lungs. It was a wonderful song, and never had Florence felt freer and more enthused about singing. She lifted her voice to the heavens and sang with gratitude in her heart. On the third verse, a gentle tap came to her arm, and Arletta slipped past her, presented her with a tentative smile, and then joined the singing. Her presence felt a bit unnerving since they had not spoken in a week, but of course, Florence held no grudge, so she put an arm around her friend's shoulder and whispered in her ear. "I'm happy to see you."

"Me too," Arletta said in return.

The song ended, the congregation sat, and Henry stepped up to the podium. He greeted everyone, read a passage of Scripture from the book of Romans, and talked about God's measureless grace and mercy. He mentioned that having a root of bitterness can grow into a wicked vine that spreads and eventually chokes out everything around it. He didn't want that for Open Door. He desired that everyone stick close together, bearing no hard feelings, but striving instead for hearts of love and compassion. He said some people allow a root of bitterness to thrive by feeding and nurturing it with hatred and disgust. That sort of spirit can grow rampant in anyone's heart, Henry said. He encouraged them to pray for Herb VanOordt, look deep within themselves to see what areas of their own lives needed forgiveness and repentance, and then to ask God to grant it. After a few more words, he invited Nora and Emiko to come forward to perform their duet. They played a beautiful arrangement of "How Great Thou Art," and Florence was mesmerized by Emiko's talent. He made the cello sing with such rich and deeply layered tones that at times she felt near to bursting with emotions. Her peripheral vision told her Arletta's gaze was upon her, but she was unable to tear her eyes away from either Nora or Emiko, and when they at last finished, she was the first to stand for the ovation, and in short order, everyone followed suit.

Henry returned to the podium, still clapping for his wife and son and saying how proud he was of both of them. He then announced that Marlene had a special story and a treat for all the children in the Sunday school room. All of the youngsters jumped to their feet and quickly filed out, leaving only the adults and parents with babies. Once the last one left, he announced his wish to have a time of prayer, but first, he asked if there were any questions about the recent events at Open Door.

"What's going to happen to Herb?" a male voice asked.

"I don't have that answer yet. The police say it will be up to the judge. We'll all have to wait and see, but I would hope we would pray for him. He's definitely hurting, I'm sure."

A woman in the back raised her hand. "What's going to happen to the Shoreline Gospel Four? Herb was in that quartet."

"I can answer that," said Edgar, a member of the group, who was still sitting on the platform. "We're going to be asking for anyone interested in singing the tenor part to contact me for an audition. We were scheduled to sing this Sunday, but obviously had to cancel."

"Any other questions?" Henry asked.

"When's the next potluck?" asked Bill Wittmyer. Everyone gave a hearty laugh.

"We'll have to get that on the schedule," said Henry. "I'll see to it that Shirley sets a date."

"I have something to say." Fred Roberts stood up, and the congregation quickly quieted. Florence sat a little straighter.

"First, my wife and I want to thank everyone for your kindness over the past two days. As most of you know, our house burned on Monday, and we lost most everything. The one thing we didn't lose was each other, and it's made me realize what's most important in life. It ain't things, but people. This church has made me rethink my life and the way I have looked at God and His people over the past several years. I always thought church was a place for weaklings and folks who don't know how to take care o' themselves. I always prided myself on being able to provide for and protect my family.

"But that fire, which shot up out of nowhere because of a short in our old wiring—well, that taught me otherwise. I ain't as strong as I thought. Matter of fact, I'm weak, and I'll be the first to admit it. I *am* someone who needs a Savior, I *am* a sinner who honestly has a doggone hard time makin' it through a day without his liquor. But let me say this, from this day forward, I'm gonna start relying on God to get me through my days. I've seen a change in my wife this past year, and well, yeah, I need to start makin' some changes of my own. I'll probably slip up, so I'll need to draw strength from some of you, but…" He turned and looked around the church at everyone else. "With all of you as my witnesses, I hereby repent of my sins, I ask Jesus Christ to forgive me and come into my life, and I commit to serving God from this day forward." There was a shakiness in his voice that attested to his utter sincerity. And then the heavyset man took a swipe at his eyes, obviously overcome with emotion. "Thank you—for lettin' me talk," he added before sitting back down. Shirley dabbed at her own eyes with a hanky and put her arm around her husband's broad shoulders. She leaned in and whispered something in his ear.

Folks clapped and cheered for Fred. "Amen!" several shouted. And the next thing Florence knew, Arletta had jumped to her feet.

"I too have something to say," she announced once the applause died down. Florence held her breath, and folks all around the room quieted, some in the front craning their necks to see her and others turning their whole bodies. There were few who didn't know Arletta Morehead and her stubborn, outspoken, and impulsive ways. Even Florence couldn't predict what her friend had on her mind or what was going to come out of her mouth.

"I've been somewhat of a nuisance around here over the years. I'm well aware of that."

A quick glance at Henry told Florence he was all ears. He stood at the front, eyes intent, hands bracing his pulpit on both sides. "I—I wish to apologize for being so difficult at times," Arletta said. "I know it draws attention to myself, and in some ways, I suppose that's something I crave, and so I—wish to say, I'm sorry."

"That's alright," someone said.

"We love you, Arletta," another said.

"I appreciate that, but I'm not quite finished. Like Mr. Roberts here, I have a confession to make. I—I—this isn't easy." She dabbed at both eyes with her white lace handkerchief.

Florence could see her friend needed support, so she stood up and put an arm around her. Arletta leaned against her for a brief second then swallowed hard and proceeded. "I—when Reverend Griffin first announced his sin of the past, it made me angry. I'll admit that. I thought to myself, 'He's been preaching all these years with that buried sin. What a hypocrite.' Yes, I thought those things. He—he apologized profusely and even told us God had forgiven him, and again I thought, 'How convenient for him. He's been forgiven, but the rest of us have to wonder how many more secrets he's kept hidden.'"

Arletta took a deep breath. She was shaking so terribly that Florence worried she might topple over if she didn't hold her upright, so she gripped her friend tighter. "It turns out that I—I was the hypocrite. I have been attending Open Door for several years, and I've always put myself on a higher level than everyone else. I thought I had all the answers, and I knew exactly what this church needed and when it needed it. I—I thought that Henry needed to learn a lesson, and so—and so I crafted a cryptic message using cut out words from a magazine and sent it to Nora. It was a warning of sorts—that her husband, that Reverend Henry, had probably had other affairs. I had no proof of any such thing, of course. I just assumed it—and I wanted Nora to think good and hard about the possibility."

A rustle of bodies and a few light gasps swept through the church.

Arletta now searched the crowd until her eyes landed on Nora, and then she moved her gaze from Nora to Henry and back to Nora. "And I want to apologize very sincerely for any grief I may have caused you by my act. And—and—if you wish to alert the police about my actions—because I know they read the message—then you go ahead and do that, Reverend, because I am ready to face whatever comes my way. I—I am guilty of doing an awful deed, and I deserve some form of punishment.

"And just so everyone knows, I have gotten down on my knees and pleaded for forgiveness from my Savior, and He has granted it. Thank you, everyone, for your attention, and that—that is all I have to say."

When she sat down, the room fell so silent that everyone could have heard a pin drop on the tile floor.

"Well." Henry cleared the frog from his throat. "First of all, Arletta, Nora and I forgive you. We're relieved to know who was responsible for that note. It's the last little piece of the puzzle we hadn't solved. Second, I don't think it's necessary to inform the police. The fact that you stood here in front of everyone and confessed it is probably punishment enough. I don't think there's a person here who wouldn't agree that your apology took courage. Does everyone agree?"

There came several head nods and "amens." Then Nora stood and faced the congregation. Another hush fell across the sanctuary.

"Henry doesn't know that I too have something to say tonight. In fact, I didn't know myself until I began to sense the Holy Spirit prompting me to speak. First, like Henry said, we forgive you, Arletta. And second, I too have a confession. Like any wife would be, I was angry at Henry. I wasn't sure for a while there if or when I would be able to forgive him for what he had done to me, but the more time that went by, the more I realized that harboring a hateful, unforgiving spirit only makes for more misery. One night, the night that Herb painted on the church door to be exact, that was the night that God spoke into my heart and told me to just let it all go. I knew I had to reach a point of surrendering my hurt and anger to the Father if I was ever going to save my marriage. Yes, I'd say we were close to separating. That wasn't God's plan for us though."

Nora wiped at the corner of her eyes with her fingertips, and Florence's heart stirred with pride for her daughter.

Nora smiled and continued. "God is in the healing business, and He desires to take our broken selves and make them fresh and whole. From the moment I relinquished all my pain and sorrow to the Lord, I began to love my husband anew. I know that must sound too simple and even trite. I don't mean to say we'll never have another argument, but what I do want to say is that I am done with the past. It's over, but today is here, and tomorrow is before us, and that is where I want to focus my thoughts and attention. There is not enough time left for us to waste it on what happened yesterday or last year, or the year before that. God doesn't want us to dwell there because nothing is accomplished if we allow ourselves to get bogged down in all our past hurts. Like that old Mercy Tree that stands out in the church yard, tall and barren now, and bearing its wounded body from that unforgiving storm, it lives on and thrives. And next spring, its branches will bud again, and new life will sprout, and that wounded tree will be stronger and taller. I pray that all of us could be more like that Mercy Tree, standing strong against the harsh winds of life, practicing mercy, resilience, and forgiveness."

She sat back down, and the silence lingered as folks pondered and prayed.

Henry closed the evening with prayer and led in the singing of the hymn "Have Thine Own Way, Lord." His voice was a bit rough and maybe even out of tune, but wholly sincere. Afterward, folks stood, embraced, talked quietly, smiled, and started making their way down the aisles to the church lobby and the exit doors, hearts light, the atmosphere warm and forgiving. Arletta and Florence lingered a moment for one last embrace. "I'm glad you had the courage to come and say what you did, Letta."

Arletta gave Florence's hand a squeeze. "Thank you for lending me your strength, Flo."

"Isn't God good?" Florence asked.

"Indeed He is. Indeed." And as best friends do, they walked down the aisle arm in arm.

That night, folks lingered in the narthex, spirits light and hearts tender as they exchanged loving hugs and warm words. Several men gathered around Fred to shake his hand and engage him in conversation, while many of the women showered Shirley with smiles and encouraging words. Others congregated in small groups, some swarming Arletta, and some simply delighting in what Nora could only describe as a Holy Spirit atmosphere. Once the crowd finally thinned, and the last of the attenders had bid good night, Nora sent the children home ahead of her and Henry, instructing them to put on their pajamas, brush their teeth, and then turn on the television so they could watch *I've Got a Secret* before bedtime. "Daddy and I will be home soon," she said. They hurried off across the churchyard, and she and Henry stepped out into the cold night. Sam Cordelle was still inside, doing what he loved, tidying the church and readying it for Sunday services.

Henry wrapped an arm around Nora's shoulder and drew her close, then nipped her ear with his teeth.

"Stop that, Reverend. I have something serious in mind."

"More serious than this?" He kissed the curve of her neck, and she giggled.

"Yes, silly. Do you have your handy pocketknife on you?"

"I always do, but what on earth would you want with that?" He reached in his pocket and withdrew his Swiss Army knife.

She stood on tiptoe and kissed him, then just as quickly took his hand and started leading him to the Mercy Tree. "It's time I carved my initials."

"Really?"

"Yes, with your help, of course."

He smiled. "I love you, Nora Beth Griffin. Did I tell you how proud I was of you tonight?"

"Did I tell you how proud *I* was of *you*? I could not have picked a better man than you to marry, not in a million years."

They stopped in front of the old tree, its branches bare, its leaves raked and burned. "Hm. I don't have a flashlight," he said.

"We have the moon though and that streetlamp."

"Yes, that should serve us well." He handed the knife to her. "Brrr. It's cold out here. Do you want to do the honors?"

"No, I want you, my pastor, to do it for me."

He smiled and turned to the old tree. "Alright then, one more set of initials it is."

When he finished carving the letters NG into the bark, he folded up his knife and dropped it back into his pocket. "There you go."

"I love it."

Arm in arm, they stared at the initials, her head nestled into the crook of his shoulder.

"It's lovely, isn't it?"

"The initials?" he asked.

"Yes, that too, but the fact that here we stand, arm in arm, facing tomorrow, and all our tomorrows, together."

"I wouldn't want to face them with anyone else," he whispered.

"Me either."

He bent and kissed her on the cheek. She turned into him, inviting a deeper kiss, so he happily obliged. It was warm and wonderful, just the two of them, melding and molding—until the sound of Sam locking up the church doors drew them to a stop.

"Uh—don't let me stop you," the wiry old janitor said from afar, his voice echoing across the still, icy air.

They both chortled. "G'night, Sam," Henry called.

"Good night now." He sauntered off down the sidewalk toward his car.

Together, they turned and headed toward the little brick house next door with the gleaming porch light and the three children inside—*their* children.

EPILOGUE

And we know that all things work together for good to them that love
God, to them who are the called according to his purpose.
—Romans 8:28 (KJV)

September 1956

C ome, Skipper!" Paige called to the family dog, an eight-month-old, rough-and-tumble Cocker Spaniel. The dog came bounding over to Paige, a long stick in his mouth, his back feet whipping up the sand as he ran to her. It was such a beautiful Saturday that Nora had decided to pack a picnic lunch. They had spread out a blanket on the beach, happy for the seclusion that September brought. Summer had ended, school had resumed, and most of the tourists had gone back to their permanent homes, giving Muskegon residents a break from the hustle and bustle that comes with a lakeside town. It was one of those days for the history books—cloudless and unseasonably warm, with a gentle breeze rustling the trees. Lake Michigan reflected off the blue sky with only a ripple of movement, the perfect day for a swim, unless you enjoyed the bigger-than-life waves that often swept upon the shoreline. A handful of people dotted the beach today, taking advantage of the perfect weather.

"Mom, Dad, watch!" called Emiko from several yards away.

"We're watching!" Henry yelled back. Emiko, standing a few feet from the shore and holding a dark gray inner tube, set off on a run into the lake, skimming its surface while lying across the tube. He turned his body and waved. Nora and Henry waved back, quietly laughing at his enthusiasm.

While the boys splashed in the water, Paige seemed content to play with Skipper.

"Getting that dog was one of the best decisions we could have made," Nora said. "Paige claims it was her best birthday present ever." Lying on her side, her elbow propped and her head resting on her right palm, she absentmindedly fingered her loose-fitting, white cotton shirt with tiny yellow buttercups. She had been so pleased to find a top that matched her elastic-waist yellow Bermuda shorts. She mindlessly ran a hand over her slightly rounded belly and relished at the notion of welcoming a fourth child into their family. Although unplanned, she and Henry had quickly adapted to the idea of adding one more. Of course, it helped that at the beginning of the year, the congregation had voted to increase the reverend's salary by a generous amount. Church attendance at Open Door had increased, as had membership and giving, and Nora could only attribute it to her husband's fine preaching, the church's outstanding music, the active teen and Sunday school programs, and the Holy Spirit's welcoming presence.

Henry patted her arm. "Oh, and speaking of birthdays, my brothers and their families are all coming up in two weeks to celebrate Dad's seventieth. The party is Friday night the twenty-eighth."

"That's wonderful! It'll be a great celebration and a good chance for all the cousins to reconnect. Haven't had everyone together since last Thanksgiving."

"It should be a happy reunion. Your mom's invited too, of course."

"Did I tell you she's taken on the food pantry project at church? Arletta's going to help her."

Henry smiled and reached over to put a few loose strands of blond hair behind her ear. "That's great, honey. Our church has been needing a food pantry for some time. It will also help us reach out to the community. Maybe Herb VanOordt can assist with the effort as part of his community service."

Nora laid back down on the beach blanket and stared up at a single drifting cloud. "What he did was criminal, but I think having to do five hundred hours of community service will make him think twice before he ever pulls any more stunts like that. I still don't understand why he did it."

Henry sighed. "We might never know, honey, but that's okay. The main thing is that we continue praying for him."

"Absolutely," Nora agreed.

"Did I tell you Fred approached me about starting a fund for a church bus? He wants to start picking up neighborhood kids and bringing them to Sunday school. As it is, he's driving his family to church, then going back to pick up five other kids who want to attend church and have no way of getting there."

She smiled up at him. "Boy, Reverend, our church is really growing by leaps and bounds. Considering how generous our folks are, I imagine they will catch Fred's passion pretty quickly and start donating. What better way to evangelize than to get children into the church? It's their enthusiasm that often brings their parents in. That's what happened to Fred, and now I guess he wants to do the same. Shirley's been telling me how much he's grown spiritually. God certainly answered her prayers."

Just then, Skipper ran past their blanket, his little paws kicking up sand as he chased after another stick Paige had thrown. The boys were now tossing a football back and forth. Nora's stomach started to gurgle with hunger pangs, so she sat up, picked a shiny red apple out of the picnic basket, and sank her teeth into it, chewing and swallowing.

Sweeping her long hair out of her face, she looked out at the children. "I've come to love Emiko so much," she said. "It warms me clear to my toes every time he calls me 'Mom.'"

Henry pulled out a few strands of beach grass growing near the edge of the blanket. "We've come a long way—as a couple and as a family."

A long stretch of reminiscent silence snuck up on them. They mulled in it for a bit.

"I wouldn't change a thing, Henry."

"Do you mean it?"

"With all my heart. We've learned a lot about love, about each other and our children, about our compassionate, forgiving Lord."

"Hm. You're right about all that," said Henry.

They sat side by side, his knees pulled up, her bare legs stretched out in front of her, the hot sun parching their shoulders. He sipped from a Coca-Cola bottle while she devoured the apple. He turned to her then and kissed her cheek. "I love you, Nora. So much. In you, I have everything I could ever want."

She smiled and dropped the apple core. "And I love you, Henry." She snuggled against him.

"Mom, Dad, come play with us!" Emiko shouted across the sand.

"Yeah, come on," said Paige and Paul in unison. Skipper barked in agreement.

"I think someone is beckoning us," Henry said.

"I think you're right."

He stood then and reached down for her. Nora took his hand, and he pulled her up.

"I'll beat you to the water's edge," she teased.

He glanced down at her stomach. "In your condition?"

She laughed. "I have never felt better, Reverend."

He grinned. "Well, then, I do so love a challenge."

"Just let me grab a cookie first. I'm eating for two, you know." Nora reached into the basket and snagged a big sugar cookie out of its container. Taking a bite, she said between chews, "On your mark…get set… go!"

They set off, but clearly, he had the longer legs. Halfway there, he slowed down and she passed him, beating him to the water by a hair.

"You let me win," she said, breathless.

"Me? Never."

At that moment, a seagull swept down and snatched the remainder of her cookie right out of her hand.

"Haw!" she cried. "Did you see that? He stole my cookie! Come back, thief!"

Henry and the children laughed as the gull flew off with its treat, while Skipper jumped around and barked wildly at the winged bandit.

Oh, how good it was to laugh with wild abandon, all the hurts of the past a distant memory, and their lives stretched out before them, God forever leading the way.

ABOUT THE AUTHOR

Born and raised in west Michigan, Sharlene MacLaren attended Spring Arbor University. Upon graduating with an education degree in 1971, she taught second grade for two years, then accepted an invitation to travel internationally for a year with a singing ensemble. Afterward, she returned to her teaching job. Then in 1975, she reunited with a childhood friend, and they married that very December. They have raised two lovely daughters, both of whom are now happily married and enjoying their own families. Retired in 2003 after thirty-one years of teaching, Shar loves to read, sing, travel, and spend time with her family—in particular, her adorable grandchildren!

Shar has always enjoyed writing, and her high school classmates eagerly read and passed around her short stories. In the early 2000s, Shar felt God's call upon her heart to take her writing pleasures a step further, so she began to pursue publishing one of the many manuscripts she'd written. In 2006, her dreams of publication became a reality when she signed a contract with Whitaker House for her first faith-based novel, *Through Every Storm*, thereby launching her professional writing career. With almost two dozen published novels now gracing store shelves and being sold online, Shar gives God all the glory.

Over the years, Shar's books have reaped awards and nominations in several categories such as the American Christian Fiction Writers Book-of-the-Year, Road to Romance Reviewer's Choice Award, Inspirational Readers' Choice Award, and the Retailers' Choice Awards, to name a few. *Their Daring Hearts* was named a 2018 Top Pick by *Romantic Times*, and *A Love to Behold* was voted "Book of the Year" in 2019 by *Interviews & Reviews*.

Her last book series, "Hearts of Honor," centers on the three Fuller brothers and includes *Her Rebel Heart, Her Steadfast Heart*, and *Her Guarded Heart*.

Shar has done numerous countrywide book signings and has participated in several interviews on television and radio. She loves to speak for community organizations, libraries, church groups, and women's conferences. In her church, she is active in women's ministries, regularly facilitating Bible studies and other events. Shar and her husband Cecil live in Spring Lake, Michigan, with their beloved collie, Cody.

Shar loves to hear from her readers. If you wish to contact her as a potential speaker or would simply like to chat with her, please send her an e-mail at SharleneMacLaren@Yahoo.com. She will do her best to answer in a timely manner.

Additional resources:

www.SharleneMacLaren.com

www.instagram.com/sharlenemaclaren

twitter.com/sharzy_lu

www.facebook.com/groups/43124814557 (Sharlene MacLaren & Friends)

www.whitakerhouse.com/book-authors/sharlene-maclaren

DISCUSSION QUESTIONS FOR GROUP STUDY

1. How did the story's premise resonate with you?

2. Did you have a favorite character?

3. Do you believe the church elders handled the matter of Henry's transgression properly? Would it have been handled any differently today compared to the 1950s?

4. Do you think Nora forgave Henry his infidelity too quickly or not soon enough? How would you have reacted in a similar situation?

5. Did any aspect of this story stand out for you or have a lasting impact? Did you reread any passages? If so, which ones?

6. Would you want to read another book by this author?

7. How did you find the book's pace?

8. From your point of view, what were the central themes of the book, and do you think the author did a good job of exploring them?

9. How thought-provoking did you find this book? Did you learn anything new from it?

10. Did any part(s) of this book strike a particular emotion in you? Which parts?

11. What was your takeaway from this story?

12. Would you recommend this book to other readers?